The floor shifted, even as the pool behind Hara erupted, spraying the Khaj warrior and the two Terrans with foul, stagnant water. Rock fell from the ceiling, along with a silting of crushed stone.

Trying to keep her balance and watch the Terran prisoners at the same time, Hara turned just as the lieutenant launched himself at her. As the force of their collision sent her to her knees, she pulled the knife from her belt and lodged it firmly in the lieutenant's side. She turned the blade and he fell away from her with a soft, surrendering expulsion of breath.

Before she could recover, the sergeant planted a kick to her right arm that sent her knife skidding across the floor. Hara was on him immediately, but even as they grappled, the door to the prison chamber burst open and a soldier of the Imperial Native Tactical Combat Force appeared. Seeing the sergeant struggling with the Khaj woman, he fired off a warning shot.

Then, as Hara broke free and rose, he took aim and fired. He let off three rounds and saw Hara clutch her right breast and right thigh as she fell backward. . . .

EMPIRE'S HORIZON

JOHN BRIZZOLARA

DAW BOOKS, INC.

DONALD A. WOLLHEIM, PUBLISHER

1633 Broadway, New York, NY 10019

First Printing, September 1989

1 2 3 4 5 6 7 8 9

PRINTED IN THE U.S.A.

To the memory of my father, Bob Brizzolara, and for my mother, Mary Jane. *Sine qua non.*

For France, a ceremony of light unto herself.

And for Geoffrey: master of imagination and joy.

All of them teachers.

Acknowledgments

First of all, I need to thank Betsy Wollheim who can pull teeth more diplomatically than any dentist.

And there are several others who helped me in one way or another in the writing of this book. I mention each of them with much gratitude and in no particular order. They are:

Peter Stampfel, France Doxey, David Brin, Amy Brizzolara, Susan Abbott, Glenn Daly, Paul Brizzolara, Michelene Zalesny, M.J., Sharon Jarvis, Jessica Rabin, Richard Bowes, Gerry and Betsy Bowes.

Thanks, all of you.

PART I

DARKATH

"The spirit of man when in nature feels the ever-changing conditions of nature. When he binds himself to things ever-changing, a good or evil fate whirls him round through life-in-death."

—Bhagavad-Gita 13.21

"Then the Lord said to Cain, . . . 'What have you done? The voice of your brother's blood is crying to me from the ground. And now you are cursed from the ground, which has opened its mouth to receive your brother's blood from your hand . . . you shall be a fugitive and a wanderer.' . . . Then Cain went away from the presence of the Lord, and dwelt in the land of Nod, east of Eden."

—Genesis 4: 9-16

"On the desert
A silence from the moon's deepest valley.
Fire rays fall athwart the robes
Of hooded men, squat and dumb.
Before them, a woman
Moves to the blowing of shrill whistles
And distant thunder of drums,
While mystic things, sinuous, dull with terrible colour,
Sleepily fondle her body
Or move at her will, swishing stealthily over the sand."

—Stephen Crane (War Is Kind)

Chapter One

Within seconds after the air lock had cycled open, Cain was covered with sweat.

He moved down the debarkation ramp with difficulty behind the priests from Vatican IV. The transport ship had increased its spin since it had reentered real space several days ago and the passengers had gradually grown accustomed to a heavier gravity, but nothing had prepared Cain for the heat which now assailed him like the expelled air of some colossal forge furnace.

"Almighty's blood!" he muttered to himself, not caring if the clergyman heard him and tried to shade his eyes with one hand. His vision was flooded with a burnt crimson; nothing could be discerned except for the shadow of the priest ahead of him. Cain stopped to put on the sun helmet that had been issued to him. The carbon mottled red of "Delgado's Star" (Darkath Prime or "Alaikhaj" as the natives called it) filled nearly a third of the sky. It took only a few moments for his eyes to adjust to the tinted light and within a matter of hours, he knew, he would be able to look directly at the surface of the red giant without discomfort.

Dust devils flew like crazed, dancing ghosts over the spaceport. Huge slabs of plasticrete lay cracked, broken or canted as far as the eye could see toward a charcoal and rose smeared horizon. To his left, remnants of Terran structures lay in ruins as if in the wake of some terrible bombardment.

Someone behind him bumped into his back, reminding him he was holding up traffic. He stepped off the ramp and began negotiating the shattered pavement toward the grouping of tents bearing the sign ENTRY INSPECTION. Hovercars waited for arriving personnel, their drivers bearing hand-held signs with the names of those they were to meet. Cain looked for his name but didn't find it.

He turned the portable holocorder on his shoulders to "record" as he approached, swung the filament mike from his shoulder to his mouth, and spoke quietly. "The evidence . . . of seismic volatility . . . is more pronounced than I had first anticipated . . . and the heat . . . incredible . . . it compares with that on, say, Cozuela . . ." The few phrases left him out of breath and he swung the mike away, shutting off the holocorder. He wondered what it was about this world that immediately recalled or . . . invoked the name of that place he had wasted so many years trying to forget. Strange, it had sprung to mind immediately. *Cozuela.*

Drone vehicles piled with passengers' cargo passed him and disappeared into the inspection area beyond a twisted metal fence. He stared, nearly transfixed, at the sight of the amorphous native shacks that came into view along the hillside beneath the Terran cantonment. The structures seemed . . . kaleidoscopic. Perhaps it was the waves of heat that rose from the desert floor, distorting things, but it was as if his eyes could not quite focus, separate one dwelling from another or apprehend sense in their shape. Everywhere he looked as he scanned the native dwellings, pinpoint flashes of colored light winked back at him or danced in clusters of variegated, shifting hues. After a moment he surmised that these were the crystals, gems, and glass the Darkhani were said to weave into the hempwork structure of their habitats. The effect, from a distance, was of a prismatic dew laced into a sprawling, delicate web.

He flicked the holocorder back on and turned to take

in a panoramic shot. He would dub something over it later when he could breathe. It would, he knew, be something like, "My first glimpse of the Darkhani hovels made me realize the extent of the squalor and ignorance the Empire has dealt with here." It was the sort of thing Holofax wanted from him, he knew. In fact, the strange, precarious looking huts made of what looked to be painted hides, crude woven rope and the winking, colored glass fascinated Cain and caused him to smile, though he would have been hard put to say exactly why. While the blasted desert landscape, the chaotic ruin of Terran artifacts and architecture seemed to mirror Cain's internal disaster area, his gnarled emptiness and melancholy, the play of bright prisms in the bizarre native dwellings seemed like coded navigational lights along some unguessed inner path.

The inspection station was a riot of noise. Passengers were advised over speakers to stay within the area cordoned off by stout ropes. The recorded message blared repeatedly over the shouting and crying of children, the arguments with customs officials, the cries of reunited families and friends. It might have been a colonial spaceport anywhere on any of a hundred worlds except for the lack of walls and windows and an air of tension that seemed to shimmer subliminally in the air like a mirage.

For one thing, there were too many soldiers. At the edges of the great tent, with their backs to the interior, Cain saw some fifty men in the blue uniforms of the Imperial Infantry. They held antique projectile weapons and short spears or lances of a kind he had never seen.

These troops weren't men, exactly, but natives of Darkath. Aliens. They were extremely short and wide. One of these turned to speak with the soldier to his right and Cain glimpsed an obsidian, blue-black face, a fold of pale flesh over the eyes that seemed almost incandescent against the surrounding blackness. He could not tell if it was one of the Dhirn or one of the

Khaj since the helmet concealed the top of his head and the back of the neck, but he felt a surge of excitement at his first glimpse of the species he had traveled so far to meet: the last sentient species to have been discovered on the farthest outpost in the galaxy.

The line ahead of him stretched for some ten meters and was moving slowly. One woman had already fainted from the heat and was being tended to by another with a damp cloth. Cain pushed his way toward the front of the line, excusing himself as best he could.

"You there," he called to one of the uniformed inspectors examining the contents of a man's handbag. "There's a woman who's fainted." Since his discharge from the military nearly ten years ago, Cain had never quite conquered the temptation to prove to anyone in uniform that he could damned well speak to them any way he pleased.

The man, corpulent and darkly tanned, glowered at him above a disheveled, sweat-stained sergeant's uniform. He turned his attention back to the job at hand. The owner of the purse was a bald, stoop-shouldered elementary school teacher from Puerto De Estrella Cain had met briefly on the ship. He fanned himself nervously with his passport.

"Well?" Cain shouted above the recorded message.

"Disembarking passengers, please form a double line behind the white ropes . . ."

"Do you intend to do anything about it or not? There'll be more of them in this heat if this line doesn't move faster. Is there a doctor here?"

Someone behind him screamed and Cain turned to discover another victim of the heat prostrate on the saffron-colored dirt floor. It was a boy this time, perhaps fifteen years old. Passengers surrounded him, patting his face and fanning him with articles of clothing and sun helmets. The inspection officials ignored the disturbance. This typical military incompetence fueled Cain's gathering impatience.

At that moment, accompanied by a basso grinding

sound, the roof of the tent began to sway. The recorded message degenerated into a roar of static and
one of the speakers fell, cutting a woman's head. Three
of the center poles collapsed, bringing down half of
the canvas and striking several of the waiting passengers. A chorus of panicked screams went up. The
ground shifted beneath him and Cain realized at once
that they had just experienced a small earthquake.
Though it was not particularly small by Cain's experience, he saw by the lack of reaction on the part of
the Darkhani, it was of no great moment. Still, it was
large enough that it was likely to be followed with an
aftershock.

He produced his Holofax ID and displayed it to the
saturnine customs official who had waved the teacher
through and seemed oblivious to everything but the
task of rifling through pockets and satchels. "Look,
you've got to get these people out of here. My name
is Cain, Martin Cain, from Hub Holofax. Surely there
is something we can do about this." Someone behind
him was crying. "We'll need a doctor . . ."

He heard his name being called. When he turned,
he saw a florid-faced man, with thinning blond hair
smiling at him gap-toothed from beneath a sun helmet.
The man pushed his way through the collapsed area of
the tent. "Martin Cain? Martin Cain?"

"Yes, I'm Cain. Yes."

"Wilson, from Starfax." The man made his way
through the churning crowd. Arriving at the table, he
spoke to the inspector. "He has clearance. It's all
right. Let me move him on." He smiled hopefully.
"Press," he added.

After a cursory examination of Cain's credentials,
the inspector checked his name against a list. The official nodded and jerked his head toward the flap in
the tent marked as an exit. Wilson brightened. "Let's
go, Cain. I've got a car."

"Yes, but these people here . . ." Cain looked at

the boy, gestured to the woman who was bleeding from her forehead and seemed pale and unsteady.

"Come on, Cain." His tone was peremptory though the smile was still in place. "Let's not stretch our luck. The car's waiting."

"This is a mess here and someone should do something about it." Cain cleared a space around the boy and lifted him; the weight was nearly unbearable. "Is anyone with him?" he asked of the crowd. When no one answered, he carried the boy to the table, elbowing past others. He looked at the inspector and said, "Please search him or whatever it is you do. *Now*. He has to get out of this heat."

"Cain, look . . ." Wilson whispered. "You don't understand. You see . . ."

The inspector ignored the boy except for a brief glance at the color of his passport. It was a drab brown, signifying its owner was a family member of an enlisted man or noncommissioned officer. He tapped the small holopack on Cain's shoulders. "This stays," he said. "If it's approved, you can pick it up at the adjutant's office in the morning." The inspector grinned. "Off with it."

"I'm a correspondent. That's a hologram recorder. You've seen my credentials."

"Take it up with the adjutant." The man's tone brooked no argument. A second official came to stand behind the first, looking stonily at the reporter. Cain was forced to set the boy on the table while he unsnapped the harness around his shoulders.

"Oh, Christ, Cain!" Wilson wiped the sweat from his forehead onto his shirtsleeve. "You've done it. You really have!"

"See about that woman, will you, Wilson?"

"Are you mad? Let's get out of here."

"Go on."

Exasperated, Wilson made his way to the woman and examined her wound. Producing a flask from his pocket, he gave it to the woman to drink. She accepted it and thanked him. He poured some of the contents onto a handkerchief and cleaned the wound. He left her seated on the floor along with a group of other shaken travelers.

"She'll be all right, Cain. Just a nasty cut. Come on, follow me."

Leaving the recorder and accepting a receipt from the inspector, he followed Wilson. Cain carried the boy toward the street and tried to keep his knees from buckling in the severe gravity. Smells assaulted him, acrid body odors, frying meat, sewage, and garbage. The streets were cluttered with Darkhani merchants, jugglers, beggars, musicians. Shrill glissandos from alien instruments struck at the air. He peered at the Darkhani, all of them Dhirn judging by the short cropped white or yellow hair stained a rose color by the sun. One elderly Dhirn was dancing alone to one of the many competing, abrasive tunes that filled the street, or perhaps he was dancing to some inner melody. He was muttering a chant that Cain could not understand despite his hypno-learning of the major dialects of Darkath. The Dhirn spun and twisted with an agility that seemed impossible given his apparent age, the gravity, and heat of the day. A pair of young Dhirn in ragged Terran civilian clothes seemed to be locked in a sweaty, rutting embrace beneath a cart of—what looked to Cain like—roasted nuts.

A native woman squatted and urinated in the middle of the dusty road. Yet another Dhirn with a white stubble of a beard and rotted teeth approached Cain with gleaming, sticky entrails depending from his blood-stained fingers. In Terran Standard mixed with Spanish and low Dhirn, he beseeched Cain to allow him to tell his fortune. "It is unwise to proceed," he cautioned Cain, "without the knowledge of events that conspire around you. Even now I see the signs of evil, the legions of warring demons that are within you . . . I can help you open your eyes. Guide you . . . the path is narrow . . . what you seek is here!'' He brandished the grayish-red guts at Cain.

Cain pushed past him. ''No. Excuse me.''

Down the street, still carrying the boy, Cain saw three Terran soldiers arresting a group of Dhirn who were attempting to ignite a funeral pyre of dried bracken on which lay two blanket-wrapped bodies. The soldiers manhandled two women and a young girl who were shrieking and tearing at their own hair. Cain had read, in the briefing material from Hub, about the health hazards around the cantonment caused by the Dhirn ritual of public cremation and the subsequent use of the ashes in birth rituals. In a nomadic context, in a sea of desert, it was one thing. In an overcrowded boomtown springing up around a spaceport and military camp, with inadequate water and waste facilities, it was something else. The military governor had declared it illegal. The Dhirn, it seemed to Cain, were ignoring his proclamation.

Everywhere he looked, he saw a seething violence threatening to erupt. Desperation, anger, and confusion suffused the streets like an electric current.

The Starfax man jabbered at him from behind. ''You could have brought that holopack through in that chaos, Cain.'' Wilson's smile had collapsed. ''There aren't any others here that aren't locked up, you know. Damn it all!''

Cain swayed beneath the burden of the boy. He felt suddenly dizzy. ''Where can we take him?'' he asked the information Liaison Officer, Nigel Wilson of Starfax, his contact on Darkath.

''Well, for starters we can take him to the hovercar. I don't suppose you have any idea how difficult it was for me to get one. No, of course not. From there, he's your problem m'man.''

The boy roused himself momentarily, lifting his chin away from Cain's shoulder blade. ''Put me down, I'll walk. I'm fine. Really.'' With that his eyelids fluttered once more and his head collapsed back into

Cain's tunic. Cain noted that the boy spoke in a Cygni dialect of Terran Galactic.

Wilson negotiated a path for them through the crowds of squat, black-faced and argent-haired Darkhani who seemed to peer sightlessly at them through their pale optic membranes. They had the appearance, Cain thought, of masked apes in an ancient photographic negative. "This way," Wilson urged him.

The hovercar was waiting across a makeshift thoroughfare full of merchants hawking pottery, hides, baubles, and herbs. Cain laid his burden across the rear seat and glanced at the driver. He was a Khaj Darkhani with a jet-faced, white-toothed smile, braided hair to one side, a raggedy blue uniform and sunburst tattoo around his eyes. When Cain had laid his charge in the vehicle, he leaned against its side and breathed heavily, trying to gulp lungfuls of air that were not there.

A Dhirn child of seven or eight, white raccoon eyes around the tenebrous face and shorn, pale hair, darted away from his family and across the street. He looked up at Cain, lowered his face, and then spat in the dust between the reporter's feet. The boy ran back to his father who cuffed his ears and scolded him, making apologetic gestures to the Terran.

Cain stared in puzzlement at the spit-stained dust.

"Welcome to Darkath," Wilson said.

The ground beneath them lurched once again and Cain was thrown against the side of the hovercar.

Chapter Two

"Soon." Hara strained against the bootgrips on her saddle and stood upright on her mount. She placed the instrument to her eye and scanned the pink sky over the basin until she found the whitish glow from the starship's retros. She followed its progress until it disappeared behind the great mesa where the Terrans had built their *Dita' Tareek* or "brittle camp." The hereditary religious and military leader of the Khaj and now leader of the Dhirn and Khaj renegade alliance clutched at the springlance strapped to the scaled beast beneath her. "Very soon now and we will know." Hara handed the lens to her companion on the rocky promontory though there was nothing left to see.

"Yes, one way or another," Sivran agreed. The Dhirn leader accepted the instrument Hara handed to him, lifted his hood back from his eyes, and studied it. It was a telescope made by Dhirn craftsmen from a puhlcalf stalk, "dragon" hide, and ground glass. A fine instrument, it gave him a sense of pride in the ingenuity of his kind. The lenses seemed a milky blend of opaque, pastel colors and it required much concentration and mastery of the iris and cornea to utilize. The Terrans found such devices useless—further evidence of the natives' idiotic fascination with crude toys—and yet Sivran knew that it was a far superior instrument to the Terrans' computerized, complicated if compact vectorscopes. For one thing, there were no moving parts other than the almost subliminal control of the user's eye muscles themselves. No sandstorm could disable a device like this. In fact that was precisely when they were the most useful. As he put it back into Hara's saddlebag—after all, it *was* a gift to her from his people—he ventured a further comment. "That is, if our people are not discovered."

Hara turned in her saddle and looked directly at Sivran. Her waist-length white hair was braided down the center of her back and it whipped to one side with the suddenness of her movement. The corona tattoo around her eyes masked any expression that might surface on an already impassive face. Sivran could never tell what she was thinking. Of course, he could never tell what *any* Khaj was thinking. "That will not happen again," she said. "We know who betrayed us and we have dealt with them."

While the Khaj and the Dhirn appeared almost indistinguishable from each other to untrained Terran eyes, no more than different tribes, or different "castes" of the same race, Sivran could not help but feel the generations of enmity, the huge cultural gap that yawned between the two of them. In nearly a thousand years of recorded history, there had never been so much as a sanctioned marriage between Khaj and Dhirn—though he had heard of unsanctioned ones, everyone had. It was now more than ever necessary to close that distance, concentrate on what they had in common if this improbable alliance was to have any hope of success. Still, the hereditary differences were so pronounced, the habit of aloofness so ingrained all Sivran could think of was the bloody-mindedness of the Khaj ways. His words came out harsher than he had intended.

"Yes, we fed their heads to the Grea' ka," he said, using the Darkhani word for their dragons. "The Terrans have executed our people in a commensurately horrific way and made a public event of it." Sivran removed the veil from the lower half of his face and lit a pipe filled with *iravka*. The wind had calmed and the desert shimmered around them soundlessly. "Then we will kill our Terran hostages one at a time which, in turn, will cause further reprisals. It is already a very ugly business and we have not yet even begun to fight each other." The *iravka* was already blunting the sadness the Dhirn leader felt.

He looked behind him at the ranks of the silent Khaj and Dhirn soldiers who followed Hara into the desert. They squatted in the sand like rows of hardy and dangerous plants.

Hara's voice, when she spoke, was low and soft. "Are you losing your stomach for this?" Her tone surprised Sivran who had grown accustomed to her terse, inflectionless way of speaking. If he hadn't known better, he would have sworn she was showing concern for him. He knew that he was important to her, that through him she had the ears (if not always the hearts and minds) of the Dhirn and he knew also that they had been through much together already, but it simply wasn't possible for a Khaj to show such a weakness. He decided that her uncharacteristic near whisper was an expression of the absolute necessity in knowing the answer to the question she posed. Could she continue to depend on his help in the bloody days ahead?

"Hara Tian Aikhan," he called her by her full ancestral name. "I think you know what you can expect from me. If the Terrans have indeed brought something to violate my people or yours, an abomination in the eyes of Darkath or Alaikhaj, I will do what must be done. The Dhirn will do what must be done and they will follow you. This I can promise. Just don't ask me to join in the sport of your hatred."

"Very well, Sivran. You wish to bury an army of butchers and their bloody god while keeping your hands clean. I will watch you closely to see how you perform this trick."

"There is yet no proof, Hara, that the Terrans plan to desecrate us or estrange us from our gods altogether. If they wanted to do so, they could have long ago. They sent their light weapons away from our world and have not forced your people to use them."

"Do you truly believe they have none of these weapons secreted among them?" She did not wait for a reply. "Their holy men torment our children with visions of their suffering god, reward the parents for sending them to the Terran schools, and penalize those who do not. With every passing year the heart of that fat Jafar who sits in power grows harder. He becomes more obsessed with his failure here. I believe what my priests say, that they have a plan to make us unclean, leaving both Khaj and Dhirn fit only for their Church of Blood."

"I, too, believe they have some plan," Sivran said. "I am only pointing out that we have no proof of it, only snatches of overheard conversation, rumors, and . . . the visions of old men."

"The visions of Khaj seers!" Hara flashed. "Do not your own holy men say that the time has come to defeat the ones from the stars?"

Sivran hesitated. Indeed there was a Dhirn myth that conquerors from the stars would be vanquished by demons from Darkath, the mother goddess, one hundred years after their arrival. The Khaj had a similar myth that conquerors would be subdued by angels. As for himself, he was no longer sure what he believed when it came to that; he thought it best not to wait for angels, demons, or anyone else. Moreover he did not wish to discuss theology with a Khaj warrior, especially not this one.

One of Hara's men, with a dye-streaked chest, appeared from a cleft in the boulders to their left. "Hia Hara. The mounts have eaten and are ready."

Hara nodded. "Thank you, Karsha." Turning to the Dhirn leader, she said, "You will return to the cantonment now, Sivran?"

"Yes, I will send a message in the arranged way when we discover the nature of the cargo on the Terran ship. It may take some time."

"I'm sure you will do your best."

Sivran spread his fingers and placed them momentarily over his eyes in the ritual gesture of greeting or farewell among the Khaj. Hara returned the courtesy by moving her palm in a brief arc over her breast, the gesture of the Dhirn. That each used the other's custom when meeting or concluding business amused them both and seemed somehow correct under the circumstances. Hara then dug her knees into the side of the beast and it wheeled, raised its wings and snorted once, leaving Sivran to puff again on his pipe to obscure the stench. He watched her glide down the broken trail, the Grea' ka—or "dragon" as the Terrans called it—lumbered gracefully toward the others below, its taloned feet touching the ground every several meters.

He sat finishing his bowl and watched the small party of renegade Khaj mount up. The sharp sound of the riders ordering their Grea' ka to rise echoed up to him.

They followed Hara into the tortured mountain pass toward Nijwhol.

Chapter Three

Commandant Manuel Velasquez Jimenez, the Military Governor of Darkath sat with his hands folded before him on the polished wooden table that had been sent from the San Miguel system as a gift from men who formerly served under him. He ran his hands over the aqua-colored wood that was now stained violet with the rays of the setting sun outside the window. The reports in front of him lay untouched. It was too hot to read, his eyes were too tired and he found his mind wandering.

He was thinking of the blue snows on San Miguel and of his daughter, when she was very young, holding on to him as they rode the sled over the gently sloping hills in the pastel forests near the starbase. His vision blurred with fatigue and the dying ruddy light of the day as he turned his hands over on the desk.

"Sangre!" he said, startling the man who sat across from him waiting for a sign to begin reviewing the day's business. It was particularly important business that day of all days, concerning the arrival of the first ship in over a year.

"I beg your pardon, Commandant?" Colonel Cristobal sat forward in his chair.

"Nothing, Colonel. I was thinking, that's all. And the sun here invades even my thoughts." The commandant was a round-faced, smooth featured man with deceptively soft looking eyes, no chin at all, and a fine trimmed mustache that merged with his side whiskers in the colonial fashion popular two decades earlier.

Cristobal was, physically, his opposite number; lean, chiseled and hairless, his eyes were the lifeless gray of long extinguished embers. "Commandant, you know the ship has brought news."

"Yes? I heard of Empress Consuela's illness." Jimenez was hoping that Cristobal was referring to something quite different, something important he suspected was being kept from him, but he would leave it to the colonel to broach the subject if he had any intention of doing so. If not, it would tell him what he was afraid he already knew.

"Yes, sir. The Empress is very ill."

Jimenez waited another beat, giving Cristobal the opening to say, "But that is not what concerns me most" or something like it. After a moment, he said, "She was an old woman when first I saw her. I was a pup then. She may be dead as we speak."

"That is possible, sir. Distressing, no?"

To himself, Jimenez thought, *Bugger the Empress!* "Hmmmm. Let's drink to the Empress Consuela, Colonel."

"If you like, Commandant."

Jimenez reached for a bottle at the end of the table and two glasses. He poured a clear liquid into each and held one of them out for Cristobal. This was a ritual usually reserved for the conclusion of the meeting, but in recent months Jimenez could be found drinking at any time of the day.

Jimenez rose and lifted his glass to the gold-framed hologram of the Empress on her throne in the ancient city of Sao Paulo on Terra. She glowered lifelessly back at them as if she had been long dead when the portrait had been made. "To Empress Consuela."

Cristobal stood and toasted. "To the Empress, may her illness be behind her. Long may she live."

"Viva Consuela."

They both drank and reseated themselves. Jimenez poured himself another, offering a second drink to Cristobal who refused.

"Commandant, the ship has brought more than discouraging news of the Empress' health."

Ah, thought the commandant, perhaps this is it.

"It has also brought the equipment you asked for two years ago and were denied. It's in the reports and manifests in front of you."

Damn the man. I *know* all that. "I know what is in front of me, thank you. A tachyon message was received here last month telling me that I would get what I had asked for after all. It only took requisitions every year for nearly seven years, the loss of nearly a hundred men, and countless failures at untold expense to install conventional fusion sources. Now I have it. What am I to do with it, Cristobal?

"There is an old axiom that warns men: 'There are only two tragedies in this life. The first is not getting what you want and the second is getting it.' I have the solar collectors now. They will work, I think, and may turn this planet into a garden. But if I try to implement my plan, I will have a bloodbath on my hands that will destroy what world there is here.

"I'm not asking for your advice, I already know what it is. 'Our duty is clear,' eh, Cristobal? I envy men like you to whom duty is always so clear. I'm not asking for your sympathy either. If I thought you'd offer me any, I'd suspect you had gone mad." Jimenez finished off his second drink.

A long silence ensued during which Jimenez hoped Cristobal would grow uncomfortable, show some evidence of the heat, or betray any sign of knowledge he was withholding. No such sign was forthcoming. Only Jimenez sweated. The colonel might have been an item of furniture in the room.

Cristobal, caring nothing one way or the other about the not-so-veiled insult, noted—and not for the first time—that the commandant had crossed that indiscernible line between fat and obese. Not a healthy, contented, or prosperous girth any longer, but a bloated, indulgent piggishness that threatened his health and by extension, the welfare of the Terran presence on Dar-kath. Cristobal was not ready for Jimenez to succumb to a heart attack. Not yet.

"I submit that we convene the council of Khaj priests, as I have suggested before. We can put it before them that the solar collectors in no way compromise the integrity of their religion. If it is made clear to them that we are not 'binding their god like a common demon' as that one fellow put it when he was discussing the hologram recorders some time ago— and infer, diplomatically of course, that it is a *fait accompli*, that they have no choice . . ."

"They'll raise hell, Cristobal! I've got enough trouble keeping the Khaj in line as it is." Jimenez got to his feet and began pacing the foamcrete-covered geodesic room. "They're animals in spite of what the good padres say—and even some of them agree. I've kept the Khaj from carving up the Dhirn and I've kept the Khaj clans from carving up each other, but I'll be damned if I'll invite them to carve us!"

"That would be a military impossibility, sir."

"Don't be so sure. I've served on worlds, fought against aliens that were outnumbered, out-gunned, out-flanked and second-guessed. Still I saw too many good men die in marginal victories or outright defeat because the enemy had *belief* on their side. Nothing more than that. It is their belief that we're up against." He slammed his fist into his palm. Lowering his voice, he said, "Our priests are failing me there."

The room shook around them. The bottle of liquor slid to the floor and splintered along with several empty glasses. Jimenez stood and watched the chandelier flicker and sway like a glittering pendulum. The tremor subsided and fine foamcrete dust fell like silt onto the table and floor, into their drinks. The portrait of the Empress hung askew on the wall.

"There are other matters, sir." Cristobal reached for the sheaf of papers on the table.

Jimenez sat again and said, "There always are."

"A delegation of priests have been sent from New Vatican IV to build a new church."

"Marvelous." Jimenez put on his glasses to read or pretend to read the sheet the colonel handed him. "Has anyone told them of the peculiar ground breaking ceremonies conducted here?"

Cristobal chuckled flatly, like a man who was unused to humor or didn't care much for it. "That's very good, sir. No, it seems their intention is to build a cathedral . . . of the people as it were. It would be constructed along the lines of a native building."

"A wobbling Darker shack." Jimenez grunted and tossed the sheet aside. "Poor bastards. Church funds?"

"Of course."

"Tell them we extend every courtesy et cetera."

"Yes, sir."

"There is an influential Padre Gillermo among them, an anthropologist. He wants to dig." Cristobal smiled.

Jimenez returned the smile. "By all means let Padre Gillermo dig."

They both laughed briefly and Cristobal returned to the sheaf of papers. "There is the usual number of family members joining military personnel, a woman writer—author of colonial dramas, you know. Oh, there is a Martin Cain from Hub Holofax."

"Yes. I've seen him on web broadcasts, though not for years. He used to be a soldier. Did well on Cozuela. Decorated, I think."

Cristobal set down the sheets before him. "He's not one of us."

"If you mean Hispanic," Jimenez lowered his glasses to peer at his advisor, "no, I don't suppose so."

"Politically."

"I don't know what you mean, Colonel. He seems solid enough. His broadcasts have always been in the best interests of the Empire as far as I can tell."

Cristobal shifted his weight in the chair. Outside, the sun had set in a rapid series of heat and atmosphere distorted configurations. Mushroom, hourglass, ziggurat, and obelisk. The temperature had cooled considerably.

"I have a dossier on Cain," The colonel said, "He has, it seems, a proclivity for going native."

Jimenez harrumphed. "Well, he's not likely to go native on Darkath, is he?"

"Perhaps not, sir. Still, we should watch him, I think."

"If you so advise, Colonel," he said almost saccharinely. "We watch all our Fax people. No trouble there."

"He had a holographic recorder with him. It was confiscated."

"That's a damned shame. He does good work. As I said, I've seen his stuff. Makes the Empire look the way it should. Maybe we can work something out for him about the holocorder. He could make us look good, Cristobal."

"That, of course, is your decision, sir."

"Yes, it is, Colonel. Would you mind moving on to the more pressing business?" Jimenez tried, without success, to think of a way to let Cain have his holocorder without allowing one to other correspondents. *Too bad, but we must all work with impossible limitations here.*

Cristobal set the papers back on the desk and folded his hands in his lap. Jimenez removed his glasses and found himself folding his hands on the table the way he had when the discussion with his "Prime Minister"—as he called Cristobal sometimes in public—had begun. In private, he sometimes referred to Colonel Cristobal as *El Raton*. So did others.

"There is the business of the native prisoners arrested at the cargo dock. Two Dhirn and one Khaj. They made their way into the restricted unloading area, disabled two servo mechanisms with handfuls of sand in their utility plates and proceeded to open government sealed crates.''

"Did they find. . . ? Jimenez half stood.

"No. They had opened some containers of church books. We found them before the ship arrived. The point, though, is that they *might* have . . .''

Jimenez cut him off. "Execution. Public execution. We have no choice. Tomorrow.'' The commandant found a cigar in a bureau drawer behind him.

"Dawn, sir?''

Jimenez found a magnesium filament and lit his cigar with shaking hands. "Dawn, noon? What difference does it make? Our duty is clear, no?''

"I would think so, sir. The point is they may have been looking for something in particular.''

"The solar collectors.'' Jimenez blew clouds of smoke at the cracked ceiling.

"We have to consider the possibility of a leak.'' Cristobal leaned forward again. "You *do* intend to go through with the solar project in Nijwhol, don't you, Commandant? If you do . . .''

"My intentions are what they are. If I find it efficacious to share them with you, I certainly will, Colonel.''

"I understand, sir.''

"The execution details are up to you. It's your sort of work. If there's nothing else, good night, Colonel Cristobal.''

"Good night, sir.''

Cristobal rose, saluted and walked away, his bootheels muffled on the dust-covered floor. Before he had arrived at the double set of plasteel doors leading out onto the courtyard and parade ground, Jimenez called him once again. "Cristobal!''

The colonel turned and called into the shadows, "Sir?''

"You're quite sure there was nothing else?''

"I . . . believe we have covered everything of importance, Commandant. Why?''

Cristobal was answered with a long pause. The commandant emitted a low chuckling from across the room. The colonel was peering into the darkness trying to make out the face of the military governor, but the overhead chandelier cast the ranking officer's face in enigmatic shadow.

"Just trying to be thorough, Colonel. It's nothing, good night . . . again."

Cristobal was momentarily at a loss. Could it be Jimenez was aware of the starship captain's detailed computerized report? That was impossible; he himself had intercepted the tachyon message long ago and made certain only *he* knew of it. The Dhirn communications technician who operated the equipment had assured Cristobal the transmission was "locked": it was received by them alone. He had further insured secrecy by transmitting a tapeworm program that destroyed even the *Pandora*'s record of its computer's analysis.

The only other receiving terminal (in the administration building) had been down as usual—and still was. The technician had met with an "accident" shortly afterward in the desert. This was seen to by Cristobal himself though he neither enjoyed it nor found it difficult, it was simply necessary. Presumably Captain Skijord was familiar with the nature of the report, but was undoubtedly far too busy with his own concerns to have given it much scrutiny. Had Skijord spoken with Jimenez already? No. Highly improbable. The fat fool suspected something; he was fishing, but fishing in the dark. Cristobal said, "Something is troubling you, Manuel?" Using the commandant's first name was an unctuous appeal.

"Always, Eduardo. Always."

The colonel smiled uncertainly into the shadows and turned again on his heels.

When *El Raton* had left, Jimenez took another bottle from the bureau and poured himself a large tumblerful. He had been summoned from sleep eight hours ago by Captain Fioricci who advised him that the terminal in the administration building was back on line and that it was storing a priority transmission from the *Pandora* it had apparently automatically filed several weeks ago. Previously there had been no way of knowing this since the display indicators had been dead, dependent as they were on conventional power. The crystal receiving memory nonetheless had something to say. Jimenez immediately ordered a printout of whatever it was. None too soon. The power died again three-quarters of the way through the print program because of the drain the old-fashioned laser print device put on the jury-rigged power facilities in the administration building. Still there was enough of it to deprive him of sleep for the rest of the night. Glancing now at the plastic hard copy of the fragmented report, he began to breathe too quickly and slammed his fist onto the desk.

Calming himself, he removed his glasses and set aside the page. So much for Cristobal's candid advisements. It didn't surprise him really, but it did disappoint him.

The Andromedans were on his moon and Cristobal did not mention it once.

Cristobal *must know.* When the report was transmitted, it must have come through the other terminal in the communications shed. No one, it seemed, after a hurried, quiet investigation, knew anything about it. The technician on duty the day it originally came through had been reported missing two weeks ago.

From what he could understand, with the help of Major Joxbov, his Rigelian science advisor, this report indicated that Darkath's moon, known as Giata to the Darkers, or more prosaically to the Terrans as "Delgado's Satellite 2," harbored an armada of unidentified starships on its dark side. Radio silent, emitting no light or heat, they nonetheless radiated erratic, but unmistakably powerful energy pulses at seemingly random intervals. "Like a small cluster of variable stars" was Joxbov's phrase. The *Pandora*'s computer, testing for conventional power sources, came up empty. Whatever they were, they were not fusion powered or ion driven or anything else in between that the computer could refer to. Mathematical language referring to pure "potential energy" recurred in the report, but this, Joxbov announced, meant nothing.

The alien, rhinolike scientist who smelled as grotesque to Jimenez as he looked, mumbled something about "subatomic particle fuel—possibly. Not unlike the way tachyons work . . . antimatter, and the manipulation of theoretical space. While our stardrives, you might say, cheat space, these ships might well travel in a way that would be analogous to 'imagining' or creating the space they travel through."

He went on to disparage his own remarks by saying, "All of this is also nonsense to me. You might as well say the things run on magic. I mean, according to this, as near as I can figure, those things aren't even really there. Or they are sometimes, but not at other times. Maybe they *used* to be there a long time ago. Or maybe they aren't there yet, but they *will* be ten years from now. They are *potentially* there. *Sort of there.* Still," he concluded, "we must assume they *are* there. I suppose." He had pointed to the spectrographic photos taken from drone probes in the moon's orbit. "It's safe to assume that their stardrive is a product of so vastly superior a technology to ours that I am like a sand wasp speculating on the manner in which hovercraft achieve altitude without wings. If they can travel in this mode without destroying themselves in the process, they should be running this Empire and not us."

Of course, the thought that that might indeed be their intention was the first thing that occurred to Jimenez.

Analysis of the spectroholos revealed that the average size of one ship was one hundred meters by one hundred meters by forty-nine meters. But the sizes varied. They seemed, some of them, to be a winged configuration though the computer could come up with no practical reason, dynamically, why this would be advantageous for space travel. Aesthetics possibly. As for weaponry, the computer again could only speculate. Given the shielded energy sources, they could well have weapons that could destroy a target two weeks before the trigger was pulled . . . or maybe they had a simple and elegant method for throwing rocks, like a zero G slingshot with very sophisticated aim. Jimenez himself had seen versions of this in campaigns against spacefaring species.

One thing was certain; while there had been reports among the Terran Starcorps for years that such ships winked in and out of Imperial space, no one had ever actually encountered them in a more thoroughly documented way than this. The computer stated with almost emphatic confidence, that these ships were from another galaxy, most likely Andromeda. And there were at least sixty-two of them.

He ran his eyes over the section of the report that dealt with the *Pandora*'s computer postulating the energy impulses as language, an attempt at communication. Several pages of this proved that even the most arcane and convoluted of methods its cyberlinguistic programs could bring to bear on the possibility produced only doggerel.

So Jimenez did not know what it meant. There was, in fact, no way to know any more than that he was in trouble. More than likely, the entire Empire was in trouble—and the possibility that he would be blamed for this, on top of everything else made him feel suddenly very very old.

Another all-too-real nuance to the problem he faced was that no one at Quadrant Headquarters wanted to hear about supposed Andromeda sightings anymore. They were up to their teeth in such reports and nothing ever came of them. This was not a strategically wise moment in the commandant's career to raise his hand

and say, "Excuse me, sirs, I think you'd better take another look here." He would be ignored and ridiculed on top of it.

That may well have been why Cristobal had not mentioned it. He would know well the weary indifference with which this intelligence would be met by Quadrant Authority. No one cared. Still, Jimenez didn't think that was it. Cristobal knew, all right. He knew everything that went on. As to why his prime minister was saying nothing, he could only speculate . . . and that provided nothing helpful. Whatever it was Cristobal had up his sleeve, Jimenez could be certain it was bad news.

In an attempt to put it out of his mind, he tried once again to recall his days on San Miguel I when his wife was so pretty, his daughter so young—but the rising moon reflected the violet light from the sun of Darkath and tainted everything in the room with the color of living blood.

Chapter Four

The hovercar rolled slowly on its flexible wheels along the streets of "Darker Heights," as Wilson called it. The "Darkers" themselves, he pointed out, had no name for the congested grouping of bazaars, smoking tents, brothels, bars, shops, shrines, and other diversions that had cropped up around the fringes of the cantonment and spaceport. Since there had previously been no such thing as a city on Darkath, the Darkhani did not know they were supposed to give a name to it. "City," in any event, was not quite the word, Cain thought. The proliferation of dwellings and population resembled, more than anything, some organic, bacterial growth, a parasitic culture surrounding the host organism of the Terran settlement. The imagery was further enhanced by the musky smell of hastily conceived waste accommodations.

It was impossible to travel faster than a few kilometers an hour through the crowd, but Cain, Wilson, and the boy were thrown backward, forward, and to either side constantly as the driver hit the brakes, accelerated, or swerved to avoid pedestrians or the Dhirn vehicles that reminded Cain of tricycles. Keeping the boy shaded with his helmet and a short tunic he had removed, Cain asked Wilson to go through his papers to see who his family might be.

Wilson glanced absently through the passport, some letters, and documents, all the while keeping up a running commentary on the events in the street as if he were a native tour guide. ". . . is what they call an

Iravka Tar. It's that one there you see, with the great yellow piece of glass hanging in those macramé sort of things and all the smoke coming out of the top of it. I'll take you there one day if you like, share a few bowls. Highly recreational. Oh, yes. You see that fellow there, with the long knife, the Khaj?''

Cain looked where Wilson was pointing. A hot breeze had come up again, stirring the dust and setting the natives' clothing flapping around them. The buildings with their hides and rope swayed easily in the wind. The dust obscured his vision so that he could not, at first, make out what Wilson was talking about. A shower of sparks caught his attention and he turned to see a Khaj warrior, veiled beneath his tattooed eyes and wearing loose, pastel robes that billowed in the dusty squall. It was the first of the sun worshiping warriors Cain had seen who was not dressed in a Terran military uniform. The Khaj held a short sword in two hands and dragged it over the surface of a large stone in the road that sent pieces of the metal flying in tiny blue-white filaments. Cain noticed the deliberate, ritualized air about his movements. The Khaj repeated the action three times. A young Dhirn stood across the tortured, winding thoroughfare bearing a similar, but more abbreviated blade. The Dhirn youth raked the edge of his blade across a small stone he held in his other hand. Sparks seemed to leap from his fingertips.

A crowd of Darkhani gathered quickly as if summoned by the scent of blood or aroused by some invisible but powerful magnet. The Dhirn among them jostled the Khaj who, in turn, shoved and threatened. Soon there were four or five subsidiary fistfights surrounding the duel. In the brief series of moments it took for the hovercar to negotiate its way past the site, the tableau had escalated from a threatening confrontation between two individuals to a mob melee.

Although Cain had been prepared to see evidence of antagonism between what were essentially two competing tribes, he could now see, feel, and smell the true level of tension between them. He had previously witnessed hostility of this kind only between two wildly incompatible alien species . . . or human, Terran religious factions. The anthropologist in Cain observed and speculated: at least a millennium of competition for what few resources this planet offered for survival, the sparse flora and fauna, coupled with deeply entrenched and divergent religious beliefs and this was the result: mindless, knee-jerk violence.

"A challenge to the death!" Wilson announced merrily as they rolled past the chaotic scene. Cain turned in his seat to watch the outcome of the fight, but the combatants were quickly lost in the gathering dust storm. "The Khaj will undoubtedly kill the boy," Wilson pronounced and then turned his attention distractedly to the papers in his lap.

"What's that all about? Do you know?" Cain asked.

"Not really. That was a whiskey kiosk they had emerged from. You can tell by the pattern of colored stones and crystals over the door. You'll catch on eventually. They were probably all drunk. Then again, maybe they weren't. This lot doesn't need any reason at all to kill each other. A Khaj doesn't decide to kill a Dhirn because he doesn't like the cut of his jib or his religious preference. Contrariwise, a Dhirn doesn't creep into a Khaj camp in the dead of night to slit throats because the Khaj threatens his family or property. No. Here the only reason one Darker kills another is because *he thinks he can.*" He paused and checked Cain's reaction. Cain's expression didn't change. "You'll know what I mean before long."

Wilson turned his attention back to the boy's satchel. "Nothing here but a bunch of letters the boy wrote, vaccination documents . . . smart of him. Nothing like any offworld visa here." Wilson produced a tiny holocube and held it up. "Well, what have we here?" He chuckled and handed the cube to Cain who saw the image of a fair-haired girl in the kind of web-robe women wore on Cygnus. Next to her was a harsh looking man in the dress tunic of a Terran corporal. In the man's arms was an infant.

Wilson pointed at the satchel. "I saw that the lad's name was Avery. Jack Avery, but I didn't connect him with the Avery I know. It's the same man in the picture though, a bit younger, of course, quite a bit. Good Lord, so 'Old Ironblood' has a son." Wilson spoke more to himself than anyone else. "Goes to show you, you never know a man really."

Cain felt faint. He had pills for planetary disorientation, but he hadn't taken one in years since rootlessness and constant sensory adaption had become a staple of his life—first as a soldier and then as a correspondent. He considered taking one of them now, but he wasn't quite sure where he kept them any longer or even if he really still had them. *Strange. Why this place? I haven't felt so . . . dislocated since . . . .* Images of Cozuela came back to him as they always did in dreams, all too often waking dreams. He forced himself to concentrate. "You know the boy's father?" He asked Wilson.

"Oh, I should say so. At least I thought I did. The old *cabrone*. A son, eh?"

Cain had little patience at the moment. He wanted to deliver the boy and find a place to rest. Somewhere cool—if indeed there was such a place. "Well, can you take us to him?"

"It's right up here. On the way." Wilson leaned forward and issued instructions to the driver in pidgin Darkhani mixed with Spanish. *"A Azteca kiyayi te, siva, siva keen. Aqui."* The car accelerated around a sharp corner, scattering pedestrians and a flock of bizarre looking birds that looked to Cain like a cross between chickens and waddling reptiles. "We'll find old Avery at the Aztec unless he's already passed out or on patrol with 'Ironblood's Lancers.' " Wilson let out a sharp whoop that exacerbated Cain's gathering headache. "Oh, I can't wait. Imagine it, Avery, here's your son from Cygnus. Oh, my."

The boy began to rouse himself. He tried to sit up, but Cain pressed him back against the headrest. "Easy, take it easy. You'll see your father soon. You'll be all right."

"Father?" The boy licked his lips and stared around him. "Darkath. Oh, yes, this is Darkath isn't it?"

"That it is, boy." Wilson barked happily again. Cain winced. "That it is."

* * *

The Aztec was a combination whiskey shop, *iravka* parlor, bordello, unofficial noncommissioned officers' club, and watering hole for correspondents. The building itself was an unlikely admixture of Terran foamcrete geodesic—crumbling and gaping in spots— held together with native hempwork, hides, and Dhirn glasscraft. Banners from a half-dozen regiments hung on the walls. Over the bar, a Dhirn sandpainting of a busty native woman riding a dragonlike beast hung next to a Terran hologram of Quetzalcoatl, the cthonic Aztec god, bearing a likeness of that same woman in his arms.

It was cool inside. An old temperature unit (secret contraband, Cain later learned) was laboring noisily in one corner beyond a group of tables where Terran, Darkhani, Cappellan, and Rigelian patrons shared a milky fluid in a beaker. All of them, except for the Dhirn and the Rigelian, Cain could see, wore Terran military fatigues in haphazard combinations.

The boy, Jack Avery, would not allow Cain to assist him to a table. "I'm fine," he assured him. "Thank you. If I could get some water . . ."

"Right." Cain approached the bartender, a fat Dhirn who was lighter skinned than any he had seen so far. The bartender wore a desert fatigue utility vest over his paunch. The vest was festooned with military decorations of every kind including the Cruz De Oro—the highest honor bestowed on an Imperial soldier—

though it was clear the barman was not military personnel of any kind. Cain resisted the temptation to ask him how he came to possess such ornamentation and asked for water.

"Agua? Water?" the expressionless Dhirn enquired. "Mil cruzeiros, Jafar. One thousand. One and three zeros for water." The bartender seemed both incredulous and amused.

Wilson came to his rescue. "Cain, you don't order bloody water here. It costs a fortune. Have a brandy. Ten croozies and good brandy, too. Drink water at the cantonment, all you want."

Cain gestured at his charge. "He needs water, Wilson."

"Yes, yes, all right. You're Martin Cain after all, aren't you? *Water!*" He shrugged to the barman. "Water *and* brandy. On me, or rather Starfax, eh?" Wilson winked at Cain in imagined conspiracy. "A brandy won't do the boy any harm either."

"I suppose not," Cain agreed.

They collected three drinks and two glasses of dirty water and brought them to a table. Jack downed the water and grimaced though it seemed to have a salutary effect on him. "I'm sorry," he said. "I remember passing out at the spaceport. I didn't mean to cause you any bother."

"The heat," Cain said simply.

Cain looked the boy over more closely. He was pale with a nascent complexion problem that normally in boys his age would become worse before it got better—but in this desert you couldn't tell. His hair was fine and dirty brown. It looked as if it hadn't been washed for a month or more. Jack Avery's eyes were large and deep set, a bright blue, set closely together. They were the eyes of a shrewd child trying to mask his fear and confusion. The boy rose hesitantly, looking around him, perhaps for an exit. "I'd better be going."

Cain, with one hand, firmly but easily lowered the boy back into his seat. He inclined his head slightly toward Wilson. "This man knows your father. He comes here, I gather."

"Yes," said Wilson, "He's not here now, but he will be before long, I'm sure." Wilson flourished his brandy. "In the meantime, this is just the place to cool off and chat, get to know one another. I'm sure you have a thousand questions."

The boy continued to look puzzled and as if he were about to speak. He leaned forward and then sat back once again as if he had thought better of his question or could not decide what to ask first.

Cain spoke. "Why was my holopack taken and how do I get it back?"

Wilson frowned. "All of our holocorders have been taken away. Someone once made the mistake of explaining to a Khaj elder how they worked. Since then they've been banned, just like the light weapons."

"They're hardly the same thing." Cain tried the water and grimaced.

"Try telling that to these maniacs." Wilson leaned toward the boy and gestured at his untouched brandy. "Are you going to drink this?" Jack shook his head absently. He continued to look about him, fascinated by the strange atmosphere of the place.

Wilson grinned, holding the brandy glass up to the fading daylight that leaked through the mesh walls. Refracted light from the red giant caught in the pulsing colored glass and crystal embedded there seemingly in a random pattern. The brandy in its snifter seemed dull and lusterless by comparison though Wilson seemed to find it infinitely aesthetic in its appeal to the eye. "As for getting your holocorder back, it's not likely, but you never know. You're famous. Maybe you can pull some strings." Wilson sipped at the brandy lovingly. "Among the many paradoxical aspects of this impossible place is that almost anything is possible."

Cain said, "I take it you don't much care for the Darkhani." Cain should not have been surprised, he thought, Wilson was exactly the kind of man one would expect on a colony world like this. Darkath had no resources to speak of, no trade potential, militarily it was of no strategic value whatever. The only reason for the Empire's presence here was that it was the farthest habitable world from the hub and so had some small value as supposed evidence of the faltering Empire's dominating, pervasive presence, its steady paternal hand on worlds from the hub to the rim. But the real reason for the colony, upon closer examination, was the increasing influence of the clergy on Imperial matters. The Church of the Universal Blood was quickly becoming the political force behind the decadent Imperium. And here on Darkath was a race of humanoid pagans crying out for the truth, the light, the blood! The kind of professional men who found themselves on what amounted to a missionary colony were the kind of men who were not needed elsewhere. No wonder Wilson was bitter, resentful, and hard. Cain wondered how long the Faxman had been marinating in his cynicism.

Wilson snorted, "Darkers, Cain. Darkers. I know all about you and your love affair with every screwball species the Empire has ever found. Kind of a missionary in reverse, eh? Wiring yourself up with Coraxians in those tanks on Marus, eating poison fungus with Rigelians and dancing naked around bonfires. I heard you even had optic augments implanted and lived among the Syngi way back on Proxima. Is that true?"

"Yes," Cain said tiredly and drank his liquor. It was reviving him marginally.

"Ever make sense of that bunch?" Wilson squinted across the table. When Cain didn't answer, he went on. "It doesn't matter. Here you stick to your own kind if you know what's good for you. We're outnumbered almost five hundred to one, just in this region alone between the mud seas and the equator. Perhaps you've noticed. I'm not even counting the nomads in the plateaus or the mountain passes. It's no good trying to be pals. They just see it as weakness." He fixed Cain with a meaningful look. "The way of things here is a boot to their backsides and then another one if they don't thank you for the first. God knows no one is *really* running the show here. You might as well say the sun here runs things—or the planet itself." Wilson paused as if reflecting on the fact that what he had just said sounded exactly like native superstition. "But for appearances' sake, *we* are running the show. That's the face we have to put on things. It's that illusion that is all that's holding this powder keg of an outpost together."

Cain set his drink down and leaned back in his chair. He was too tired to conceal the dislike he had taken to the information officer. "At least we can all be grateful that *you're* not running things, Wilson."

The senior man from Starfax bristled, his jaw tightening. "See here, Cain. I'm telling you this for your own good. There is nothing noble or deep about the Darkers. They're just a pack of homicidal monkeys. If you wander off making playmates, you're likely to be found outside the cantonment walls minus your head . . . like those poor bastards the other day." Wilson peered at Cain to see if he had generated any curiosity. Cain looked blankly back at him, but Jack Avery stared in horror at the newsman. Wilson caught the boy's expression and grinned.

"Didn't know about that, did you? No, you couldn't possibly. A cartographic party; two Terran soldiers including a lieutenant, a Dhirn surveyor, and a Khaj guide accompanied by a priest and a nun who had ideas about 'reaching out' to the renegades in the mountains, set off and disappeared a month ago. Then one night, about a week afterward, a Dhirn and a Khaj, neither of them Imperial Native Troops, but outlanders from the north, were discovered going through the files in the adjutant's office late at night. They were captured and executed outside the walls. The Khaj was staked to the ground, blindfolded—a great humiliation, died without seeing the sun, you know—and

flogged. The Dhirn was tied to the walls—again a humiliation, in his case because his feet weren't touching
good old Mother Darkath when he died. He was
flogged to death, too. The idea, of course, was a good
one as a deterrent; neither of them will get into their
respective Darker heavens now." Wilson smiled and
drank from the smoke-tinted Dhirn glass. Outside, the
sun was now setting with uncanny swiftness.

"So last week the headless bodies of three of the
surveying party were discovered near the execution
site. One of them was the Terran corporal and the other
two . . . and this is the strange part, were the Darkers,
the Khaj guide and the Dhirn surveyor. Their heads
were torn from their shoulders by dragons. Undoubtedly this was a reprisal of some kind for the execu-
tions, but no one can figure why they killed *both* the
guide and the surveyor. The thing is, if it were one or
two Khaj, then it would be logical to assume it was
renegade Dhirn who killed them. Or vice versa. But
one of each?"

"Maybe they were considered traitors to a renegade
alliance of both Khaj and Dhirn," Cain offered. If
Wilson expected Cain to be shocked or frightened by
tales of local unrest, he intended to disappoint him.

Wilson grinned but waved away the possibility. "It
does add fuel to the rumor that the renegades have
united. Khaj and Dhirn side by side. The thought
would be frightening if it weren't so hard to imagine.
Rumors may abound, but I give you my personal as-
surance that no Khaj and Dhirn could abide each other
long enough to organize a spitting contest, much less
anything else. The only reason the army's had any luck
in keeping them in the same units is that we've got
better weaponry. *That* they can understand. But no,
the two they found in the adjutant's office were just a
couple of thieves, not agents of some renegade Darker
conspiracy. As to what happened to the surveyor and
the guide and why . . . that's anyone's guess. Even
yours, Cain."

"What about the rest of the party? The lieutenant, the priest, and the nun?"

Wilson shrugged. "All I can tell you is I wouldn't want to be one of 'em."

"Hostages?" Cain ventured.

Wilson produced a half smoked reddish cheroot from his shirt pocket and placed it in his mouth. "You just never know here, that's what I'm trying to tell you. The Darkers don't do things that make sense in any human way. Care to try a bit of *iravka*, Cain? How about you, lad? You look unsteady."

Jack Avery did indeed look pale. His eyes seemed to have enlarged in the fading light, offset by the colorlessness of his cheeks. "I'll be all right," he said thinly.

"You've frightened him, Wilson. Do you enjoy frightening children?" The edge in Cain's voice seemed to be lost on the older reporter.

"No, Cain, I don't. But he might as well know what it is he's gotten himself into."

Cain looked at the boy and back at Wilson. Jack shifted uncomfortably in his hard chair. By way of explanation, Wilson produced a well-thumbed journal that had been among the boy's possessions. He handed it to Cain and Jack tried to grab it away. "That's not yours. It's none of your business. Give it back!"

"You'll get it back, son," Cain assured him and leafed through the tightly written handscript. "Is it true? Did you run away?"

"My father was going to send for me when I turned seventeen anyway." He sank back in his chair defensively. "I'm old enough *now*."

Cain examined the entries in the journal. The later ones seemed filled with phrases that conveyed the terror of living for weeks in the livestock hold of the *Pandora*, but it was *why* Jack had done this that interested him. His gaze lit on one entry written nearly two months ago.

"*. . . copied the signature from the personnel dispatcher's desk . . . Mother won't care, it will*

*be a relief to her when I'm gone . . . I will know
soon if my father is the way I've always thought
of him. I know he isn't what Mother says, but it
doesn't matter even if she's right . . . they can't
send me back once I'm there, not for over a year
at least . . . I have discovered where Mother keeps
my passport and I've had a new holo made that
is the right size. . . .''*

At length, Cain looked over at the abashed juvenile
and said, ''I'm not sure how you managed it, but it
doesn't matter now, you're here. What you did was
terribly clever.'' He handed the journal back to him.
Jack grabbed it indignantly and put it away beneath
his tunic. Cain went on. ''It was also monumentally
stupid. At the very least, you will have gotten your
father in considerable trouble.''

''I haven't seen my father in five years and then it was
only for a day,'' Jack offered by way of justification.

Before Cain could comment, Wilson said, ''Well
feast your eyes, boy. There's Old Ironblood now.''

The man who had just entered the Aztec was wearing a dusty sergeant's uniform and plumed helmet. He
was tall enough to have to duck the top of the foamcrete doorway when he entered and he was as broad
in the shoulders as any Darkhani. (A significant comparison since most natives of Darkath were almost bizarrely wide in the hips, thighs, and shoulders. Avery
Senior was the first Terran Cain had seen who looked
as if he might give a good account of himself in a
wrestling match with any of the native troops under
his command. After the initial impression of size and
strength Sergeant Avery made, Cain noted the antique
machine pistol that hung from his hip in a web holster.
His gaze traveled upward and Cain saw ample evidence of Avery's tenure on Darkath; the man's skin
was coarse and so weathered that his face appeared
mottled: ravaged by sun and sand. A symmetrical scar

descended from over his left eye onto his cheek. His eyes, so often blistered and swollen from desert exposure were mere slits, sunken in shadow beneath a prominent brow.

Jack half stood in his chair and Cain reached out to steady him.

"Avery!" Wilson called out. "Over here. There's someone I'd like you to meet."

The sergeant removed his helmet and took a bottle from the Dhirn bartender. He walked toward the table carrying the bottle and a glass. Jack looked as if he might laugh, cry, hit someone, or bolt into the night.

"I thought you were meeting some offworld muckety-muck faxbender from the starship, Wilson." Sergeant Avery seated himself between the two reporters and spared the boy a cursory glance.

"So I have, John. Meet Martin Cain from Hub."

John Avery nodded, produced a grunt, and poured some native wine into his glass. "Used to see you on the holos," he mumbled at Cain.

Cain merely said, "Yes." He studied the boy across from him and then the boy's father. During their conversation he had watched Jack begin to register the full knowledge of what he had done; for a boy his age he had held up well, presented a strong, even manly facade in view of his surroundings and Wilson's pronouncements of the danger on Darkath. Now the boy looked half his age, staring at the man who was his father with a mixture of emotions his callowness could not contain. "Sergeant Avery, this boy was on the ship with me. He's your son, Jack."

A silence lay over the table. Lengthened. The sergeant looked at the boy and set his glass down. He stared at the lanky youth with narrowed eyes. Cain noted a mirroring of the determined mouth on both boy and man as well as the long flared nostrils and even the matted hair. The eyes of the boy, however, were blue and cool, shrewd and almost feminine while the older man's were ruined, deep set wounds.

At last, Wilson spoke in a whispered aside to Cain.
"I wanted to tell him, Cain. You've ruined my fun and
there isn't much of it around here."

"Shut up, Wilson." Cain said quietly to the older man.
John Avery said, "Jack?"

"Yes." The boy put his hand to his mouth to stop
it from moving.

"It's not possible. God's blood . . . I . . ."

"I had to come, I'm sorry," Jack said with both
defiance and supplication; Cain was sure the boy would
release the tension between the two by weeping, but
Jack fought the tears and after a few moments, won.
"Why didn't you ever come back?"

The elder Avery looked at Wilson, then Cain. He
did not look at his son. "It was better all the way
around."

"Not for me it wasn't." The boy's accusation hung
in the air and seemed to twist in the breeze that wafted
through the ropework and jagged holes in the foamcrete walls.

The sergeant roused himself as if from some unpleasant reverie. Frustration and anger fell over his
features. "What in all the hells are you doing here? I
won't ask you how you managed it. I can see you are
a devious one just like your mother. Have you inherited her witchery?" The sergeant did not wait for an
answer but plunged ahead with his tirade. "What did
you expect to find here on this bloodsoaked ball of
dust? Did your mother fill your head with nonsense
about me?" More to himself, John Avery muttered,
"I couldn't have gotten any farther away. Don't you
understand? I don't want to be reminded, boy. Ever
again. I can see her laughing at me from your eyes."

The boy sat glaring at his parent with anger, awe,
hatred, and love. The sergeant stared incredulously
back at him as if simultaneously trying to reject and
retrieve his past. Wilson cleared his throat, stood and
took his glass to the bar to be refilled. Cain stood also.

"We'll leave you two alone. You must have a lot to talk about."

"No." Sergeant Avery stood. "We have nothing to talk about. I'm taking him to the adjutant's office. He can be put on the starship going back. Thank you for helping him, but he has no business here."

Cain looked levelly back at the sergeant's flint-hard eyes. "That's your affair, naturally."

"I suppose I am in your debt for helping him." Avery appeared to be excruciatingly uncomfortable at the prospect of being in anyone's debt.

"No," Cain said, "forget it." He turned to join Wilson at the bar and urge the reporter to show him to his quarters in the cantonment. "Good luck to you, Sergeant Avery . . . and your boy."

The soldier put a hand on Cain's arm, staying him. "I know you think I'm a hard man, Mr. Cain, but you don't know the facts."

"No, I don't. It's none of my business." Cain genuinely did not care to know the facts. It would not change his opinion of Avery which was that the soldier was, in fact, a hard man. "Now if you'll excuse me, Sergeant."

Cain joined Wilson at the bar. At his back he heard, "If there's anything I can do for you, Mr. Cain . . ."

Cain turned to nod tiredly and try to smile. His expression froze when he noticed the table behind John Avery, the table where they had all been sitting a moment ago. It was empty.

Cain looked up and down the room. Avery turned and shouted, "Jack?"

But the boy was gone.

Chapter Five

When the first band of violescent light from Darkath's titanic moon appeared on the desert horizon, the Khaj scout signalled Hara's party on the canyon floor below. The scout could already be seen silhouetted against that light as he stood on the lip of the escarpment and put his hand to his mouth reproducing the cry of the *kagra*. Below, Hara hissed the order to dismount. It was a good place to stop for the night. She estimated they were more than halfway between the Terran camp and the Nijwhol plateau. They would rest for three hours, eat and leave before sunlight to arrive back at the caves before midday. They had encountered no Terran patrols and Hara expected none. Since the execution of the three surveying party members, the Terrans, like timid sailors, had hugged the shore of their island and ventured no farther than was necessary into the desert sea.

When her party had dismounted, tethered their beasts to rocks and began gathering puhlcalf to feed them and start a fire, she herself poked at the side of her Grea' ka with the spike on her boot. The animal let out a low whoofing sound and a cloud of gas from fermented vegetation. She took no notice of the momentary stench. As she slid from the saddle, the animal turned to bite her on the back of the leg. She grabbed one of its horns and brought her fist down just above its eyes. The beast retaliated by spitting a stream of hot, pungent cud at her feet. She cursed, wiped the viscous, steaming drool from her boot with the hem of her robe and silently prayed that she would soon capture a Terran hovercar for her personal use. Once away from her trusty Grea' ka she breathed easier. The relatively cool night breeze funneled its way through the canyon carrying the scent of night blooming desert flowers.

Nos, the corpulent Dhirn shaman, unstrapped himself from the crystal sled behind the mount in front of her and approached Hara. "It is time for the prayer to *Giata*, Hara."

"Yes, go on." The ritual invocation, while it had been, in a way, her own idea, had begun to annoy her. The time could be better spent in planning for contingencies such as the possible capture of her people at the spaceport, but she knew her presence was necessary. The recent alliance between the Dhirn and the Khaj could be effected by nothing less than worship of a common god. And so Hara and Sivran had turned to *Giata* as a perfect compromise. The Dhirn, who worshiped Mother Darkath herself and the Khaj, whose spiritual allegiance lay with the Sun Father, found a mutual religious mentor in *Giata*, their moon. Child of Alaikhaj (*Giata*'s father) and Darkath (his mother), the satellite god was a perfect symbol of unity between factions and could serve them both.

For both Dhirn and Khaj, this joint worship was particularly timely as *Giata* was the focus for an ancient prophecy among them concerning invaders from the stars who would be vanquished one hundred years after their arrival by beings from *Giata*'s dark side.

The prophecies of Dhirn and Khaj differed only in the nature of the avengers: the promised liberators tended to be perceived as angels by the Khaj and demons by the Dhirn. At the time of the next rains, it would be one hundred years exactly since the arrival of the Terrans. The timing, while it disturbed Hara on some inaccessible level, could not be more perfect for her purposes.

And so, she dismounted and joined the circle of less than five score renegade Khaj and Dhirn who came together over a smoky fire of slow burning leaves and lifted their prayers to the rising moon.

> *Oh, Giata, Son of Alaikhaj, Father of us all*
> *and Darkath Our Mother,*
> *guide our movements this night.*
> *Cloak us from our enemies*
> *and illuminate their treachery.*
> *Send forth your demon spawn to rend our foes.*
> *Send forth your angels to armor us.*
> *Your children are the hope of our children.*
> *The grandchildren of Alaikhaj and Darkath*
> *are the hope of our grandchildren.*

Nos spoke alone. *As it was written in the flesh of your mother.*

The Dhirn among them repeated the phrase.

Hara provided the Khaj response. *As it was shown to us in your father's fiery heart.*

The Khaj echoed her.

In unison, nearly one hundred voices ended the prayer with the word, *Tirat.* It was the same word the Terran priests chose in native translations of the ancient *Amen* at the close of prayer. It meant, not so much, "So be it" as "It is unless the gods change their mind." It was a word indicative of the ambiguous nature of their language, their gods and their lives.

Hara unrolled her knitted bedding from the panniers on her Grea' ka and found a place on the canyon floor next to Nos and Karsha. She lay staring at the ruddy, bruised surface of Giata and tried to meditate. Her hopes for sleep were almost nonexistent; when it did come, it was laden with dreams of slaughter. She thought of the Khaj soldier she had sent with Sivran's men to examine the starship's cargo. He was little more than a boy, but he was stealthy and brave. She had spotted him in the streets near the cantonment stealing bulbs of Terran liquor. He had piled his tunic with a dozen of the containers unseen by anyone but her. When she had confronted him, he was mortified. More, she thought, because he had been caught than for any other reason. Hara, of course, cared nothing for the victims of the private's thievery, but she instructed him to put his talents in her service. The young warrior thief was honored. Now, as she lay staring at the moon, she wondered how he fared. As she wondered, she drifted into a kind of sleep, but not before she saw, or thought she saw, several tiny white flashes from the surface of Giata. It was almost as if the young god were winking at her.

She thought no more about it and slept a dreamless sleep for the first time in weeks.

She was awakened by Karsha. It was time to move on. Giata had moved across a third of the sky and she could hear sand and rock sifting through the fissures in the pass wall. A large tremor was coming. As she automatically prepared to travel again she found herself wishing that the tremor would split the starship like an egg and leak its poison cargo over the useless, artificial rock of the spaceport. It had happened before, more than once. If luck were truly with them . . . but she could not count on luck. Success was something she would have to insure with her actions.

The caravan of Grea' ka and their sleds ascended in darkness, gliding over the increasingly rugged pass toward the summit. Just beneath them, the ground shook and tossed as if Darkath writhed in her sleep, tormented by the dreams Hara had herself escaped for a few hours. At dawn, when Alaikhaj erupted over the horizon setting the mountains and desert on fire, the Khaj among them turned to look into the fireball and silently recited the morning's prayers while the Dhirn shifted uneasily in their sleds and talked quietly.

The morning's invocation complete, Hara wheeled on her Grea' ka and turned to face the great sprawling plain below them known as the Nijwhol basin. Still in the mountain's shadow, the basin appeared to be the very edge of the world: a great yawning void where nothing could possibly live. In fact, very little did live there. The basin was the most stable area on the planet, a vast tectonic plate, hundreds of kilometers wide and half again as thick, made of imprevious, volcanic stone that tilted almost imperceptibly with the gyrations of the planet's core and surrounding surface. Except for a rare crazed Khaj holy man who would wander out there to die in the unblinking gaze of Alaikhaj and a few species of hardy weeds and insects that lived symbiotically off each other, the plain was empty—hostile to any life since there was no water. Not a drop. Elsewhere on Darkath's surface, lakes would appear and disappear with the capriciousness of the mother goddess. Streams and rivers would form, flow, dry up or seek out the bowels of the planet again only to reappear years later—or not. But Nijwhol was dry. Bone dry. Drier than the eyes of a Khaj widow it was said. Only once every eighteen months when the torrential rains fell would the basin flood and then, with the first major tremors, send wild, turbulent tides crazily against the foothills of the surrounding mountains where the earth would open up and drink its fill. Nijwhol meant ''God's Mouth.''

Travelling along the mountain peaks, Nijwhol to one side, the jagged descending peaks on the other, Hara's troops arrived at the caves—the stronghold for the Khaj/Dhirn alliance—by midday as planned. Nos organized his people and led them to the caves assigned to them by Hara. Hara's troops dismounted and went to their respective ''barracks.'' Here they could sleep, cook meals over a fire and await the news from Sivran. The caves were made up, in part, of the same integral stone as that of Nijwhol's floor making them the most stable natural habitat on the planet. Streams of water would appear with some regularity through the network of caverns, and puhlcalf, arghasch (a leafy, lettuce-like cactus) and daric root grew in abundance. It was, in short, a subterranean oasis that had been a freehold for centuries, though controlled historically by the Khaj.

Beyond the caves, at the very peak of Ayeia Alaikhaj, the highest point on Darkath, was the temple, the hewn obelisk that bore the crystal used in "The Ceremonies of Light"—The Eye of God. It was here that Hara went to meet Juum, the blind Khaj holy man. Juum was seated at the end of the dark stone corridor on a woven mat. Before him was a bowl of cold soup and a long wood-like instrument similar to a recorder. His hair was yellow with age and worn loose, not braided. His face resembled a desiccated eggplant gaily painted with bright tattoos around cataract eyes. He stared, without seeing, through a window carved in the rock wall and hung with jewels in a web net of leathery fiber. Beyond the window, The Eye of God caught the midday ray of Ailakhaj and spun and refracted that light into a protean play of prismatic beams that danced over the old seer's face.

"Hara," his voice sounded like the sifting of gravel in a mild quake. "Your footsteps speak of weariness."

Though his back was to her, Hara did not seem surprised that he recognized her. "Troubled sleep, Father."

"Yes," he nodded as though that were proper, expected. "News?" he asked tersely.

"Not yet. We must wait. Tonight there will be a celebration at the cantonment for the new arrivals from the ship. At that time Sivran's people will signal us."

He nodded once again and proffered the bowl of soup. Hara seated herself next to him and drank the salty brew. They sat in silence as she lost herself in the colors of God's Eye. Presently Juum began to play: soft slow melodies that spoke of desert winds, the colors of light and the death of warriors. She fell asleep listening.

Chapter Six

Jack Avery found himself in trouble.

He wandered through the labyrinthine streets of alien buildings that were more like tents or shacks, keeping to the shadows and alleyways that would dead-end as quickly as they opened. He had no idea where he was going, in which direction or why. He only knew that the meeting with his father had been a failure, that he had traveled over a hundred light-years to be treated like a stray dog. It was true, then, what his mother had told him, that Jack Avery Senior was inhuman—their little joke (long since turned sour) since she had no Terran blood—that the man had no feelings, his only passions being discipline and bloodshed. His maternal grandmother, never one to say an unkind word toward anyone, called his father "intemperate and uncheerful." Well, Jack would not blubber or pine. It had been a calculated risk from the start, his own idea, and now he knew. He would summon all the coldness and lack of emotion that he might have inherited from "Old Ironblood" and make his own way. He resolved to need no one.

This was decided almost unconsciously and in a matter of moments since the greater part of his attention was engaged in negotiating the darkness of the alien "streets." He dodged furtive figures shambling to and from doorways, the small, chickenlike animals that seemed everywhere underfoot, and several reclining bodies, dead or asleep, stretched out upon the ground or leaning against structures that seemed too frail to support them.

Thoroughly lost, he fought down his fear and approached several passing natives: Dhirn by the look of their shorn hair. He asked directions to the Terran cantonment and was met with silence, curious pale stares, or incomprehensible mutterings. He knew that the network of native shacks and haphazard streets surrounded the cantonment in a rough crescent configuration—he had studied a crude map on the starship that was several years old. The Terran settlement was built into the side of a mountain formation on a great outcropping and he should be able to see its lights, but no matter where he turned he saw only the starshot blackness and the glowering, rubious moon overhead. He had read that the native "village" tended to take on the form of a series of plazas where wells formed or water merchants would set up shop and short streets or alleyways would radiate out from these plazas like irregular spokes on a wheel. Therefore it was not only possible, but highly likely, that—unless you knew exactly where you were going—you would find yourself getting farther away from your destination rather than closer to it, even if you could see it plainly.

Suddenly, one quarter of the night sky exploded. Flowerlike eruptions of red, gold, white, green, and blue flooded the heavens accompanied by a barrage of deafening sound. The fireworks illuminated the jagged abutment and plateau on which the Terran cantonment was situated. It lay directly ahead of him. All around him, Jack saw the faces of the natives turned heavenward, heard them gasp and ahh at the display in much the same manner as any Terran family might on an evening's picnic. But interspersed with the conventional sounds of awe, he could hear curses and shouts, see arms and hands upraised in gestures of disdain, anger, or protest. Children ran into their mothers' skirts to hide their faces. The chickenlike reptiles darted for shadows that appeared and disappeared in the strobelike effect of the stuttering lights. The jewels and colored glass stones that hung in the ropework of the native tents winked in repetition of the phenomenon overhead. Momentarily lit by the explosives, faces loomed out of the darkness. Tattooed and white-masked, they seemed like demonic visions from some fevered nightmare. Some were looking at him, shouting, pointing at him. And then two of them, with long braids, began to move toward him.

Jack's instincts told him to run. He did. He attempted to leap over a pile of overflowing Terran sanitation containers, but the heavier gravity announced itself mercilessly and Jack found himself sprawling amid the overturned, foul-smelling contents of two battered plasteel trash cubes. He got to his feet with more effort than he had anticipated and bolted lumberingly toward a gap between two shacks. The braided aliens ran after him.

One of them grabbed a momentary handhold on Jack's clothing. It tore away and he was running free, minus his tunic.

He found himself in one of the plazas. He stopped and turned frantically in every direction, the strobe-light and shadowplay of the fireworks making things even more confusing than they were in the previous darkness. Pain knifed through his chest and his legs trembled with exertion and adrenaline. In the center of the plaza was a stone-ringed pit some five meters wide. Three Dhirn sat on the edges like gargoyles and studied the sky without expression, until Jack burst into their field of vision. They turned and stared at him, each blinking slowly.

When the shouts of the men chasing him could be heard, the three Dhirn got up slowly and spread themselves out to intercept Jack. Jack feinted to the right and when they converged, dodged left and around them. This time allowing for the denser gravity, he launched himself up onto the stone ring of the well and broad jumped the narrow opening. He nearly overcompensated and missed his footing on the other side. He scrambled up and over, fell, rolled, and came up running. He knocked into a group of young Khaj, his own age, he estimated, or the local equivalent. He fled into darkness.

The shouts of the men chasing him grew fainter and he slowed marginally. A good thing, because as he turned, still running, to see what was behind him, he ran full into a beam of Terran plasticrete that supported a large, dimly illuminated tent. He was thrown backward, dazed. He felt blood run from his forehead onto his left eye.

He could hear the shouts grow louder and he scurried on all fours looking for an entrance to the tent. He lifted away a flap of woven rope and crawled inside.

The room was filled with smoke and aliens of both sexes. Some of them formed a circle in the middle of the space around a large glass bowl with tentaclelike hoses reaching away into the corners. The glass was filled with burning embers and leaves. The room's other occupants were stretched out on pallets of rags and frayed pillows. A sweet incense tried to cover a sour, charred odor that emanated from the pipe and the bitter smell of alien perspiration. A hollow, holed instrument and another with stunted strings played by the same musician provided a discordant drone in the background that some swayed to arrhythmically. No one noticed his presence.

Jack quickly buried his head in one of the pillows, to silence his rasping attempts to fill aching lungs and covered his body with a dusty, thin mattress. A moment later, the two Khaj poked their heads in the door, peered through the gloom and just as suddenly disappeared, their excited jabbering growing fainter as they continued the search elsewhere.

He lay for a moment trying to still his heart, calm his shuddering body, jamming the pillow into his face to clog his nostrils against the bizarre odors. Outside, the boom and crump of the fireworks provided a plodding backbeat to his labored breathing and racing heart.

As he lay there, he thought: If I were back on Cygnus right now I would be in school, staring out the window at the spaceport beyond the trees, listening to Doña Estoban recite the principal products of Altair IV. Or I would be at home with Mother and Grandmother watching colonial dramas of conquest and romance on distant planets . . . or playing Empire and Bugs with David and Enrico, or asleep in my own bed, all the while wondering—about Father, Darkath, real aliens. He let out a muffled laugh into the pillow. The laugh threatened to become tears and he pressed the crude cloth into his face until the feeling passed. When it did, he became aware of how hungry he was. He couldn't remember the last time he had eaten. There was nothing he could do about that now. He would try and rest here for a moment and gather his thoughts.

He lifted the pillow a few inches from his face and breathed the acrid, sweet odors of the room. The smoke smelled much like the cheroot the man Wilson was smoking when he met his father. As he breathed, he remembered thinking: I wonder what those Khaj wanted with me? And then his thoughts took on funny, cartoon shapes that eased him into a twilight trance between sleep and wakefulness. Sometimes the images that fluttered beneath his eyelids were benevolent and grand and at times they were frightening, nightmare images of menace. He lay there for several hours unaware of the sheen of sweat drenching his body and the mattress. Unaware that he was taking in the fumes of a powerful drug with each breath.

* * *

Just after sunset, Cain and Wilson left the Aztec with Avery. They stood with a group of the cantina's clientele and watched the firework display overhead. Wilson, on his fourth brandy, announced, "It's to celebrate the arrival of the starship. The Darkers don't like it!'' He grinned boozily at Cain.

Cain, wanting very much to find a bed of some sort, turned to Avery. "What about your son?"

"I'll put some men on it," he said as if discussing a latrine digging detail. "Boy could get himself into worlds of trouble out there." He gestured with his chin at the maze of streets winding upward toward the mountainside settlement.

"Should I notify the adjutant's office?"

"I'd rather handle it first. Once I've got him, I'll turn him over myself."

Considering that he had done what he could under the circumstances, Cain put the boy out of his mind. He turned to Wilson. "Shall we go? I need to sleep and get clean."

"Of course. Where's our bloody driver?" Wilson picked him out of a group of native soldiers tossing dragon's bones in some kind of game for money. "*Aqui*, tirav!" He whistled through his teeth. The driver scooped up his money and flashed a brief smile at the other players. In a moment he had brought the car around in a swirl of dust and settled it in front of them.

They bid Avery good night and glided uphill through the streets on a cloud of air and churned, dirt stained, variegated colors in the light of the fireworks. Wilson prattled on.

"There'll be a reception tomorrow night at the governor general's. Drinks, dinner, Darker caterwauling. You're expected to be there, of course, along with those priests and that woman, Amalia Dubois, who writes all those trashy colonial dramas . . . wonder what she gets for one of those bits of nonsense? Anyway, if you mind your manners, you should be able to swing getting your holopack returned. If you're planning to tattoo yourself like a Khaj or start worshiping dirt, I wouldn't mention it if I were you . . ."

They climbed steadily away from the concentration

of Darkhani streets until they came to a checkpoint manned by two Terran soldiers. They were waved in and drove through darkness for nearly a kilometer until they came to a high plasticrete wall reinforced with titanium beams that had buckled, cracked, fallen, been repaired and re-repaired. They passed another checkpoint uneventfully and Cain found himself gaping at the ubiquitous, almost comic ruins of Terran architecture.

It looked like hundreds of other military colonial settlements elsewhere in the galaxy: rows of Terran style homes, shops, office buildings, and barracks all in popular Argentinian or Brazilian architecture, grafted-on symmetry from another world that never quite took. The exception here was the crumbling atmosphere of resignation and abandoned maintenance. The cantonment looked blighted by some colossal force of nature, which in fact it was. Cain wondered how, if he ever managed to retrieve his holopack, he would manage to make this look like a thriving colony of the Empress. It occurred to him that, aside from the religious aversion the Khaj might have to holocorders, there might be other, more practical reasons for their proscription. Any footage of the living conditions for Terran colonials on Darkath would be an indictment, a documentation of imperial failure.

They drove past buildings that Cain knew must have housed the families of enlisted men and noncommisioned officers. Children, streaked and smudged with dust, darted in and out of gaping holes in the prefabricated walls of the all purpose, military family units. Electric lights flickered occasionally from within, but more common were primitive petroleum lamps that glowed dimly in doorways and windows. Women sat on field chairs in the dried ruins of abandoned gardens fanning themselves with wide, hand-painted, native made fans.

As they climbed the streets toward the governor's mansion and walled parade grounds, the broken crate buildings gave way to the more capacious and expensive homes of the officers. While these buildings featured long porches supported by colonnades and porticoes, bay windows framed in rococo, gingerbread embellishments and many more electric lights, they too were subject to Darkath's inhospitable thrashings. Windows were boarded over, roofs sagged, columns lay shattered on dying turf lawns.

They passed a cluster of domes and tents that Wilson pointed out as "The Beetle Compound." These were quarters for Rigelian and Cappellan personnel, on Darkath in a variety of capacities from ordnance advisors to engineers to linguists.

At one point, Cain turned to look behind him and saw, far below, the spaceport laid out in the moonshadow of the mountainside, the crazy, jagged streets and plazas of Darker Heights illuminated by campfires, lamps, the sporadic dying fireworks and the huge moon, Giata. The irony of Wilson's name for the native encampment became clear.

The driver stopped at a row of foamcrete bungalows and Wilson pointed with his sun helmet at the first of them. "Home," he said and wiped sweat from his head onto his shirtsleeve.

They climbed from the car and Wilson said something to the driver that Cain did not understand. The driver, however, nodded to both men before driving off. "He'll bring round the luggage tomorrow or the next day. Whenever they're finished with it at Inspection. If you haven't got it by tomorrow night, just mention it to Jimenez. He might pull some strings for Martin Cain."

Wilson guided him to the bungalow and opened the front door with his shoulder. The door scraped reluctantly against the uneven wooden floor. Wilson passed his hand over the light switch and a ceiling fixture flickered unevenly above them revealing a bed, two chairs and a table. A ceiling fan hung uselessly by its wires from cracked foamcrete. "Not much," Wilson pointed out, "but it's all yours." He walked to what looked like a closet and opened the louvered, wooden doors. Inside was a holoplayer set that was two decades old. "It works, more or less. I hope you'll have the discretion not to flaunt it in front of the Darkers. They all know we've got things like this, but as long as we don't make a spectacle of them we don't ruffle their feathers too badly."

"That's very sensitive of you, Wilson," Cain said, but the irony seemed to be lost on his companion. It was clear Wilson had no intention of leaving him in peace.

"Your boy, Raith—he'll be around in the morning with breakfast—knows it's here, of course. The holoplayer I mean. He's Dhirn. It's all the same to him." The man from Starfax busied himself placing a cube cassette he had produced from his pocket into the cradle of the machine. "Power is supplied by a generator that runs all four of these huts. Half the time it's out, but it seems to be all right now. By the way, I'm just next door. Beyond me are two bungalows that have been empty till now. I imagine they'll be putting up the woman, Dubois, in one and the priests from Vatican IV in the other."

"What are you doing there, Wilson?" Cain gestured at the holoplayer.

"I'm showing you the score here. This is a recent broadcast of mine that was censored by the administration, probably *El Raton*, that's Cristobal." Wilson passed his hand over the wall switch and plunged the room into darkness again. Cain resigned himself and stretched out on the bed. Colors sprang into being in front of the unit and Wilson's voice could be heard over a three-dimensional stillshot of Darkhani schoolchildren in white and blue uniforms who seemed to be playing the ancient Terran game of Star Rover.

Wilson's voice: YOU SEE HERE A SCENE THAT WOULD BE FAMILIAR ANYWHERE IN THE EMPIRE. YES (chuckle) FROM PUERTA DE ESTRELLA TO THE COALSACK, FROM

COPERNICUS TO TERRA HERSELF I GUESS KIDS ARE PRETTY MUCH THE SAME. THE DIFFERENCE YOU SEE HERE IS THAT THESE CHILDREN ARE ABORIGINAL NATIVES OF DARKATH, THE FARTHEST OUTPOST IN THE TERRAN GALAXY AND THE THIRD GENERATION HERE TO BE EDUCATED BY THE SISTERS OF THE UNIVERSAL BLOOD.

Cut to holostill of Dhirn adults in laboratory looking at microscopes, placing test tubes in centrifuges.
Cut to Dhirn laborers constructing Terran style schoolhouse.
Cut to the Khaj infantry wheeling on parade in dress uniforms.

Wilson's voice: WHILE THEIR PARENTS ARE HARD AT WORK BRINGING TERRAN TECHNOLOGY AND DISCIPLINE TO BEAR ON SOME OF THE CONSIDERABLE PROBLEMS POSED BY THE ENVIRONMENT AND THE MILLENNIA OF IGNORANCE AND SAVAGERY THAT IS THEIR HERITAGE . . .

Cut to native children sitting in classrooms facing Eduscreens.

. . . THESE KIDS ARE SPENDING THEIR TIME PRETTY MUCH THE WAY YOUR OWN KIDS DO. WHILE THEY MAY LOOK LIKE UNLIKELY CANDIDATES FOR SCHOLARS, ENGINEERS, MILITARY, AND RELIGIOUS LEADERS (chuckles again), THAT IS EXACTLY WHERE THESE CHILDREN ARE HEADED. IN THE LESS THAN ONE HUNDRED YEARS SINCE THE ARRIVAL OF OUR FIRST SHIPS HERE, A CADRE OF DEDICATED MEN AND WOMEN OF THE EMPIRE HAVE FORGED A PATH TOWARD A BRIGHTER

FUTURE FOR THESE KIDS AND HUNDREDS
MORE LIKE THEM ON THE FOUR CORNERS OF
THE PLANET.

Abruptly, Wilson turned off the machine. He passed
his hand in front of the light switch again and faced
Cain. "You get the idea."

"Yes." Cain sat up. "It seems like pretty harmless
pap to me. What was the problem?"

Wilson walked over to a cabinet beyond the table
and chairs. He opened it and produced a bottle of clear
liquor from Nueva Brasilia. "A housewarming gift
from Jimenez. Join me?"

Cain shook his head and Wilson poured himself a
drink. "They wouldn't say, of course. It just came
back from the adjutant marked 'rejected.' In fact, when
you think about it, it isn't surprising. Oh, everything
looks peachy enough in the stills—and believe me, that
wasn't easy to stage—but the problem is, I believe,
that it raises expectations. Imagine poor old Jimenez
sitting up there filing reports on his projects: the ter-
raforming, unsatisfactory, the irrigation projects, un-
completed, the spaceport, all but nonfunctional, the
school buildings, demolished.

"Where, Planetary Affairs wants to know, are the
exchange students? The local scholars being sent offworld to the universities? The military academies?
What kind of trade situation have we set up here and
by the way, how's the manned station on the local
moon coming? 'Well, you see, sirs, it's like this. The
mud eaters won't leave the planet and the sun maniacs
are only fit for soldiering—but only if it means slaugh-
tering the mud eaters, themselves, or us; they have no
quarrel with bugs on Rigel, no interest in policing
slime-based life-forms on Corax, miners on Niflheim,
or colonists on a gas giant. The schools and churches
won't stay built, see; and, well, we can't even keep
the damned lights on in the officers' mess.' "

Cain saw the problem, all right. It corroborated the
thoughts he had while passing the family housing on

the way up. It didn't surprise him that the military would want to closely scrutinize any outgoing news, but it seemed to him that Wilson was doing his best to give them what he would have supposed they wanted. He asked the obvious question. "What do they want, then?"

Wilson mounted one of the chairs backward and folded his arms over the headrest. "Depends on who you ask. If you talk to Jimenez, well, he'd probably like the piece you just saw. He's okayed a dozen others just like it, but Cristobal's policy is 'No news is good news from Darkath' and Cristobal is slowly becoming the real power behind the throne here. If you ask me, Cristobal would like to egg the Darkers into a fight, make it look like Jimenez's fault, and then turn us loose with holocorders to get all the gory details of his military triumph. Snatching victory from the jaws of Jimenez's failure. Now, you may be an exception, Cain, but most of us here, including Jimenez and Cristobal weren't exactly sent here as a reward for our sterling careers. You can go where you like, you've a reputation for wandering the highways and byways of the Empire and entertaining the folks back home with bite-sized little pieces of alien culture, but most everybody else is on this spastic dust ball because they've either botched something royally elsewhere, see Darkath as a last ditch opportunity to make a military name or monetary fortune for themselves in gems or drugs, or are just plain expendable in the eyes of whoever sent them."

"So what are you saying, Wilson? What's your professional recommendation as to the nature of my dispatches from here?" Cain thought he knew where the man was going. He got up and took the bottle from Wilson and poured a drink for himself in a glass he found in the cabinet.

"My advice is to go the way the wind is blowing. Cristobal is going to have his fight one way or the other and he'll be in command here before long. Rumor has

it that Jimenez wants to risk a major solar installation
northeast of here. Cristobal is on record as being
against it because that will provoke the Darkers. It is,
of course, exactly what he wants, but he'll go about it
his own way, behind Jimenez's back. That way he can
say, 'I told you so,' relieve the commandant of command and put down an uprising that will make him
look like a hero. As to what he has in mind to provoke
the Darkers, I don't know. In the meantime, get on
Cristobal's good side and don't take offense when your
dispatches are canceled. Just bide your time and wait
for the footage you'll get when the shit hits the fan. I
have a feeling those holocorders will become available
just in time.'' Wilson winked at Cain.

Cain tasted his drink and felt a mild tremor beneath
his feet. The ceiling fan swayed slightly above them
and the lights flickered for a moment. "Why did you
hope I'd get my holopack through Inspection, then?
What could you expect me, or us, to do with it?''

Wilson shifted his weight and looked slightly
pained. "You may think of me as a scum-sucking
toady, Cain, but in fact I have my professional side
and I'm not a military man. I wasn't exiled here by
Starfax because I'm third rate; I've done good work
for the company in the past and I see Darkath as my
ticket to retirement. You know, the memoirs, 'My Life
as a Correspondent on Two Dozen Worlds,' that sort
of thing, with Darkath as the payoff. 'We Were There'
by Nigel Wilson and Martin Cain. You like it? We
could put together footage that Jimenez or Cristobal
never have to see. Smuggle it out on next year's ship.
They've got a temple of crystals and gems up in those
mountains,'' he jerked his head toward the west wall
of the bungalow, "that would make smashing holos
from what I hear. Nothing like it in the universe. When
this place goes Cristobal's way, there won't be much
left to shoot but rubble and smoke. Great for Cristobal's purposes maybe, but for us, a before and after
kind of thing would be an incredible story.''

Cain ignored the proposition for the moment. "What makes you think Cristobal won't just do everything he can to facilitate the solar project while appearing to cry foul the whole time?"

"Good point, but you have to know Cristobal. He's not called *El Raton* for nothing. He's got a corkscrew mind if ever there was one. No, he's got something else up his sleeve. It might be light weapons. I don't know."

"I see," said Cain. He got up and walked to the door. "Well, thanks for the information, Wilson. I need to sleep on all this."

Wilson put down his drink and allowed himself to be shown out. "Of course, we could call it, 'We Were There' by Martin Cain and Nigel Wilson. Naturally, you'd get top billing, but I was here first and all that."

"Naturally," Cain said and closed the door. "Good night, Wilson."

"Right," he heard through the closed door.

When Cain's head hit the pillow, he was already asleep.

* * *

Sivran puffed on his pipe and watched the workers clear the parade ground of wood and paper debris from the firework display. The applause from the viewing stands had trailed off and the group of fifty or so notables, including Jimenez and Cristobal, their escorts, and the wives and children of the highest ranking Terran military personnel, had begun to file their way to the reception area for complimentary beverages, idle chat, and speculation about long awaited shipments from home. Sivran lingered for a moment as if savoring the memory of the wondrous Terran spectacle, all the while choking back cordite and gunpowder. At length, he met the eyes of the Dhirn who had supervised the detonation of the noisy, menacing sky blossoms. He nodded and the Dhirn approached, wiping his hands on his waistcloth. Sivran placed his hand over his chest for a moment and moved it in a left to right gesture. The supervisor mirrored the greeting and said, "I can hear the Khaj grinding their teeth tonight." He jerked his head at the sprawling, flickering lights or what the Terrans called Darker Heights at the base of the mountainside. "I don't think they appreciate the . . . *artistry* of the Terran toys."

Casually, Sivran lifted a satchel from beneath the folds of his tunic. It contained several hundred Terran cruzeiros and a handful of small semiprecious gems. Payment to the Dhirn on the detail for detonating the fireworks in a certain sequence. The supervisor surreptitiously accepted the drawstringed bag while looking away, not entirely unaware that he had been an accomplice in sending a coded message to Hara and Juum at Ayeia Alaikhaj. He had followed Sivran's instructions. As to why the Dhirn leader wanted this done in such a way was none of his concern, though he sensed its importance and had no doubt as to the wisdom of Sivran's purposes.

"You are right, brother. The Khaj have reason to be unamused . . . And so do we all tonight."

The elder Dhirn, the wise Sivran who, it was said, alone could make sense of the arrogant pale soldiers from the stars, fixed the Darkhani with an *iravka* washed intensity. "Tell me. You take Terran coins and Darkath's gems with equanimity for you know not what end. Where is your heart if you were asked to choose between them for the rest of your days?"

The workman showed his yellowed teeth and shrugged. "*Epile* and *Arziaj*," he said, naming two of the gems he had asked for in payment, "delight my little ones and my woman. They are fine gifts that please those who matter to my heart. The Terran coins . . ." He laughed and scuffed at the dust, dancing slightly while the parade ground shook and cracked with a mild quake neither he nor Sivran seemed consciously aware of, ". . . are ugly and only of use for buying the silence or blind eyes of the Terran Jafars. If I wish to make my prayers three times a day when I am supposed to be doing something idiotic for them, like making a hard tent to shit in that will only fall down tomorrow, then I give the Jafars some coins, they call me mad, and let me be." He suddenly looked very earnest. "I am a religious man, Hia Sivran. I meditate in Korjh, the second level of Darkath's bosom. I have many times."

"I commend you." Sivran himself, supposedly a religious leader of unquestioned integrity, had not attempted such spiritual rigors since his youth. He doubted the veracity and even value of such things in these days of more urgent, worldly concerns. He felt a vague nostalgia and sadness.

When Sivran did not speak for several moments, the other Dhirn asked, "Are things going to go badly with the Jafars, Hia Sivran?"

The diplomat, priest, and now spy looked at the extinguished embers in his pipe and sighed. "What is your name, brother?"

"Raith, Hia Sivran."

He met the younger Dhirn's eyes and gave in to the temptation to speak directly, without dissembling, duplicity, or couching his words in nonsense. "They already are, Raith. And, yes, they're likely to get worse. You take care of your family."

"Of course," Raith said with a trace of indignation. "But you must count on me if you have need, Hia. I may be just a big kagra to the Terrans, to be harnessed and put to work at idiot's tasks, but I assure you I am more than just a strong back. There is nothing wrong with my heart or my brain. I may not be a hot-headed Khaj warrior, but I would not sit idle while the Terrans trample my people beneath their boots like so many insects."

"Of course not. I'll remember. And no need to call me Hia Sivran. It now puts me in mind of all the ridiculous honorifics the Terrans have for each other. It is comical. Just as well to call me Jafar Sivran.''

They both laughed. "Oh, I would never do that," Raith said. Jafar was a term of many connotations from "the largest turd" to "the biggest male sex organ."

Raith pressed his point, at ease with the older Dhirn leader now. "Seriously, perhaps I can be of use. I know, for example, that the reason you wished me to ignite the Terran sky bombs in the order you had written was to make a signal in the old Khaj colored mirror code used at the siege of Ayeia Alaikhaj five hundred years ago. I remembered some of it from the poem I heard from a bard when I was a child. Two red slowly and then three yellow in quick succession, slow green, then blue, white, white, white, another long slow red, this was the signal to the Khaj troops in the stronghold from their relief that they had been cut off and could not reach them. 'All is lost' it meant in the poem. Many Dhirn children heard this song of their victory over the Khaj generations ago, but not many are as smart as I am and remember." He smiled widely.

Sivran studied him in silence, amazed and horrified. Could anyone else know? No, no. It was extremely unlikely. This one before him was clever. Uncomfortably clever. He decided to bluff. "Very interesting, Raith. A fascinating coincidence, a wild notion, but I'm afraid you're wrong." He attempted a good-natured laugh.

"The poem is written on the walls of the Moonrise Cavern not five days from here. When it reaches the part about the colored mirror signals, it consists of single brush strokes of paint: two long red ones, three short yellow ones, a long green, blue, white, white, white . . . I wish I could remember more, but I do not. Certainly this is no coincidence, Sivran. If all is lost, I would wish to know."

"All is not lost, Raith. Believe that." Seeing he could not carry on the lie, he put his hand on Raith's shoulder. "Perhaps we will talk again, but we mustn't anymore. Not now. Do as I say and take care of your family. Perhaps travel north where the mud dissuades the Terrans."

Raith backed away from Sivran and ran his palm over his breast once again. "I will take care of my family. I will also be here to help . . . if I can. I would be pleased if you thought to call on me for any small service I might afford." In a low voice he added, "Perhaps I will seek out the Khaj priestess Hara. It is said she is prepared to raise her springlance to save our kind, both Khaj and Dhirn, from Terran toys that are not so playful." He began to walk away and Sivran stopped him, calling his name.

"Stay! I would consider myself in your debt if you stayed nearby until we can speak again. You have a rare spirit, Raith, and it will be needed. I must go, I am late." Sivran turned and walked toward the reception area, his leg muscles sore from the long walk across the desert that afternoon. To himself, he thought: *This one will play a part. He sees more than what is before him and he listens with his ears and heart to Darkath. He will be valuable when it begins.* He was overcome with an ineffable sadness once again he could not place. He sensed that Raith would somehow fall victim to events once they were set in motion though he didn't know how or why. He chalked it up to the fey sentiments and intuition that comes with old age. *Mark that,* he thought, *and be wary of it. Hara is right.*

He paused at the door to the reception chamber and composed himself. He took one last look out at the parade ground and saw the silhouette of the Dhirn worker in enigmatic shadow.

He put a smile on his face and advanced into the gaily festooned room.

It is beginning.

Chapter Seven

"Tell me what it is like," Juum stood next to Hara on the natural rock balcony of the temple that had been embellished by artisans over the centuries with abstract reliefs of flowerlike sunbursts and mandalas. The desert wind blew in updrafts from beneath them, lifting their robes and whipping them around their faces sporadically.

Hara held tubes of colored dye in one hand and a rolled hide in the other. She lay the hide against the lip of the balcony and let it unfurl. She looked alternately at the markings on the hide: two long red daubs, three short yellow, long green, blue, white, white, white . . . "They are showers of sparks that explode and fall from a great height," she said distractedly. "It is to impress Terran children perhaps."

She did not see Juum smile in the darkness beside her. Already she knew that the message contained bad news. Sivran was using the opening line of the old poem commemorating the historic Khaj humiliation at the hands of the Dhirn. She wondered if Sivran took some measure of relish in his choice of words, "All is lost."

"I think I would enjoy it." Juum was saying.

"No, Father. I don't think you would. The message reads, 'Spies captured . . .' " She studied the colors and their duration in the sky. Jotted paint on the hide. " ' . . . execution probable . . . cargo still unknown.' "

She put down the tubes and the hide, staring at the

sightless white eyes of her father and ignoring the now
meaningless exposition in the night sky. She waited
for him to speak. When at last he did, it was with a
voice that held both implacable resolve and regret.
"We must not allow the Terrans to kill them. Send
them the eye of one prisoner, the Terran officer, the
tongue of a second, the priest, and the finger of the
third, the woman who serves the God of blood. Tell
them we will exchange their lives for the lives of our
people and the disclosure of every item that arrived
aboard their ship."

"I will go myself." Hara made to leave.

"Wait." Without turning, Juum put out a hand and
caught her forearm. "We cannot risk you. Send someone you trust completely, yet is expendable."

"Father," Hara fumed for a moment. "No one I
trust is expendable. Sometimes I think you are as mad
as they say. I . . ." She trailed off when she saw the
indulgent smile form at the corners of his mouth and
realized that this was yet another of her father's les-
sons: an example of his paradoxical humor designed
to make her confront and master her passion and remind her of the grim nature of her role. She relaxed
in his restraining grasp and said, "I will call an assembly and ask for a volunteer party."

Juum took his hand from her. She turned and summoned a temple servant. Within an hour, word was spread
through the caves that an assembly was to be held in the
natural courtyard beneath the temple balcony.

They arrived in small groups bearing torches, both
Dhirn and Khaj. When their ranks had swelled to
nearly a thousand adults and children perched on
rocks, seated on the floor of the amphitheaterlike hollow below them, and filling the mouths of the facing
caves, she raised her hands above her head to still the
excited murmurings that rippled through their ranks.

When silence had fallen, she paused, looking out
over the play of dancing torchlight and shadow that
seemed to animate the faces below her with seething

menace and bridled violence. She placed her palm, fingers splayed, over her eyes and the Khaj beneath her mirrored the gesture. She ran the same hand over her breast and the Dhirn among her following returned the greeting. She was momentarily pleased to see that there was a roughly equal distribution of Darkhani factions. "Bring the prisoners here," she called out. There was a brief flurry of activity at the base of the temple and in moments, three hooded and bound figures were brought forward into the ring of torchlight beneath the balcony. They stood upright and Hara judged that they had not been harmed.

"Children of Darkath and Alaikhaj! The time has come to bargain with the Terrans. They have ignored our entreaties that we be allowed to accept or reject the things that are brought to our world from the stars and have denied us the knowledge of these things in order to protect ourselves. Our attempts to exert our rights have been met with brutality. Three more of our agents have been captured and await execution at the hands of the pink butchers. This must be prevented. We must make known to them now that we hold three of their number as well. Their safety will depend upon the return of our people and the revelation of their intention to compromise our gods. I ask for ten volunteers to take this message, with proof of the hostages, to the fat Jafar. Your lives will be in great danger."

An uproar from a hundred or more volunteers echoed off the living rock. Hara could see Karsha with his brightly painted chest waving a springlance in one hand and a torch in the other. She nodded to him and he stepped forward from the crowd. "Karsha, my friend, select nine of the others and come forward." When this had been done, she gave him another order. "Remove the tongue from the Terran priest."

Immediately, two of the hooded prisoners began to writhe against their bonds. The third, the priest, stood immobile as his hood was removed. A muffled protest from the captured lieutenant resounded through sudden silence. Two of the volunteers grasped the priest by his head and shoulders and arched his back. Karsha came forward with his knife glistening in firelight. He bent over the priest and in the next moment an involuntary cry went up into the night. The priest was allowed to slump to the ground as Karsha held the bloody flesh above his head. His gesture was met with shouts of approval as he turned in a circle and displayed his grisly trophy. Next was the lieutenant. Karsha removed his right eye with his thumbs and severed the connective cords with the knife. The lieutenant endured this in silence. The nun sobbed as Karsha severed her small finger and placed it with the eye and the tongue in a hide cloth. With each dismemberment, the guttural shouts of Hara's followers grew louder.

Her face remained impassive as she forced herself to watch the execution of her orders. When a relative quiet had fallen over the courtyard, she spoke in a firm, but lowered voice. "Carry these things to the Terran Jafar and give him our message. You must leave at once if you are to arrive before our people are killed. Select ten of the fastest Grea' ka. Go. Quickly." With that, she turned from the balcony, taking her father's arm more for her own support than his.

* * *

Karsha and his party of five women and four men, three of them Dhirn and six Khaj, flew through the canyons on the backs of their Grea' ka. Karsha had no illusions that male warriors were in any way superior to those that were female, though he could not break himself of the habit of thought that Dhirn, of either sex, were useless mud suckers. He brought a token three along so the Terrans would see that they stood— albeit grudgingly—shoulder to shoulder and could not single out the Khaj for reprisals with impunity from the Dhirn. It was not easy to find Dhirn willing to mount and fly. He hoped that their presence would be registered by the Terrans, an indication of a desperate cause, desperate times. Their mounts soared ten meters above the canyon floor and glided almost effortlessly on the rising thermals and cool surface air currents that made the sunken mountain passes into wind tunnels at night. Every kilometer or so, the beasts would raise and lower their wings, scooping at the air to regain altitude.

Tucked into one of the panniers behind his leg was the cloth that held the eye, tongue, and finger of the three hostages. It was exhilarating for Karsha to travel at such speed on a mission of such importance. He was confident they would reach the walls of the Terran Dita' Tareek by godrise if they had to exhaust their animals to the point of death. This, however, did not worry him overmuch since the wind was at their tails. He had ridden harder and longer without the beasts suffering any lasting ill effects.

As he rounded a great promontory to his right, he heard the rumblings of Darkath beneath him and saw rivers of stone and sand cascading into the canyon. Too late, he turned to point at the collapsing rock wall, hoping to catch the attention of those who followed. The promontory broke into three large pieces and a dry, sighing groan reverberated below. Boulders the size of a dozen men fell onto the backs of three of the Grea' ka, spilling their riders. Their cries carried on the air and echoed long after they lay silent and crushed beneath the avalanche. Karsha did not look back again.

It was with six riders that Karsha arrived at the eastern wall of the Terran cantonment. The Grea' ka glided slowly up the windward side of the mountain in the false dawn, their talons dancing, seeking purchase on the rocky slope, their wings rampant. A Terran sergeant drilling a platoon of native infantry across the parade ground was the first to see the seven airborne riders crest the peak of the east wall and sail downward, pausing at the last moment to wheel overhead in formation. A cloth packet fell from the sky at his feet and his troops halted their movement clumsily. He shouted an order to present arms. Half of them obeyed. "At ease!" he called out. Some of them stood at ease and others fingered their rifles tensely. Slowly, he bent to pick up the fallen missile, alternately studying the riders overhead and his own skittish soldiers. When he opened the cloth and saw its contents, read the ultimatum written in pidgin Imperial Spanish/Darker and addressed to Jimenez, he paled but managed to croak a faltering, "Dismissed," at his charges. Many of them left the parade ground in desultory fashion while many others remained where they were, clutching their weapons and searching the sky for the mounted Grea' ka that were now disappearing into the suddenly rising fireball of Alaikhaj.

The sergeant forced himself to walk at a dignified pace off of the parade ground toward his commanding officer's bungalow, the blood-soaked cloth firmly under his arm. Once out of sight of his men, he broke into a run.

* * *

Cain slept for a few hours and awoke before dawn. He could not say what it was that had roused him from a badly needed rest, but if he had to describe it, it would, he thought, be something like excitement. He ignited a petroleum lamp and resigned himself to the fact that he would get no more sleep that night.

Something here, on this world, was waiting for him like a half formed circuit needing only for Cain to reach out to it, touch it in order to close and form . . . what? Some vital current, some unknowable connection to a dormant, patient power he sought and had no name for.

Leaning back on his bed he exhaled slowly and dissipated the not unpleasant tension the dreamlike thought had aroused in him. A wish fulfillment dream, that's all. This world was no different from any other, give or take a few degrees of temperature and gravity, some curiosities of culture and then, ultimately some brand or other of disappointment. The only thing different here was that there really was nowhere else to go anymore. He laughed to himself without any real happiness and tried to summon sleep again from wherever it had gone.

It occurred to him that a dose of soporax would be very welcome and smiled to himself again that after all these years without the drug he still had not quite gotten over his occasional craving. In fact, he thought about it fairly regularly. After the revolt on Cozuela he had been introduced to the drug in the hospital and that had begun a two-year high on the hypnotic that nearly killed him. Then there were the other drugs he had sought out, the exotic, alien compounds that altered his perceptions, depressed his spirits or raised them, opened his senses or closed them, induced trances or stupors that would last for days or sometimes weeks. But it was soporax to which his nerves felt a ghostlike chemical allegiance. When he had kicked soporax finally (a single visit to a psychestim center and six and a half painless seconds of current to the frontal cortex) he was forced to confront the dreams he had avoided by twenty months of REM suppression. With minimal psychestim treatment he could avoid the resultant psychosis while he was awake, but in dreams he would be plunged back into the maelstrom of insanity that was Cozuela.

* * *

His regiment was the first to make planetfall there. They landed at the equator in the eastern hemisphere. He was a young man then, though after six months he would never again be mistaken for a youth. The rest of the division arrived ten days later and touched down at the temperate southern pole. Cain's regiment (the 119th) as well as two others were the top pincer in the ill-fated strategy. Thousands of years of military history dictated that an army should not divide its forces, but they were led by the General Priest, Vasquez, who spoke with God. Before they ever encountered the rebel army, the isolated 119th was decimated by heatstroke, poisonous insect bites, a bizarre form of malaria that baffled Terran doctors, and the monsoons that drove radioactive particles to the earth from a monstrous cloud held in check by trade winds. The cloud was born of the colonists' seizure and detonation of an arsenal in the western hemisphere that left millions dead and thousands dying.

The villages and cities they marched through were populated by refugees, mostly women and children. All of them colonists and therefore all of them revolutionaries, enemies of the Empire. They were herded into camps, those who did not resist. Cain oversaw the disposal of the bodies once belonging to those who did resist. Incendiary pits were effective for the most part, though occasionally city wells would suffice and accommodate as many as ten thousand Cozuelans. Skilled demolition teams sunk drill detonators where necessary, followed by a ton or two of phosphorus weighted with brick and stone from the rubble that was everywhere. This was capped by an energy shield that would force the explosion downward. The mass would burn and sink nearly half a mile in a matter of hours. This, followed by quick decomposition chemicals used on board deep space transport ships, dropped in huge payloads down the wells and craters proved very effective. Cain had been given a medal specifically for such work in stemming the tide of the mutant malaria among Terran troops.

He saw almost no combat until they reached a vast plain in the south where the Cozuelan insurgents moved triumphantly and in incredible numbers on vehicles armed with weaponry captured from the 293rd Imperial Battalion. The battle lasted two months. During most of it, Cain was alternately frightened senseless or numbly bored. The

Terrans gained ground and lost it. Their perimeter was overrun and recaptured almost weekly.

In the final days of the campaign, Cain found himself in the front lines of the advancing Terran Army as his division effected a massive rout of the Cozuelans. It was his first experience of the glorious hysteria of victory. He was among the spearhead battalions driving the enemy across the plain and into a narrow mountain pass where a great ion curtain had been erected by an advance tactical force. Cain remembered firing and reloading, firing and reloading, emptying his weapon into the ragged rearguard of the enemy soldiers who tried to delay their inevitable disintegration. They fell before him and he advanced with the others, walking over the dead and dying.

Some of the Cozuelans threw away their weapons and marched deliberately into the invisible particle wall that blocked their retreat. Some tried to surrender and were cut down. Cain could not remember how many he had killed, but what he did remember filled him with a nightmarish self-loathing—the tormenting realization that for him there was nothing quite as pleasurable in this life as taking it.

But Cain's torment had only just begun.

From hastily established emplacements in the mountainside, the Cozuelans hit Cain's regiment with a barrage of plasma artillery, pulverizing the front ranks of Terran troops with their own captured weapons. The earth erupted under the 119th and their world became a supernova. The sounds of explosions and screams and small arms fire became one homogeneous cacophony of white noise and when it was over, Cain was in a metal cage.

The cage was shorter than Cain so that he had to squat. Where his knees touched the metal that baked in Cozuela's sun, two infected burns formed. A slightly larger one left his back a festering mass of singed meat. The cage filled with the stench of his own rotting flesh, sickened him constantly and sometimes woke him from a tortured doze that was more frightening than wakefulness.

He was fed scraps and fouled water. Cain lost forty pounds. For several weeks, his existence was comprised of nothing but delirium, fear, and pain.

But his captors were dying as well, by degrees, of starvation and sickness and the continuous assaults from fresh Imperial troops.

He was evacuated by a drone ship, he and ten other men who helped him into the cargo hold. By the time the drone ship deposited them on Iando's World, Cain was diagnosed with, among other things, malnutrition, radiation disease, and Belgrad's Syndrome, an incurable form of psychotic depression all but unheard of since generation starships had produced only corpses or madmen as colonists two thousand years earlier.

He was left in the hospital facility on Iando's World with every expectation that he would die and he was most eager. But his luck continued to run foul and he did not die. The anti-radio treatments stemmed but did not reverse the rad damage and his body slowly allowed itself to be fed and healed in a near coma state. His depression was masked by various somacoid drugs in heavy doses and he was weaned onto soporax. The doctors at the Institute on Iando knew he was a time bomb of self-destruction because they could not risk intensive REM therapy, but Cain played the game with the psyches, convinced them, and he walked.

He found himself heavily decorated for things he was certain never occurred, at least not in the way he was told, but he didn't argue. Cozuela no longer existed. It was a ball of radioactive wind by the time he was released, discharged from the military, and decorated with the Cruz De Oro. This was interpreted officially as a triumph for the Empire and Cain was a hero. He was seen as something of an embarrassment at certain levels—because of his lack of jingoistic enthusiasm—but presented a good figure on the Fax networks for the folks at home.

It didn't matter. Cozuela no longer existed. Cain recited this to himself like a mantra. He joined arms in that galactic conspiracy of denial.

He was given a sinecure as "Frontier Correspondent" for the Imperial Armed Forces and that led to an even better paying and easier, almost silly job with Hub Holofax.

He had a ticket to ride out whatever destiny it was he had been spared for and though he hadn't a clue as to what that might be, he knew he wanted to ride, all right. Whatever it was he was meant to live for and witness, he suspected was very far away.

Very very far away. And he was patient.

And here was a way to go far without being in the bloody sick stinking rutting Army.

Still, the doctors on Iando were right. Cain could not seem to reconcile his need for oblivion with his miraculous survival. He could not understand why he had not died when it was so eminently clear that was what he deserved.

It was the dreams that drove him to the series of suicide attempts.

The overdose of Cortomine that should have killed him instantly, merely made him deathly ill as a result of the antitoxins in his system—introduced as a precaution during the addiction therapy. Cutting his wrists in the lagoon on New Proxima should have worked, but he was found by two of the stick creatures of that world who stanched the flow of blood with their milky secretions.

He lost his nerve when attempting to walk into a particle beam in the weapon shops on Rashi—hesitated just long enough for a lensmith to fling him out of the way. And again when he was about to jettison himself from the air lock aboard the *Hidalgo*. The alarms had gone off during that ten-second tremor of intent between conception and execution when he could have entered the crawlspace.

It seemed that the circumstances of his life conspired to keep him alive without offering any clear reason to do so. It was after his failure of nerve on the *Hidalgo* that Cain had read somewhere, in one of the hundreds of documents and books he would scroll through at night to keep from sleeping, that ". . . suicide is a perversion of the impulse toward transcendence." He could not remember where exactly he had read it, but it started him on a course of thought that led him thousands of light-years across the void.

He began to immerse himself in the cultures of colony worlds. He studied and actually tried in any way he could to become something other than human, convinced as he was that he had done and thought everything *humanly* possible to understand the particular existential non sequitur he was living.

The surgical alterations had been another compulsion, after all, to simply get out of his skin—like the drugs—and not, in the end, transcend it as he had told himself.

He had gone from woman to woman, bed to bed, even with aliens most Terrans would consider repulsive and that, he knew, was another form of addiction. Oh, the women: the female Terrans and Cygnans, the Sirens of Raynal with their rose-colored skin softer than six-hundred-year-old *isqualia* from the cask. The musky monkey women of Eislon and the hard, chitinous spasms that drew blood with the Cappellan Pleasure Bonders. It both sickened him and aroused him to remember.

Transcendence.

The word haunted him and the image of his spirit soaring from his flesh. The myths of Iguajigchu, Paleodeomacer, Jesus, Vazxicir, and Bodhisattva were themes that plied the corridors of his gradually healing dreams.

Then the religions and cults and rites of a score of worlds. The high he was searching for now was God and he pursued it as surely as any drug, sexual thrill, or cybernetic transformation—with the same ungratifying result. It was as if there were an unfillable abyss in him: a black hole whose relentless pull drew him ever into some internal void he tried to outrace as he fled across the galaxy. Always he was obsessed with something outside of himself, convinced as he was that he contained only a yawning need, an emptiness that would devour him like a cancer. He sought the thing that would fill him, the antidote to himself, and he had run out of universe looking for it.

As he lay in the relative coolness before sunrise, he inventoried the sensations of being on Darkath. The gravity seemed to press him into the bedclothes, it was as if there were no blood in his veins or his muscles had turned to useless lead. A cloud of tiny insects, barely visible in the faint light, swarmed about his head, producing an almost subliminal drone. A chitinous, clicking sound drew his attention to the floor. He sat up on one elbow and saw a dozen or more beetles or roaches the size of mice fighting each other for the half ounce of sweet liqueur that lay in the glass next to his bed.

From the pocket of his tunic which he had used for a blanket, he produced two small books. One of them was his journal and notebook, the other was titled, "Incidents of Travel on Satellites of Azaroth and Delgado's Star." A computer log. Delgado's Star was, of course, Darkath prime: Alaikhaj. The book had been written almost one hundred years before by a missionary priest named Monteleone and was Cain's main source of information about Darkath after Holofax briefings and Government information. He thumbed past a chapter on Dhirn metalworking, the erroneous chapters full of misinformation on the Khaj whom the priest had almost no contact with (basing his facts on Dhirn informants who were, in essence, lying; entertaining themselves at the expense of an offworlder who had an imperfect grasp of the language to begin with) and found the chapter on indigenous life forms. Here Monteleone seemed to be reliable. He found descriptions of the beetles and as he suspected, they were classified as highly poisonous and nocturnal. He glanced at the floor again and saw them retreating from the pool of light cast by the lamp. He made a mental note to sleep with the light on in the future.

He leafed through the volume at random. Though he had nearly memorized the well thumbed book, he turned to the early pages.

ARCSYNVECTOR822987
POE. REAL SPACE:
PUERTO DE ESTRELLAS/MEDIA/AZAROTH
H.M.S.S. AMAYA
Entry: XVII
Monteleone, Javier, S.B.J.
August 25, 5108 A.D.

Document title: Incidents of Travel on Satellites of Azaroth and Delgado's Star.

Entered by: Father J. Monteleone, Society of the Blood of Jesus.
Run Excerpt: . . . . .

With the aid of the ship's computer I am now able to comprehend enough of the aboriginal language to ascertain that they call their world Darkath and themselves Darkhani [computer's spelling] though there seem to be two separate and distinct factions among them.

I have been among the food gathering nomads who call themselves Dhirn. They labor under the apprehension that their desert planet itself is a deity. This is quite a literal concept rather than a metaphorical or symbolic one. The Dhirn have welcomed me somewhat guardedly. They are relatively peaceful except in proximity to their traditional enemies, the Khaj, who, it is said, regard the red giant star, their sun, as the one true god. Both cultures are, in this way, monotheistic.

I have not seen members of this other caste, the Khaj, other than in depictions by Dhirn artists who have rendered them in likenesses fashioned with dyed sand. From all appearances they look much like the Dhirn except with exaggerated, vulgar features and tattooed faces and limbs. I would speculate at this point that they are racially identical to the Dhirn. Their exaggerated features in the renditions might be an artistic tradition informed by generations of warfare.

Identifying characteristics, Khaj:

Waist-length hair, sometimes braided (white or yellow in color as with the Dhirn. Speculation: severe ultraviolet exposure). Extensive body coloration by needlepoint etching with permanent dye (archaic anthro term, "tattooing") on scalp, face, torso, arms, legs, buttocks, groin, feet. Pale nictitating membrane from brow to cheekbone, sometimes painted. Spec: ultraviolet, infrared evolutionary adaptation. If human stock, implications of time scale are problematical.

Note. I have glimpsed what must be the Khaj from a distance. They ride winged reptilian mounts. These I have personally witnessed (see Entry IX). Dhirn abstain from travel in this manner for religious reasons.

Characteristics, Dhirn:

Same optic membrane. Same physical structure. Blue/black skin. Heavily muscled. Very powerful.

Short cropped hair, occasionally dyed earth tones, but never permanently. Body decorations: jewelry, scarves, robes dyed in earth tones. Excellent craftsmen, hunters of small animals, gatherers of herbs, berries and succulent plants, merchants and tradesmen. I have seen musicians, artists, and sand painters as well as singer/poets. Warriors are primarily skilled in something other than combat. Quick to laugh at expense of Terran personnel. Illusion of superiority to humans and Khaj. Ignorant and uncurious, they are not overtly hostile.

Cain turned back several pages and read one of his favorite passages. He wanted to see this with his own eyes.

ARCSYNVECTOR822987
H.M.S.S. AMAYA
Monteleone, Javier S.B.J.
Entry IX:
August 2, 5108 A.D.

Run Excerpt. . . .

An observation worthy of remark is the flocks or herds of winged, horned reptiles that graze on succulent desert plants and are capable of extended flight. These creatures that range in size from 2-7 meters in height, 5-15 meters long with a wingspan of 8-20 meters are known as Grea' ka [computer] and are the chief methods of transportation for both Khaj and Dhirn. The Khaj (apparently) keep herds of them, train them to be saddled and bear riders through the air, while the Dhirn harness them only with sleds to pull passengers or burdens along the surface of the planet.

Unfortunately, it has become a popular sport among Terran military personnel to hunt the dragons from hovercraft. In the six weeks since planetfall I have witnessed the slaughter of hundreds of these beasts. Already the cargo hold of Her Majesty's Starship Amaya is laden with over 100 kilograms of dragon horn. If the present rate of slaughter continues, the population of the Grea' ka will be decimated within one generation.

The singular cause of marvel I must note here is that these creatures, "dragons," exist at all. On a world with such a thin atmosphere coupled with the dense gravity, they literally fly in the face of what is known to be possible. There are species like this on many worlds—unexpected wonders of

*creation—but none so magnificent, none so flam-
boyantly symbolic of the mystery at the heart of
all things.*

Tired of reading, he set the book aside and mas-
saged his eyes.

While he waited for the sun, Cain meditated. He concentrated on his breathing, allowing his thoughts to
dissipate until his mind seemed to hover, detached from
his body in the middle distance of the room. It was
then he became aware of a presence. Though he could
not see anyone and the room remained silent except
for the soft buzzing of the gnatlike insects and the
diminishing click of the beetles who had begun their
retreat from the dawn, he was certain he was not alone.

The fey sense of excitement he woke with returned
as a fluttering in his stomach. Though not unpleasant,
he could not get a handle on the sensation. It was
maddeningly elusive. An intimation of urgency, something of moment, a heady, slightly euphoric anxiety.
He felt that something was just beyond the door to his
room and that if he opened it he would see some unfamiliar reality, some vista of truth he was unprepared
for. He sat up in bed and carefully set his feet onto
the floor. This was ridiculous, the feeling had begun
to annoy him now, or rather his reaction to its lack of
grounding in anything he could point to.

He moved slowly to the door.

Cain was certain someone would be there although
whatever clues he reacted to were subliminal. Oddly,
he was reminded of the last time his brother had visited him on Antares, surprised him in his quarters after not having seen him for five years. It could not be
David, though. David had died of Quintana fever a
long time ago. Why did he feel it was possible to see
him if he opened the door?

His hand shook as he reached for the latch.

When his fingers closed over the mechanism, he

took a deep breath and prepared himself to see a ghost, a hallucination, a dancing fish or a beautiful woman.

Cain opened the door.

Darkath's red giant sun flooded the horizon with a blinding red that Dopplered in shades across the horizon. He blinked as the moment of dawn caught his eyes off guard. In the next moment he could see dim shapes of buildings across the dusty lane. He looked down.

Squatting in the dust at his doorstep was a native, a Dhirn with his hair cut unevenly close to the scalp. He wore a brightly colored waistcloth and his whitish optic membranes were closed over his eyes, giving the appearance of a wide, mindless stare toward the horizon. The alien remained motionless for several minutes, his calves hunkered at an angle, his arms folded, until a tremor rocked the ground beneath him. Cain lurched in the doorway and fell to his knees.

When he looked up, he saw the Dhirn flat on his back laughing.

"Who . . . What's so funny?" Cain managed to say. Another tremor rocked the floor beneath him and he held on to the doorjamb.

The Dhirn opened his eyes and got to his feet with a fluid motion. "I was meditating," he said. "Meditating on Darkath. My mind kept wandering as I tried to think only of the ground beneath me, to become heavy and sink through the sand and rock, but I kept thinking of other things. In the end, Darkath announced herself to me, you see?" He chuckled, an oddly high-pitched sound coming from such a formidable frame. "Perhaps one need not search for God when God is searching for one."

He smiled at Cain, who looked back at him without expression, stunned by the coincidence with his earlier thoughts and the anticlimax of seeing this ragged, hulking Darkhani instead of . . . whatever it was he thought he would find. The alien allowed his smile to fade and brushed sand from his waistcloth.

"Buenos dias," he cleared his throat, all business now. He repeated the phrase in Terran Standard Portuguese. "I

am Raith.'' He bowed. "I have been assigned to you. I
will clean, cook, take care of your garments . . . my religion forbids that I drive an aircar, but I can pedal a sithe,
one of which I happen to own.'' Raith exposed his teeth
at Cain, a parody of his former grin. A sithe must be one
of the rickshaw tricycle contraptions Cain had seen yesterday. "I forgot your breakfast,'' he confessed, then
asked, "are you hungry?'' without waiting for an answer.
"You can pay me what you will.''

"Come in, Raith. I am Martin Cain.'' He extended
his hand and Raith, awkwardly, took it.

"Yes, yes, I know. What can I do for you, Martin
Cain?'' He picked up the glass next to the bed and placed
it in the sink beneath a plasteel hand pump. He then picked
up the carcasses of several dead beetles which he put in
the folds of his waistcloth. He looked around for something else to do. Cain wanted something tart to drink, to
wash the taste of the night's thoughts from his mouth. His
tongue and lips were dry, from the gathering day's heat
that already filled the room and the effects of his bizarre,
almost psychic anticipation of something that still seemed
to hang in the air unresolved.

As if guessing his need, the Dhirn extended a hide flask.
"This is good for the morning. Here.'' Cain drank it and
was gratified by its effect. It was something like wine and
cut through the dryness, dissolved the bollus of memories
the night had proffered. When asked what it was, the Dhirn
tried to grope for the concept in Standard. In the end he
said *calijin* which Cain understood to mean roughly "tea
wine" or distilled tea.

"Sit down,'' said Cain offering him a chair at the
table. "What you can do for me is teach me.'' He
heard his own voice as if another man were using it.

"Teach?'' Raith hesitantly seated himself looking
up at Cain.

Cain sat opposite from him and nodded. "Yes,'' he
said, though he wasn't sure why. He looked at the
floor, his hands. He began to laugh, "Yes. Teach.''

Raith laughed along with him and drank from his flask of *calijin*. "Teach you what?"

Cain shrugged, still smiling. For the first time he could remember, he had the feeling that he was exactly where he was supposed to be with no compulsion to be anywhere else. "I don't know," he said. His laughter was the kind that comes with the release of a long held breath in a child's game.

Raith joined him. "Oh, I see," he said, and maybe it was that the Dhirn was used to humoring crazy Terrans, but it really didn't matter. "In that case . . . fine. I'll teach you."

Chapter Eight

Manuel Jimenez stood at the entrance to the reception hall wearing his full dress uniform of gold and blue that smelled of the stasis container it had lain in for two years. On that occasion he had worn it in honor of the Quadrant Authority representative on the inspection tour that resulted in the approval of the request for unconventional power equipment. He felt conscious of the mass of metal and ribbon decorations that tugged at the front of his jacket, both proud of them and embarrassed by their ostentatious size and colors.

On his right stood Eduardo Cristobal looking carved from teak: ramrod straight, his bald skull gleaming with reflected light, his jaw set above his spotless uniform. Behind them were five Khaj honor guards bearing rifles and outfitted with plumed helmets.

Across from them were Sivran, his empty pipe protruding from his teeth, and Jiliad, the female Khaj elder, withered and hunched, peering inscrutably from beneath yellow tresses that hung to the floor. Behind them were five Terran color guards in uniforms identical to those of the Khaj opposite them.

Jimenez greeted the dozen or so guests from the starship, welcomed them to Darkath and introduced Cristobal, Sivran, then Jiliad, Nigel Wilson, other civil servants, and military functionaries. Padre Gillermo and his acolyte, both from New Vatican IV, were the first to be announced, followed by Amalia Dubois the famous dramatist, Nils Skijord the captain of the transport ship *Pandora*, and Martin Cain.

After the introductions were made, the guests of honor were escorted by servants to a sideboard offering wines, liquor, meats, breads, and cheeses from several worlds—courtesy of the starship's arrival. While more guests filed into the room, mostly Terran officers and their wives, the celebrities from the ship had an opportunity to chat with each other briefly. A quartet of Dhirn musicians on a raised dais played low, atonal melodies on string and wind instruments. In the middle of the room, four long tables were laid with plates and cutlery enough for forty diners. Cain observed the high domed ceiling above them was wisely devoid of any fixtures that might become dislodged during a quake though it gave the room a barren, hangarlike appearance.

Amalia Dubois spoke first. "This is the first room I've been in since I arrived that has any temperature control at all . . . and I'm still terribly warm." She was a short, rotund woman with a doll's face and lively eyes. She wore a formal summer evening dress that exposed her fleshy shoulders and trailed to the floor in shifting pastel colors.

"Yes," Wilson commented and introduced himself. "There are four of them in this room and I think two of them are working. At any given time there are no more than fifteen or sixteen of them operating on the entire planet."

"The power difficulties," she offered.

"Yes, madam. The power difficulties." Wilson took on the job of introducing everyone to each other.

Gillermo was a saturnine man in stark black broken only by his blood red collar and gold crucifix. His salt and pepper beard was neatly trimmed and mirrored his tonsured pate. He smelled vaguely of perfume or perhaps incense.

His companion looked to be no more than seventeen years old. A severe complexion problem made him look flushed as he peered nervously around the room with narrow, secretive eyes.

The ship's captain was a tall man in his fifties, Cain estimated. He stood erect, his eyes scanning the room with the thousand-parsec stare of the veteran space pilot. His conversation consisted of grunts, nods, and mmms as he glanced at his wrist display, obviously ill at ease in such surroundings. Cain followed his gaze as it fell on the armed men positioned every few meters around the room. He noted that every one of them was Terran. The Khaj guards at the door were window dressing, tokens.

"Perhaps they're expecting trouble," Cain commented to the captain.

"Mmm." The taller man nodded and tasted his wine. "They'd be wise to." He said it so softly, Cain wasn't quite sure he had said it at all.

"What makes you say that?"

The captain studied Cain's face, drained his wine and spoke. "You've been around, Mister Cain. You should be able to smell it as well as I."

"Yes," Cain agreed. "there's quite a bit of tension here. Like a . . . desert before a summer storm."

"Or a battlefield just before dawn." The captain supplied. "I just hope my lift-off does not become an evacuation."

"How long will you stay?"

"Two weeks. No more before the window from Azaroth to Puerto de Estrella closes. If I miss that, it will be six standard months."

Amalia Dubois ruffled up beside them and joined the conversation. "Tell me Mister Cain, what do you think of Darkath so far?"

"Fascinating. And you?"

"Oh, lovely. Absolutely beautiful. In a harsh, primitive way, of course. I intend to set a drama here. A love story concerning a young girl from Betelgeuse, an archeologist who falls in love with a wild Khaj warrior. I intend to break many hearts with this one."

"I'm sure you will," Cain obliged her. "And you, Padre Gillermo, what are your plans on Darkath?"

The priest, who had just joined the trio, smiled as he pulled, with delicate fingers, at a piece of meat wrapped in bread. "Ah, always the newsman, Mister Cain. I am here with a delegation to build a new church. The old one, as you know, is all but a ruin."

"Yes," Amalia chirped brightly. "I saw it this morning. But you are an archeologist and not an engineer, isn't that so?"

"Indeed it is." The priest bowed, slightly pleased possibly that his reputation had preceded him. "I am afraid I am not much help in building new structures. My specialty is finding old ones."

"And you will conduct a dig here?" Amalia seemed delighted at the prospect. "What in heaven for?"

"Well, as you may know, the first interstellar empire, the African empire, seems to have reached farther than anyone had previously supposed. There is evidence of their planetfall on worlds as distant as January and Azaroth."

"I had heard something about that." Cain encouraged him.

"Then you must read very widely." The priest complimented him. "These are relatively new discoveries."

"Do you think there may be evidence of the Africans here?" Amalia widened her eyes.

"No one knows. Ten years ago, a metallurgy survey drone orbiting Darkath detected certain anomalies. Their nature remains a mystery. They may be nothing at all, or . . ." He spread his arms to embrace a myriad of possibilities.

For the first time, since he had spoken to Cain, Captain Skijord contributed to the conversation. His tone seemed to indicate a certain aversion to the priest, as if he found it distasteful to be speaking with him at all, but could not easily contain his curiosity. "Where were these anomalies detected?"

"They are scattered in a linear pattern over what the aboriginals call the Nijwhol basin. The terrain there is very dense rock, like granite covered with a relatively thin layer of sand and so I was able to persuade the commission that a dig there would be possible.''

"A linear pattern,'' Skijord suggested, ''could indicate the breakup of a spacecraft entering the atmosphere.''

"Exactly, Captain.'' The priest nodded.

"It could mean many other things as well.'' Skijord pointed out so quickly, it was almost as if the idea of agreement with the priest on anything was an embarrassment.

Cain noticed the disdain in which the Starcorps man held the priest and knew the phenomenon well. Skijord's profession was one that carried tremendous responsibility, competence and pride. It was, in fact, the Starcorps rather than the Quadrant Authority, Hub bureaucrats and politicians or the Imperial Military that was maintaining the Empire's faltering hold on rimworlds. Starcorps was increasingly resentful of the church's influence on everything from trade routes, exploration policies and even the very selection of colonies. Darkath was a prime example of this. The Church of the Universal Blood and their mission to convert the Darkhani was the entire *raison d'être* for the Imperial presence here. Skijord undoubtedly thought this a poor justification for a colony and believed that Starcorps resources, his own skill, experience, and time could better be used elsewhere. Cain, privately, would have to agree.

Still, Cain felt, *there is something here. Some vital and as yet unguessed element.* Some unforeseen reason that all of them were present. It was a fragile, insubstantial kind of certainty, but he felt certain nonetheless.

"Well,'' said Gillermo, breaking a momentarily awkward silence, ''I hope to find out what I can about it.'' He smiled pleasantly. ''I'm very eager.''

It took Cain a beat to realize the priest was referring again to the anomaly in the Nijwhol basin.

Amalia took the priest's glass to refill it with wine. "You must let me accompany you, Padre. You simply must. I am composing a drama about an archeologist."

"Perhaps that could be arranged." The priest seemed dubious, but unwilling to cause offense. "I would be delighted, of course. Have you ever been on a dig?"

"No. I haven't. I've always wanted to."

"I can only promise you dust, discomfort, and boredom, I'm afraid. You dramatists have invested my profession with a romanticism that is all too rare in reality."

"Oh, come now, I'm sure it's fascinating." Amalia fairly bristled with visions, Cain surmised, of mummified African colonists.

The priest smiled. "I must say I do find it so, but it isn't for everyone. Most often it is unrewarded drudgery."

The conversation shifted to other topics as guests found their way to the sideboard and mingled with the celebrities. Cain rejoined Wilson as the older man was regaling Gillermo's novice with tales of his interplanetary travels.

After an hour of polite conversation the guests were herded to tables and served reconstituted fruits, vegetables and flavored pastes. Cain noted that Cristobal insisted on being seated next to Captain Skijord where he engaged in a hushed, one-sided conversation with the reticent pilot. He also noticed Jimenez, at the head of the table, trying to overhear the conversation between the captain and the colonel while pretending not to.

* * *

The commandant weaved his way through the throng of guests, smiling and shaking hands, looking grave or concerned when appropriate, nodding, even laughing. But his thoughts were elsewhere.

The business of the ultimatum and the bloody proof that the renegade aliens held the three missing Terrans had weighed heavily on Jimenez. His conference with Cristobal that morning had been heated and inconclusive. His direct order to delay the execution of the prisoners apprehended at the spaceport had been met with steely disapproval from *El Raton*. The ranking colonel had insisted on filing a formal protest by tachyon to Quadrant Headquarters. Fortunately, the communication equipment was down as usual and by the time Cristobal's complaint would be sent, the matter might yet be resolved peaceably. An exchange of hostages had to be made with as little fuss as possible. In the meantime, the solar equipment had to be offloaded in secrecy and transported under cover of nightfall to a staging area in the northern desert. A handpicked crew accompanied by a detachment of Terran cavalry in armored hovercraft was effecting that now.

As for the starship computer's report of Andromedan spacecraft on Giata, Captain Skijord confirmed that sensors had recorded a cluster of shielded, mobile, energy sources of a type that matched previous reports and rumors of unidentified spacefaring vessels, and that they did not originate in any known quadrant of Imperial space. No one, until now, had ever gotten close enough to one of them to gather any data about them other than the fact that they were huge, fast, uncommunicative on any known frequency and unlike anything ever encountered before. All previous reports of them had come from the outer quadrants, the galaxy's rim. Now, there were dozens of them on the blind side of Darkath's moon and Jimenez had no way of knowing what it meant. Skijord emphasized that this was the first time any real data had been gathered, vague as it was. This was the first real possibility for contact. The Starcorps man had stiffly requested that he be allowed to take the *Pandora* on a reconnaissance mission for a closer look.

With regret, Jimenez turned him down. The situation here demanded that he think of the starship as an evacuation vessel in a worst case scenario. The ship could only remain a short time before the "window" would close. Jimenez would need every day of that time as insurance. Skijord had merely said, "I see," turned on his heel, and left with the minimum of required courtesy. The starship captain would undoubtedly think him a timid fool at best, a coward at worst. But Skijord had no way of knowing all the facts. Oh, he could surmise from the cargo, that native unrest might be on the horizon, but a man like Skijord would find this insignificant in comparison with the discovery of possible extragalactics so near at hand. The fact that no representative of the Empire felt galvanized to seize this opportunity, but instead wrung their hands like nervous schoolteachers at the unruly antics of their unwilling students, undoubtedly filled the pilot with disgust.

Eventually, if events permitted, Jimenez could launch one of the two shuttles for reconnaissance and perhaps even attempt contact, but he simply did not have the Terran personnel to spare. Especially not now, when mutiny was in the air. The Dhirn scientists he had at his disposal might be a natural choice for such a mission, but their tenacious beliefs forbade them to leave the planet: even those that proclaimed their Christianity would balk at such an order, he was certain. The Khaj would be useless in such a context; they were warriors pure and simple. Perhaps at some future point, he might prevail upon the Rigelians and Cappellans along with, say, a few civilian Terrans, like the priests, but not before he could be sure those shuttles weren't needed for combat mobilization or, if worse came to worst, *evacuation* with little hope for the passengers' rescue. The word was pregnant with despair and he was loath to think it.

Evacuation.

Yet one more thing troubled Jimenez. He could not quite say why it made him so uncomfortable, but it was something the old Khaj woman, Jiliad, had said to him just before the party. She had placed a withered, plum-colored hand on his arm and said, ''They came to me in my dreams last night. The angels of Giata. They are here, Commandant. My people are no longer alone.'' Crazy old woman. There was no way she could have known about the Andromedans. None. They said she was a seer, though. It is why she was held in such regard by the Khaj. It was also rumored that her daughter organized renegade resistance to the Terrans. Rumors, dreams, old women, *angels*. Still it troubled him and he was vaguely embarrassed that it did.

He tried to return his attention to Cristobal's conversation with Skijord, but he was distracted.

''I saw the most amazing sight this morning, Commandant.'' Amalia Dubois was talking to him. He could make out nothing of what the starship pilot and *El Raton* were saying anyway. ''Darkath's famous dragons.''

''Ah,'' Jimenez smiled noncommittally.

''Yes. Just above the parade ground. There were six of them with beautifully painted, half naked Khaj warriors on their backs. They wheeled gracefully over the compound and dropped something from the sky only to disappear as quickly as they had come into the mountains and the rising sun.'' The dramatist made graceful, flying gestures with her hands mimicking winged flight.

''Your reputation for depicting the colorful is well deserved, I see,'' Jimenez complimented her.

''Why, thank you, Commandant. Were they executing some military maneuvers?''

Jimenez registered the look of interest on a half dozen faces at the table. ''Er . . . yes. You could say that.''

''They certainly look fierce, but so graceful. Tell me, do you employ the dragons in your cavalry?''

"To a limited extent, yes. They are uniquely suited for local use. They have certain advantages over our hovercraft here. They are inexpensive to maintain, nearly tireless, they can function in sandstorms without difficulty—unlike our hovercars—and they have their own sort of armor. The bladders on their undersides which enable them to fly are somewhat vulnerable, but they are sectioned and quickly self-sealing so that it really requires a rather large wound to debilitate them. Of course, I prefer the odor of one of our hovercars."

This brought a wave of polite laughter to the table and steered the conversation away from the morning's incident. As dinner was served, Jimenez ordered another bottle of wine for himself. He saw that he had finished the one before him all too quickly. When it arrived and was poured he lifted it to his lips and met Cristobal's eyes over the rim. *El Raton* seemed to laugh coldly at him and the commandant only pretended to drink. Making a face, he handed the bottle back to the servant and requested another. "Devil of a time keeping wine in this heat," he remarked to Doña Dubois.

* * *

Jack Avery drifted upward from the depths of languid dreams. Cold fire played slowly over his body like the tendrils of nightmare creatures at the bottom of a methane sea. Slow visions of dancing angels gave way to angry black faces with white masks for eyes, painted cheeks in startling colors, lips twisted away from pink gums and jagged rows of teeth. He felt the tug of powerful hands lifting him, carrying him somewhere and then he was facedown, tied with thongs that bit into his wrists and ankles. There was a blindfold over his eyes and his mouth was stuffed with cloth, making it difficult for him to breathe. He sensed this was not a dream, but could not be sure. The pain provided a focus for his thoughts and intensified as he was jostled roughly, his face and stomach pounding against the surface he lay on. He was being moved on the back of a large animal. A stench of rotting meat met his nostrils and he fought down the sickness that rose in his throat, knowing that to give in to it, meant to choke and drown. To drown in a desert; the thought made him smile crazily and with that came the full recollection of where he was. Darkath.

He tried to struggle and free himself, but his limbs would not obey him. *What's happening? I must have been hit on the head . . . or drugged.* He remembered running through the streets being chased, evading his pursuers in the tent. All the smoke . . . like what the man Wilson had been smoking. How could he have fallen asleep? He didn't know, but the very idea of sleep seemed to beckon him back down into the embrace of lurid dreams. He fought it and forced himself to inventory the harsh sensations that insinuated themselves over the gauzy blanket that smothered his thoughts.

Oh, God, Lord of the Universal Blood of your son, forgive us the flesh and deliver our . . . something . . . to something else . . .

He couldn't remember the rest of the prayer. It seemed more important to concentrate on other things, first of all breathing. As his breath came more regularly and his heart slowed, he could time the contraction of the muscles in his neck and stomach to meet the jogging of the beast under him. He could hear harsh shouts in an alien tongue and feel the whipping of cool night winds laden with sand against his cheek.

Abruptly, the jogging ceased and Jack knew that he was airborne on the back of a dragon. In spite of his fear he wished he could see it. He had studied holos of the Darkhani Grea' ka and they seemed to him to be the most fabulous creatures in the universe. With the remaining detachment the drug afforded him, he resented being deprived the full experience of flight on one of the legendary beasts.

Gradually, the night winds cleared his head and exhilaration gave way once more to horror. The journey continued for over an hour while Jack frantically groped for a course of action to save himself. For the time being there was nothing he could do.

At last he felt the impact of solid ground beneath him and he was nearly thrown from the mount. Arms caught him and dragged him from the animal. He was forced to stand. Hands tore away the blindfold and he blinked into the bruised purple light of Darkath's giant moon.

Two Khaj in tattered Imperial uniforms glared at him. One held a short sword at his heart while the other gestured at him to be silent, pantomiming that his gag would be removed if he complied. Jack nodded slowly. He felt dizzy and lowered himself to the desert floor. The one with the knife cut away the cloth around his mouth and conferred with his companion. Jack took the opportunity to look around him. Long, graceful sand dunes studded with prickly vegetation rolled to the horizon in the bluish-red light, their peaks spouting a fine spray of sand into the wind like powdered sapphires. In the distance behind him, Jack could see the lights of the spaceport and guessed that they were some fifty kilometers to the north of the settlement. Farther ahead, he thought he could see a procession of vehicles moving slowly across the horizon accompanied by a train of human looking silhouettes. His mind was still fuzzy from what he had decided were the drug fumes he had inhaled in the tent, but backlit by the brooding moon and almost phosphorescent low clouds, distorted as it was by heat mirage and distance, Jack was almost certain that what he was looking at was a Terran military convoy. If only there was some way to signal them . . . but there was none.

He was resigned, there was no chance of escape. Even if he were to break away from his captors, he would not get far.

Continuing his inspection of his surroundings, he

shifted his position in the sand that had yet to give up
its heat from the day. His first sight of the three dragons made him suspect he was still in the grip of hallucination: they stood higher than a man, their scaled
backs winking in moonlight. Great, stupid eyes, rolled
in leathery sockets beneath a stub of bony horn. Slow
scarves of viscous smoke trailed from their nostrils to
be caught by the breeze. They crouched on hugely
muscled legs culminating in three pronged talons
longer than the Khaj's sword. Their tails snaked lazily
behind them in the sand like independent serpents for-
aging for food with flat, spiked heads.

He tore his fascinated gaze from them. The two Khaj
seemed to reach an agreement of some sort and signaled an end to their discussion by splaying their fingers across their eyes. The one with the sword
motioned for Jack to stand. He obeyed and was lifted
back onto the dragon he had been lashed to. This time
they allowed him to sit upright without the gag or
blindfold. His hands were secured to a pommel on the
saddle and with a loud cry and a prod from his sword,
the soldier ordered the beast to rise again. Jack held
on grimly as the animal lurched beneath him and began to taxi across the sand. Within a few meters the
creature let out an expulsion of foul gases, shrieked
like a tortured bird and unfurled its wings, their span
twice the length of its body. Air caught beneath it;
dragon and rider sailed into the sky. Wings struck at
the air in great, ponderous movements that seemed to
echo the bizarre choreography of his recent, *iravka*
induced dreams. Jack turned to see the two others
mounted and lifting into the night behind him. They
quickly closed the distance and rode to either side of
him. The convoy of troops was even more defined from
this height, but he forced himself to look away, un-
eager, though he was not sure why, to call his captors'
attention to it. When he turned forward again, he could
see they were headed toward a mountain peak at the
head of a long, low range visible now to the east.

Still, it looked for all the world as if the dragon were taking them into the heart of the strange, violet moon.

* * *

Cristobal and Skijord strolled across the parade grounds beneath the great amethyst satellite called Giata. Streamers of luminous gas clouds laced the heavens studded with dense constellations and gay clusters of stars. Darkath's night sky seemed more festive than the decorations inside the hall. Each man walked with a brandy and a Terran cheroot, laced mildly with *iravka*.

"What you are asking," Cristobal spoke slowly, as if making sure he was getting this right, "is that I authorize one of our shuttles here to make a preliminary investigation of the vessels your ship sighted on Giata?" He gestured at the ponderous moon above them.

"That's right, Colonel. Jimenez has told me he is worried about the political situation here. He needs the *Pandora* as a possible evacuation vessel. I could defy him. I could investigate anyway. It is my ship and I have enough friends with influence at Starcorps and Quadrant Authority so that I would not be overly worried about the consequences to my career, but I don't wish to gamble with people's lives. Jimenez may be right about things here and my ship could hold several hundred refugees if it had to. But this opportunity is unprecedented."

"Hmm." Cristobal sounded thoughtful and though he frowned, he was loving this. Here was *his* opportunity to do what he intended to do all along, but now with the backing of Skijord, Starcorps and the pilot's friends at QA. "I don't know, Captain. What you're asking is for *me* to defy the commandant instead. I just don't know. The Empire isn't interested in these sightings of Andromedans. They don't want another inconclusive report about this. It isn't a priority at this time.''

''Not a priority?'' Skijord's face darkened in the mauve moonlight. ''This is a pivotal moment in the history of the Empire, in the history of starfaring. The Empire isn't interested because it is becoming more and more the tool of priests instead of the species it governs. It doesn't want any more . . . theological anomalies. It is a poor sort of religion that shrinks from the universe.''

''What you say sounds like heresy.'' Cristobal managed to look slightly shocked.

Skijord gestured with both arms to the heavens. *''That* is my religion. And my ship is my church.''

''But you offer your ship as an evacuation vessel standing by, in exchange for my authorizing a shuttle mission without the commandant's knowledge?''

''I don't care if it's with or without his knowledge. I only have authority over my own ship. I have no authority over your shuttles and Jimenez will not use them, but you can.''

''And if I refuse?'' Cristobal stopped his slow pacing and stood firm on the parade ground.

The starship pilot stood motionlessly beside him, breathed in the thin, night air and shrugged as if to work tension from his shoulders. He turned to face Cristobal. ''Then I will take the *Pandora* and return in five days. I will do this with regret, but it is a choice I am willing to make. I will accept responsibility for the consequences.''

Cristobal looked pained, but inwardly he was experiencing a kind of glee.

Skijord added, ''I will lend you the use of some of my crew if necessary. I myself would like to go, but that would add insult to injury. I have no wish to make an enemy of Commandant Jimenez.''

''Quite right.'' Cristobal said. ''Quite right.'' He seemed momentarily distracted. ''Er, no . . . no . . .

that won't be necessary, but thank you for the offer. I think I can manage a crew of our own people."

"Then it is agreed—you will send a shuttle?"

Cristobal lifted the last of his brandy in a toast. "Very well, you leave me little choice. For the time being, I think it would be best if we do not discuss this."

"As you wish."

They touched glasses and drank. Cristobal smiled, but Skijord did not.

* * *

"It is unfortunate, Mr. Cain, but we cannot release your holocorder at this time." Jimenez lit a cigar and offered one to Martin Cain who accepted and Padre Gillermo who declined. The three men stood to one side of the main group of milling guests who, flushed with wine and after dinner drinks, chattered louder than was necessary. "As much as I loathe handicapping your fine work, the situation here has become far too ticklish in recent days to provoke the Darkhani. I trust it will all die down as usual after a week or so and at that time I promise you I will do what I can."

Cain swirled his brandy and peered at the glowing end of his cigar. "In what way, 'ticklish,' Commandant?"

"Oh, nothing to be alarmed about. Just the usual sort of sensitivities. Something in the air lately. I've seen it in the past, just before the rains. The natives get a little peevish." Jimenez seemed far too eager to brush off the topic.

"Wilson told me about the cartographic party and the missionaries. Any word as to what might have happened there? There was some talk of rebels holding them hostage for certain religious demands. Anything in that?" Cain was going out on a limb and didn't expect a straight answer. His answer would be in Jimenez's face and body language.

Jimenez frowned, shifted his considerable weight. "Nigel is a good correspondent, but a bit of a doom-sayer on the subject of native disaffection. No, I'm afraid what we have here is simply a case of an inexperienced party getting lost in a sandstorm. You must have heard that three of them met an unfortunate end at the hands of . . . brigands. There are some damned ugly renegades outside these walls, but they are few and not as organized as Wilson might have you believe. We're searching for the others, naturally."

Jimenez took another brandy off a passing tray and surrendered his empty. Cain could see that the commandant's knuckles were white where he held the glass. "Perhaps I could be of help," Cain offered. "I would like to tour the surrounding desert with my man, Raith, who has promised to show me a thing or two. If I can be of service . . ."

"Mr. Cain, I can't forbid you to wander outside the cantonment walls, but I heartily urge you to reconsider for a few days. I cannot be responsible for your safety. I can't spare any men to accompany you."

"I wouldn't hear of it." Cain countered pleasantly. "I've been around a little, Commandant, and I don't need a chaperone."

Jimenez grunted and turned to Gillermo. "I'm going to have to ask you to delay your excavations as well, Padre. For the same reasons."

"That things are . . . ticklish?" The priest grinned.

"Unsettled, yes," he answered, regretting his previous choice of words.

"You yourself said that the rains are due anytime. I cannot conduct a dig when the Nijwhol basin floods. Once the rains begin, it will be the better part of a year before the area is workable."

"I cannot control the weather, Padre. I can offer you safe conduct in a few weeks to the basin. There you can join up with an engineering party I have dispatched there for some surveying. They will be there for the better part of a month. During that time we will all be praying for clement weather until their work is finished. That is the best I can do. I have no authority over Mr. Cain, but the clergy is here on sufferance of the military governor."

The priest's smile faded. "I am aware of that, Commandant. I will cooperate in every way. Excuse me." The priest walked away, lifting his full snifter as though it needed replenishment.

Since he had Jimenez to himself for the moment, he decided to press his advantage. "Tell me," Cain began, then noticed Jimenez following Cristobal and Skijord with his eyes toward the door. "Does your surveying party have anything to do with installing solar collectors? It seems the Nijwhol basin would be ideal for that sort of thing, though I can't see how you'd get around the flooding problem during the rains."

Jimenez's eyes flashed. "There are many problems with such an idea, primarily Khaj superstition. If I were to entertain such a notion, the flooding problem could be bypassed with a system of interlocking pontoons to support the chain of panels. However, the subject is far too delicate to discuss seriously at this time." The older man fixed Cain with a pleading look. "Far too delicate, you understand, Mr. Cain?"

"Yes," Cain nodded. "I understand."

"Good. I knew you were a sensible man." Jimenez drank his brandy and sighed almost imperceptibly with relief. "I believe we have some Dhirn dancers for entertainment this evening. I think you'll enjoy them. Shall we?" He inclined his head toward the dais where the musicians had cleared a space.

"Delighted," Cain agreed and followed the large man who waddled unsteadily across the room. He had seen many military commanders in his time in a number of stressful situations. *This one*, he thought, *is a good man at the core, but tired and with the stink of desperation on him. He's ten years too old for this and he'll buckle in the first strong wind.*

Chapter Nine

Hara toured the caves. She exchanged jokes and greetings with her followers, squatted over cooking fires to sample foods and offer compliments, carried children on her shoulders and in general made herself accessible to those who had thrown their lot in with her under the blue banner of Giata. She repeated to those who asked of news concerning the captured agents, "There has been no word yet, but they are alive. The execution order must have been suspended. We will wait and see."

Everywhere small fights ensued between Khaj and Dhirn. This was a fact of daily existence that no one took note of in any real measure. That the ancient foes could coexist together at all was a marvel. In Hara's presence, these squabbles dissipated. Each combatant froze in the wake of her charisma like embattled *ikas* stunned by torchlight. Her pause and silent gaze was reprimand enough. She made her way through her people alone.

She walked downward through the winding labyrinths she knew so well, the passageway alternately narrowing to the width of her shoulders—sending any passersby on their way up scurrying quickly back the way they came to allow her passage—and then widening enough to accommodate as many as ten abreast. She entered a cavern with a natural rock vaulted dome arcing overhead. The cavern was larger than the largest Terran-made room on Darkath and yet it was a relatively average size chamber in the Alaikhaj network.

Its only distinguishing characteristic was the hole in the ceiling where rock had fallen away, exposing the cave to a wide shaft of fire orange sunlight.

Inside the cavern were several hundred Dhirn. Hara could see that a wedding was in progress. She situated herself in the shadows to watch unobtrusively as eighteen nubile Dhirn brides-to-be sat cross-legged on the floor in the center of the room. They wore only a small cloth at their waists, ankle bracelets, and finger jewelry. Their faces were veiled with shimmering diaphanous cloth which fell from the turbanlike hats they wore which, in turn, rose in gauzy folds from their heads. Each headpiece was connected to the one next to it by a length of cloth, in fact all eighteen wedding hats were formed from a single, very long bolt of fabric which remained uncut. This signified, Hara thought to herself, the solidarity and interdependency of Dhirn women; a kind of check and balance system in the dance—as in life—that could easily become bondage if it were allowed to.

From her unobtrusive place in the recesses of the chamber Hara watched as the musicians, all male, began to play their stringed *aljians,* pipes and staccato, stabbing *krikitiks.* The women soon began to beat out a tattoo on their thighs with their palms and the musicians followed the tempo the women set. Then the bridegrooms stepped into the space cleared around the women. Naked and painted with brilliant colors in abstract, geometrical designs, they began to dance slowly around the brides to the mounting beat. In and out of the wide cone of fiery sunlight slanting in from the roof, the men would dance with increasing urgency and variation of movement. The women pounded their thighs with their palms as they drummed the dirt floor with their feet and knees. Faster and faster the women beat, some swaying, some tossing their heads back, threatening to break or tangle the symmetry of the headdresses. Some were moaning with eyes closed or hungrily drinking in the sight of the reeling men. Sweat broke out on the backs and thighs of the writhing grooms. Around they spun, snaking, leaping, grunting. The musicians furiously followed the insistent, nearly maniacal slapping and thudding of the women with shrill runs and jangling glissandos from their instruments that echoed in the cavern like the plaintive mating calls of demonic birds. The men danced around and around, circling and spinning where they stood, moving in large circles and small. Some began to shake, their bodies taken in spasms of vibration, their eyes crossed or squeezed shut while they groped at the air or their genitals.

Faster now they reeled. The women moved their shoulders as they worked their hands and thighs. Their faces were contorted with pain and arousal.

Some of the men, spittle running from their mouths, shouted incomprehensibly into the shaft of sunlight, their eyes crossed, others danced and shook until they fell unconscious to the ground in spent ecstasy, some ejaculated onto the earth, sank to their knees and wept.

When the women stopped suddenly, the musicians fell silent. Two men were left standing among the dancers and they would have their choice of brides. Hara moved away through the shadows, stepping over several copulating wedding celebrants. Later, she knew, when they would drink the wine and smoke *iravka,* the feast would begin in earnest.

She walked out of the cavern and continued on her way through the stronghold at The Eye of God.

She passed a group of Khaj warriors practicing with their springlances. "Hia Hara!" one of them called to her. "Would you care to show us how it's done?" The three warriors laughed, each bowing almost imperceptibly in her direction. They had painted a target, a crude circle the width of a human head—with painted eyes and whiskers to resemble Jimenez—on a wall of smooth stone. To either side of the circle, great gouges were bitten from the rock by the tines of the lances.

They had been throwing from a distance of thirty meters and one of their lances had carved out the lower left corner of the face.

Hara smiled and took one of the proffered lances. She held the hilt of it and dug the base into her thigh. With her other hand, she pulled the cocking mechanism against the spring until it clicked home and all three of the prongs were wedged beneath the restraining ring. This one was made of the finest Dhirn-crafted steel and its handle was decorated with filigree work that also served as a grip, insurance against sweaty palms. She lifted the lance and rested the broad point on her forearm. Sighting low, with one eye down the length of the lance, she held her breath, stooped slowly and then with an expulsion of breath and with a rising cry, shot to her feet and hurled the weapon: lifting with her forearm and at the precise moment, throwing it like a javelin with her other hand. Her powerfully muscled body followed through the motion. The sound of metal on stone rang and echoed against the cave walls. In unison, the four of them ducked as they heard the violent snapping of the restraining ring. The three prongs of the springlance opened inside the rock like a deadly, blossoming orchid and chunks of rock the size of fists flew through the air over their heads with a deep whooshing sound. When they stood, they saw that the entire target was obliterated with only a few streaks of paint to indicate it was ever there. In a moment the huge wound in the rock began to bleed water in a slow trickle.

The Khaj warrior who owned the lance frowned at Hara. "We were only practicing aim, not mining water."

Hara grinned at the other two who seemed delighted by their companion's abashment. "That is the finest springlance I've ever raised. I'd welcome you and your lance beside me in battle." This brought a wide smile and a noticeable bow from the Khaj, his pride inflated once again. She moved on toward the Dhirn metalworks, clapping the warrior on his shoulder, leaving the three of them to pry the weapon from the mountain.

After visiting at the forges and complimenting the smiths, she climbed upward on stairs cut into the stone toward the site of her secret project. She emerged in a circular clearing open to the sky, but protected on three sides by spires of rock. Here, a small army of Dhirn workers labored at stitching the bladders of Grea' ka into gigantic balloons. Others busied themselves at weaving baskets from puhlcalf and hide. Hara's auxiliary air force of five hot air balloons would be ready, she was assured, in three more days. Each would carry three Khaj armed with explosive grenades and Terran machine rifles and could stay in the air indefinitely. They would sustain multiple bullet or projectile punctures, though not artillery—or light weapons if it came to that—and could travel, literally, as fast as the wind itself. Steering difficulties had yet to be worked out.

Hara continued to walk. She gradually left the camp-sounds behind her and climbed toward a place she had often come to as a child. It was a narrow plateau that fell away sharply on every side of its oblong perimeter. On its surface, low, windworn rock formations gave the place the appearance of a graveyard for giants; their great mute skulls, worn smooth by the sand laden wind, peered plaintively toward the horizon. As she walked among her sullen childhood playmates, she listened for the low singing of the wind through weather-worn holes: the eye sockets. There it was, like a sad melody half apprehended in a dream. What a fitting place this was for her as a child. How it prepared her. What more perfect rehearsal for the leading of her people to their slaughter than to wander alone as a child among the rows of death's heads, her imaginary friends, under the fiery scrutiny of her god. It seemed the most natural thing in the world, a place uniquely her own that spoke only to her and now she knew why.

For perhaps the first time in her life Hara admitted to herself that she would have wanted to play with the other children her age. But, as the daughter of Juum, this was out of the question. Her destiny was to seek the visions and spiritual paths of her father, to prepare herself to guide her people on a lifelong journey into the blazing heart of Alaikhaj. She was what the Terrans would call a priest. But the Terrans would never credit a woman with such spiritual integrity. She wondered why. It made no sense. Still, like the Terran priests, physical love was denied her. It was not, as with the Terrans, a law, written with blood on stone or however it was they did such things, but simply the way things *were*. It was assumed that the daughter of a seer, on a spiritual journey toward God, of whom religious, social and military leadership was expected, would no more seek a physical lover than she would throw bones for the gems in The Eye of God.

An image of the naked Dhirn bridegrooms and courtiers sprang into her thoughts. The patina of sweat over knotted muscles, the erect, urgent members that seemed to guide their movements toward the women like dowsing rods.

No. It was forbidden. Not *forbidden* and yet . . . so out of reach. She needn't have hidden herself in the shadows that way. She would likely have been welcomed into the wedding party, coupled with one or more of the honored men, but the punishment would have been swift and sure. Not from any outside agency, her father or her people, but within herself the retribution would surely follow. She simply *could not*. When she did one day, it would be an act of surrender to a part of herself she could not now afford to recognize. Besides, she really didn't know how it was done.

One day . . . One day. . . .

She thought of these things as she walked, the wind lifting her robes and hair, her palms playing over the reassuringly smooth skulls of her old comrades. She came to the rock she called her Grea' ka as a girl. It seemed much smaller now, but it was basically unchanged. She fitted herself into the worn saddle and gripped the stone neck. *Kari*, she whispered the secret name for her beast friend. *Kari, it has been a long time. Do you remember how you used to speak to me?* But Kari did not answer. Hara smiled and looked about her at the rest of the stones. Sometimes they became her fleet of dragons when she led imaginary warriors against the Terrans she grew up hating. In some secret inaccessible place inside her she always knew what she would do, what she must; the imperative that was the price of her birthright.

Everything, her whole life had been a rehearsal for what was to come.

But it wasn't a dream any longer or a game. It wasn't pretend anymore. The skulls lying bleached beneath Alaikhaj were now real. The dragons real. And on the heels of that thought, the loneliness returned. *That* had always been real.

She rose and walked to the edge of the plateau where her warrior friend, chief lieutenant, bodyguard, sentinel, and lover once stood scrutinizing the desert floor—watching for Hara's enemies. The stone had been cracked in two by a quake. A natural rock formation, only the child in Hara could see *Tikan,* the life-size stone doll that served as mentor, advisor, and tender friend to the girl Hara. Now only a broken stump remained. She put her hand to it and then clenched her fists. She tightened her eyes as she willed away the upwelling image of a lover with his arm around her, lifting her, brushing her face with his lips. Her heart hammered in her ears and she lifted her head, staring eye to eye with God. The tears dried as they formed. The low, almost subliminal moaning of the wind through the rock seemed to rise until it was an unbearable shriek in Hara's ears. When she realized the sound was coming from her own throat, she stopped and turned her face away from the sun.

Nos, the Dhirn shaman, found her. She was kneeling on the ground, her arms folded around a jagged stump of rock at the edge of the plateau. Her shoulders were rising and falling though no sound came from

her. Unwilling to interrupt her religious rapture, but
knowing the urgency of the news, he said tentatively,
"Hia Hara Tian Aikhan, we have a new prisoner. A
Terran child. He has just been brought by two of our
riders."

Hara's shoulders stopped moving and for a moment
Nos thought she might have left her body, perhaps forever. She remained motionless for a hundred heartbeats. When she turned to look at the shaman, it was
with her full sense of self-possession and more than a
trace of anger and disdain. "How has it come about
that we are now taking children as hostages, Nos?"

No answer presented itself and the Dhirn merely
averted his eyes to the horizon.

Hara got to her feet. "Take me to him," she said.

* * *

Colonel Eduardo Manosa Rodriguez Cristobal sat
behind his desk and studied the three Dhirn officers
before him. Their uniforms were clean and the color
of the Terran sky on a clear day. Their boots were
polished and their crimson berets bore their rank and
area of expertise. Koros was a physicist and astrono-
mer; the eldest of the three, his rank was lieutenant.
Vija, a Dhirn junior lieutenant and specialist in lin-
guistics and what she called "soft communication sci-
ences" was the youngest. Ganar was a middle-aged
sergeant major who was little more than a bureaucrat,
an administrator of Dhirn military office personnel.
Among the three of them they had a total of eighteen
weeks military training and though this was the second
time they had worn their full uniforms in the past week,
(the first being at the reception and firework display)
it had been nearly a year before that since they had
worn anything but fatigue tunics and their traditional
waistcloths. Their military status was ornamental,
honorary. They were no more soldiers than the nuns
across the compound, but for what Cristobal had in

mind, he needed Imperial military personnel. Imperial military *Dhirn* personnel.

The primary quality these three Dhirn had in common was that they all visibly and audibly professed to be Christian. Each of them had left behind the old ways of Darkath worship. Or so they said.

Ganar, Koros, and Vija undoubtedly wondered why they had been called into Cristobal's office. In a moment, the colonel would relieve their curiosity, but first he would sit in silence for a moment to impress upon them the gravity of the situation.

The Dhirn looked around the immaculate office. It must seem to them almost preternaturally clean, dust free . . . sterile. Cristobal smiled inwardly, it was a subliminal symbol of his personal triumph over his environment, the planet itself. He had his staff clean every hour on the hour, rifts in the foamcrete or wandering doorjambs that might potentially allow sand and dust would be detected and repaired before they could undermine the integrity of his microcosm.

He stared at the three he had summoned. He *forced* himself to stare at them because he found the Darkers, all Darkers, maddeningly repulsive. Every day that he must lay eyes on them was a reaffirmation of his inner discipline. The fold of pale, slimy translucence over their eyes sent the gorge rising unbidden into his throat. He wished to pry it away with a razor and expose the beady, treacherous cataracts of evil that hid from the sun. He had done this, alone and unobserved, with prisoners and corpses and it somehow made him feel clean, purged, afterward. Their jet blue-black bodies seemed filthy to him, especially when they burned in the sun and their skins would molt gray, like serpents. He beheld the enemy. No matter what the Empire, guided by fools and priests proclaimed, this was the nemesis of humanity: a perfect negative of the Terran aesthetic ideal.

He noted Koros looking at his prize holo of his kill on Marus. The Darker squirmed with discomfort as he took in the folds of slaughtered black and red flesh.

The hunt had been good that day and he wished he had holos of the other cetaceans he had mutilated with his photon lance. Whales and dolphins. Such a pretentious species: idle, rutting, fouling the waterways with their litters. Hard to imagine they were once very rare on Terra before the Africans cultivated the herds on Marus. Their legendary or fabled intelligence—when the subject was brought up—annoyed Cristobal to the point of distraction. They weren't intelligent enough to avoid his lance. Ah, now Ganar was looking at his shrunken bottle nose dolphin skull collection and the mounted sea lion penis on his wall. "That," he pointed out archly, "is from Terra herself. It was one of the last dozen or so in arctic waters. The skill involved in tracking that beast is undoubtedly beyond your comprehension, but I assure you it cost me more standard credits than you'll see in a lifetime and an inner discipline you can't imagine. I lost twenty pounds. Frostbite cost me three toes. Why I'm telling you this is that it was a function of my single-mindedness. It would serve you in good stead to mark that here and now."

Vija was staring in fascination and apprehension at the chair in the corner of the office. Cristobal let a grin appear briefly at the edges of his mouth. The chair was covered in a hide that looked for all the world like it might have once belonged to a Darkhani. "Killer whale." Cristobal announced. "From Marus. Got it with a detonating harpoon to the skull, otherwise I would have had the head stuffed." He knew its effect on the Darkers which was why he had it on display. He would have loved to show off his Rigelian hide and the shrunken Khaj head he had in his secret hold or "bunker" beneath the church, but these were proscribed by law. One day they would grace his office. One day soon, when *he* was the law on Darkath.

Until that day, there was much to do and he was patient. He forced his thoughts back to the matter at hand.

Cristobal still had no idea whether Captain Skijord

believed his story about Jimenez's deteriorating mental condition. But the seed had been planted in his mind. He had urged the captain to make a full report to him, Cristobal, rather than Jimenez since the commandant could not be expected to make a rational judgment in response to the Andromedan presence on Darkath's moon. Skijord, however, had reported to Jimenez anyway. No harm done. Cristobal had underestimated Skijord's fascination with the Andromedans.

Cristobal's plan had come together at last. With the protest of the hostage situation filed with Quadrant Authority and Planetary Affairs, the conversation with Captain Skijord to establish a background of Jimenez's feebleness and the military governor's certainly suicidal attempt to install solar units in the backyard of the rabid Khaj stronghold, and now Skijord's demand to reconnoiter Giata—in fact his almost blatant blackmailing of Cristobal to do so—no military authority could call Cristobal's actions into question. The presence of the Andromedans on the moon had to be dealt with, or at least the appearance of such in order to appease the fanatical starship pilot in exchange for the *Pandora*'s services as an evacuation vessel. Yes, that's how it would appear to any court of inquiry.

Of course, he had intended to send the Dhirn up anyway as a show of power, an unmistakable statement of authority. But now his position was strengthened. It was politically necessary, militarily necessary. Any fool could see that. Surely he would be commended for taking matters into his own hands in the absence of a decisive leader. The beauty of it was this: he, Cristobal would be seen to be making a savvy judgment by sending expendable, native troops on this phantom chase, thus keeping vital Terran personnel nearby in a time of emergency. Cristobal would order his three Dhirn and one Terran trainee to pilot the shuttle to Giata to investigate and attempt contact. He did not believe that they would disobey his direct order. He could not, for a moment, seriously entertain the idea that these three would throw away their life's work, their careers, their very *lives* because of some primitive superstition about leaving their goddess of a planet. Jimenez had coddled the Darkers on these matters and Cristobal was confident that that was precisely the wrong approach. He would now prove it. Once the precedent was established that a Dhirn crew had flown a mission offworld, he would have them forever. They would be broken and the rest would fall in line.

The mission itself was unimportant, but it could be accomplished. An uneventful reconnaissance flight over the silent mysterious ships, a few holograms, the shuttle's computer cobbling together the first maps of the place, a few hours of attempted greeting transmissions to the extragalactics (if, in fact, that's what they were) and Skijord would be satisfied. The point was that Cristobal would then have established his iron control over half the native population. The Dhirn. They would be his.

One way or another, Jimenez was certain to be relieved—especially when his solar project blew up in his face and Cristobal pulled his chestnuts out of the fire for him.

If the worst should happen and the mission served to disaffect the Dhirn *en masse,* well, he had other plans to fall back on. He had cached more than trophies in his bunker beneath the church.

At last he cleared his throat and fixed each of the Dhirn with a challenging stare. "I have selected you three for a mission of critical urgency and utmost secrecy. It is also a test by fire of your loyalty to the Empress." He paused. "If there is any reason why any of you would hesitate to obey the verbal orders I am about to give you, speak up now."

Koros, Ganar, and Vija looked at each other. No one spoke.

"I must have your sworn loyalty before the fact, because I cannot risk divulging the nature of the mission to anyone less than absolutely committed to its completion. Again, if there is any doubt in your minds that you can do what I ask, now is the time to withdraw from the room. There will be no repercussions.'' Cristobal was aware that each of them knew him and his reputation sufficiently to understand that what he had just said was a veiled threat. If they let him down, he would ruin them. Possibly, they would "disappear" which was the fate of others who had run afoul of *El Raton*. Having no idea what it was their choice really consisted of, they remained silent.

"Very well, then. I knew I could count on you." Cristobal then outlined the reconnaissance mission. He watched their faces become horrified. It was Koros who spoke first.

"What you ask of us is . . . a great deal. To leave the surface of Darkath would be . . . at the very least, a betrayal of our traditions. We would be seen as unclean, rendered outcasts among our kind. As much as we would desire to cooperate, Colonel, it would be construed by our people as an act of religious mockery."

Cristobal had, of course, been prepared for just such a reaction. He sneered in disgust. "I cannot believe my own ears. Three highly educated officers of the Imperial Army, two of you scientists, and you speak to me of losing your souls because of a short flight to your own moon?" He walked to the transparent alloy window and stood with his back to them, staring out at a handful of native mechanics making unhurried repairs on a row of hovercars.

"Do you not call yourselves Christians? Don't I see you and you and you at the mass on Sunday?" He jabbed a finger at each of them in turn. "Haven't you, Vija, had your son christened by the monseigneur only last month?"

Vija said, "Yes, I am a Christian. Of course." She seemed hesitant, frightened, choosing her words with great care. "I think that what Koros is saying is that, politically this might be unwise. That Terran crewmembers might be more appropriate. . . ."

"I have ears!" Cristobal struck his desk with his

fist. "I can hear Koros perfectly well. Are you suggesting to me that your political sensibilities are superior to mine? Do you imply that you are better suited to make command decisions?"

"No." Vija flinched backward a step. Her optic membrane fluttered nervously.

"Don't speak to me of politics! I am asking you to demonstrate your loyalty to the Empire as well as the sincerity of the faith you profess, or are they both just convenient 'political' fictions. Eh? How about you, Ganar?"

"No, er, yes." The stolid looking sergeant major said, "That is, I am prepared to follow orders as always, Colonel."

"Good. Because, now that you know the nature of the assignment if you will not go, you force me to detain you until the mission is accomplished with other personnel. That goes for the rest of you as well. I can't have you speaking of this to the superstitious rabble you call 'your people.' The Empire is 'your people.' The Church of the Universal Blood should now inform your beliefs, your traditions. Once you return, perfectly sound, your souls fully intact, I assure you, having done vital work for the Empress you shall be heroes, an example to all Dhirn. I am offering you a unique opportunity to show all of Darkath, all the Empire, what the Darkhani are made of, what being a soldier, a Christian, and a scientist really means. Let us leave the primitive, groveling heathen of one hundred years ago behind, shall we? Once and for all. Fulfill your destiny and light a beacon for those behind you to follow."

There it was. Leave Darkath and compromise their traditions, their beliefs, their spiritual past. Or rot as Cristobal's secret prisoners in a distant hole in the ground somewhere. No one would ever know they were there, and they undoubtedly would never leave it alive. Each of them knew Cristobal that well.

At length, Vija said, "May we have a moment in private to discuss this, Colonel?"

Cristobal took a cigar from his desktop and nodded. "Of course," he said. "You have five minutes."

He left the office and strolled along the parade ground, smoking and smiling to himself. When he returned, he was accompanied by two armed Terran soldiers. "Well?" he asked. Ganar was wringing his hands, Vija did not meet his eyes.

Koros said, "When do we leave?"

"Tonight. These men will accompany you to the spaceport. Everything you need is on board. Your orders are recorded. They will be played once and then deleted. When you return in a week you will report directly to me, no one else. All communications on every channel will be monitored by me personally." He put out his cigar and grinned coldly at them. "You have made the right decision, of course."

As they filed out of the room, Cristobal called to them. "Isn't it customary to salute a ranking officer when dismissed?" All three of them saluted desultorily and turned away. The guards escorted them to a waiting hovercar.

Chapter Ten

Three days after Cristobal's interview with the three Dhirn shuttle crewmen, Cain and Raith sat cross-legged on the desert floor some thirty kilometers to the north of the cantonment.

Cain studied the method his servant and teacher used to cure the poisonous beetles he called *ikas*. First they were soaked in water and herbs gathered from the flowers of two desert plants and then allowed to dry in the sun in the solution—this took less than an hour. As they waited, Cain squeezed the gummy residue of a puhlcalf leaf on the sunblistered skin of his face and arms. Despite his sun helmet, his lips were cracked and his eyes burned painfully, the flesh around them swollen from the heat, sun and reflection from the desert floor. They had been walking for two days and two nights. They had toured "Darker Heights" and visited various members of Raith's family. When Raith's sister announced the birth of a daughter on the very morning they arrived at her home on the outskirts of the Plaza of Hidesmiths, Cain was invited to join in the baptismlike celebration. He stripped naked, smeared himself with mud from an urn filled with water, sand and the ashes of Raith's ancestors for five generations and he danced and drank blue wine. He danced by himself and with Raith, he even danced with the baby's mother who seemed none the worse for having given birth eight hours earlier.

The next day they visited a Dhirn temple. The room was made of hides, rope, and glass like every other native structure. The dirt floor was intricately patterned with dyes and sand paintings of Dhirn shamans, seers, prophets and various holy men. On a squat stone dais Cain saw a copy of the Book of the Land or Book of the Ground (Raith's loose translation of the title) laid out for inspection. Cain wanted to stay and study the document, but Raith insisted it would mean little to him just now. "First, you must truly meet Darkath, the Mother."

Raith led them north into the barren, low dunes between the spaceport and the great mud seas. Stopping three times a day to recite prayers to Darkath, Raith was astonished at Cain's patience and seeming ability to enter a primary meditative state within a few minutes. He had never heard of a Terran with any interest in such matters let alone an intuitive understanding of the principle. Still, Raith was unsuccessful in conveying the method of meditation that was at the heart of Dhirn spirituality: the dissolving of barriers between the consciousness of the individual and the planet itself.

"We will each eat three of the *ika*," Raith proposed. "This will facilitate travel out of the body. You must, once again, try to envision a cave, a hole in the ground that descends endlessly downward. You will know you are successful when you see the walls of the tunnel or cave become luminous. Then you will begin to see water and . . . creatures, small animals unlike any you have ever seen before. Your success will depend entirely on your desire to accomplish this end. Once in the bosom of Darkath, the rewards are . . . ineffably apparent."

Cain, his vision watering, the pain of his blistered, swollen skin threatening to eclipse every other sensation but his hunger after a three-day fast, nodded. If it had occurred to Cain, he might have thought this venture was foolish: to ingest an unknown drug in the middle of an alien desert with a humanoid, but barely scrutable creature he had known for only a few days—but it did not occur to him. He had set his feet on a path that seemed providential in a way he could not explain, as if he were dancing to a tune he could not quite hear but felt compelled by nonetheless. The words from some ancient scrap of literature sprang to mind though he could not remember exactly where it was from: *Faith in the substance of things hoped for, the evidence of things not seen:* Shakespeare or Saint-Exupery or Silverberg, someone like that, one of the pre-Imperial classicists. He reveled in a sense of unfolding correctness that would be revealed to him a little at a time, like a mountainside announcing itself in the dawn.

When the *ika* were prepared, Raith handed three of them to Cain and kept three for himself. ''The poison is neutralized, changed into a powerful drug now.'' He then began to chant something that Cain could not apprehend and when Raith put the first of the insects into his mouth, Cain followed suit. There was little taste. If anything, just a trace of bittersweetness. The texture was nauseating, however; the crunching sound caused bile to rise in his throat. It was, Cain reminded himself, not the first time he had eaten insects. This was only a small comfort.

When they had each ingested the three beetles they sat in silence, Cain hugging his knees, Raith squatting with his arms slung between his massive thighs. The red sun began its accelerated descent to the horizon. A violet circle in the middle of Delgado's Star resolved itself into the features of Giata. Cain's vision wavered as he attempted to concentrate on the image Raith had suggested.

Instead, colors, lights, sounds, faces and patterns of every description began to parade themselves before Cain's eyelids. Everything but the subterranean imagery he was trying to maintain. He heard a low crooning and could not be sure if it was Raith singing in impossibly high and beautiful tones or if it was some auditory hallucination. It began to seem as if the surface beneath him, the entire desert was singing: the wind and sand playing glissandos of pain and loneliness, loss and longing. Cain was convinced now that he was hearing the voice of Darkath herself as the mood of the music became transcendent, triumphant.

In that moment, for the first time, he felt in his heart that the Dhirn belief in the sentience of their world was based in fact and not superstition. He sensed the awareness of the desert, the planet, the miles of dense rock beneath him, but he could not merge with it. He was one consciousness confronting another, one being recognizing another, but separate and distinct. And he could not seize upon the imagery of a tunnel or cave in which to bridge that gulf. He simply hallucinated wildly, all the while trying to steer his mind back toward that merging point.

Once, he was convinced he had shed his body, but instead of flowing downward to the earth, he soared above it. He became a dragon, an angel, a meteor hurtling in an orbit that gradually decayed, flamed, exploded, and met the desert in a hundred scattered pieces.

When he began to come out of it, he was lying on his back staring at a thousand stars. Giata hung low on the horizon. Raith tugged at his sleeve. "Cain, Cain. We must go! Something has happened."

Cain sat up slowly. His head felt like a centrifuge. "What? What has happened?"

Raith stood and pointed to the northern horizon. Cain could see the sporadic glow of something burning. A tower of smoke was illuminated from below and climbed toward the heavens obliterating stars with a churning oiliness.

"A ship has crashed. Not far from here. We must see what has happened. There may be survivors."

"Of course." Cain followed after Raith who set a grueling pace. As he hurried after him, following the dimming beacon of smoke and fire, the fog in his head began to lift. He tried to remember something very important about his experience eating the *ika*, something he had learned, something true and vital and extraordinary—but it would not return.

It seemed to Cain that they traveled for hours, but he could not be certain. It took all his concentration just to keep moving. The flames on the horizon never seemed to grow any closer, though whether this was because they were gradually becoming extinguished or because they were making less progress than he had supposed, again, was unclear. The *ika* experience had left him both dazed and moved by something he did not understand . . . but then the same could be said about his life in general in the years since Cozuela.

"Wait! Raith!" He could not compete with the alien's advantageously muscled frame in this gravity. His companion seemed to fly over the shallow dunes while Cain stumbled and fought the thin oxygen and dense gravity. His chest was on fire with exertion.

At last they were close enough to breathe the smoke from the conflagration. As they topped the last dune, they could see twisted metal blackened with carbon spread out before them in an area several hundred meters wide. Much of the wreckage still burned with various degrees of heat and in flames of white, red, orange, and blue. Cain and Raith looked at each other, silently acknowledging that what they had discovered was the wreck of a Terran space shuttle. They each wrapped a scarf around their noses and mouth to filter the acrid smoke. Cain gestured that Raith should search to the right for survivors while he circled ahead and to the left.

Skirting a glowing mass of metal he identified as a freight compartment, Cain peered inside but could see nothing. Debris was everywhere and his progress was slowed. He stepped over machinery, computer parts, gnarled landing assemblies, fragments of zero G toilets and countless less identifiable components of the spacecraft. He wandered among the smoldering remains, despairing of the possibility of any survivors when he first smelled and then saw the charred flight suit and skull of the pilot. Only the upper torso and one arm remained intact. The skin around the face—flaking, black, and desiccated—pulled away from the bone to give the corpse the appearance of mindless levity.

As Cain stared, trying to think, brushing away the last tendrils of the drug's hold, he heard Raith's voice call to him in the distance. He moved in the direction of the sound and now saw other mutilated body parts and the crisped rags of utility flight fatigues dispersed among the metallic ruins.

When at last he found Raith, the Dhirn was huddled in shadow, outlined only dimly by Giata's light. Beneath him was a body still strapped to an ejection seat that was more or less intact. The arm strapped to the seat moved and when Cain advanced he could see that it belonged to a Darkhani though he couldn't tell if it was a Khaj or Dhirn: the light was poor and any hair was singed completely.

Raith turned to Cain and said, "He's alive. Barely. His name is Ganar, he is a military administrator of Dhirn personnel at the cantonment. I'm trying to find out what happened, what he was doing on a spaceship. It is beyond credit. He mentioned something about *El Raton,* Cristobal."

Cain moved closer, but the dying administrator was speaking in a Dhirn dialect he could not understand. Raith seemed to be reassuring him of something and the word Darkath was repeated again and again, agitatedly. It would not, Cain knew, be different from a Terran dying in pain in another's arms repeating the word "God."

Raith and Ganar spoke in hushed tones for several minutes. Raith gave him some water from his flask, mixing some powder into it that, in an aside to Cain, he said would ease the transition into death. Ganar was severely burned and he bled profusely from the chest and legs. While they were speaking, an earthquake rocked the landscape. Cain was thrown to the ground and he heard metal against metal as the shuttle's wreckage bounced, shifted, and resettled itself into the desert. When it was over, Raith announced, "He's dead."

"What did he say?"

Raith said nothing for a long time but began to cover

the body with handfuls of sand. At length he stopped, looked at Cain and said, "Help me." Cain did. When the body was completely obscured and the first faint rays of sunlight appeared at the edge of the world, Raith seemed to have arrived at a decision. He recounted what Ganar had told him about the mission, the Andromedans and the Dhirn crew members who had entered into a suicide pact to crash the ship after overcoming the Terran pilot with sleeping herbs. "They did what they had to do, Martin Cain."

Cain said nothing, but followed Raith again back in the direction they had come from.

"You asked me to teach you," Raith reminded him.

"Yes. I did."

"Then learn this. They had no choice. They did what I would have done. They believed themselves to be Christian. They thought they could do it, but they could not. Once beyond the atmosphere of Darkath, they experienced a crisis in their faith. They became empty, their souls had been left behind. Each of them felt this and could not go on. The god of blood did not help them. Darkath beckoned. They went mad up there, Cain. They had to return, but not to the death Cristobal would give them."

It was several moments later before Cain said anything. "I think I understand." After another long silence that stretched through the dawn, Cain asked, "What will you do?"

"Sivran must know." Raith answered simply. "He will know what to do."

"Oh, yes, Sivran." Cain wondered what the diplomatic Dhirn's reaction would be. He sensed it would be the same as Raith's. *They had no choice. They did what I would have done.* Cain could only foresee disaster. He once again noted how much the color of Alaikhaj, Giata, and the sands of Darkath conspired to evoke a world ocean of blood.

After some time he looked up to where the horizon bisected Darkath's moon. In the daylight it looked like a translucent lavender dome. He thought of the Andromedans who had crossed such an immense gulf of space to arrive here. The implications of their presence were myriad: frightening, promising, puzzling and most of all, he understood, threatening to the Terran Empire. He wondered what they could be like, but mostly, as he walked in silence with Raith, he found himself wondering what they believed.

* * *

Jack was determined to show no fear, but he knew that he probably looked like a boy playing at bravery. He was certain that mortal terror was plainly evident on his face. His captors had brought him to a series of canyons and caves that ran through the highest point in the mountain range. He was marched through narrow passageways, tunnels, and vaulted caverns with his hands tied painfully behind his back and to a rope cinched around his neck and waist.

When he was led to a wide rock clearing, a mesa or plateau, he saw hundreds of dragons, thousands of armed Khaj and Dhirn—men, women and children. The children ran up to him first. The little ones with their braided blue-white hair and their long knives danced around him, jeering and shouting something he could not understand. He dodged away from the thrusts of their knives and realized that they were terrified of him as well. He may well have been the first Terran these children had ever seen. The oldest of them, only a few years younger perhaps than Jack himself, leaned his face close to Jack. The boy shouted something in a rising, questioning tone that ended in a shrill keen. It sounded to Jack like, "illiakiji . . . tikyatikya . . . kiiiiiii!"

And then the boy spit into Jack's face. Jack lost all control. Head down, he launched himself at the young Khaj and caught him in the stomach with his head, the boy went down with a whining expulsion of breath and a look of animal terror in his face. Jack then launched a kick at the boy's head and caught him beneath the chin. He raised his foot for another kick and something exploded at the back of his own skull. The next thing he knew he was facedown, sand mixed with blood in his mouth and he was hearing the sound of running water. He looked up and was momentarily blinded by the giant red sun. He saw a female Khaj silhouetted in a crouch over him and felt a stream of warm, gamey urine against his cheek. He rolled away painfully and the sound of laughter deafened him.

He was jerked to his feet by rough hands and pushed forward. Sticks and lances were placed in his path to trip him and he had to take care to keep his feet. He was pelted with stones and blood ran from his scalp into his eyes.

At last he was taken down damp stairs carved into rock into an enclosure that sent his footsteps and the whispering of phrases he understood to be Terran, echoing around him. Phosphor torches glowed dully against one wall and after several moments Jack could make out the slumped figures of three Terrans, one, he saw immediately was a nun and another a soldier. The third man was a formless shadow seemingly folded into itself.

The Khaj guard behind Jack sent him sprawling face first onto the stone floor. The Terran soldier helped him into a sitting position and whispered, "I'm Lieutenant Chun. Imperial Infantry 303rd Battalion. What's your name, boy?"

Jack told him.

"I know another Avery. A sergeant."

"Yes. He's my father."

"Oh," the lieutenant said. "I see."

Jack waited for something more, but there was nothing else. At length, as he tried in vain to find a position of relative comfort, he mumbled, "I don't."

The officer seemed to drag his voice up from somewhere deep inside him. In tones laden with fatigue he said, "How did you get here?"

Jack told him about stowing away, the incident at the spaceport, his meeting with his father and his subsequent flight and capture. He kept his voice level. He was dazed by events and this produced a kind of numbness that passed for calm. When he finished and the lieutenant said nothing, Jack asked, "What will they do with us?"

"They want to exchange us for their spies. Jimenez won't treat with them if he's smart, so they'll kill us unless we can escape."

It suddenly dawned on Jack who he was talking to. "You're the lieutenant from the cartographic party, the one that man Wilson was talking about."

"Yes. I was leading the mapping party north to the mud seas and the mountains east of them. These two," he indicated the nun and the sleeping man, "were along to make converts of the nomads out there. I had a corporal, man named Sanchez, under me and two loyal Darkers—one a Dhirn surveyor, the other a Khaj guide who knew the mountains. We were caught in the mud by a dragon party and brought here. A while ago they came for the corporal and the Darkers. I don't know what happened to them."

When the officer paused, Jack told him, "Wilson said they were found outside of the cantonment walls without their heads. He said . . . the dragons . . ."

"Yes, they fed their heads to the dragons then." The lieutenant said softly, "It's their way." Jack noticed for the first time the details of the soldier's face. His left eye gleamed faintly from the light of the phosphor torches, but where his right eye should have been there were blood-caked, sunken eyelids. His right cheek was a scabrous blotch of dried gore. Lieutenant Chun continued. "They bury the victim to the neck, then cut the scalp. They leave them there until the blood dries and draws insects. Then they bring the dragons. The dragons will only eat carrion, you see. When the head is swarming with flies and they smell the old blood, they think . . .'' Chun broke off when he heard Jack's retching sounds in the darkness. ''Are you all right?''

''Yes. I'm fine.'' Jack forced himself to breathe normally, grateful for the dark to hide his shame. ''Your face is bloody. Have they tortured you?''

Chun told him what happened in the courtyard. Jack looked over at the nun who stared sightlessly ahead into the blackness and worked her lips silently. He looked for the missing finger, but her hands were hidden in her sleeves. ''The priest is sleeping,'' Chun explained. ''He has lost a lot of blood. A brave man, but he won't make it far.''

''You have a plan to escape?''

Before Lieutenant Chun could answer, footsteps and new torchlight drew their attention to the cave entrance. Three Darkhani appeared. Two of them held lights and the third, Jack could see presently, was a female Khaj.

She approached alone, taking one of the torches, and stood before the prisoners. She was a striking figure with her braided hair secured in a loop at her waist, and then slung again over her right shoulder where it was held in place by a pin fashioned with the vertebra bone of a dragon. She bore a corona tattoo of startling primary colors across her forehead and cheeks. The muscles of her calves seemed to strain at the sandal thongs that bound them and her thighs gleamed black and smooth over knotted cables of sinew as stout as a man's arm. Her torso was encased in sleeveless, form-fitting chain mail of shifting metallic-rainbow colors. Hanging from a belt around her waistcloth was a jeweled dagger, a pouch made of hide, and a Terran machine pistol. Around her shoulders was a cloak of plain, rough cloth, fixed at the throat with a chain and ornate clasp into which was set a large amber jewel. The hand that held the torch was wide and strong with thick, short fingers that bore three rings mounted with blue, red, and yellow gems. Her jaw was wide and

strong, her lips thick, the color of dark plums beneath
nostrils flared like gun barrels. Her eyes were impassive slits of blackness surrounded by the swollen white,
masklike membrane. When she spoke, her voice was
husky and inflectionless though not cruel, as if, once
hard and edged, it had been worn away, eroded by
years of dry heat and sandy winds.

"Who are you?" she asked.

"My name is Jack Avery."

"What were you doing in an *iravka* parlor, boy?"

Lieutenant Chun spoke. "Say nothing to her. She
is the enemy."

"Silence or I'll have your tongue as well."

When Jack said nothing more, she asked him again.
Still he was silent. Hara lowered herself on her
haunches and took his face in her left hand. It bore no
rings, but Jack saw a thick bracelet of worked, gray-blue metal. Her touch was soft. "Are you injured?"
After looking to Chun who nodded almost imperceptibly, he shook his head from side to side. "Good."
Hara stood and said something in Darkhani to the
guards. The one on the left came forward and cut
Jack's bonds with his short sword. As the blood rushed
back into his hands, he stifled a cry of pain.

"Come with me," Hara said. "You are a brave Terran pup and that's good. You have nothing to fear from
me, however. If I need more blood on my hands,"
she looked down at Chun, ". . . I'll take his."

Jack was taken out the way he had come. Everyone
they passed acknowledged the woman's presence with
splayed fingers over the eyes or palms arcing across
breasts. Children ran to her and tugged at her waist-cloth chanting *Haraharahara*. She laughed and tousled their hair, speaking to them in Darkhani. They
ascended endless stone stairways that coiled upward
into the rock and at last they came to a high, airy
cavern that looked out onto thousands of meters of
desert through a series of wide archways. The walls
were hung with embroidered cloth and ropework set

with colored stones, glass, crystal and gems. She guided him to a low table set with bowls of berries, nuts, vegetables, and cold meats he did not recognize. "Eat," she said. "Jafar Chun is right, I am the enemy, but I am not your enemy."

Jack was starving. The aroma of food, even alien food, was overpowering. He hesitated for a moment and then ate, slowly at first and then with more urgency. It was delicious. Suddenly, he stopped and spat out what he had in his mouth. Hara laughed and took a sample of food from each bowl. She put it in her mouth and chewed, swallowed. "No," she said, "it's not poison and it's not drugged." He watched her for a moment longer and then fell to his first meal in days with abandon.

After he had taken the edge from his hunger, he remembered something he should have told Chun about: the miragelike caravan of Terran troops and vehicles he had seen on the desert horizon to the north. He was certain it was no mirage, but as to what it meant or whether it could spell help for himself and the other hostages, he had no idea. One thing was clear, however; he must keep it from the woman Khaj they called Hara and every other Darkhani in the renegade camp. The convoy had been moving in this general direction and if enemy scouts had not yet seen it, Jack was determined not to call their attention to it.

If he had thought about it, he would have realized that very little moves in the desert without either the Khaj or Dhirn knowing about it—whether or not they discuss it with each other would be another matter—that the space each of them inhabited was defined by horizons, heaven, and the depths of the world itself and not just flesh. And if Jack had any idea where he was and what it meant he would have known that nothing is hidden from The Eye of God.

* * *

Cain could not go on. By midday he was thoroughly dehydrated and found himself swaying with each step. He had finished the water in his bag hours earlier and could not bring himself to ask Raith for any of his. To lose face with the Dhirn now, in light of their discovery last night, could cost him his life as surely as the desert and his thirst.

"It is the *ika*," Raith, several yards ahead of him, said over his shoulder. "The poison robs the body of water. Here." He removed his own water bag and tossed it through the air at Cain. Cain staggered toward it and lifted it, hesitated while the Dhirn looked on. "Go on. Drink it or you will be dead before my evening prayer."

"What will you drink, then?" His voice sounded like the crackling of old leather.

Raith gestured everywhere around him. "There is watersign here." Cain saw nothing except sand dunes and tiny, desiccated looking, thorned weeds that bound them together. Occasionally a small flower blossomed in white. "And by dusk we will reach more."

Cain knew that it was commonly thought the Darkhani could go for much longer than Terrans without drinking and that it was rumored they could extract water from the sand itself. He doubted this, suspecting it was an exaggeration of necessary adaptations they had made to their environment—until now. He grinned up at Raith. It hurt his lips to do it and he felt blood run down his chin. "Teach me," he said.

Raith hesitated and then nodded abruptly. He retraced his steps back to Cain and then squatted. He placed his hand between two of the rugged little weeds and then burrowed with his fingers beneath the sand. Cain realized as he sat, that the temperature was perhaps thirty degrees hotter near the ground, that if he remained there he would pass out. He tried to stand, but couldn't. He had to trust Raith. He drank from his companion's water bag, trying not to drink all of its contents. He managed to leave a few centimeters at the bottom. Meanwhile Raith, his blue-black hand buried just past the wrist, pulled at something less than half a meter down. He tugged gently so as not to snap the root and it came away without difficulty. It was a fibrous network of thin, but flexible vegetation. Taking a length in both hands he offered one end to Cain.

"Here," he said. "Take this and tug firmly but gently. Follow it until the root becomes stout and will no longer come away easily. Then we will see where the khat drinks."

Cain nodded and took the ropy weed. He crawled on hands and knees exposing the root of the khat plant until he had a trail behind him that extended for nearly half a kilometer up the slope of a dune. At length, Raith's voice could be heard behind the next dune. "Over here, Cain!"

Cain scrabbled back down the shifting hill and up the next one. Once over the crest he saw Raith poised over a cleared hole with two fistfuls of fat, liver-colored tubers extending straight down. Raith turned and signaled for Cain to approach. "Here, you see?" The Dhirn took his knife and sawed away at the fattest of the root trunks. He then placed his mouth over it and began to suck. He paused and looked at Cain. "Well, what are you waiting for? Do as I do."

Cain took the knife from his belt and hacked messily at one of the tubers. When he had severed it, he placed his mouth on it in imitation of Raith and sucked, pausing now and then to spit dry, bitter splinters of the khat that he had loosened with his blade. Nothing. The exertion of trying to draw water from an obviously dried root made Cain angry and light-headed. He threw it down in disgust, squinting up at Raith who sat placidly sucking away with his cheeks collapsed.

"Raith. Are you . . . drinking?" He ran his tongue over his lips but he may as well have rubbed them with a stone.

"Not yet." Raith looked at him in mild disgust. "This is not a Terran tap." As an afterthought he added, "It helps if you pray." And then, in deference to Cain's paganism, "To Darkath, of course."

Cain summoned the strength to keep drawing on the plant, but could find no prayers within himself. He imagined a huge subterranean lake with crystalline icy water racing up the root into his throat. As he was passing out, he thought he sensed moisture forming at his lips. His head throbbed, but he renewed his efforts.

It was warm and bled into his mouth with maddening slowness, but it was water. After several minutes it came in a full trickle and Cain nearly lost a mouthful as he laughed.

Later that day as they walked, Cain restored enough to believe he would live after all, Raith asked him, "Did you pray?"

"You mean back there when you were doing your midday prayers?"

"No, no. When you were drawing water from the khat."

"Well, I tried to pray. . . ."

"A man dying of thirst with a straw in his mouth and a well at the other end, with little strength . . . How can he not pray?"

"Well, I did concentrate very hard."

"Ah! That is prayer. Bring your mind to one point and you will know God!" Cain looked at his companion for a long moment, turning the words over in his mind. After a moment of this, Raith shrugged. "You asked me to teach." And then he turned away, his eyes fixed on the horizon.

It was just past dark. They were still two days' walk from the northern Terran watchposts beyond the edge of the spaceport when a dozen mounted Grea' ka swooped from the darkness and surrounded them. As if on cue, twenty armed Dhirn showed themselves from behind a dune before them. They fanned out around Raith and Cain, leveling rifles and short swords.

"Say nothing," Raith instructed Cain.

One rider dismounted from his dragon and stepped forward. He looked Cain up and down first and then Raith. It was too dark for Cain to make out his features, but his tattooed face flowed wanly in the moonlight. He spoke to Raith in dialect and Raith answered him. Cain heard both their names. The Khaj spoke again and when Raith answered, drew a springlance from its place across his back. He leveled it at both of them and signaled for them to prostrate themselves on the ground.

"What's happening?" Cain asked.

"Quiet," Raith whispered. "His name is Karsha, a general of the Khaj leader Hara. They saw the spaceship crash and believe we were in it. They want to know what our mission was. I told them we were not on the ship, but that we have information I will deliver only to Sivran of the Dhirn. They are taking us prisoner."

"Almighty's blood! I've got to get back."

"Quiet." As if to underscore his point, the one called Karsha crossed the distance to Cain and kicked him in the side. The air went from Cain's lungs and sand filled his nostrils. The next kick was placed to his head and the desert night exploded into a painful blur of colors before subsiding into total blackness.

Chapter Eleven

Sergeant John "Ironblood" Avery arrived back at the Aztec at sunset as planned. Three of his lancers were already there, the other three were still combing the rocky hills above the cantonment for his son, but would be at the rendezvous point at any time now. He turned to Lance Corporal Virik, his Khaj platoon leader who was the best soldier on the planet, Avery reckoned—with the exception, naturally, of himself. Virik had volunteered himself and the five others to aid the sergeant in his search for Jack. Jack Senior had kept to Darker Heights with two Khaj whose names he couldn't keep straight. He called them both simply "soldier." While he knew every "man" in his five platoons well enough, these two were brothers and had names that sounded like gargled glass in a Terran throat. To mispronounce them would be an unaffordable weakness so they became "soldier" or "you" or "private," both of them.

"It's been fifty-six hours, Virik." He downed his own glass of wine and presented Virik and the two soldiers with glasses of wine as well as water: an extravagant demonstration of gratitude for their help. They understood this to be an effusive thanks from their officer, the only one forthcoming. "The boy is dead or a prisoner . . . up there." He gestured with his glass to the northeast where the rebels had their stronghold. "Unless your boys found him in the passes somewhere, then they've got a hold of him somehow. I know it."

"A father knows these things," Virik said in halting Spanish.

"A soldier knows these things," Avery corrected him. And then, more to himself than his companions, "Dead. Or a prisoner."

"Maybe he went back to the starship." One of the soldiers, whose name was Riliaviriakikia, said.

"No." Avery shook his head. "He wouldn't." He looked at his three companions who blinked back impassively at him and he knew the unspoken question: *How do you know?* "He wouldn't because he's his mother's son. He didn't travel across half the galaxy to slink back like a cowed dog. He's his mother's son. More importantly . . . he's *my* son. I saw it in him. Like looking in one of your damned twisted Khaj mirrors where the true reflection is behind the distorted one." He allowed a crooked grin to rearrange the lines and scars of his face into a mask of gnarled satisfaction. "He wouldn't go back to the *Pandora*. A father knows these things." He drank and his men joined him.

Behind them, the other three Khaj lancers lifted the dusty tarpaulin that served as door to the Aztec and entered. Every head in the room turned at the sight of the huge, heavily armed soldiers bearing the insignia of the elite Imperial Native Tactical Combat Force: a sun shot through with lightning superimposed on a death's head. Avery took pleasure in the effect their entrance made on the patrons of the Aztec. He had created the insignia himself and it had become a symbol of fear and respect among Terrans and Darkers alike. Only on Darkath could he, a sergeant, have wielded such a command.

The tallest of them (still a good head shorter than Avery) saluted and announced, "Corporal Jaralaj reporting, sir."

"Right. Anything, Jara?"

"Maybe, sir." He stood, seemingly ill at ease in the unaccustomed atmosphere of the Aztec. Jaralaj would be aware of the place's reputation for Darkhani who were more Terran than Khaj or Dhirn and he was not among them. He was a good warrior, in the service of the Terrans, but a Khaj warrior first and foremost. Avery wondered more about such conflicts of loyalties with every passing day.

"Have a bloody drink." Avery ordered water for three more men. (Alone, those would cost him half a week's pay.) He also ordered another bottle of the Dhirn flower wine he was partial to. "Well?"

"We did not find him, Sergeant. We did hear, however, of a pale boy from the starship captured in an *iravka* parlor near the Plaza of Those Who Lend Money. He was taken by some Khaj in old uniforms."

"Renegades."

"It may be." The corporal drank his water slowly, savoring it. He tried the Dhirn wine and set it down. He never picked it up again.

"Well, what the hell do *you* think?" Avery fixed him with a frightening, one-eyed stare.

Jaralaj blinked twice and began to take a step back, caught himself, and did not. "Rrrr . . . ahh . . . nagedes." Stumbling over the Terran word, he repeated, "Renegades. Yes. Those who follow the woman Khaj who leads Dhirn, too."

"The daughter of the seer," Avery pressed. "The one up at The Eye of God. Whatsername? Harry or Harriette?" He laughed heartily to mask his fear for his son. Virik and his two companions mimicked the Terran sound to appease him.

"Hara is her name, sir." Virik's smile faded and he drank the last of his water, turning his attention to the wine.

Jaralaj nodded, "Hara. Yes. It is possible he was taken there."

"Well, damn my eyes!" Avery studied the dregs of the bottle. "How do we visit *Doña* Hara without mussing her feathers?"

There was silence for a long time. The temperature

unit behind the bar had ceased to work. With an air and sand gun, the Dhirn bartender washed glasses that were already clean. Avery realized their conversation was being listened to by everyone in the place. "God's blood! I guess there's nothing we can do, lads. Let's get some sleep."

He paid his bill and "Old Ironblood" with six of his lancers went out into the night's heat that lay like a blanket over the street.

At the staff car, Avery paused, lit a cheroot. He looked at Virik, to Jara, and at the stars. "How would you men like to go renegade and take the old man prisoner?"

Virik produced one of his own Terran cheroots and smiled. "It would be gratifying to give you orders for a change."

Avery looked up at him in mild surprise.

"It would be gratifying to give you orders for a change . . . sir!" Virik spoke around a mouthful of smoke, starlight glinting on his teeth.

He laughed and climbed into the aircar. Before ordering the car to proceed, Avery looked at the purple mottled moon on the horizon. Rumors had been spreading since the arrival of the starship that something had been seen up there on Giata, some kind of alien fleet from God knew where. The Khaj said angels were mustering celestial armies to overthrow the Terrans, the Dhirn maintained that they were demons from the heart of Giata come for much the same reason. Either way, it laid another layer of tension over the world he lived in and every bone in his body cried out to act. His son's sudden arrival and just as sudden disappearance provided a reason to do *something*. *Anything*. An unfamiliar, but not unpleasant sensation moved through him. He did not know what to call it, it was a mixture of exhilaration and frustration. And if he only knew the words to evoke, he might have admitted that the feeling contained elements of gratitude to his son for this catalyst, gratitude and perhaps something else, something like love . . . or close enough.

"I bet it would, you bloody ape," he said and ordered the driver on.

* * *

Padre Gillermo sat in his quarters next door to those of Martin Cain whom he hadn't seen in several days, and those of the woman he had come to think of as the human gadfly, the dramatist Amalia Dubois. He should never have told her that he would take her on the dig. He was counting on Jimenez or Cristobal to quash any notion and save him the embarrassment, but neither of them seemed anxious for her company either. That morning he had spoken to Jimenez after church, asking when it would be possible to set out on the expedition and the commandant had told him he could not foresee any authorization in the near future, the situation was too dangerous beyond the small Terran island. Well, Gillermo had more than a little influence on Vatican IV and, by extension, with Planetary Affairs, Quadrant Headquarters and even Cardinal Cota, spiritual advisor to the Empress herself, long may she live. As he packed his things, stepping over the rubble of dislodged window sashes, overturned chairs and cabinets all covered with foamcrete silt— the wreckage of last night's quake—Gillermo satisfied himself that he could justify taking the responsibility for the expedition in spite of the situation. The church had gone to enormous expense to send him halfway across the galaxy and investigate this matter and he would not disappoint them because of the timidity of the local military leaders. Besides, martyrdom on the sands of this world was not something he feared . . . in fact . . . but no, that was pride pure and simple. He doubted he was worthy of such an honor. He finished securing his equipment into four neat bundles of durable Altairan flexfabric and waited. All that re-

mained was for Cheverny, his acolyte, to return with
the hired guides and to slip away without undue notice. Especially from the woman Dubois.

As he sat, he looked out the window at the gathering
cumulus clouds on the horizon to the west. He stared
at them in fascination for several minutes before he
realized that they were the first clouds he had seen in
the skies of Darkath since his arrival.

A knock at the door roused him and he sprang up
from his dusty bed to greet Cheverny. He swung the
door open and was met with the smiling, sunburned
and cherubic countenance of Amalia Dubois. She was
dressed ludicrously in colorful, flowing Dhirn robes
of the type worn during ritual celebrations: weddings,
funerals, pagan earth worshiping feasts. On her head
was an Imperial issue sun helmet with visor, gaily tied
off with a Khaj war scarf. Her face was smeared with
white Zirian oxide ointment to protect her skin, he
supposed, from further damage from the fierce ultraviolet of Delgado's Star though the stuff was more
suited to a day at the beach on a temperate, resort
planet. She looked, Gillermo thought, like a player in
one of the gaudy dramas she perpetrated so profitably
on the Terran viewers. "Ah, Doña Dubois. So good
to see you this morning." His smile felt leaden in the
gravity he was suddenly aware of.

"Good morning, Padre Gillermo! I've been to the
shops. You like it?" She spun, modeling her outfit.

"Very colorful."

"Oh, and practical." Not waiting for an invitation,
she brushed past him in the doorway. "Gillermo, that
means William in old English. My late husband's name
was William. I see you're packed." She spun and faced
him again. "Does that mean we're leaving? For the
dig?"

"Well, I . . ."

At that moment Cheverny arrived accompanied by
two Dhirn dressed in dusty, frayed, civilian Terran
clothing. One of them wore a crumpled, three cor-

nered sombrero with the faded colors of a monsigneur's office. Gillermo smiled at him, but the Dhirn remained impassive.

Cheverny introduced them as Ty and Rik. Gillermo greeted them in formal Dhirn dialect and Rik, in the monsigneur's hat, answered in pidgin, "We'll take you to Nijwhol, okay, but it will cost you two million croozies. You want Darkers to dig, okay. Another million croozies. Ten Darkers."

Gillermo was about to agree when Dubois exclaimed, "That's robbery! The padre will not stand for such insolence! Two million cruzeiros for the lot of you and that's that."

"Who is she?" Rik peered up and blinked slowly at the bizarrely dressed woman.

Gillermo, as graciously as he could, introduced Doña Dubois.

"Two million five." Ty conceded.

Amalia remained firm "No," she said. "Two million is what you will be paid. Take it or leave it."

The Dhirn consulted with each other in rapid dialect, the drift of which, Gillermo caught to be "Where else would we get two million cruzeiros?"

"Okay," Rik said, "but only five Darkers to dig."

"Eight." Amalia folded her arms over her ample breasts and punctuated her resolution with an abrupt nod which caused the sun visor of her helmet to fall. She looked comical, but steadfast.

When they both looked at each other and then back toward Amalia and nodded agreement, she turned to Gillermo and said under her breath, "You see? Perhaps I can be of help after all. I just saved you a million cruzeiros."

"Yes." the padre said, adding to himself, *and lost me two men to dig.* When Ty, Cheverny, and Rik began to carry the bundles from Gillermo's quarters and throw them onto a carrier rack behind the sithe they had arrived in, Gillermo turned to Amalia and tried to explain. "Doña Dubois, I am embarking on the expedition without the permission of the military governor. I am willing to take the risks and responsibility for such defiance, myself. Unfortunately it would be impossible for you to accompany me under such circumstances. You understand, I'm certain.''

''If you're not afraid of some backwater tinhorn commandant, then neither am I.''

''It is not simply a matter of the commandant, it is a matter of your safety.''

''I can take care of myself, Padre. I have traveled to a half dozen worlds, slogged through mud and slime, grown moss and funguses there aren't names for, lived in an environment suit for two weeks orbiting Niflheim, and dealt with creatures that would just as soon cut your throat as smell you!'' She delivered this speech with flamboyant gestures that sent her robes swaying wildly around her in different directions. Gillermo was certain it was a speech she had written for one of her dramas. ''Do I look like a faint-hearted female to you, Padre Gillermo?'' She drew her considerable bulk upward: shoulders back, chin out.

''No.'' He wasn't sure *what* she looked like. ''That isn't it at all. I cannot, in good conscience, allow you to accompany me. Please accept my regrets.''

''Very well, Padre. If that's the way you want it. Good luck to you.'' With that she stormed past him indignantly in a multicolored flurry of cloth smelling of Zirian oxide and sweat.

Well, he thought, that wasn't so difficult after all.

He joined Cheverny, Ty and Rik as they pedaled the sithe around to the rear of his quarters. There he had stockpiled supplies: tools, cameras, concentrated foods, tents, clothing, a few books and 200 liters of water. There was also a pistol that fired flares, pellet shot, and smoke cylinders. He wasn't sure how to use it, but it didn't look difficult. While Ty and Cheverny loaded more of the supplies and made their way separately to the main gate of the cantonment, he waited for Cheverny to bring another sithe for the rest of the equipment.

He sat and studied the clouds again and read from his breviary. Every time he looked up, there seemed to be more clouds.

Cheverny arrived within the hour and they were loaded, slowly making their way through the streets of the cantonment. At the gate, he told the guards he was bringing religious articles to distribute among the natives. He lifted a flap of the tarpaulin and exposed a box of crucifixes and religious tracts written in pidgin. The guard waved them through.

With Delgado's Star at its zenith in the sky, they reached the rendezvous point at a well in the center of a plaza known as the District of the Musicians. There they were met by three Khaj with tethered dragons that trailed sleds made from a siliconelike glass. They loaded the equipment onto the sleds and made themselves comfortable in the shade of a kiosk that sold khatberry juice. There they waited for the other five men Rik was to round up and for the onset of darkness. Gillermo listened to the cacophonous droning of Dhirn musicians playing incomprehensible melodies and watched the clouds on the horizon extinguish the ruddy glare of the sun. There was a momentary hush in the plaza when this happened. After several minutes, the musicians resumed their playing and activity on the streets returned to its chaotic pace, though it seemed to Gillermo there was an added element of urgency to things. Perhaps it was his imagination.

Before long it was fully dark. Gillermo had his eight men, two guides, one acolyte, and three dragons. They began their trek north to the desert beneath the gathering clouds.

* * *

Jack sat across from Hara on a low pillow and eyed the ancient, jeweled springlance that hung on the rock wall over the firepit. They had been discussing Jack's story of stowing away aboard the *Pandora,* crossing thousands of parsecs of space to see his father. Hara praised his audacity and acknowledged that many would give all they had for a demonstration of such filial love. "Not him" and "Anyway, I don't love him," Jack had said. To which Hara said nothing. Jack had told her about his childhood on Cygnus and as the daylight began to transmute itself into shades of mauve on the sands beyond the archways, he found himself speaking to her with a gradually increasing ease.

The notion that this woman was his father's enemy, the enemy of the Empire, began to lose its hold on him the longer he was in her company. In a sense, he began to feel that even if it were true, and it was—it made no difference. The Empire found enemies everywhere. If they could not find them, they created them. It was almost as if Hara had reluctantly accepted the job, simply because it was open; waiting for the day when she could do the work of her choice. The fact that she was indeed a warrior and a leader of a warlike race seemed somehow incidental. After all, her weapons were toys compared to what the Terrans could bring to bear.

No, Jack saw her in a different role, but one he could not put a name to. He only knew it had nothing to do with killing. As she said, she was not *his* enemy and he sensed the truth in that through a window of perception that often closes as a boy passes into manhood. Her presence in the dungeon when he had first seen her was terrifying, fierce, alien, a vision of barbaric violence, but in the high room with just the two of them she seemed to shed that persona like some oppressive burden. The ugliness he initially saw in her features, skin, and form, he now saw as a kind of economy of musculature, bearing, and strength; her clothing and body decoration he examined with a dawning appreciation of its artistry. As he spoke to her of the loneliness of his boyhood—a half Terran, half Cygni child who looked predominantly Terran in a world where Terrans were tolerated as conquerors, but thought of as dull-witted, violent animals—he sensed a kind of empathy. Certainly it was neither pity nor sympathy, but a tacit recognition was there in her flashing black eyes when the white membranes parted in interest at something he said.

"Go ahead and touch it," Hara said, gesturing at the mounted weapon. "It is a springlance."

"Yes, I know." Jack ran his hand over the shaft that was as thick as his calf. The inlaid filigree work was black with carbon and age.

"That one is older than any on Darkath. It has been hanging there since before the arrival of your first starships. Made by the finest Dhirn weaponsmith that ever lived, Puradan. His name means 'bowels' in Terran. It is a high concept in Dhirni. It relates to Darkath itself rather than human bowels, but it is always a good joke among the Khaj. They are a strange race."

"Which? The Khaj or the Dhirn?"

"A good question. Both undoubtedly."

Jack turned his attention from the weapon he could not lift from the wall and faced Hara. "Aren't you really the same race?"

Hara smiled at him without malice. "There are many among both Khaj and Dhirn who would kill you for uttering such a thing. Don't worry, I'm not among them." Hara stood and walked to an archway. She looked out at the crepuscular landscape below, moving with a fluidity no Terran could manage in this gravity. Jack tensed as he watched her. It occurred to him that she had spent hours talking to him, a Terran boy of no consequence when undoubtedly she had more pressing matters to attend to, a nation to prepare for war. Why was she wasting her time? Or was she? What did she want from him? She continued. "The answer is, I don't know. Your Terran priests say that we are and that is a heresy to both Khaj and Dhirn."

"Some also say that you are the same race as we are, human. Bipedal life-forms with humanoid symmetry have developed independently on many worlds. Also there are those they've found who've descended from the Africans. They were a starfaring Terran race that established an empire thousands of . . ."

Hara held up her hand. "I know all about it."

"Well, it's just another possibility in favor of what the priests say, that the Darkhani are members of the Universal Blood."

Hara sounded tired and a little arch. "That is another idea that pleases no one greatly. Including myself."

Jack had been trying again to lift the springlance from the wall. Hara crossed the room and with one hand, easily hefted the weapon. She laid it in both of Jack's outstretched hands. He was able to hold it out for a few seconds before his arms began to tremble. She took it from him and grabbed the collar ring, pulling down and driving the angled tines flat against themselves and the length of the shaft. It was now cocked. Thrown with the kind of force Hara was surely capable of, those tines would spring open on impact and tear a man to pieces at thirty meters, pry the armor plating off a section of hovercraft at twenty, and at ten, rend a native dragon limb from limb.

"Is it true," he asked, "that no Terran has the strength to even cock a springlance?"

"I have never seen a Terran cock a native-made springlance and I know of no one who has." Hara replaced the lance in its resting place. "It is a matter of musculature and gravity. Perhaps one of your soldiers with cybernetic limbs could do it, I don't know."

Jack helped himself to more sweets that lay on the table circling the firepit. The room was darkening rapidly. Neither of them spoke. He wondered when she would light a torch or whatever it was she used to see at night. From the shadows, only her hair and optic membranes dimly visible, she spoke. "What is so important to Terrans about their blood?"

Taken by surprise, at first, he didn't know what she meant. Then, "Oh, you mean religion? The Church?"

"Yes. I was raised here at The Eye of God and never attended one of your priests' schools, but I have read many cubes, had long hours of conversation with the monsigneur who died during the last rains. I have even spoken with Khaj who have become believers in your church. No one has ever explained to me so that I may understand: what is so important about this universal blood? Perhaps an honest child can tell me."

Jack didn't know what to say. This was a matter for scholars, theologians, at the very least a diplomat with linguistic skills who had days or weeks or years to explain the complexities of dogma and ritual, tradition and faith and DNA and all that stuff.

"Well," he began, "it has to do with, like, if you've got the right blood then you're saved from hell because Jesus got killed a long time ago and I guess he had this certain kind of blood, God's blood. I guess all Terrans do, I think. Anyway aliens who have the same kind of blood or have enough humanoid characteristics . . ." He trailed off, at a loss. He was a good student at most subjects, but religion just went right by him. He knew it was an exact science and everything, based on thousands of years of study, but he was damned if he could ever get it straight. He continued, in a voice of renewed confidence and patience, to try. "You see there are very exact biological and spiritual criteria for candidacy in The Brotherhood of Universal Blood. I don't know them all. Many scholars have debated about it for so long and I can't begin to speak for them. The thing is, in the early days of the Empire, when the missionaries found so many sentient life forms, they thought, I guess, that Jesus might have died for them, too, or some of them, see . . . depending. The priests thought that a lot of them should be able to go to heaven, too, if they, uh . . . studied the faith and believed. . . .'' He was making a mess of it, he knew. Here he was in a position, possibly, to convert the most hostile alien on the planet and he didn't know what he was talking about. He wished he had studied harder.

''Do *you* believe?'' Her voice from the darkness was soft.

''Sure. I guess so.''

''Tell me how this Jesus dying makes it possible for men and others to go to this heaven?''

Jack fidgeted in the darkness, hoping she couldn't see him. ''That part I'm not too sure of. I mean exactly how it works. I think you'd have to ask a priest.''

''I have.'' Silence.

''Well it might sound strange, I admit. But it's no stranger than worshiping a sun, which is just a star. Stars aren't God.''

''How do you know?''

''Stars just . . . *are*. Gases and matter. They just burn. They don't *do* anything.'' Jack was beginning to get nervous. How did he get himself involved in this insane, dangerous conversation? He wanted to change the subject back to the springlance.

''What is God supposed to *do?*''

After a long silence, in absolute darkness except for the winking of stars beyond the archways, the dim patches of white that were Hara's teeth, hair, and membrane mask, Jack said, ''I don't know.''

''Do you think you'd know a God if you saw one?''

''I . . . don't know. Maybe.''

Hara stood; he sensed her movements in the dark and he took a few steps backward, afraid that she was about to do something frightening, violent, or even supernatural. All she did was to ignite a lamp with a hand filament. She moved around the room doing the same to other lamps set into the rock walls. Shadows rearranged themselves wildly. Her jewelry seemed to dance on her fingers and at her throat. She lit the kindling in the firepit and in a moment the puhlcalf stalks caught and blazed, giving off a pungent sweet scent and causing his eyes to tear. Gems set into the rope-work around the archways stuttered colorfully with reflected light. When she closed the thick, blown glass of variegated hues around the wall lamps, the room seemed to be bathed in a single color he had no word for. The walls and arches seemed to have receded and he felt as if he were suspended in a womb of luminescent mystery.

In a moment his eyes adjusted and the dimensions of the room were restored. The predominant color he could not describe lingered. "It's a trick," he said. "Some kind of trick of the light."

"Yes," Hara said. "A trick of the light."

"That wasn't God." He looked defiant, but unsure. Maybe he was supposed to say that it was.

"No," Hara said and seated herself once again. "Just some of his . . . blood." Her smile exposed all of her teeth. Jack smiled back at her, feeling suddenly off balance. "Tomorrow I will show you the rest of him if you like."

Before Jack could respond to that extraordinary remark, a dim figure appeared in the archway leading to the stairway they had climbed earlier.

"Hia Hara," the shadow said in a low, guttural voice.

"Yes, Karsha. What is it?" Hara stood and the one called Karsha entered bowing. He stood and quickly performed the Khaj greeting as if dashing invisible water onto his face. He was the same height as Hara, but his hair was unbound and filthy. His chest was naked, but streaked with crude paints to offset long, curving scars from his shoulders to his stomach. Around his waist was wrapped the faded, shredded remnant of a blue and gold Imperial tunic. His boots were the scuffed Phylaxian leather of the Imperial native infantry and, judging by his protruding toes, appeared too small for his feet. He cast a harsh look at Jack which set his scarred and tattooed features into stark relief in the firelight. Dismissing him, he turned again to Hara.

"Hia Hara, a Terran spaceship, one of their shuttles, has crashed north and east of here. Among the crew were three Dhirn and a Terran. All of them dead. At the site we captured another Terran, a civilian named Cain and with him, a Dhirn who calls himself Raith. At first we thought they were among the crew, but the Terran looks as if Alaikhaj had been roasting him out there for days." He grinned a little and jerked his head at the archway and desert beyond. "This Raith says he spoke to one of the Dhirn crew members before he died. He will only relate what was said to Sivran." He paused, waiting for Hara to digest this.

Jack stood, unable to understand the rapid Darkhani except for the word Cain. That was the man who had rescued him at the spaceport.

Hara made some exclamation in idiomatic dialect and then said, "What would Dhirni be doing in a Terran ship? Even the most cynical of them . . ." She searched the corners of the room for the answer.

"I can make the Dhirn tell us here. It would take days to arrange a meeting with Sivran," Karsha said.

"No, if he is tortured, we could lose all of our Dhirn." She paced, thinking.

"There is more, Hia Hara."

"Go on then."

"A large Terran convoy has been spotted through The Eye of God. They are headed toward Nijwhol. *Around* the mountains, two hundred kilometers to the north. They did not wish to be detected." Karsha smirked contempt at this folly. "They have ten hovercraft, gravity sleds, and they travel with a full company of infantry and a squad of outriders on Grea' ka. They are carrying so much heavy equipment that it could only have come from the starship. Whatever it is we have feared, it is moving across the desert tonight. By godrise they will be in Nijwhol."

Jack felt suddenly in danger though he did not know

why. Hara rounded on him. In Terran she spoke, her voice no longer soft, but edged with threat. "What was aboard that starship? Tell me. You were in the cargo hold. What did you see? What is the Terran convoy carrying to Nijwhol?"

Jack stepped backward two paces, looking from Hara to Karsha. "To Nijwhol? I don't understand." So they found the convoy he had seen on the horizon. In a way he was tremendously relieved that he no longer had to withhold this information. The only thing he could possibly have told them and it was now was something they already knew. Still, would they torture him anyway? Was he worse off because he now had nothing to bargain with?

"Speak! Or Karsha will help you. What was in the cargo hold aboard that ship?"

This was the other Hara. The one before him now, nostrils flared, breasts rising and falling like bellows, struggled to contain some obsession, some demon. She took a step toward him. Jack looked for an opening to bolt, but Karsha advanced toward him and closed the distance quickly. He caught the boy by the shoulders and clamped his hands over him, squeezing like servo pincers. He fought back a cry, but could not keep from wincing. He was driven to his knees.

"Weapons?" Hara demanded. "What kind of weapons? Lasers? Light weapons? Speak!"

"No," Jack hated himself for talking, but Karsha was slowly separating his arms from their shoulder sockets. "No weapons." Would their disappointment in what he had to tell them only provoke them further to kill him, like an armed thief who kills in disgust when he realizes he has chosen a beggar for his victim? He tried to breathe so he could speak. How could this same woman he was speaking with so easily a few moments ago allow this?

"What, then? What was in the cargo hold?"

"Nothing. Just junk. Machinery and stuff."

"What kind of machinery?"

"Old-fashioned power stuff like they use on farm worlds, orbital colonies."

Karsha released one shoulder only to take a fistful of Jack's hair and jerk his head back. Jack screamed.

"Tell me! What kind of power equipment?" Hara turned her back as if to say she could not watch what Karsha would do next.

"Solar collectors. A lot of solar panels. That's all."

Karsha released his grip and Jack fell to the floor. When he turned his head, expecting a blow or the thrust of a knife, he saw only Hara and her general looking at each other in silence.

After a moment Hara repeated the words as if they were an incantation that summoned something unclean.

"Solar panels."

Chapter Twelve

Jimenez swallowed another pill. The first one had not produced the desired calming effect. He would have to speak to the doctor once again and have something more potent prescribed. He paced the chamber, swatted at foamcrete silt on his desk, dusted and straightened the portrait of Consuela that forever seemed to hang askew no matter how it was fixed to the wall. He seated himself and was about to attempt contact once again with the adjutant's office, but remembered that, yet again, the power was fluctuating madly and he would undoubtedly be connected with the ordnance building, or the east wall sentry house or with anyone except whom he wished to speak to, if he didn't just get a screen full of static that is. *How dare Cristobal keep me waiting?* He wondered again if he shouldn't have witnesses here when *El Raton* arrived. His lies would hang him if he could catch him out and, of course, the recording device had been a useless sand trap for two years. He paced to the liquor cabinet, changed his mind, and walked to the door. He would get a guard in here to listen to the conversation. No. It could work the other way—against him. Cristobal could turn everything around somehow. Better to have it out man to man and then call in a witness if needed. First, hear him out.

The door swung open and Cristobal entered, his sun helmet tucked under his arm, his uniform impossibly spotless. They stood face-to-face, less than one meter from each other and Jimenez absently wondered how the colonel managed to look so damned clean all the time.

"Commandant. You wished to see me." Cristobal sounded unruffled. If there was a trace of fear in him, it didn't show.

"You're damned right, Cristobal. Sit down." Jimenez walked once again to his desk and seated himself behind it. He noted that the chair across from him where *El Raton* was sitting was too high. It put them at equal height. He would have to get another chair immediately. He jotted this down on a plastic sheet. Sand clogged the pen and the note was unreadable.

"Two days ago, Cristobal, I received a report from the radio hut that somebody was jamming five different bands. I asked him where it's coming from and the communications officer said it could only be coming from right here. He checked his equipment. Everything was working as well as it ever does here. It had to be from the starship or one of the shuttles. There's no other broadcasting equipment that sophisticated on the surface here and there's nobody in the damned satellites, is there? He contacted the *Pandora*. Nobody's jamming anything from there. He checked with the shuttles and found we've only got one and it's surrounded by guards. Your orders. No one can get close to it. Where the hell's the other shuttle, I ask? He doesn't know. An hour later he comes to me with a readout on the homing signal from the *Gryphon*. It's down. I send two aircars out and find it: in the desert about twelve kilometers from the spaceport . . . in pieces. Four dead crewmembers and a garbled flight log that indicates they went up, achieved orbit with a trajectory to Giata . . . and then the orbit decayed. *Intentionally.* The pilot made sure it came down right in our laps. Voiceprint authorization for the flight was made by you, Colonel, and automatically erased."

The commandant fell silent, staring at Cristobal who appeared to be shocked, flustered, and then angry in convincing degrees. "Now I understand," he said, smacking one fist into his palm.

"Understand what? I would like to understand, too, Colonel."

Cristobal stood and walked to the door, stood for a moment with his back to Jimenez and then turned suddenly on his heel. "Two days ago, one of my Dhirn agents aboard the *Salvadore,* the other shuttle, came to me and said the *Gryphon* had launched just before dawn. It had been stolen, he said, by Dhirn spies in the employ of Sivran. I have their names here." He produced a folded plastic sheet with personnel printouts on Ganar, Koros, and Vija. "The pilot was most likely taken forcibly at gunpoint. I told him that was impossible, that the *Gryphon* could only launch with my voiceprint authorization or . . . yours. At first I thought he was jumping to conclusions, that you had ordered a mission of some kind and thought it unnecessary to advise me. I could not think why, but that is not my concern. I assumed you had your reasons.

"My immediate reaction was to come to you about this, but then my agent said that it was my voiceprint that was used for launching. He played an eight-second recording that survived the crash. I recognized it as a composite of words spliced together from a recording made at the reception. Before I came to you, I was determined to get to the bottom of this in order to make a full report. I could not believe his accusation, that Sivran was behind this, but nonetheless I ordered his quarters searched. . . . This was found." From his tunic he produced a holocube and set it on the desk.

"There is no visual, only sound." He activated the device and the room was filled with the sound of silverware and plates, laughing, the rattle and clink of jewelry, wineglasses, and background conversation. Cristobal's voice dominated the others as he spoke casually with Nils Skijord of the *Pandora.* The words "Giata," "flight," "launch," and "mission" were punctuated by Cristobal stabbing his finger at the cube to draw Jimenez's attention. "I think you see how it was done." Cristobal turned off the cube and reseated himself. "An ordinary vocorder would not be delicate enough to pick up a voiceprint with the required accuracy, but the highly sensitive audio receiver on a holocorder, concealed beneath his formal robes or beneath the table . . ."

The tranquilizer was beginning to do its work on Jimenez. In fact both of them seemed to kick in at once and he felt himself getting euphorically fuzzy. He regretted taking them now. He needed all of his faculties. On the face of it, it looked pretty convincing. Still, some remaining sentinel in the back of his mind warned him of duplicity. As to what quarter it was coming from, he could not say with certainty. "Sivran spliced words from this conversation together in order to effect a launch of the shuttle? Why? What possible reason?"

"It only remains to question him. But I have a theory."

"Well?"

Cristobal leaned forward and in a conspiratorial tone spoke quickly. "Manuel, it occurred to me that if Sivran were, in fact, a traitor, just such an incident might serve his purposes. If an offworld mission of some kind seemed to be ordered by myself or you, crewed by Dhirn to whom such an order would be abhorrent, he could arouse the dissident Dhirn who only need an excuse to join the Khaj rebels. As it is, the rumor of the *Pandora*'s cargo bearing something to compromise the solar deity is of no consequence to the Dhirn. Up until now they have had no stake in this Hara's crusade. If she has gotten to Sivran, with promises of power or wealth after the overthrow of Terran rule, something exactly like this could be his part of the bargain: to deliver Dhirn support in an uprising. A reason would have to be trumped up, do you see? A mission offworld, seemingly ordered by the Terran government here, consisting of Dhirn personnel would do just that.''

Cristobal sat back in his chair, satisfied. For emphasis, he smacked his fist into his palm once again. ''It all fits, don't you see?''

Jimenez hesitated before he spoke. He wanted a drink or a stimulant to offset the tranquilizer's clouding of his thoughts.''Hmm,'' he said. That was safe. It bought him a moment. ''Sivran? It's hard to believe. He seems such a peaceful man.''

''Yes?'' Cristobal pressed. ''He was overheard telling the fax man, Cain, at the reception that his function here is to make us think things are not as bad as they really are.''

''This is diplomatic humor, Cristobal. Hardly incriminating.''

''Perhaps, Manuel. Perhaps.'' He folded his hands in his lap, the figurative ball returned to Jimenez's gravity field once again.

Jimenez shook his head to banish the encroaching pharmaceutical cobwebs. ''Why did you take control of the *Salvadore*? My own man could not get close to it.''

''My regrets, Commandant. Naturally I thought if one ship was stolen, it would be best to cut losses. Make damn sure the other was not, eh?''

''And you felt no need to consult me? I am the military governor here. Your commanding officer.''

''As I said, I wanted to gather the facts before I made a full report to you. Besides, I needed to jam transmissions immediately. We can no longer be sure of our native personnel at the communications compound. If they had intercepted this intelligence before us and there was a traitor among them. . . .''

Jimenez caught himself before he said, ''Good work, Colonel.'' It did make a certain, horrible sense. Instead he said, ''Wait here, please.'' He left the room and crossed the hall to his personal secretary, Captain Fioricci.

The captain stood and saluted. Jimenez returned the salute and asked, "Do you have coffee?" He could see there was none and quickly added, "Never mind. Get Ambassador Sivran here immediately, Captain."

"Yes, sir!" The captain launched himself out the door and trotted across the compound, calling for his corporal. Jimenez returned to his chamber.

"I have sent for Sivran. We will wait." He sat back heavily in his chair. Cristobal was at the liquor cabinet pouring a drink. *The nerve of the man,* thought Jimenez. Cristobal poured a single glass of brandy from Nueva Brasilia and offered it to his superior.

"You look like you could use this, Commandant."

Jimenez hesitated for only a moment. "Thank you," he said and drank it. It was a large one and he was secretly grateful. He must trust someone. Cristobal showed so much initiative, but was that a crime? Maybe it was what he needed on this hellworld. Still, he did not like the man. Was that necessary, though? Of course not. "Have one yourself, Colonel."

"Thank you, sir." Cristobal poured another, much smaller drink.

They sat in silence for several minutes. Jimenez was aware of his sweat-stained uniform, the beads of perspiration on his brow. *Why doesn't the bastard sweat?* he wondered, examining his colonel silently. Gnats and mites swarmed around his prime minister, but otherwise he seemed untouched by the environment. When the silence stretched to the point where Jimenez found himself fighting off sleep, there was a knock on the door. "Come in," the governor called out.

Captain Fioricci stood in the doorway, his face and neck flushed with exertion. He saluted. Jimenez lifted a hand to approximate a return salute. "Sir," he said, panting, "Ambassador Sivran is not in his quarters. His servant said he left quickly this morning. He packed some things. He did not say when he would return."

Jimenez looked at Cristobal who nodded back at him as if to say I told you. "We have our traitor."

"Find him, Captain. Take a car and a squad of men. Terrans. Bring him back here."

"Yes, sir!"

The captain turned and left, leaving the two older men to study each other in wary silence.

* * *

Karsha had gone himself, accompanied by two flanking riders and weighted down with a dragon sled as if he were a low caste tirav. It was the Khaj general's own idea to drag the one called Raith through the mountain passes lashed to the sled, leave him at the foothills under guard, fly to the escarpment over the cantonment, and send for Sivran. When the old Dhirn ambassador completed the climb—half carried and half dragged up the cliff face by one of Karsha's men—he was placed on the sled and pulled (at a less debilitating, more respectful speed) to the foothills where Raith waited to tell the secret of the crashed shuttle. Karsha cursed the idiot superstitions of the Dhirn sand humpers that made such clumsy, time consuming arrangements necessary. It would have been a simple matter to fly through the canyons with Raith strapped to a dragon, bringing him to Sivran, and they would have had their information by godrise. But the rock-headed dust sucker refused to speak if he was forced to leave the surface. Very well, the sled. They had dragged the fool at windspeed through the canyons. He was now bloody, bruised, and barely conscious, but his religious integrity remained intact.

Karsha observed Hara's ally as he seated himself on a rock and listened to his fellow Dhirn. Raith propped himself against another boulder and wrapped his waistcloth around a bloody gouge on his shoulder. Blood from a scalp wound flowed freely down the Dhirn's face and turned his short, silver hair pink in the morning light. Sivran listened, motionless, expressionless, the wind ruffling his plain robe and his pale hair that he had allowed to grow a little to approximate the Terran style. He produced a pipe and lit it with a Terran filament.

Karsha grunted. Turning to one of his men, he spoke in a low voice. "Look at him. His Terran manner and fire stick, sucking away on *iravka* constantly. This is the one Hara relies on for the dirt lovers' support. Have you ever seen anyone so useless looking?" His lieutenant laughed in agreement. To himself, Karsha admitted that despite his personal feelings about the Dhirn, he was a general after all and whatever means were available to swell the ranks of the army he wielded must be abided. Personally, he felt the Khaj warriors that he alone commanded could crush the Terrans, but Hara was right: the cost might be so high that they would, in turn, be vulnerable in a second war with the Dhirn. Alliance was vital to insure, not only victory against the Terrans, but survival for the Khaj afterward.

At last, Karsha saw Sivran rise. Sivran handed Raith a packet of *iravka* to smoke and gently touched the other Dhirn's foot. It seemed to be unbroken but considerably swollen. Karsha's lieutenant grinned at his general and Karsha returned the smile. The unspoken acknowledgment being: *It will cost a Dhirn to dictate to the Khaj.*

As if purposely intruding on their shared smugness, Sivran approached Karsha and in a voice that brooked no argument, said, "Take Raith back with you to Ayeia Ailaikhaj. Travel slowly. You have nearly killed him getting him here. Tell Hara that I will deliver ten thousand more Dhirn to her cause by this time tomorrow. Tell her that they will want to fight immediately, there will be no holding them, no more waiting." And then Sivran told Karsha what Raith had told him. "When word is spread that Cristobal has done this, there will be few Dhirn who will not turn their hand against the Terrans. It cannot be concealed from them for long and nothing I or anyone else can do will prevent the killing.''

With that, the Dhirn turned his back on the Khaj general and descended the foothill toward the desert. His form grew smaller and shimmered in the morning's heat until the mirage swallowed him. "Where does he think he's going?" Karsha asked. Receiving no answer, he cursed and ordered his men to mount up and strap Raith to the sled once more. He turned once again to the desert, trying to make out the form of Sivran and thought he saw him weaving his way unhurriedly through an obstacle course of boulders in the distance. *Who can understand a Dhirn?* he thought. He grudgingly allowed himself momentary admiration of the ambassador. Maybe the old man hadn't grown so soft. He was clearly unafraid of the desert. More than that, he was clearly unafraid of Alaikhaj and that was more than Karsha could say for himself.

From the north a wind blew, swirling walls of sand in the air, driven ahead of the clouds that rolled on the horizon. *Good,* thought Karsha. *The rains always follow the sandstorms.* And when the rains subside, Darkath would be theirs once again. It had been promised long ago.

* * *

The two hovercars Jimenez had dispatched to investigate the homing signal on *Gryphon* were manned with mostly Terran soldiers: one Lieutenant Luther Meshach and a squad of nine infantrymen. One car was driven by a young private named Geoffries and the other was driven by a Khaj private of about the same age. His name was Jhitivik. Both drivers were friends of sorts and they raced the engines of the aircars as they passed the spaceport.

Flying over dunes, sometimes nosing the craft almost vertically, then slamming back earthward onto the air cushion or fishtailing, spinning out over the level stretches, they were cheered on by the shouts of their mates who had been bored to death for days.

Even Lieutenant Meshach, who was hardly a year older than the men/boys he commanded, seemed to enjoy the ride until he reasserted his authority and ordered them to slow. This was met with general groans and protests. The lieutenant shrugged, "We're almost there," he said, holding up the hand-sized homing tracer.

They created a series of higher dunes and within minutes they could see the haze of smoke smudging the horizon and the lower face of the fire-pink sun.

Once again, the lieutenant ordered Geoffries and Jhitivik to slow, but they already had. In the daylight, the scene of wreckage could be seen to spread to the horizon, blackened metal and gnarled refuse lay over the desert to the east and west. Sand had already begun to silt over the smaller bits of debris. It was as if someone had scattered inscrutable but disturbing sculptures over the landscape or as if the desert were sprouting some smoldering, cancerous growths.

The lieutenant ordered the men to spread out and look for survivors. When the bodies of four crew members were discovered, Meshach quickly ordered Jhitivik back to the car. The Khaj driver knew then that there was something here he should not see. As he walked back toward the craft, he barked his shin on a piece of blackened instrumentation from the crashed shuttle. Something dislodged itself from the tangle of crystal and wire and titanium plating. Jhitivik bent to pick it up.

It was an electronic flight log. Still warm, it fit into his hand. On its face, to one side, was a small screen. Next to it were forty or fifty buttons, like a keyboard. He tried pressing the buttons, but there was no response. The keyboard was jammed. He pressed a stud beneath the screen and immediately it lit with a crowded jumble of numerals and characters he could not understand. One line at the top of the screen almost lept at him however. It was in Portuguese Terran Standard.

He read: FLIGHT LAUNCH AUTHORIZATION: VPRINT POS+COL.E.R.CRISTOBAL. Beneath that he read the word "crew" and the names Manuel E.

Resetez, Koros, Ganar, and Vija. Private Jhitivik didn't know this Resetez, but he knew all three of the others. Not well, they were Dhirn, after all, but he knew them well enough to know that: they *were* Dhirn. What were they doing on a flight ordered by Cristobal?

He thumbed the stud once again and darkened the screen. He placed the log in his tunic and returned to the aircar, awaiting the lieutenant and the others. While he waited, he asked himself how much of this was his business. He was a Khaj, not a Dhirn, and he fought with the Terrans, not against them . . . at least theoretically. His ancestors had always fought the Dhirn, what should he care that they had been ordered from the face of their god? It wasn't his god. Maybe it was the idea that they were ordered by someone other than Darkhani. Maybe they weren't ordered at all. Maybe they went of their own free will. It was impossible for him to conceive.

The longer he waited for the others, the heavier the log felt in his tunic. When the lieutenant returned with the men, dragging four large sealed bags, he showed him the device. "It doesn't work, though, Lieutenant. It has been damaged."

The lieutenant took it, barely glancing at it, and placed it in his pocket. Jhitivik could still feel its weight somehow, the ghost of it tugging at his tunic.

All the way back, the others did not look at the Khaj driver. Even Geoffries in the other car drove slowly and somberly. This time there were no vehicular acrobatics.

Upon their return, Jhitivik was dismissed. Geoffries as well. His friend, the Terran driver, asked Jhitivik to accompany him to a whiskey parlor where painted Dhirn women danced with sand serpents. The Khaj declined. "I have something to do," he said.

"Sorry," Geoffries mocked an apology. "I forgot you were such a bleeding busy Darker."

Jhitivik ignored him and hailed a sithe pedaler. He gave him instructions to take him to the Plaza of Fortune Tellers. There he would ask advice.

He consulted a Dhirn Grea 'ka bone reader named Lok. Lok gave him no advice. Instead, the seer fell to the dirt floor of the tent, babbling in Dhirn dialect. His wife came in and he told her what Jhitivik had told him—again in dialect the Khaj could not fully understand. Lok's wife ran from the tent, shouting news to her sisters and the neighbors. As Jhitivik left the Plaza a crowd was gathering at its center, shouting angrily, "The Terrans are coming for us to put us in their ships!" or "The Terrans are killing Dhirn!"

As his sithe pedaler rounded the corner and the plaza was lost to sight, Jhitivik could hear the shout, "Death to the Terrans!"

He no longer felt the weight of history beneath his tunic.

* * *

Cain sat in darkness, slumped forward painfully, his feet and hands bound together. His back ached from the position he was forced to maintain as well as from the series of shallow wounds his captors had inflicted as they prodded him with their short swords. Well, he had discovered what became of the cartographic party, all right. Lieutenant Chun sat several feet away from him in the darkness, half out of his head from starvation and infected wounds. The nun moaned or prayed constantly when she was conscious but was beyond any conversation. The priest was dead across the cavern from him. He could hear the insects rasping and clicking as they worked to pick the bones clean. Chun had managed to tell Cain to shift his position regularly, that if he remained immobile, the insects would mistake him for dead and begin eating him alive. The nun, he said, was dying from the beetles' poison already. Chun told him how long they had been there— as close as the lieutenant could reckon it in the unchanging blackness—and Cain was amazed that they had not joined the priest long ago.

Chun also told him about the boy, Avery. "They took him away some time ago. I don't know how long, maybe a day, maybe two. The priestess, Hara, their leader, she came herself for him. God knows what she has done with him. She said she wouldn't harm him, but she's a butcher. They're all damned butchers—every one of them! We should have killed them all eighty years ago." Chun ranted until Cain could no longer make sense of what the man was saying. Eventually he fell silent.

Cain told him of the events that had transpired outside. Everything from his arrival and encounter with the boy up until the discovery of the crashed shuttle and his own capture. Not knowing if the soldier had heard him, he, too, fell silent. After a long time, during which Cain managed to roll onto his side and control the pain with deep breathing and "containment imagery" he had learned in the hospital on Cozuela, Chun said raggedly from the shadows, "There are tremors now and then. The rock behind me is split, its edges are sharp. I've almost frayed the hide around my wrists, but I'm too weak to continue."

Cain made an effort to adjust his eyes in the dark. His optic augments were designed to heighten bands of light in the ultraviolet spectrum of another sun—and here there was none at all—but with an act of will and concentration he was able to bring them to bear on the available light within the cavern. He could see the lieutenant, the nun, and the writhing mass of *ikas* as pale, luminous patches of heat. Flecks of mica and phosphorescent fungi provided the only other traces of illumination. He forced himself to concentrate on these things, bring them into sharper focus, and amplify their effect. At last he could see his surroundings as well as he was going to.

The chamber was roughly egg shaped, some ten meters by fifteen or so. In the center of the canted floor was a natural pool of stagnant water. Dark stains that must have been blood indicated where the captives had dragged themselves to drink. Chun confirmed this, adding that every time the guards returned, they made sport of dragging the prisoners back to the walls and away from the water. The walls themselves were worn smooth except, as Chun had discovered, where they had cracked during countless years of earthquakes. Chun had positioned himself in front of the largest rift, concealing most of it with his body—slim insurance against the guards noticing what he was up to. The ceiling was high, perhaps thirty meters, and craggy. Pieces of rock had broken and fallen, small pieces were scattered on the stone floor. The guards removed these every time they entered. It was not the maximum security holding units of Hades V, but it was effective.

A period of time passed when Cain slept, or thought he slept. He found himself in complete darkness once again and realized that someone was speaking. He opened his eyes and listened. It was the lieutenant's voice. He was saying something about the nun. ". . . dead or will be soon. If I can stay alive long enough to cut through this hide, I will free you. You call to them, tell them the nun is dead, demand she and the priest be buried. Make a lot of noise until they come. Usually there are two of them. One stands at the door and the other enters. If we can overcome them, maybe strangle them with our bonds . . ."

"Forget it," Cain said, sitting up painfully. He went through the exercises necessary to refocus the augmented parts of his pupils and again the cave came into a marginally sharper relief. "Neither of us are a match one-on-one for an armed Khaj, even if you weren't as weakened as you are."

"I refuse to die here."

"Good, then stay alive."

Chun laughed. To Cain, the sound bordered on hysteria. When the laughter had trailed off, the soldier began to sing weakly: a military song about the honor in dying beneath a sun fighting and the horror of dying in the void between worlds. Cain joined him, trying to remember the words. He shifted and inched himself as close as he could to the nun. After they had sung the song twice, Cain found himself among a swarm of the *ika*. He quickly rolled away, bruising his face on the rock floor. The nun was dead. He had mistaken the faint glow of the live *ikas* for her rapidly fading body heat. He broke off the song and cursed.

In the next moment he was blinded. His eyes, finely adjusted to the near total absence of light, were painfully unprepared for the two torches that suddenly sent *ikas* and shadows scurrying everywhere. He cried out and shut his eyes. He was lifted to his feet and dragged by four powerful hands. As they passed the slumped form of Lieutenant Chun, Cain tried to think of something encouraging to say to the man, but could not. Instead Chun called out after him, "Die in the sunlight, Cain! Even if it's their bleeding sunlight!"

They ascended what seemed to be an endless series of stairs carved into the stone. Long past the point when it seemed certain they must be aboveground, they continued to climb in darkness. Cain was sure not to lag, though the effort cost him fire in his legs, chest, and head: it was better than being prodded any more in his back that felt studded with small puncture wounds radiating lances of pain in all directions. At last they emerged in scarlet sunlight. Along either side of the stone alleyways they traversed, Darkhani men, women and children slept, cooked over small fires, copulated, threw dragon bones for money, played instruments, wove fabrics, sharpened, oiled, loaded or unloaded weapons, strung jewels, painted their faces, wove their hair, chattered, and bartered. When Cain passed with his two guards, all activity ceased, heads turned, and a path opened for him. A momentary pool of quiet grew and then closed behind them, activity and conversation resuming in their wake.

When he slowed and fell finally, scrambling quickly to his feet and dodging the cursory jabs of his guards' short swords, his eye caught a sharp, silent explosion of almost white light directly ahead of them. He looked up and saw the needlelike projection of Ayeia Alaikhaj like an ancient skyscraper of Terra. On the Terran maps this was called simply Khaj Point. In Monteleone's journal he referred to it as "The Needle of the Sun" though the priest had only seen it from a distance and was not allowed to approach. Cain was hoping for a glimpse of this landmark, though he would have preferred different circumstances. It reached toward the heavens some hundred or more meters from where he stood, its height was difficult to gauge, but it was easily a kilometer from its base to the top. From the desert floor itself it was many times that. As his guards forced him forward, he continued to stare at the obelisk, carved smooth in spots and in angular patterns in others. He felt a fey attraction to the half natural, half fashioned artifact. "What was the light?" he asked his guards.

They looked at each other. One of them decided it would do no harm to speak. "Since you will soon be dead, I wager, it will not matter that you know. It was The Eye of God, Terran." He smiled over at his fellow Khaj. "Winking at himself. Few Terrans have ever seen it and lived."

"None," the other guard corrected him.

"None," the first guard amended.

Cain made no reply, though he found himself intrigued by this notion. He allowed himself to be encouraged a little and indulged in a half smile. He had been told several times, by several aliens on a number of worlds that he was privileged to see what no Terran had ever seen and lived. It sometimes appeared as if that were his only real talent.

* * *

Sivran walked until midday. He rested on a dune where the khat provided some refreshment. He soaked the hem of his robe in the slow trickle of water and continued walking with the cloth torn into a wedge and tied onto his head. He was decidedly too old for treks like this, but it was more vital than ever that no one thought so. By midafternoon he encountered a caravan of gem, herb, and water merchants who pulled wagons made of defunct Terran vehicle parts on great, flexible wheels that wobbled crazily as if trying to go in different directions at once.

He was recognized immediately and the Dhirn caravan master offered him water, food, and drugs. Sivran accepted none of these but told him of the flight of the *Gryphon*. He asked the caravan master to spread the story, to urge no violence, but instruct every Dhirn within and outlying the cantonment to withdraw into the mountains and seek out the Khaj stronghold where Hara ruled, promised sanctuary, and . . . vengeance. He wished them speed and safety and resumed his journey on foot. "I need to tread the Mother's sands now to prepare myself." The caravan master, barely containing his fury, bowed, ran his hands over his breast and left the older man to himself, insisting on leaving him with a flask of tea. The party made for the cantonment with considerably more speed than they were making previously.

Sivran encountered two other parties that afternoon. One a family of Dhirn on foot who were coming to the cantonment to visit relatives and another party of both Khaj and Dhirn who followed the Khaj's dragons on sleds. The hired Khaj tiravs stood stolidly by and said nothing as Sivran told his tale to the Dhirn kagra merchants who were transporting the caged animals in Terran crates marked in Spanish: COSMETICOS. One of them drew a knife and knelt before Sivran, symbolically offering his life in service to the religious leader. Sivran reiterated his wish that they take no action other than to evacuate the cantonment and surrounding area of all Dhirn personnel. He pointed at the mountain range behind them and said, "Offer your blade to the Khaj priestess Hara and you will serve

Darkath as well.'' The merchant reluctantly nodded and they left Sivran to walk.

A sandstorm engulfed him near sunset and he shredded his robe to wrap about his face. He drank all the tea except the dregs full of leaves and grit. Storm clouds obscured the rising of Giata and the setting of Alaikhaj. Wind and sand obscured the surface of Darkath. Tremors shook the planet beneath him and he made his way by intermittent starlight.

A Terran priest had told him that over 20,000 stars were visible to the naked eye on Darkath and Sivran chuckled, thinking of the Terran's idiotic determination, the frustration the priest must have undergone to count them night after night, losing his figures in confusion, never quite sure if he had counted this one or that one before, never quite certain that he had not overlooked that one over there or this one rising . . . and should he count the one that just sank below the horizon? Well, it wasn't like that probably. They had a computer count them, he supposed, but still it was a funny idea that they should be counted at all. This proved the Terrans to be impressively knowledgeable supposedly and the Darkers to be oblivious of their own world? Wasn't it enough that the stars were there and plentiful and shone like the eyes of children in a sea of mystery? The amusing nature of the priest's proud, crisp pronouncement kept Sivran's spirits high as he walked through the sandstorm. He allowed himself to think: *What wonderful fools! The Terrans*. It was like the joke the sledsmith told.

How did it go?

Sivran remembered and told the joke to himself.

A Terran Jafar of some kind sees a Dhirn sledsmith baking the gum and residue of melted epiliaj and durijiam before molding it into a large sled shape for a rider. The Jafar asks the smith what he is doing and he says he is making a sled that will glide over the sand like the wind, without friction.

''This stuff increases speed?'' The Jafar asks, pointing at the molten liquid.

"Exactly," replies the smith.

"Ah, then give me some of that!"

The smith is obliged to part with much of his solution and the Jafar takes it and begins to brush the boiling, foul smelling compound on his servant's feet. The servant howls in pain, the skin scalded from his feet and races away into the desert.

"By God, you're right. It works!" cries the Jafar staring after the running man. "I'll take ten bottles of it."

It went something like that anyway.

Maybe it wasn't exactly the same kind of thing as counting the stars, but it was a good joke and he needed to smile. It certainly illustrated the Terrans' penchant for seeing only what they wanted to see, for proving to themselves again and again that their preconceptions were correct even in the face of much evidence to the contrary.

Sivran knew that when pain enveloped you or fear, when anything troubled one's spirit, it was because you were clinging to something that must be released, allowed to pass. Pain, fear, and worry were aberrations, like disease. *The correct state of existence is always at the brink of laughter*, it said in the Book of the Land. He realized then that the source of his unhappiness in recent months, the thing that he clung to past its time, like a dry khat, was peace.

It was several hours before dawn when the sandstorm dissipated. He lifted the veil, crusted with sand and sweat from his face. Scanning the horizon ahead for the lights of the spaceport, the cantonment, and the surrounding Darkhani settlements he found them, but there was something else, something wrong. The sky above the cantonment and Darker Heights brooded with low storm clouds lit from below by sporadic fires that burned out of control. He quickened his pace and gradually began to run. As he got closer, he could see silhouettes of moving figures streaming away from the area and toward him. Most were on foot, though some seemed to be in carts or on sithes. Bundles of possessions weighted the backs of figures and vehicles. In the distance he could hear the rattling and popping of gunfire, the occasional crump and rumble of artillery.

He was too late. Word had preceded him somehow. He had not been able to save a single life with his plan of orderly action. He did not know how the news had spread so quickly, but it didn't matter any longer. He had never felt so useless, so despairing. He stopped running and dropped to his haunches in the sand. He put his face in his hands and wept.

The refugees streaming past paid little attention to him. They moved around him as if he were a boulder in a river. No one recognized the dusty, sobbing wretch as Sivran, spiritual and political leader of the Dhirn.

War had begun.

PART II
ALAIKHAJ

"That splendor of light that comes from the sun and which illumines the whole universe, the soft light of the moon, the brightness of fire—know that they are all come from me."

—Bhagavad-Gita 15.12

". . . and lo, in heaven an open door! And the first voice, which I had heard speaking to me like a trumpet, said, 'Come up hither and I will show you what must take place after this.' At once I was in the Spirit, and lo, a throne stood in heaven, with one seated on the throne! And he who sat there appeared like jasper and carnelian, and round the throne was a rainbow that looked like an emerald. Round the throne were twenty-four thrones, and seated on the thrones were twenty-four elders, clad in white garments, with golden crowns upon their heads. From the throne issue flashes of lightning, and voices and peals of thunder, and before the throne burn seven torches of fire, which are the seven spirits of God; and before the throne there is as it were a sea of glass, like crystal."

—Revelation 4: 1-6

"And God shall make thy soul a glass where eighteen thousand Aeons pass,
And thou shalt see the gleaming Worlds as men see dew upon the grass."

—James Elroy Flecker
Gates of Damascus

Chapter Thirteen

Isabella Xavier, wife of Major Jacinto Ismael Xavier awoke to the sounds of gunshots and the unintelligible cries of Darkhani outside the window of her home in the officers' families' sector. The room was dancing with shadows and reflected firelight whose origin, she quickly determined, was the burning home of Captain Lichtenberg and his family across the compound. Still mostly asleep, she watched in horror and fascination as half-naked Dhirn, armed with rifles, pistols, and swords emerged from the inferno bearing candlesticks, statues, chairs, draperies, and cooking utensils. Convinced she must be having another of the nightmares that had plagued her for months after her arrival here with the children, she ran a hand over her face. *The children!* She ran from the window and closed the distance between the window and door to the hallway. Her six-year-old daughter Macinta was rubbing her eyes and saying, "Mommy, what's happening?"

She swept the child into her arms and lodged her on one hip though Macinta was too old to be carried that way normally. "Where is Paul?" She ran into the children's bedroom only to find it empty. "My God! Where is he?"

"He's under the bed, Mommy," Macinta informed her.

Darting for the bed, she stopped when a hulking black silhouette appeared at the window, a short lance clutched in the Dhirn's left hand. He entered in a fluid motion brushing aside the curtains, paused beside the bed, and raised the lance as if to run the woman through. She could see the row of white teeth exposed by the savage smile of the intruder. Just as quickly, she saw the smile disappear and the lance fall from his grip as he bent suddenly to grasp his foot. The Dhirn let out a cry of pain, doubled over, and Isabella saw her son's head and arms emerge from beneath the bed, both hands clutching the hilt of a bayonet that was lodged firmly in the howling figure's ankle. Paul crawled out and wrenched the bayonet away from the wound. The boy drew his twelve-year-old frame up to its full height, the blade over his head and his mother watched, sickened and relieved simultaneously as her son stabbed the hunched form once, twice, and a third time in the back. The Dhirn slumped, fully prostrate and groaned, but made no effort to rise.

"Paul, come with me!" The boy hesitated, staring at what he had done and then broke away, obeying.

In her husband's study, seldom used and little more than a place to hang his decorations, holostills of previous campaigns and major's uniforms, she found her way to the desk. She set Macinta underneath it. Groping inside, she found the machine pistol and fumbled with the magazine and breach.

"*Mom!*" Her son shouted and pointed to the door of the study. Two Dhirn armed with knives and wearing infantry uniforms stood frozen for a moment. Isabella raised the pistol with both hands and pulled the trigger. The gun jumped and an arc of bullets tore the door, wall, and doorjamb into splinters. The first native turned and fled, the other crouched and rolled to the side. She lowered the pistol and fired again, killing the one who darted down the hall. His body flew several meters with the impact of the bullets. Isabella fired a concentrated burst into the thin, Imperial issue wood and foamcrete wall until a gaping hole revealed the blood-spattered form of the other Dhirn.

Macinta was screaming. Isabella searched the drawers for another magazine of ammunition and shouted, "Paul, you get under the desk with your sister!" Her son had produced another clip from the drawer and handed it to her. Ignoring his mother's command, he than ran to the body of the dead soldier by the door and took the knife and the small spring mechanism from the corpse's belt. "It's a spring knife, Mom!"

"Paul, get over here now!"

After she had shoved the desk into a corner, the three of them huddled behind it and Isabella Xavier tried to calm her daughter. Paul showed her how the Dhirn knife fit into a spring loaded casing, locked, and released to create a projectile of deadly accuracy. The smell of smoke was beginning to choke them. She wondered if her own house was now burning and how much time was left for them.

More Darkhani voices. Louder. Closer. The window of the study.

Paul lifted his head above the surface of the desk and raised the spring knife. "No! Paul!" She reached for him. He released the trigger and the blade found its way into the chest of the Dhirn at the window.

In the next moment a gunshot deafened her and she saw her son's head erupt with bone and blood. His body was thrown against the wall where it remained motionless.

With a strangled cry rising from her throat she aimed at the window and pulled the trigger until the gun was empty. She remained leaning over the desk, still screaming her inarticulate rage and grief, her knuckles white around the useless weapon.

When she felt the impact of the bullets, she was absently surprised to note there was no pain. She found herself on the floor and saw the torch land on her husband's cot where he sometimes fell asleep in the afternoons. She watched the flames catch on the bedding, lick at the walls. The curtains were on fire, but there seemed to be so little light. It was odd. *Macinta* she tried to say, *Macinta*. And her daughter was the last thing she saw, being lifted by two muscular arms the color of the darkness that engulfed her.

* * *

Eduardo Cristobal marched across the compound ignoring the hail of bullets that flew around him. The insurgent Dhirn were crouched behind the rows of hovercraft that were positioned haphazardly to one side awaiting repairs. Cristobal estimated there were no more than five or six of them as he continued to walk at a brisk pace, without appearing to hurry. He shouted a command to one of the men that followed him in a crouching run. "Get gas canisters and use it on those bastards over there!" He pointed at the men who were shooting at him as if there could be any doubt as to who he was referring to. "You two!" He pointed at two others that followed him and provided covering gunfire. "Follow me."

One of the hovercraft exploded with a deafening whoosh, sending metal flying upward and out. Flame and viscous smoke poured into the night sky as if the ground had opened up and hell was escaping from beneath them. Cristobal threw himself on the ground for a moment, waited until the flying debris had settled, and then stood, brushing at himself. "I don't want to lose any more of those cars. Get that gas, soldier!" He felt at the back of his neck where something warm and wet soaked his collar. He brought away his hand and saw that it was darkened with blood. Cursing, he removed one of his gloves from the satchel on his belt and pressed it to the wound. With his other hand he drew his pistol and gestured at the two Khaj soldiers behind him to get up and follow.

As they did, Cristobal renewed his brisk, stalwart pace, taking aim at intervals and firing his pistol at the huddled rebels. Once across the compound, he led his escort through the maze of buildings and lock facilities that were the military and civilian jails. He shouted orders ahead of him to open up and titanium-barred doors swung wide to meet him. He entered a doorway that led down two long flights of stairs. Here, carved into the bedrock beneath tons of sand, was the chamber where the three spies were held hostage. Two Dhirn and one Khaj, each in separate cages.

Cristobal stood in the center of the room. There were five, man-sized cells altogether. Two of them were empty. Neither provided any more room than was required to stand or crouch over the chemical sanition fixtures that slanted at an uncomfortable angle from the wall. The Dhirn spies looked half dead. They lay slumped against the bars of the cell, their once burly frames shriveled from starvation and thirst. The Khaj prisoner stood with his arms folded, his legs apart defiantly. His face was sunken and shadowed in the dull, flickering glow of the electric lights and his stomach was shrunken beneath his rib cage. Cristobal ran his eyes over him and, though he hated him, he also approved of him. *That is the way to conduct yourself as a prisoner.* Cristobal himself once served an eight-month sentence on Cozuela while awaiting a court-martial for killing unarmed civilians during a truce. He was eventually acquitted and the charges dropped, but the incident resulted in his posting to Darkath.

"Open those two cells," he ordered his men, indicating the cells containing the two Dhirn. The Khaj guards moved to the wall of electrical switches and closed the circuits on the ones corresponding to the numbers of the indicated cages. The doors began to move, then stalled as the power fluxed and dipped. They waited a moment and the power surged a little. One door opened and the occupant fell forward onto the cracked, stone floor. The other was stuck. Cristobal moved to examine the problem. Pulling the door on its track, he saw that tremors had caused the frame to buckle. He pulled and tugged at the top of the door without effect. In the next cell, the Khaj prisoner reached a hand out and gripped the first bar of the adjoining, immobile door. Before Cristobal could protest, the Khaj had pulled away the metal from its frame. The door sagged forward enough for the guards to pull the other Dhirn free.

"Keep your hands at your side!" Cristobal waved his gun at the Khaj prisoner. The prisoner complied, smiling. "What is your name?" he asked the prisoner.

"Dalak," came the reply.

"No. You are number three. That is a lucky number. You will live, number three . . . as long as you keep your hands at your side." Cristobal then turned to the Khaj guards who seemed to be studying Dalak warily. "You," he spoke to one of them, "give me your braid." He meant the ornamental braid at the shoulder of the Khaj's tunic. The Khaj untied the knot and handed the meter-long piece of pseudosilk to his colonel. "You," he commanded the other guard, "get water. There." He pointed at a trough against the far wall. "Revive these two spies."

While the second guard was fetching the water, Cristobal strung the braided cord around a beam in the ceiling. The Khaj returned with the water and at Cristobal's command, dashed it into the faces of the prostrate prisoners. They roused themselves marginally and Cristobal nodded at the first Khaj, then looked at the dangling rope. The Khaj understood. He fashioned a loop and knot and then lifted the Dhirn who struggled weakly and mumbled in dialect. The guard placed the noose around the Dhirn's neck and held his hands firm. Meanwhile the remaining two prisoners looked on in silence.

Cristobal waited. After a full minute he ordered the Khaj to release the hanged native's hands. As he did so, the Dhirn brought them up weakly and tried to pull the rope from his neck as he was strangled. It was taking too long. Cristobal took aim and shot him in the forehead. "Cut him down and hang this one," he ordered.

They obeyed. The second one struggled more. Just before the braid closed over his head, he said in Terran, "May Darkath chew you and spit you out!"

"It may yet, you little Darker bastard. But you won't

live to see it." Once the cord was around the Dhirn's neck and his tongue began to bleed where he had bitten down on it involuntarily, Cristobal shot him as well.

"That leaves you, Darker number three, whatever your name is."

"Dalak," the Khaj repeated.

"Darker number three. If there is any trouble from the Khaj, you will be among the first to die. You have my promise. It won't be as quick."

"Ah, so there is trouble from the Dhirn." Dalak smiled. "The Khaj will follow and the Khaj are warriors and will bury you and your toys in pieces. We are not as easy to kill as the Dhirn." He winked—an oddly Terran gesture, Cristobal realized—at the two Khaj guards, ". . . are we?"

Cristobal looked at his men who remained expressionless. It must have been his imagination that he saw something pass between them in that brief second of eye contact. Something that immediately compelled him to reestablish his authority over the moment. "Take these bodies and bury them. Then report to me in the compound."

* * *

Jimenez stood on the balcony at his bedroom window. From the second story of the crystal steel building that had withstood forty years of earthquakes, a slow, graceful sand dune flowed beneath him. The first floor was completely claimed by the migrating sands and it was only with constant effort, daily digging details, that the second floor was salvaged from the implacable march of the desert. The administration building next door was similarly engulfed by the slow tide of sand movement. Only its third floor was functional. The building seemed to be toppling in slow motion as if caught in a freeze framed holo of a disaster in progress, a piece of Terran flotsam tossed on a curry-colored flood tide. Beyond the administration building was the compound, parade ground, utility field, and common area of the cantonment. Smoke and clouds of gas, luminescent blue-pink beneath the moon, poured across its flatness on the winds that bore the sand.

The area was secure for the moment, but beyond lay the officers and noncom Terran personnel quarters. It was a conflagration stoked by the winds. Everything had been burned to the ground. The wind also bore the sounds of the wounded, dying, and surviving mourners. Now and then a burst of small arms fire or grenade explosions would punctuate the relative silence. Darker Heights was ablaze with rampant fires. Refugees streamed away into the night by the hundreds. He had ordered a regrouping of all Terran personnel, military and civilian, behind cantonment walls. Jimenez had ordered *Pandora* to stand by for evacuation. A radio message to the detachment on the Nijwhol expedition had warned them of possible hostility and he had promised reinforcements as soon as possible if necessary. An empty promise: they were on their own. Once the regrouping had been effected, he would know where they stood. Yesterday at this time Darkhani military personnel outnumbered Terran troops by five hundred to one. Things would not have improved during the night. He had to establish how many civilians remained. He would issue them weapons, any women or children old enough or strong enough to fight, and inform them they must prepare for a long siege. Jimenez was certain the convoy of power equipment would be discovered at any moment and he had to assume the Khaj would rise against him now as well. Already, Skijord was sending a tachyon SOS relay to Quadrant Headquarters, but he could expect no help in less than three months—if he were lucky.

Then, of course, there were the Andromedans. What could he expect from that quarter? No news there and no way to investigate now. He had to assume a threat, but as to the nature of it, that was speculation. The most he could hope for was their indifference to events on Darkath, but no matter how alien and imponderable they might be in human terms, the soldier in him could not believe that an armada, albeit small, was sequestered on Darkath's moon with indifferent motives.

He fingered the vial of powerful sleeping medication the doctor had prescribed for him and considered the extent of his failure. A handful of pills and respiration and heart rate would cease painlessly within minutes. He held the vial up to the moon and admired the play of light through its beveled surface, counted the capsules. A woman's cry came to him on the smoky, sandy nightwind: a widow or orphan or casualty—someone in pain. He set the pills on the ledge of the balcony and felt ashamed. He turned from the balcony and picked up his sword and pistol. He left the sliding airtight and transparent crystal doorway open. *Let the desert take the damned place.*

An aide awaited him in the hallway. "Get the captain of *Pandora*. Tell him to strip the vessel of everything not essential and prepare to evacuate civilians. Ask him how many we can save."

"Sir, I was just informed a moment ago that *Pandora* has been overrun by hostiles. The ship is occupied by Dhirn, sir. And they are . . . dismantling it."

* * *

Nigel Wilson crouched behind the makeshift barricade of furniture, sanitation containers, broken sections of foamcrete walls, and sand bags. In one hand he held a rifle and in the other an old-fashioned vocorder. The bodies of seven Terran soldiers and three civilians, one of them female, approximate age, fourteen, lay slumped in various poses of violent death. He peered through the smoke at the entrance to the adjutant's office and spoke into the recording device. "Uh . . . this night will forever go down in the . . . uh . . . annals of infamy as the . . . Night of Dark

Death . . . no . . . The Night of the Bloody Moon . . .
wait, no . . . The Night of the Springlances! That's it.
The Night of the Springlances!''

There had been no movement from inside the building for nearly ten minutes. Smoke poured from the
doorway and windows and the adjutant's staff sergeant's body swung from a piece of cable above the
doorway. The Dhirn had hit the building, butchered
its occupants, ransacked the contents, found little of
interest to loot, and moved on. The ten dead Terrans
behind the barricade had tried to stop them. Wilson
had observed the brief firefight from an already gutted
building a block away. He had not fired a shot; in fact,
he had not even checked to see if the rifle was loaded.
He had taken it from the body of a dead soldier inside
the Aztec earlier that night after the Dhirn in the place
had unexpectedly erupted in a barroom brawl that
quickly escalated into a pitched gun battle leaving some
twenty bodies, Dhirn, Terran, Khaj, and one Rigelian,
who must have taken nearly one hundred bullets
through its rhinolike layers of hide before collapsing.

From his hiding place in the hempwork ceiling, Wilson had made a recorded note, rather well put, he
thought, about the valiant fight of the Rigelian and the
river of copper-colored blood that flowed from the
great creature as he brought down one Dhirn after another with his bare claws. He decided it was now or
never and he leaped the barricade and ran, hunched
over, across the street into the building.

Inside, all was chaos. He quickly worked his way
through two rooms with overturned desks, file cabinets, computers, and smoldering stacks of printouts.
He absently noted three more bodies. Down a hallway
and up a low flight of stairs he found the room he was
looking for marked CONTRABAND: AUTHORIZED
PERSONNEL ONLY. The titanium door was riddled
with bullet holes but remained intact and locked as if
the looters had briefly tried to blast their way in and
given up. Wilson retraced his steps and searched the

drawers of the sergeant's desk for a folder of metal key tabs imprinted with the adjutant's I.D. code. He scuttled back to the locked room and tried each one. The fifth one slid the door back far enough for him to enter.

Stacks of sealed lockers bore plastic tags with names scrawled by hand with permadye pens. His eyes ran over more than a dozen, looking for his own name, when he saw M. Cain, Hub Fax. That would do. He checked his rifle, pressed a stud, and a single bullet snicked into the chamber. He stood back and aimed at the lock, pulled the trigger. He ducked as metal flew past his head and the bullet ricocheted around the room. He threw open the locker and lifted out the lightweight holopack. A newer model than his own. In the next moment it was strapped over his right shoulder, microphone filament in place at his chin and he was bounding through the doorway to the street.

As he ran, wincing against the gathering sandstorm that blew from the north, checking that the lens shield was disengaged, he began his narration into the microphone, "Night of the Springlances," he pronounced in a no nonsense baritone, "Your correspondent, Nigel Wilson. . . ."

* * *

Captain Nils Skijord of the Imperial Starcorps had ordered all airlocks sealed and all personnel aboard to arm themselves. Half of his men were to take up rifle positions in the cargo bay, the other half were to man the bridge and outer flight deck. His crew of forty-six men responded quickly.

The cargo bay was vulnerable because the door assembly had been removed for repairs. There was no time to reinstall it.

The Dhirn came at them in waves. Skijord's men sent most of those first two waves to whatever passed for Darker hell. If they had not been obliged to strip the ship of all light weapons before departure at Puerto De Estrella, the outcome would have been different.

As it was, the third and fourth waves took the ship with homemade smokebombs—deadly toxic—as well as rope and grappling hooks. Within minutes, the men in the cargo bay were overrun and slaughtered. The Dhirn fixed their grappling hooks to one of the three stabilizing struts anchored in the distressed plasticrete of the spaceport, secured the other end to a captured drone tractor and toppled the *Pandora* with relative ease.

As a result, Skijord and twenty-two of his men were thrown around their various compartments and Skijord himself suffered a broken ankle. On the bridge with him were his first lieutenant, navigator, real-space pilot and co-pilot, as well as two members of the ship's engineering complement. His lieutenant had hit his head and was unconscious. The rest of his men were on the outer flight deck, separated from him by a bulkhead. Those on the bridge could hear their screams as they died from the smokebombs and small arms fire.

"They will be able to cut through the bulkheads before long." Skijord pointed out. "They have the tools, they know how to use them. I'd say we had less than an hour."

"That sounds about right, Captain." One of the engineers agreed. No one suggested starting the engines and blowing themselves up with the Dhirn: they would have taken most of Darkath's northern hemisphere with them. "What can we do in the meantime?"

"Whatever you like. Pray, play cards if you have 'em, drink if you got anything, sing."

Another engineer was playing with the communications console and getting nothing but noise. Some of the others started to sing: "Beneath the Terran Moon." Skijord looked after the unconscious lieutenant, placed his shirt beneath his head and positioned him comfortably.

He emptied the bullets from his pistol.

"Anyone want to play a hand or two of Matrix Sprouts? We can use these for markers. Won't get to use them on the enemy. They'll get us with gas."

"We've got suits, Captain." The engineer, whose name was Thornton, pointed to the bank of lockers at the rear of the compartment.

Skijord shrugged. "Use them if you want. They'll buy you a few minutes. You can take a handful of Darkers with you, I suppose. Me, I don't see how killing makes dying any easier." He waited while the co-pilot and one of the engineers found suits for themselves. "Anyone in for a hand or not?" He waved his bullets in the air.

"Sure." Thornton squatted next to the captain and emptied his weapon. He scattered the rounds in a random pattern on the bulkhead/floor. Skijord picked up three of them. Thornton puzzled for a moment and picked up one. He raised his voice softly to the tune some of the others were singing. No one's voice broke.

Skijord didn't join in the song. He had no nostalgia for Terra. His nostalgia was for places he hadn't been. Places he would now never see.

It took less than half an hour. The men and women on the bridge sang "Voidbound" and "Keep the Glory." Skijord won ten bullets. He smiled and joined in on the last chorus, his voice a surprisingly clear tenor.

When the bulkhead glowed white, then blue, then red and the smoke entered the compartment, Nils Skijord started to reload his pistol, holding his breath. He got two bullets in the magazine and his hands shook. He tried to lift the pistol, but couldn't. He let out his breath, said, "Damn," and inhaled.

* * *

Lance Corporal Virik, Platoon Leader of the Imperial Native Tactical Combat Force, turned in his saddle and signaled to the three riders behind him.

Sergeant Avery nodded and with his knees, guided the dragon into a slow descent to the canyon floor. To either side of him, Jara and Private Rilia something or other followed them down. At an altitude of one hundred meters they were enveloped in whipping sheets of stinging sand. Avery closed his visor against the onslaught but could still see very little. He depended on his men with their protective membranes to guide them from here. The fireball of Alaikhaj, muted behind a bank of charcoal clouds, became nearly invisible as they approached the ground and entered the sandstorm.

Virik guided them to a bend in the mountain pass that afforded them some shelter. He gave the order to tether the mounts and Avery grunted his assent.

"Sergeant, beyond this next rise is the approach to The Eye of God. From here on we can expect to be spotted if we haven't already."

"All right, you're in charge, Virik. Make it look good."

"We'll have to bind your hands and feet, of course. And blindfold you."

"Yes, yes. Get on with it."

"What do we do, sir, after we turn you over to Hara?"

"We'll have to feel our way along. The main thing is to locate Jack and learn as much as you can about their plans here." Avery was bound and blindfolded. Jara guided him back onto his dragon. "Take off your tunics and rip up your leggings a bit or something. Look like deserters, renegades. Stay close to wherever I'm taken and prepare to brazen our way out of there with hostages. You, Jara, try to find the old seer, Juum. Get an audience with him or something and prepare to stick a weapon in his gums and march him out in front of us. If not him, some holy man or other should do. I don't reckon we'll get to Hara herself."

Jaralaj and Riliaviriakikia exchanged looks Avery could not see. Though they remained expressionless the message that passed between them was: *Is he mad? Yes*.

"If things go sour, you, soldier," he meant Rilia-viriakikia, "ride for the cantonment and bring the Lancers. We'll fix it with Cristobal later. If they kill me, get Jack and get out. If Jack isn't here or they've killed him, again get back, report to Cristobal. He's got spine. Tell him they've got me and I recommend a cavalry strike with shuttle support. He'll love it. Any questions? Let's go."

Virik shrugged at his two fellow Khaj as if to say "So much for questions" and they mounted up.

They ascended the approach to The Eye of God and within an hour they stood before a sentry post. Virik announced that the three of them had defected from the Terran cavalry and had taken the Jafar prisoner for Hara's interrogation. They were directed through a series of sharply turning canyons. Avery could hear voices, curses and shouts, felt spittle on his face. He was pelted with rocks and blood flowed from his forehead and chin. Virik shouted a threat and the assault ceased.

At length they came to a halt and Avery could sense a throng of hostile Darkers pressing in on them. Jara whispered in his ear that Hara had been sent for. He felt hands tugging at him and he was down. He was kicked and prodded, dragged and pushed. He called out for Virik and his men, but there were only the hate-filled curses and babble of Khaj dialect echoing against stone walls and a high ceiling. When his blindfold was cut from his eyes. He blinked into darkness and was thrown against another body. The body stirred.

"Avery," the voice came from next to him, very weak, a dry croak. "What are you doing here?"

"Who is it? I can't see."

"Lieutenant Chun . . . 303rd."

"Thank God you're alive, sir. I'm here to rescue you. Has a boy been taken here? I'm looking for my son."

"Yes. He's here. Or he was. The woman Hara came for him. Are you going to rescue him, too?"

"Yes, sir."

"Well, that's just excellent, Sergeant. Do you mind telling me how?"

"No, sir. I'm going to kick some Darker ass."

"Ah. Did you notice there are several thousand armed renegades between here and the passes."

"Yes, sir."

"Did you come with the entire Imperial Army?"

"Better than that, sir. I brought three of my lancers."

"I see. For a minute there I was worried."

"Let me do the worrying, sir."

* * *

Padre Gillermo shook his head. "No," he said, "We cannot go on." The sand flew through the canyons as if propelled by colossal fans. His face was a plaster of hardened grit. His eyes glued together, his nostrils and mouth sealed despite the tightly wrapped Terran fabric he wore in layers around them.

"It's okay," Ty insisted. "No difficulty. I know the way. Straight up." The Dhirn in the three-cornered monsigneur's sombrero pointed at a sharply sloping rockfall that confronted them in this blind alley where the trail ended and a huge sand dune grew before the priest's eyes, Where the dune crested, the sheer face of a mountain peak rose for nearly one hundred meters before being lost to sight.

"That's all very good, but I can't go on and Cheverny needs rest as well." They had been traveling without pause for two nights and three days. Cheverny was lashed to one of the dragons, too weak from exposure to carry on without help. The boy suffered from muscle cramps due to the unaccustomed gravity, dehydration as a result of an inability to hold down food or water because he had lost his planetary disorientation pills in one of the three quakes they endured within the canyons, and suffered a blow to the head from a falling rock. The third quake which had nearly claimed Cheverny, was responsible for the avalanche that closed the mountain pass ahead of them. With the sandstorm showing no sign of abating, Gillermo, at last, gave in to the consequences of his folly. "We'll find shelter nearby and return to the cantonment when the winds stop."

"No way, Jafar. The winds don't stop. They bring rain. We wait here and we will be buried." Ty indicated the rapidly mounting mass of sand ahead. "We don't get buried, we sure as blood drown when rain floods the canyon."

"You must find us shelter." Gillermo observed the sand beginning to close over his boots and calves. He forced himself to move again.

"Okay. Back maybe two kilometers where little Jafar got hit on the head. Rockfall will break the sandwind."

"Back?"

"*Si.* Back or up." Again, his guide indicated the sand dune and above it the sheer mountain face.

"We can't go up." Gillermo muttered, exhausted.

"No difficulty for Grea' ka. We leave all the garbage here and . . ." He made a winging motion with his hands.

"We can't leave the equipment."

"Okay, Jafar. We go back."

"All right. Back."

The retracing of their steps took what was left of the daylight. They fought the winds head on and each meter was a hard won victory for Gillermo. Ty and Rik trotted ahead, untroubled by the diabolical reality they called home. Somewhere, in some chamber in the labyrinth of corridors on Vatican IV, teams of hyper educated Neo-Jesuit theologians were arguing in favor of a Manichean status for Darkath; for the first time Gillermo found himself wondering if they might not be correct, if this world was not indeed some creation of the Fallen One.

At last they reached the break of boulders in the pass from which they had recently fled. Now the jagged configuration of stone and sand that made a fork of the wide arroyo served as a temporary haven from the wind. The dragons were tethered and fed, the equipment off-loaded and the Dhirn made pit-dens for themselves out of rock and sand, digging with only their hands. Gillermo imitated them. First he made a place for Cheverny and then, without enough strength to dig another shallow hole and potential grave for himself, he huddled against a drill motor casing and slept.

He woke with a start in pitch blackness. The wind was a constant, low crooning as it continued to blow past the rock break. He blinked and groped around him. His hand closed over the arm of one of his Dhirn guides. It was Rik. Rik's other hand closed over Gillermo's mouth for a moment and then was removed. He was being signaled to remain quiet. "Two riders," the Dhirn announced in a whisper. "From the west. Very close." Gillermo could see and and hear nothing at first. When his eyes adjusted, he made out the forms of their own dragons curled into themselves with their tails under them, their heads tucked beneath the flat, spadelike configuration of leathery flesh that shielded them from the drifts of sand. He strained to hear above the oboe and cymbal droning of the sandstorm and after a moment he could hear a human voice calling his name, "Padre Gillermo! Padre Gillermo! Where are you? Can you hear me?"

It was the woman, Dubois. God's blood! What was she doing out here?

Rik gestured for him to follow and climbed the shifting wall of various sized rocks that had formed their natural lean-to. Gillermo scrabbled after him, slipping and losing ground, eventually gaining purchase. At the top of the rubble, sand blew like spray from an ocean swell. Gillermo could not open his eyes enough to see anything whatsoever. "Is she alone? Can you see?"

"Two Grea' ka. One Khaj rider in front. One woman Jafar."

Gillermo had no choice. He must offer her whatever shelter he could from this hellwind. "This way, Se-ñora Dubois. Follow my voice!"

"The Khaj will find us." Rik said. "No difficulty," he added. This was something the Dhirn guide said constantly, usually preceding some unguessable hard-ship or near impossibility. He proved correct, however. By the time they had both climbed back to the canyon floor, Gillermo could see the woman trailing behind a native dressed for the storm in pale robes that whipped around him and a hoodlike cloth fixed to his head with a scarf. He took Rik's word for it that the native was indeed a Khaj. They rounded the windbreak and dis-mounted. Their beasts had been traveling low to the ground and seemed rather old and tired to Gillermo, judging by their flaking scales and slow movements.

"Well, Padre Gillermo. I've found you at last. I really did have to come. Please don't be angry with me, but as you can see, I'm quite capable of fending for myself." She seated herself against a fall of small stones that settled beneath her and removed her sun-helmet. Despite her precautions, her eyes were puffy and swollen, the skin of her face blistered.

"You've followed me all this way?" the priest asked in amazement.

"I employed a scout. He tracked you marvelously. I'm afraid I bring some terrible news." Amalia Du-bois told him of the Dhirn uprising at the cantonment and surrounding area. She related the garbled story she had heard of the commandant ordering several of their number offworld for some purpose or another she did not understand.

"I don't believe it." Gillermo looked incredulous. "For what purpose would Jimenez do such a thing?"

"It's possible that it is just a rumor, with no basis. But it caught on and spread with disastrous results. There are hundreds of Terrans dead, and many Dhirn, of course."

Gillermo instinctively looked over at his own Dhirn guides and the eight Dhirn laborers that accompanied them.

"Of course, I know what you're thinking," Dubois leaned toward him and spoke quietly. "Your Dhirn know nothing of this and I have paid my scout to remain silent. Still, we shouldn't count on his loyalty staying bought. I suggest we take turns keeping watch. You look exhausted. I'll take first watch while you sleep. I brought this." She produced a small machine pistol from her robes. "Then you or Cheverny can keep watch. We'll rotate that way so that at no time can we be taken by surprise."

Gillermo then told her of Cheverny's condition.

"It's a good thing I arrived then, isn't it?" She said matter-of-factly.

Gillermo said nothing. He did not point out the obvious, that if she hadn't followed them in the first place, he would be assured of his men's ignorance of events at the cantonment—at least for a time. "I'm exhausted, yes," he told her, "but I will be unable to sleep. I will take first watch."

"Very well, then, hold on to this." She offered him the pistol and he shook his head.

"No, I would be unable to use it anyway. I have a flare gun with some smoke and pellet canisters."

"Well, maybe that will suffice. Let's hope we won't have to find out. Wake me in two hours and I'll relieve you." With that, she replaced her helmet on her head and leaned back against the gravel. Within moments, Gillermo could hear muted snores from beneath her faceplate. He sat with his arms resting on his knees and prayed. When he saw that all of his Dhirn were asleep, he wandered to the bundle next to the dragon where he knew the flare gun was packed.

As nonchalantly as he could, he removed the weapon from beneath a bundle of maps, pretended to study the maps for a minute, and then returned to his place between Cheverny and Dubois. All the while his eyes were fixed on the inert, seated, but upright figure of Amalia's Khaj "scout." Still hooded, he could barely make out the pale membrane of the native's eyes. He could not tell if they were open or closed.

When his wrist display registered the passage of two standard hours, Gillermo woke Amalia. Silently, she nodded and sat up, her hand closing over the pistol still hidden beneath her clothing. Gillermo gestured to the Khaj who remained in exactly the same position. He assumed he was asleep. Dubois acknowledged his presence and whispered, "Don't worry." It sounded disturbingly like Rik's refrain of "no difficulty," but he laid his head against a rock. It would be dawn in less than an hour, he reckoned. He fell asleep almost immediately.

. . . and woke for the second time that night to hands shaking him roughly. He sat up quickly and groped for his flare gun. Amalia bent over him, prodding him with one hand and with the other, firing her machine pistol into a chaotic flurry of sand. The popping report from her gun sounded like a child's toy and echoed briefly against the canyon walls. Gillermo stood and noted that it was almost daylight. He leveled his flare gun in the direction Amalia was shooting. "What is it? What are you shooting at?" He could see nothing. The Khaj was gone. So were his Dhirn.

Amalia let go of him and raced into the saffron flurry. He heard her pistol for another moment and then it fell silent. He was poised to run after her and hesitated. He looked quickly around him and saw his equipment scattered and broken in several places. A packet of maps flew crazily into the sky on an updraft. A surveying tripod was wedged, broken in half, between two boulders. Boxes of dehydrated foods had been cut open, their contents spilling into the air with each renewed gust from the storm. The two dragons Amalia and her Khaj had arrived with were still tethered where they had been when he fell asleep, though now they were upright and stirring at the commotion. Almost as an afterthought, he turned to check on Cheverny. The boy lay, seemingly undisturbed, in the place Gillermo had dug for him. He stepped toward him and felt a hand on his shoulder.

He spun, leveling the flare gun, and confronted Amalia Dubois. "Blood of the Savior! I almost shot you."

"At least that would be quick." Her words were muffled beneath her helmet. She thumbed a stud on her pistol and an empty magazine fell from the grip.

"What happened? Why didn't you wake me?" He peered at her faceplate, now beginning to opaque in the gathering daylight. She lifted it slightly and spoke.

"I watched the Khaj and your two guides as well as I could. A little while ago the storm picked up and I couldn't see anything, not even my own hands. I got up and moved down a few meters and discovered the Khaj was no longer where he had been. He might have been waiting for just such an opportunity. I moved around blindly for a while trying to see where he had gone. I couldn't find him or anyone from your party. I must have gotten turned around. I was lost for ten or fifteen minutes until I nearly stumbled over one of the dragons again. By that time the storm had settled back down enough for me to see that your men were looting supplies. One of them was bent over Cheverny. I fired at him and he ran, along with the others, in that direction." She pointed with the gun toward the mountain face Gillermo knew lay ahead of them. "The Khaj must have told them what is happening at the cantonment. I ran to check Cheverny and then woke you. They're gone. All gone. We're lucky to be alive."

"Cheverny?" Gillermo let the question hang. He rushed to the acolyte's side and turned the boy's head in his hands. Blood seeped from a deep gash in Cheverny's neck. There was no pulse. Gillermo cradled the young man's head in his arms for a while and felt stunned. Emotion would come later, he knew. For now he was in a mild state of shock. He got to his feet and walked toward some of the thrown satchels. He was looking for the oilcloth bundle containing ointment, stole, holy water, and items he could need to administer the Last Rites. Amalia watched him wordlessly.

After several minutes Gillermo abandoned any hope of finding what he needed and returned to Cheverny's side, reciting the words of the sacrament by heart and using what little spittle he could produce to anoint the body. When he was finished, he tossed a token handful of sand onto the body that was already in the process of being buried more efficiently than the two of them could together. He stood over the boy for a moment until he felt Amalia's hand on his arm once more.

"We should keep moving, Padre. I don't think it is safe to go back to the cantonment, however. They left us two dragons. They are old and I think sick, but might take us some ways."

Gillermo roused himself. "Yes. Let's salvage any supplies we can. You know how to . . . ride the thing."

"Once I get it moving, yes, More or less."

"Then let's get about it."

"Where will we go?" she asked. Gillermo noted with some surprise that this was the first time he had ever seen Amalia Dubois at something of a loss.

"Up," he said. "Over the mountain face if the things will carry us. To Nijwhol."

Chapter Fourteen

Cain stood before Hara in her chambers. His impressions were that of bizarre beauty, bridled, raw personal power, integrity of spirit and not a little ruthlessness. An uneasy mixture of revulsion, fascination, fear, and an attraction he did not understand warred within him for prominence. As he studied her—kneading his wrists to renew circulation after his bonds had been cut—*she* studied him. He felt her gaze burning through his own, her hooded eyes were dark wells of mystery and charisma. While she was, he had to admit, physically repulsive in conventional Terran terms, he felt an inexplicable, almost erotic rapture in the prolonged, silent eye contact. Like a mongoose entranced by a cobra, he felt, to some degree, paralyzed in her power. The thought made him bristle and he was the first to look away. She smiled and the spell was broken.

"The Dhirn, Raith, tells me he was sent to you as a servant and you asked him to serve only as your teacher." Through the arches behind her, Cain could see the renegade camp below stirring with activity: supplies and people were being moved from one place to another with a sense of furious purpose. Mounted dragons floated up over the mountain peaks to and from the stronghold on random errands. Beyond the mountains, beneath an ash-colored sky, he could see the vast stretch of desert beyond with its sheets of sand moving like waves on a troubled sea. From here, Darkath looked like a great cauldron being stirred by colossal but indecisive and invisible forces.

"Where is Raith? Is he alive?"

"He is here. And yes, he is alive. He tells me you wish to know our Gods here: Darkath and Alaikhaj. Is that true?"

"I wish to know the source from which the Darkhani draw such strength." Cain answered evenly.

Hara arched an eyebrow with interest. "You perceive us as strong?"

"Yes."

"To most Terrans I think we are perceived as disagreeable but domesticated animals. Strength?" she mused, "Most Terrans would think of our strength in terms of beasts of burden."

"I don't know most Terrans."

Hara smiled again. "I thought it was your work to know the *minds* of most Terrans." As quickly as the smile formed, it faded. "Tell me what you mean by strength."

Cain swayed on his feet momentarily. He wondered if it was a tremor or exhaustion. He felt faint. "May I sit?" He indicated the floor.

"No."

Cain smiled a little. Though he lacked any inclination to defend himself, he knew he was on trial. Hara might be listening for obsequious lies, but he would give her none. Not out of any desire to save his own life which seemed of less and less importance in recent years, but simply because it would require an expenditure of energy that, in this heat and gravity, seemed pointless.

"It's really very simple," he began. "Most cultures the Empire has encountered have been . . . less advanced technologically than our own. This has surprised everyone, but is true nonetheless. It is true here as well, but with a large, puzzling difference. Nearly every inhabited world I know of that has been contacted and assimilated into Terran rule has suffered a collapse of their indigenous culture; their institutions and traditions seem to break down as if suffering a certain failure of confidence in their own systems of belief. They are eclipsed by Terran technology and thought. There are some notable exceptions, but they are due, I believe, to the sheer alienness of the beings involved. There is no basis for an exchange of ideas, each race is and probably always will be completely inscrutable to the other. We exist in different modes.

"Here, you are not so different from us at all. You are humanoid and bear far more similarities than differences to human, Terran stock, but you are technologically backward. The Empire has encountered hundreds of races like you and by all indications the Dhirn and the Khaj should be fairly degenerate by now after one hundred years of Terran rule. We should have assimilated you easily, made broken puppets of you, but it is the reverse that is happening here. With the exception of a relative handful of Darkhani, your cultures remain idealogically autonomous. It is the Terrans who are suffering a collapse in confidence, a breaking down of organizations and systems. It is we who are falling apart here, not you."

Hara said nothing for a long moment after Cain fell silent. Cain suspected she was weighing his words, hefting them in her mind as if trying to detect the hollowness of patronization. He wondered why he interested her at all. As if in answer she said, "There is something different about you. I haven't seen it before in a Terran." He waited for her to elaborate. After a minute, she inhaled, cocked her head to one side, studying him, and then let her breath out in a long measured sigh. "You are like a man who has been aroused from a dream and the others of your kind are sleepwalking." She fell silent. After a moment she straightened her head again, "You may sit," she said.

"Thank you." Cain lowered himself to the floor with relief.

"Do you know what is happening at the cantonment?" she asked.

"I haven't been there for several days."

"As a result of Cristobal's lunacy, his mission to Giata, the Dhirn have risen against the Terrans. Among other things, they have destroyed the starship *Pandora*. The carnage is considerable. We are at war."

"You don't sound pleased. Surely this is what you have been preparing for here for some time." Cain accepted a small cup of water in a beaten metal chalice from one of Hara's servants. He drank gratefully. All too quickly, it was gone.

"No, I am not pleased. Only madmen like Cristobal are pleased with war. Oh, I am a warrior, and a leader of warriors, but that is by virtue of my lineage. I am from a long line of spiritual leaders. To the Khaj, battle is a path to God. I have no problem with that. Everything is a path to God. As a military strategist I may leave much to be desired by Terran standards, but here it requires little training—though I have it. The Khaj are natural fighters, if uneducated ones, they only need a . . . figurehead. My father is too old and he is blind from looking into The Eye of God, so I am their leader."

Hara paused. Cain sensed she was unused to speaking at such length.

"What bothers me," she looked at her hands as if they belonged to someone else, "is that the Dhirn are different. They are bad fighters. This insult to them was unforeseen. I cannot hope to lead a concerted attack on the Terrans now. I can only follow up the Dhirn's rashness and lay siege to the cantonment. I had hoped to drive them from our world, but now there is no means to carry them away from here since your starship is disabled. I must wipe them out or be their jailer until the next ship arrives. Then, of course, I must fight the Terrans that arrive at that time and I cannot hope to win against the weapons they will bring. No one can win this war, you see. But we will fight it anyway."

Hara sounded resigned, tired, yet resolute. She was not the wild-eyed fanatic Cain had half expected. Nor was she the cynical opportunist he feared. She was simply caught in the center of a web of destiny she could only hope to influence in its details. She could be the author of her planet's epitaph, if only an unenthusiastic collaborator in its destruction. Still, Cain thought, history might well note as an aside, based on dispatches by the likes of Nigel Wilson, that Hara led a suicidal holy war against all odds. This would be a paltry approximation of the truth, but Cain was far too versed in the machinations behind recent recorded history to expect more accuracy. Still, he could hope to be wrong. It was one of the few kinds of hope left to him that had any basis in reality. He wondered if he was expected to say something. "Because battle is a path to God?" he asked.

"I think I already mentioned that everything is a path to God. Did you listen to Raith's teachings so selectively?" She did not wait for an answer. "I hope not. Raith is a devout Dhirn. More so than I am a devout Khaj perhaps. There is a kind of perfection in you selecting him as a teacher." She said it distractedly or regretfully and then, "But there is a perfection in everything. Whether it is seen or not." Cain could tell she believed it, but he sensed she was unhappy that it was not *her* idea of perfection one could see in things. "Would you care for some Khaj liquor? It is basically distilled Dhirn wine with a mild hallucinogen called *upaya*. Sometimes it refreshes, sometimes, I find, it only . . . complicates things. It's up to you."

"I would join you, though I wonder. Do you always offer your prisoners such amenities?"

"I do not intend to poison you or drug you. You are not important enough. You are different from most Terrans. Like me, in some ways. Everything, to you, seems to be a . . . lesson in something or other. No? What I would like to know is what *you* know." Hara rose and poured two glasses of red liquid into metal cups.

"What is that?" Cain asked.

"That we, as Darkhani, are strong somehow, and that the Terrans are weak."

"I didn't say the Terrans are weak. Outnumbered, yes." Cain drank. the stuff tasted like sweet alcohol, nothing more. The kind of drink he found disappointingly common on too many worlds. Still, it was pleasant. "That's not the point, is it?"

Hara stood over him. He looked up at her and felt a surge of unbidden blood flowing in unaccustomed places. His desire for women had been long dormant and he did not welcome its return now. Especially not now with this distorted muscular caricature of a female human towering over him. She said, "What *is* the point?"

"God," he said, invoking something like an old chestnut, a safe fantasy that would steer him away from the rocks on the shore of this conversation. "Or Gods, whichever you prefer." The drink had gone to his head after all.

"Ah," Hara breathed. "God or religion? Strange word: re-ligion," she pronounced. "A Terran word."

"Yes. But, that's the thing, you see. With Terrans it is religion, an area of study, theory, dogma, faith, duty. An abstraction several times removed from the heart. With the Darkhani it is . . . something else. More along the lines of, say, breath, functioning, eating, making love, surviving. Surviving! Life itself. Your God lives. Ours dies for a living. Bleeds. It seems so limited a thing for a god to do, in the end. Bleed and die."

"There is rebirth in your religion, no? Eternal life."

"Not in a literal sense. There is a vague promise of reward and punishment."

"So I've heard."

Cain roused himself from the profound tiredness that had nothing to do with his recent trials. "But you don't want to hear about Terran religion. You've heard enough and I don't have much to say about it anyway."

A servant appeared in the doorway. Hara did not

look at him but spoke as if to Cain. "Bring Raith and the boy to The Eye. We are on our way."

"The boy—Avery." Cain said.

"Yes. You and he are to be witnesses. I will show you Alaikhaj the way no Terran has seen him. It is for my own purposes. I wish the Terrans to know what it is they have set about destroying here. Come with me."

Cain rose and followed Hara out of the chambers up a flight of steps and into the overcast day. They crossed an expanse of flat rock punctuated with carved obelisks the height of a man. Wind and sand had worn the glyphs on their surface nearly smooth over the years, but Cain could still make out the angular, stylized figures of stick men with halos or coronas. He asked about them and Hara shrugged. "They are ancient. It is said they were carved by the angels that live in the heart of Alaikhaj. They have always been here."

As they approached the base of the great jutting stone that resembled a needle from a distance, Cain felt a gathering awe traverse his spine. The giant obelisk was carved from living rock with tools that must have been far beyond the technical grasp of the Darkhani. The stone was sheared at angles with a proportion and precision that spoke of power sources that would be proscribed, even if they were available to the Khaj or Dhirn.

Only a starship with light weapons could have formed this structure. A starship with lasers in the hands of master artisans and not soldiers, for the thing was a work of art on the order of a cathedral: a towering spire crested with a glowing white crystal enclosed on the top and two sides by stone. A needle with a huge eye containing the largest gem he had ever seen. Aerial holostills of the mysterious construction did not prepare him for the majesty and symmetry he beheld.

At the base of the needle they paused before an archway that opened to a narrow, winding staircase ascending the interior of the rock. Cain watched the approach of five figures across the plateau. In a moment he could see that one of them was Raith and the other, the boy, Avery. They were accompanied by two guards and the hunched form of an old Khaj whose black face was tattooed in a riot of color that mirrored the dyes in his robes.

"Your father?" Cain inquired.

"Yes. Juum."

When they had crossed the distance, Cain smiled at his friend and teacher. "Raith," he said.

"Martin Cain." Raith returned the smile. "I see you have managed an audience with yet another god."

"Silence." One of the guards prodded the Dhirn in the back with a springlance. The wind whipped at their clothes. Above them, clouds swollen with rain churned against each other.

Jack Avery looked up at Cain in recognition and nodded. Cain smiled briefly at the boy and decided he had not been mistreated. The boy seemed healthy though apprehensive.

Juum spoke. "Why do you do this, Daughter? You would reveal the heart of Alaikhaj to our Terran enemies and to a Dhirn?" He smiled as he spoke as if his daughter's decision pleased him greatly.

"Yes, Father. The man Cain will be a witness to what the Terrans have violated. The child may see what an adult Terran will not allow himself to and the Dhirn is a teacher. If Sivran is killed, which may already have happened, Raith, if he will, could take his place and unite the Dhirn again with our cause. With Darkath's veil of clouds between her and Alaikhaj, their sight will be spared. There should be no blindness. Will you conduct the Ceremony of Light, Father?"

"Of course. Follow me." Juum walked unhesitatingly to the stone spiral stairs, a path his feet knew well. At the first step he paused and turned toward Raith. "The stairs are carved from the living rock of Darkath. They are of a piece with the stone beneath your feet. It is no compromise for you to follow."

Raith nodded. "I understand. Thank you."

The guards remained at the base of the tower and Cain followed Juum. Behind him were Jack, Raith, and Hara. The walls were barren, worn smooth by countless hands that had gripped the sides for support up the steep stairwell. There was no light and they ascended in darkness for several minutes, climbing and turning at a slow, deliberate angle. At length, a soft blue light began to suffuse the dry air. The only sound was Cain's labored breathing and then Juum broke the silence.

"It would be best to pause here and allow your eyes to adjust to the glow of God's Eye." He stopped and Cain halted abruptly. Jack bumped into his back. "Remember that when you look into The Eye of God, The Eye of God also looks into you. Resist nothing that occurs. If there is pain or fear, remember it is only the phantoms of the mind clutching at itself. You will have no choice but to let go of it. The sooner you release your grasp on what you think you know, the less you will suffer. There is nothing in The Eye of God that can harm you. The danger is in you."

They resumed their ascent into the gathering blue-white glow, pausing twice more. When at last they rounded the final turn, Cain blinked at an archway above them that framed a pulsing spectral light that seemed to dim and brighten erratically with a dozen colors at once.

"I will go first and draw His Eyelid," Juum announced and climbed the remaining stairs. He seemed to dissolve gradually, slowly becoming one with the light he entered. Presently, the eerie, yet somehow inviting fluorescence dimmed to the tolerable intensity of any brightly lit room.

"Go on, Cain," came Hara's voice from below him. Cain put his arm on Jack's shoulder and climbed into the archway.

The room was circular, perhaps thirty meters in diameter. Two wide, gracefully curved stone pillars buttressed the vaulted ceiling that was lost to view. The space between them was open to the sky on two sides. Cain could see the planet stretching away to the horizon in every direction except the extreme north and south where the huge curved pillars blocked the panorama of sky, desert, and mountains. They stood on the highest point on the planet. In the center of the chamber was a circular pit, ringed by a jewel-encrusted wall that rose to the height of Cain's waist. Embedded in its center was the base of a colossal, faceted crystal that was the source of the intense illumination. Cutting off the view of the mass of the semitransparent stone was a great dragon hide tarpaulin suspended by ropes and pulleys that could be drawn or rolled back to the walls of the pillar behind them: God's Eyelid, undoubtedly. Cain could not guess at the mass or dimensions of the mammoth stone that was Ayeia Alaikhaj. Nothing in his experience or imaginings prepared him for the sheer, mind numbing size of the thing. How it was formed, where it had come from, he could only guess at crazily.

"The outer edge of The Eye," Juum was saying, "is of another order of density than the center." He began to walk around the jeweled wall that contained the colossus. Cain followed and behind him, Jack. Raith remained next to Hara and he could hear the Dhirn reciting a low prayer in dialect. "Anything on the surface of Darkath for a week's journey in any direction can be seen by looking through the edge of The Eye, even that which appears to be beyond the horizon." Cain now noticed the stone monoliths that surrounded the wall, each rising gradually higher than the next and each one with finely worked ladders of bone and puhl-calf fixed to its side. As Cain followed Juum around the curve of The Eye and a medium sized block came into sight, he saw a Khaj, formerly of the Terran cavalry judging by his uniform, perched on one of the risers and watching something in the crystal intently. Hara appeared behind Cain and spoke rapidly in Khaj to the sentry who raised his spread fingers to his eyes and climbed down.

"Go ahead, Cain," Hara indicated the narrow platform. "He is watching the northern reaches of Nijwhol where my troops have intercepted a Terran convoy bearing the solar collectors." While Cain climbed the short ladder, Hara conferred with her sentry and seemed satisfied.

At first Cain could see nothing but the steady glow of prismatic light. As his eyes moved over the surface of the crystal, the opaque quality of the thing gave way to transparency.

"What do you see?" asked Juum.

"My . . . reflection," Cain said slowly. While it was himself he saw as if in a mirror, there was an unsettling quality to the image he could not, at first, identify. When it came to him, it did not dispel the uneasiness. The facet of the bizarre stone he looked at presented his image faithfully, but it reflected nothing else, not the wall of the pillar behind him or the view of the desert over his shoulder or even the carved rock on which he sat. He saw himself sitting cross-legged in a sea of light, as if he were floating. "I see myself."

"Of course," Juum said as if that was not what he meant, but an acceptable answer nonetheless.

"Is that all there is to it? I look into The Eye of God and all I see is myself? This is certainly more than just a trick mirror, I trust."

"It is Ayeia Alaikhaj. You will see what you will see. For many, looking into The Eye of God and seeing only oneself would not be a disappointing thing but a cause for marvel. Still, continue to look. It is, of course, more than a mirror. It is a telescope, an observatory, you would say, a magnifying glass that enhances the image of the world and the soul, a cosmogram, a psychocosmogram and just a bloody big rock, too." Juum laughed. "Go on and look, Martin Cain. You have traveled a long way to see as God sees.

Look into His Eye. You will be the first to blink, I assure you.''

Cain stared hard into the surface of the light, but could not seem to gain visual purchase on what was before him. The nagging thought that he was being played for a fool of some kind danced at the corners of his mind. He tried to banish the notion and concentrate. His mind seemed to race, flitting from one image to another. He breathed slowly through his nose, expelling his breath in measured cadence through his mouth. He tried to empty himself, simply *be*, without expectations. He heard Juum's retreating voice behind him as the old man moved away, ''Whatever you focus on will expand.''

Cain wondered if these were operating instructions or just general philosophical advice.

The former seemed a promising avenue of experimentation and he chose a small circle directly at eye level to scrutinize. Still breathing evenly, slowly, relaxed, he found he was seeing clouds on the eastern horizon moving with a hurried grace as if he were viewing them from the porthole of a ship entering the atmosphere. He could almost reach out and touch them. He let out a small sound of delight. The sensation was like a dream of flying. With a slight effort that was somehow without effort, he adjusted his perspective a few degrees downward. Now he was seeing the floor of the Nijwhol basin. Sand flowed in swirling opalescent patterns, driven on the winds, repeating the roiling ballet of clouds overhead. The illusion of flying was more pronounced now as he flowed over the landscape at will, kilometers of scouring sand rushed beneath him, fell behind, rose up toward him. He thought he should feel the wind, but on the heels of that thought came the realization that, in a sense, he *was* the wind. He reveled in the experience, felt impossibly light, unfettered, unlimited. It occurred to him that he could travel anywhere in this way, all he had to do was think of where he wanted to go and . . .

Smoke whipped by fierce air currents swirled up from the desert. Black, oily smoke that streamed like vaporous blood from the ruins of Terran hovercraft. To either side of him and below him, dragons wheeled, dove, and lifted away from the scattered train of the Terran convoy. Cain could see the riders leveling their rifles at the remaining pockets of soldiers below them, huddled beneath hovercars, drone vehicles, and equipment sleds. Solar panels tumbled across Nijwhol like crumpled rectangles of paper. From the rifle muzzles, small silent flowers of fire blossomed. During brief lulls in the sandstorm's fury, in the wake of reeling walls of sand, Cain could see the dead scattered like stick figures, broken, charred, posed in aspects of flight, still clutching weapons. The bodies of fallen dragons punctuated this motif at intervals. There must have been several hundred dead or wounded, Terran and Darkhani, but mostly Terran.

He was watching a massacre.

Abruptly he was back in the vaulted chamber staring at himself in the blue, glowing glass. Hara's voice behind him seemed small and incongruous, the voice of a child rather than that of a commander who held the leashes of such destruction. "Is it over?"

Cain turned and met her eyes. He thought he saw her begin to step backward, check herself and stand fast, but he could not be sure. "Why don't you look for yourself?" he said. "A glorious victory."

"Yes." she said. Her voice once again contained her customary surety. "I know what 'glorious victory' looks like."

"Look, damn you!" Cain rose and pointed at the crystal.

"Very well."

Cain came down from his perch and Hara climbed the ladder. She looked into the gem, dimming now with the failing daylight. Cain watched her for several moments until she turned away. She remained seated, her head averted and her eyes closed.

"Does it look prettier through The Eye of God, Hara?"

She did not answer, but roused herself and climbed back down.

Cain moved to follow her, but she stayed him with a hand. "Remain here, Cain, and look into The Eye. Someone will come for you in the morning." It was not an invitation but an order.

"What about Raith, and the boy?" Cain gestured at his fellow prisoners, both of them perched on stone platforms and gazing slack-jawed into the dim, pulsing transparency.

"They are with Alaikhaj. I suggest you join them. It is what you want."

"How do you know what I want?" Cain asked without apparent anger.

"Your eyes are empty. Fill them." With that she turned and left him.

Juum remained behind. The Khaj Elder walked the circumference of the tower with a slender torch he used to ignite seven torchlamps set into the walls at intervals of ten or fifteen meters. As he did this, he recited a low, singsong chant that reverberated around the chamber and seemed to vibrate up through the floor and into the soles of Cain's boots. With each lamp that he ignited, Juum closed a colored glass window over the flame and secured it. With the onset of nightfall, the lamps' multicolored prismatic effect reflected in the great crystal, filled the room with rainbow shades that melded into one color that Cain could not name: a cross between amber and violet, but neither of those at all.

Completing a full circuit of the room, Cain selected another stone platform situated at what he estimated to be a middle height; close enough to Jack and Raith that he would not feel separated from them. He called each of their names and though he was less than a half dozen meters from either of them, they did not seem to hear. They were undoubtedly hypnotized as he had been during the illusion of flying. The word *illusion* was not quite right, though. This thing before him was not merely some oversized conjurer's device, but undoubtedly some alien artifact; a cross between an objet d'art and technological feat, possibly a monument or a shrine as well. Juum had said it was an observatory. This interested Cain. He wondered if it would function in this capacity with an overcast sky. What else had he called it? A "cosmogram" and a "psychocosmogram?" As he reached his perch he made himself comfortable and once again tried to gain some visual traction on the protean light source.

Within a few moments Cain was suspended in the light. It seemed to be made up of all colors at once and yet colorless. Confusion gave way to euphoria as he allowed the sensation of warmth and well being to envelop him like a radiant bath. He briefly wondered if the thing was radioactive and immediately realized he didn't care. Besides, he was inexplicably certain it was not.

His next sensation was that of euphoria giving way to satori. The light around him dimmed and he was once again floating, weightless and motionless in deep space. Distant and not so distant stars moved in a slow arc above him, below him, ahead of him, and behind him. He could see gas clouds and nebulae now, whole spiraling galaxies like powdered diamonds wheeling ponderously in their own dance while maintaining a harmonious motion with each other. He sought the single point of reference about which they seemed to move and understood at once that that point was himself.

This startled him and at once he felt panic. Satori fled. Where was he? What quadrant? Would he find his way back to where he belonged? Where did he belong? The questions rose in a silent clamoring inside of him and he groped for a sense of place. He picked a nearby star at random and focused on it. It rushed at him as if he were shot at it or it at him. He entered the field of white hot light, sucked on solar winds and screamed. . .

Patterns.

Jigsaw-kaleidoscope images. Fractured, distorted.

Himself as a child, not as he was, but as he remembered himself.

Alone. Afraid.

Cozuela.

Fires. Smoke, Pain. Blood. The bodies, all the bodies . . .

No. No. Nonononononononononoooooo.

Women. Soft. Good. Parades of faces and limbs and lips and thighs merged into one woman who was all women with a thousand faces and a thousand arms and legs like a daisy wheel of flesh dancing and spinning with a terrible grace and beauty around a tongue that darted from between her teeth like a spear and the jewel in her forehead flashed with the light of ten million suns.

Blind. He was blind. And then he was not because he could see . . .

The Coraxians probing him with lobster-eyed indifference. What he learned from them: the-universe-does-not-care. Is that what they knew? Is that what he was supposed to learn?

The campfires on Rigel. They cut his skin. He ate the poison. He danced and became . . . a beast.

To become a beast is to forget the pain of being a man.

Who said that?

Pain.

Fever. The sickness on Betelgeuse. So many dead. No more ships. Quarantine. How many? Thousands dead. Why?

Why?

WHY?WHY?WHY?WHY?WHY?

You know where you are, Cain. You've been here before. You're inside that little cage that is your mind.

What drug is this? No drug, Cain. You. Your show. All you. The Eye of God. Darkath.

God.

God?

He was in a fetal position, his arms clutching himself to contain everything. In his solar plexus was Darkath and her moon and red giant sun. His head was in a gas cloud near a red dwarf star falling slowly toward Alaikhaj. His feet were splayed over the scattering of stars being spit in slow motion from Puerto De Estrella. Everything was falling into him . . . he was growing to encompass . . . everything. This galaxy and the next rushed into him. Another, a fourth and fifth. They flowed into him between his legs. His belly grew and he felt the unutterable pain of the beauty, aloneness, longing, the love and silence and sickness and peace of a thousand million living souls. He was Mother. The Mother. A Goddess. The Goddess.

His loins erupted in pain and he threw back his head to articulate a howl into the blackness, but no sound came forth. He gave birth to the Universe, returning it to itself. He searched for a sound to articulate the beauty of the pain, the horror and joy and awe.

Laughter welled inside of him. Ghosts of tears. He put his hand in front of him. No hand. Laughter. No sound, but laughter. *Can't stop. Hysteria. Cosmic hysteria. Ha ha ha hahahahahahahaaaa!*

The sound burst from him in a deafening torrent and it was the sound of wind and rain and oceans and solar winds and great frozen glaciers jostling each other in decaying orbits around gas giants and the chitinous laughter of Cappellans mating and men and women screaming and singing and things unseen and things that were and things that might be and something, one thing *become itself.* One deafening, beautiful note that was every song, one song that contained vast eons of silence. His laughter. Him.

Me.

I.

* * *

The I that was Martin Cain and that was also everything else was equipoised between that what was behind his eyes and what was before them.

He *was* . . . wanting nothing, rejecting nothing.

He had passed through a scheme of disintegration from the One to the many and into a reintegration of the many to the One. He had reached the end of evolution while he contained its origin and its course. There was nothing to search for within or without.

There was nothing to achieve.

Still, he was curious. A pleasant curiosity in which patience was implicit. God contemplating himself at leisure.

Certainly he *was* God. Here were his angels. Dozens of them, showing him around happily. Beings. Alive. Small faces with sketched, unfinished features that hinted at childhood and play and endless stretches of time that fed back into itself. Something quite like men about them: faint brush strokes for limbs/wings that were mostly suggestion. Something of bilateral symmetry there. Perfect creatures, just the way they should be. So familiar . . .

He wondered where they came from and the answer was there.

Andromeda.

Cain searched himself for the source of that information. It came from a voice directly behind and midway between his ears. It was his own voice and yet it was not. It was silent and yet clear, unmistakable. It was as if he had searched his memory for the word "Andromeda" and part of him had whispered it to himself.

The "angels" did not call themselves such, nor did they call the place they lived "Andromeda." These were Terran words. They called themselves *Xi* and they appeared to Cain as luminescent hourglass shapes of gold-yellow light. At the top of this configuration was something that might be a head, but was not, at least in any conventional sense. What Cain saw was a rainbow fingerprintlike configuration that he knew was energy traces visible in the spectrum of light he could perceive. A dark trace of a raccoonlike mask could barely be discerned where the eyes should be. They were, basically, auras without bodies, evident only in a narrow band of light in colors from ultraviolet to orange to near white. The name they gave to Cain for the blindingly bright and hot world they inhabited near the outer rim of the Andromedan galaxy, orbiting a blue-white sun was something unpronounceable with a human tongue, but looked something like this in their written language.

$$\hat{\blacksquare} \, 0 \, \text{\frownie} \,) \approx \odot \blacklozenge \, \backsim \# \text{\texthookx} \, \mathbf{X}$$

To orient Cain, to make him more at ease with contact, they presented more familiar images, culled from Cain's memory and unconscious mind.

He saw an open door, much like the entranceway to The Eye of God chamber he had been led through sometime (days? hours? minutes?) ago. A voice, not human, but recognizable that sounded to Cain like a note blown through a fine glass instrument said, "Come and I will show you what must take place." He stood before a huge throne the size of the monumental Autarch sculptures on Altair I. The being seated on the throne was a riot of colors that never coalesced into any single shape or hue, but Cain had the overwhelming impression of power, vast, inconceivable, benevolent power. Around the being, at the foot of the throne was a moat of heartbreakingly beautiful green light.

Surrounding this throne in a wide circle, Cain counted twenty-four lesser—or at least smaller—thrones. At first he thought he was standing on a vast, featureless plain that stretched to infinity all around him, but then the horizons of his perceptions defined themselves more clearly and he now knew he was standing in a room that was a mirror image of the dimensions and pattern of the chamber at The Eye of God. But he was certain he was *not* in The Eye of God in any vital sense any longer. His body was there, *he* was on a world two million light-years away.

Cain saw the seven lamps set into the walls, the torchlamps Juum had ignited as he had chanted the appropriate invocation for The Ceremony of Light—or lamps identical to them. Around the center throne in the twenty-four lesser thrones were seated men with long beards, with flowing white robes and crowns of gold upon their heads that winked in the reflected light from the center throne and blinded Cain.

The image of the twenty-four bearded men shimmered, dissolved, and mutated into various visual patterns. One would become an infant squirming in the throne, another would look exactly like Cain's mother, still a third would revert to the hourglass aura mode and Cain knew these were Xi. He also knew that the rainbow profusion of warm colors he bathed in was a manifestation, a representation of the presence of Godhead and that he had never been away from it for a moment in his life. Even when he was covered in the ashes and blood of the thousands on Cozuela, in the darkest reaches of his own personal hell, when he had killed and killed and rutted with aliens in a bestial hysteria that had nothing to do with love, he had never been out of the presence he beheld now.

He had never been deserted. He had never been more than a heartbeat away from the primal harmony he searched for across nearly a million light-years. He had, he now knew, always been loved.

Cain tried to look away, lower his eyes in shame, relief, gratitude that he was forgiven, never tried, judged and damned. He tried to weep, but his grief and joy were beyond tears.

He tried to turn his face away, avert his eyes, but neither was possible. Instead, he hung in a kind of void he created for himself, a dark pocket of self spun from illusion, fear, ignorance, and shame. It was a place like a small, silent, and darkened room in a large house filled with light and voices. He had no idea how long he hid, but it seemed to him a long time and then he emerged. With an unacknowledged act of will he stepped from the shadows of himself into the light once again, like a shy child, drawn out and curious about the music and laughter at an adult party.

They were there. Waiting. Cain had the impression of patience on a scale he could barely conceive.

Another impression nagged at him, but he could not name it. Something frightened him here. Not the godhead vision, but something about the Xi themselves signaled a reaction of muted alarm. It was, perhaps, their sheer potential, their power. While they seemed benevolent, wondrous, even beautiful, he felt there was something dangerously unpredictable, something *random* or capricious about their nature that chilled him.

"We wanted you to see that your search has come to an end so that you will hear us without distraction." The voice again, was his own, but seemed also to come from each of the twenty-four entities that hovered around him. The thrones were gone. The trappings and furnishings of his unconscious mind, provided by mystical images from ancient scriptures, disappeared. There was only the Xi and the sea of crystal before him that the Darkhani called The Eye of God.

"You are on Darkath's moon," Cain said, bewildered, wondering what they wanted of him, at the same time desperately glad that they wanted anything at all.

"We have ships there that travel through the physical modes of space though very few Xi need to travel in this way. In the past one thousand Terran standard years we have made a series of accelerating evolutionary leaps and we continue to. We are in a boom phase of our species' development. Soon, very soon, we will completely master the physical parameters of existence. Already we have no enemies that threaten us, war is an embarrassment of the past. Our strength is in our complete lack of need to defend ourselves. Our technology, our ships, while incomparably advanced from your own, is already a worn-out encumbrance we drag with us out of the necessity to make our presence known to those who cannot perceive us in this mode."

Was it arrogance he sensed? "Why are you telling me this?"

"Because you are able to perceive us, you are willing to, you wish to, and so you make it possible. You must be our emissary to the Terran and Darkhani leaders. You must tell them the fighting will cease or we will prevent them from continuing their war and they will die as a result. It is a passive measure on our part. We have no desire for the deaths of any creatures."

Cain was not sure exactly what they could mean by this, but there was a more pressing question.

"Why? Why do you care what happens here . . . there. On Darkath? If what you say is true . . ." Cain was certain that he had been told the truth, but perhaps not all of it. ". . . why meddle in the affairs of ants?"

"Because the Darkhani are our descendants. They are also yours."

"What are you talking about?"

"Whom you call the Africans. They were wrecked on Darkath in their ship called the *Slovo*. That was some one thousand of your years ago. Just as the Xi were embarking on a new phase of racial existence. We had a small colony here. A seedship with less than two thousand colonists . . ."

The image sprang to Cain of Xi starships carving the needle at The Eye of God with laserlike tools, carving the network of caverns into the mountainside above Nijwhol. He saw them as they looked in their primary bodies. Albino white with pink, white, gray, or even black membranes over the eyes like the Darkhani. Colorless silver hair. Their bodies, of necessity had been artificially protected from the ferocity of their sun on their homeworld for millennia. Their eyes had evolved the protective membrane, but never truly developed what humans would term normal vision. Their eyes remained almost useless and it was the vision behind them that fueled their ascendancy as a race.

"It was, in a way, accidental, our coupling with your species. The forced landing of your ship coincided with a rapidly diminishing gene pool among our own colonists who had neither the fuel nor transphysical knowledge to leave the world called Darkath. The Eye of God was built as an observatory and method of communication with the homeworld. We could be apprised of events, but until recently we were unable to cross the gulf between galaxies. Once able to, it took us many years to locate the world. We investigated hundreds of planets with similar suns set in similar constellations. Meanwhile we learned that the crossbreeding of Xi and human—after certain homeokinetic biological engineering done on a survival basis (skin pigmentation, musculature, etc.), a process we were just beginning to master at the time—created a hybrid species that was uncannily suited for metaphysical or what you might call, spiritual evolution. The Darkhani, both Khaj and Dhirn.

"You have seen for yourself the beginnings of extraphysical knowledge among the Dhirn who can travel through the mass of the planet itself by means of certain promising disciplines not unlike your own Terran traditions: yoga, or what you would call shamanism, meditation, arresting the mind and bringing the will into harmony with the universe. The Khaj have misinterpreted over the centuries of chaos, but beheld nonetheless the visionary realm that is the sentient birthright. This they have accomplished with the artifact, The Eye of God, but beyond that they have come to know their primary, their sun, for what it is: a profusion of thought. It is the nature of all stars. This they have learned because their survival demanded it. It is the way of learning.

"Now you must take this knowledge to them, the Darkhani and Terrans both. You must be the forerunner of what is to come. Our destinies are linked. If you are unable to make this known to your people, we will render their weapons useless, isolate them, and their gradual discorporation and passing will be a suicide. We can show them the mythology of the future, the patterns we have seen, what should begin here.''

Cain was listening, enraptured. A dozen, no, a hundred questions sprang into his mind, but one surfaced with a clarity surpassing the others. ''Is . . . was that God that I have seen?''

The answer came in the quiet, authoritative voice that was recognizable as his own. ''You must no longer persist in asking, 'What is God?' It is more useful to ask yourself now, 'What isn't God?' ''

A silence stretched over the light-years, a silence comprised of all sound, past and future that was ever discerned by any thinking thing in any range of audibility. In this silence, Cain and the Xi simply *were* . . . with all the time in all the worlds.

And that was a fine answer to his question.

Still, there were others. Were the Xi, in spite of their magnificence and mastery of so much, in fact, mad? Just a little? Who was to say that a species so accomplished, so evolved, so *different* could not be subject to foibles and flaws similar to those that plagued every other creature born from the heart of a star?

Even if he had perceived a choice, Cain would have been willing to do what they wanted. There was a pivotal moment in the history of, not one world, but thousands, perhaps billions. The advent of the Xi universe would be ineluctable no matter what his choice. With the knowledge that, in the end, he might be ushering in nothing more than a new kind of evolutionary, existential imperialism, Cain told them, ''I will do what you ask.''

For what they had given him could never be taken away.

''Yes,'' was the response . . . as if there had never been any question.

He would.

Chapter Fifteen

"Tougher than a Rigelian's tit! Blood of my mother!"

While Hara was introducing Martin Cain, Raith, and Jack Avery to her God, Jack's father, Sergeant John Avery Sr. was busy rubbing at the dragon hide bonds that held his wrists against the metallic edge of his boot toe. Avery decided that at this rate he could cut through them in a few days if he could maintain circulation in his wrists, saw constantly with no breaks, avoid bleeding to death, dying of thirst, gangrene, severe muscle cramps and, of course, discovery. If he could manage to do all this, by that time his son might be dead and he would be too weak to walk out of there under his own power. He stopped sawing and cursed again.

"I have never in my life seen anything like this bleeding hide, I could make a fortune selling this stuff back on Cygnus."

"Plenty are," Chun pointed out from the shadows. "Cygnus and other places." Avery was heartened to hear Chun's voice. While it sounded weak, at least he was speaking. The ranking officer had maintained a disconcerting silence for several hours and the sergeant had wondered if the man was dead. It hadn't kept him from keeping up a running patter throughout the day, however. He spoke about the ripe prospects for a decent war on the planet, how armored hovercraft maneuvering tactics could be translated to a mounted dragon force with light armor weapons and how popular Chun was going to be with the ladies when they got out of there and fitted him with a proper eye-patch.

At last he fell silent and asked, "How are you feeling, Lieutenant?" Avery leaned back against the rock wall and flexed his fingers painfully.

"I feel like I've been thrown into a dungeon on some godforsaken hellworld for about a month or more."

"Ah. Well, it won't be long now. My boys will be watching for Hara when she comes or sends for me. They'll create a diversion and . . ."

"And what, Sergeant? You have no plan of any kind do you? You had yourself brought here with three of your men to get arrested with a half-baked idea of breaking your son out of here. You did this without any authorization and with no intelligence about the strength or deployment of the enemy." Chun didn't sound angry, only exhausted: the musings of a dying man contemplating his almost comical dearth of luck. "It is undoubtedly why you are as old as you are and still a sergeant posted to this backwater."

"No, sir." Avery explained patiently. "I asked to come here. Where else could a sergeant major command his own tactical company? Avery's Lancers they're called, as you know, sir. And me only a sergeant, like you say."

Avery shifted closer to the lieutenant. He could make out that the younger, Oriental Terran officer was still patiently rubbing lightly with his bonds against the jagged edge of a fissure in the wall. He seemed to put little exertion into it, as if he were doing it out of habit, an almost unconscious mannerism. He wouldn't get anywhere like that, Avery thought, though it certainly wasn't his place to say so. "Anyway," he continued easily, "there *is* no intelligence about this place. With all due respect, the brass don't know a bloody thing about who or what's up here other than it's bad news. It's a situation that requires, er . . . considered improvisation, you see. There wasn't time to clear channels and I know I done wrong, but I'm willing to take full responsibility.''

The lieutenant said nothing for a moment and stopped his absent, measured rubbing against the rock.

''Sir,'' Avery asked at length. ''You all right?''

''Shhh!''

''Eh?''

''Quiet.'' Silence. ''You hear that?''

''Hear what, sir?''

''Tremor. A big one.''

Avery strained for any sound other than the scurrying of beetles in the gloom and the steady drip of water from the ceiling into the pool at the center of the chamber. He might have heard a low, distant rumbling, like quarry machinery in the distance. ''Right,'' he said, ''I think I hear it.''

''It's louder than I've heard it before. The aftershock's going to be very big or very close. Maybe both and probably soon.''

''God's blood,'' Avery muttered. ''I won't be buried alive in this place.''

A rattling of chains and the ponderous screeching of metal against stone eclipsed any other sound. Both men blinked into a sudden riot of torchlight. ''Wait here,'' they heard a female voice say in high Darkhani.

It's her. The bitch! Avery thought. He brought his legs up beneath him and squatted, poised to act if the opportunity should arise.

Hara entered bearing a torch. ''Sergeant John Avery?''

''That would be me, your royal highness.''

''I am Hara Tian Aiakhan of the Khaj, priestess of Alaikhaj and commander of the combined Darkhani forces under the banner of Giata.''

''That's splendid, Ma'am, and I'm king of the bloody beetles here,'' Avery said.

Chun's laughter echoed mildly against the dank walls.

Hara moved the torch toward him, partially to make him flinch if she could—though he only squinted against the flame—and partially to mask her smile. "Your son traveled a long way to see you. I don't know why. You're not much to see."

"Where is the boy? If you've harmed him, I'll have your liver on the end of a lance on the cantonment walls."

"Your concern is touching, if somewhat late. You demonstrated no such paternal devotion when he came to you."

Avery said nothing. He studied her wide form, gauging her center of gravity to be just above her knees and registering the fact that the only weapon she carried was an ornamental dagger at her waist. *Ugly bleeder and that's a fact,* he added to himself.

"Jack is at The Eye of God. We have become friends of sorts. He told me of your God and now I am telling him of mine in the only way I can. He is fine. In no danger. I am releasing him with the man Martin Cain. They will be escorted back to the mouth of the canyons to make their way back to Terran lines. We are at war. Did you know that?"

When neither of them responded, Hara outlined the events of recent days concluding with the apprehension and slaughter of the Nijwhol convoy.

"Steady, Sergeant. She's lying." Chun advised him and reached out in the shadow to touch Avery on the arm, letting him know that his hands were free.

Hara played the torch toward Chun and the lieutenant scurried to replace his hand behind him before it could be discovered. "Believe what you like," Hara said evenly. "It doesn't matter to me. You are both prisoners of war, but at Jack's request I will have you brought to the compound aboveground, have your wounds dressed, and feed you. Jack wants to see you," she indicated John Avery, "before he is released."

Avery wasn't listening. He was frantically trying to figure a way to utilize Chun's new freedom of movement. That the woman Khaj had entered the dungeon alone and relatively unarmed was a mark of her arrogance and a mistake, he hoped, one stroke of luck for him. That Chun had at last managed to free himself somehow was another and if he could stall for a few moments yet another piece of luck could tip the scales. He began to talk, saying anything that came into his head, mixing fact with improvisational fancy.

"I haven't been any kind of father to Jack and that's certain. His mother was Cygni, you know, and while it's not exactly against military law, it *is* against the tenets of our church to mate with them. Well, I did anyway. I gave her whatever I could, tried to provide, but all I know is soldiering and she could never understand that. She wanted me to desert the army and herd pilders up at the pole where they'd never find us. I couldn't do that, you see, and she turned me in to the local padres for committing the sin, technically, of bestiality—or sexual fraternization with a nonhuman species. That's all rot, of course, the Cygni are as human as you or I—er, as me and the lieutenant—but it's because of the psi thing that the church says they're more like animals with instinct instead of regular brains. Anyway, the priests had a word with my C.O. and the next thing I know I was up on charges. She'd connived to have me thrown out of the army figuring I'd have no choice but to milk those great stinking beasts in the freezing cold on her father's land. That's no life for someone like me, so I asked to be sent here. No one in their right mind asks to be sent to Darkath, with all due respect, Your Worship. Well, if I did harden my heart a bit toward young Jack and leave him without a proper old man, I reckoned I was doing the lad a favor, see, because I just wasn't cut out for it and when he showed up here, I thought, God's blood, the best thing I can do for him is to send him packing. . . ."

"Shut up, Sergeant." Chun croaked in a voice that was a study in weak, dying breaths. Avery noted that he sounded much weaker than he really was. "You're talking too much. Do I have to remind you that this is the enemy here. Any information, no matter how seemingly harmless, is out of order, a violation of the San Miguel Prisoner of War Conventions."

Avery paused and played along. "Well, the way I figure it, sir, is that we aren't at war, strictly speaking. This is a mutiny or a police action, you might say."

Hara suspected that they were up to something. The banter was too calculated. They were stalling, but for what, she didn't know.

In the next moment she had her answer. The walls of the cavern trembled and the floor shifted beneath them. The pool behind her erupted, spraying all of them with foul, stagnant water. The tremor shook them violently and she sensed a sudden movement next to her where the lieutenant lay.

She turned to see what Chun was doing as she spread her feet apart to steady them. Rock fell from the ceiling, along with a fine silting of crushed stone. As she turned, she saw Chun had both his arms free and was attempting to rise to his feet. She felt the two hundred-pound form of John Avery as he launched himself at her, burying his head between her lower thighs and pushing off the wall with his feet. She staggered backward, dropping the torch, but kept her feet under her despite the bull-like charge of the sergeant. She felt arms around her neck, slippery with blood from the lieutenant's recently eroded bonds. The three of them swayed, bucked, and struggled together as the floor beneath them seemed to sink a full inch into its bed of granite.

As she went down to her knees, she pulled the knife from her belt and lodged it firmly into Chun's side, just between the ribs. She turned the blade and the lieutenant fell away from her with a soft, surrendering expulsion of breath. Avery had gotten to his feet somehow and planted a kick to her right arm that sent the knife sprawling across the floor. She took hold of his boot and twisted until he fell beside her. Immediately he scrambled on his knees toward the fallen, smoldering torch and thrust his wrists, still bound behind him, into the stuttering flame. He screamed as his flesh burned and the dragon hide seemed to melt and elongate, searing into him.

Hara was on him and tried to wrench his hand in a neck-breaking turn that Avery resisted only by moving with it, relaxing his shoulder muscles. The thongs that bound him were now sufficiently charred and weakened that he had a full half meter of hide between his hands. He brought it under his feet and up. It caught on his knees and he pulled painfully. He had no feeling in his hands, but brought them up over his head and wrapped the hide around Hara, crossing his wrists beneath her neck. He pulled crosswise, bringing every muscle in his upper body into the effort. Hara brought a fist up into his crotch and Avery saw black, his groin and stomach filled with pain, robbing his chest of air.

The door to the prison chamber burst open and a single figure stood silhouetted against a fallen torch that sputtered behind him next to a body. The figure paused for a moment, trying to see into the confused shadows of the cavern. An aftershock reverberated through the walls and more rock and dust fell. A fresh gout of water bubbled up from the newly tapped underground spring and extinguished Hara's fallen torch completely. A brief second before the cavern was plunged into blackness, Lance Corporal Virik of the Imperial Native Tactical Combat Force saw Ironblood Avery slumped in the arms of the Khaj woman who had to be Hara. He fired his rifle at the ceiling with one hand and pulled a magnesium flare from his utility belt with the other, tossing it into the far corner of the room. When the flare exploded with uneven light, he saw Hara rising in slow, strobelike movements. He took aim and fired. He let off three rounds and saw the woman clutch her right breast and right thigh. She fell backward.

Virik rushed to the fallen sergeant and, still leveling his gun at the prostrate form of Hara, lifted the Terran onto his left shoulder. Avery goaned and Virik paused long enough to see that Hara was motionless in a gathering pool of blood. He turned, still clutching his sergeant, and jogged out of the chamber.

On his way up the stone stairs he shot two rebel Khaj who rushed toward them with leveled rifles. He set Avery down next to the second one and examined him. Avery stirred, batting Virik's hand away from his chest.

"Get your hands off me. The bleeding spawn of the great whore punched me in the balls, that's all. I'm all right. Get that soldier's weapon, give it to me." Virik handed him a machine rifle and two spare magazines from the dead Khaj's belt. "What about Lieutenant Chun?"

"Everybody's dead down there," Virik announced simply.

"You got her? Good. I always said you were the best soldier on the planet, besides me. Too bad about Chun. Where's Corporal Riliawhatsisname?" Avery checked the action on the weapon.

"He's waiting at the top of the stairs. We set fire to some ammunition and they're all running around up there like kagras on *iravka*. We've got maybe a few minutes."

"Okay. Where's Jack?"

"He's in the tower, Ayeia Alaikhaj. We need a dragon."

"We'll get one. Where's Jara?"

Virik paused and fixed Avery with a troubled look. "He's with *them*."

"What is that supposed to mean? He's with *who*?"

Virik shrugged and looked away. "I mean he defected . . . sir. He's the enemy now."

The sounds of a high caliber machine gun firing explosive rounds echoed through the stairwell, deafening them. They ducked, but realized after a moment that no one was firing at *them*. "That must be Riliaviri-akikia, sir. We'd better go."

"Move it, then," Avery waved the muzzle of his gun upward, indicating he would follow. He noticed he was keeping the gun trained on Virik's back and moved it a few degrees left. He had to trust someone. Virik just saved his life and killed the rebel bitch leader. He couldn't ask for better credentials than that.

* * *

The Dhirn had overrun the spaceport, taken control of Darker Heights, and surrounded the Terran cantonment. The Terrans had fallen back behind the walls and created makeshift, but effective barricades of everything from sandbags, gutted hovercars and chunks of plasticrete to priceless pieces of antique furniture and musical instruments. Inside, there was enough water in the reinforced titanium cisterns to last for a week and enough preserved food for perhaps a month. The cantonment wells had been destroyed and warehouses of food burned. Now and then, Terran troops would make sorties into the streets of Darker Heights in hovercraft or groundcars to retrieve personnel who had been pinned down or cut off in rebel held territory. As often as not these sorties ended badly. While many of the Dhirn had evacuated the entire Terran area, enough remained so that the Terrans were still outnumbered almost two to one. Twenty-four hours after the uprising had begun, the Imperial colony and its surroundings were relatively quiet save for the occasional stuttering of weapons in an isolated skirmish, a belated explosion, like an afterthought, caused by the fires that raged throughout the night and the sounds of Dhirn shouting, dancing to native instruments and discharging weapons into the air.

In the Plaza of Those Who Sell Women and Boys, Sivran sat and ate from a bowl of steaming meal he shared with a Cappellan envoy sent by Jimenez. The envoy, whose name was Moumya, used two of her arms and pincers to hold the bowl as it was passed to her and two arms to gesture with as she spoke. Her remaining two appendages were folded beneath her in an imitation of the Dhirn squatting posture. Her bony, planed face culminating in a small, trumpetlike snout sucked up the Dhirn food noisily in an effort at politeness. Two antennae played behind her head nervously as armed Dhirn paced at her back, periodically making faces of menace or repulsion at the alien.

"The smell of death is everywhere," the Cappellan said. "Too many bodies. No facilities. Your people will become sick if they remain here. Your wells will be bombarded by Terran artillery. You have no alternative but to disperse or surrender, Sivran. I do not tell you this to frighten you or threaten you. I say this to save lives. I think you can understand that."

"Moumya, the rains will come; if not tomorrow, the next day. Do not presume to tell the Dhirn they will die of thirst without Terran help. Do not presume to tell us we don't know how to manage. And please do not presume to tell me that it is the Dhirn who are—what is the expression?—over a barrel here. We, too, have captured artillery, Moumya. We also have . . . the Khaj. Darkath help us." Sivran took the bowl from the Cappellan and offered her *iravka*. The alien turned her head sideways, considering the diplomatic imperative of ingesting the toxic stuff. Sivran laughed, "Do not feel obliged, Moumya," and withdrew the pipe from the envoy. If it were possible for the Cappellan to demonstrate relief, she would have.

"Jimenez wants only to put an end to the killing." Moumya said.

"Possibly. But it is Cristobal that worries me." Sivran smoked and then held up a hand as a Dhirn soldier came to him with news of Terran civilian prisoners. He instructed the soldier to escort the prisoners back to the free fire zone around the cantonment and to return immediately. The soldier looked disappointed, but gestured obeisance with his right palm over his chest. He returned his attention to the Cappellan who had certainly taken this in. "Tell Manuel it is my concern to minimize the blood as well and that it was a good thing to send you, neither Terran nor Darkhani, to speak with me. I approve. Tell him further that if he wishes the same thing truly, in his heart, to kill Cristobal. Send me his head and we will speak again."

Moumya fluttered her antennae and tried to stay Sivran, who rose to indicate the conclusion of the interview. "But Sivran, what you ask is impossible and it does not suit you, a being of peace and not war."

Sivran stood over the Cappellan who looked at the guards who closed toward her. He said, "A being of peace, yes. But it is a time of war. Cristobal is the enemy. His life for thousands, that is the exchange."

"And the Khaj priestess will then want the head of Jimenez," the Cappellan pointed out reasonably. "And this one," she gestured to one of his Dhirn guards, "will want the head of the Terran priest who offends him. And this one," she indicated his other guard, "then will want the throat of the Terran teacher who insults his children and what else, Sivran?"

"I understand you, Cappellan. It is war. That is something else I understand. And you would do well to believe that. What I am telling you is that now, today, the head of *El Raton* will buy peace with the Dhirn. Tomorrow, who knows? It may be too late." Sivran placed his veil over his face and turned from the envoy. The conversation was finished.

The Cappellan rose in three stages into an upright position, her rear vestigial carapace trailing agitated patterns of dust in the sand. She called after him, "Do you guarantee the Dhirn will cease hostilities if Cristobal is executed? It might be arranged."

Sivran did not answer but began his rounds, speaking with the wounded who had been brought to the brothel tents in the plaza.

As Moumya was escorted back to her hovercar bearing a white sheet of truce over the hood, she attempted again to elicit a promise from the Dhirn leader. "Do I have your word, Sivran? If I can convince Jimenez of a summary court-martial and to execute the colonel, will the Dhirn cease hostilities? Do I have your promise then, Sivran?"

The Dhirn diplomat turned to the Cappellan, looked at the twenty or so Dhirn who were studying him as eagerly as the envoy from the cantonment and said, "No." He disappeared into the brothel/hospital.

The clouds parted for a moment. The wind stilled. A few drops of rain began to fall onto the sands of Darkath for the first time in eighteen standard months. One year on Darkath. Through the bloodshot light of Alaikhaj the rain spattered the dust lightly: the color of wine and tears.

* * *

Cristobal cruised in the armored groundcar along the perimeter, noting with satisfaction the large number of fit civilians, including women and children, who manned the walls along with Terran regulars and loyal Khaj. The Khaj might prove to be a problem yet, but, he told himself, no sense in borrowing trouble; he would deal with that when the situation presented itself. The women and children stood by to reload weapons, deliver ammunition where it was needed along the walls and to make bandages, refill canteens and distribute food. Some were armed, others were not. At sunset he would order an artillery barrage on the wells in Darker Heights where the greatest concentration of Dhirn were sure to be and then, at the sound of the great guns as a signal, launch the aptly named *Salvadore* into orbit armed with air to ground missiles. Nothing too powerful, the targets were too close, but enough to reduce Darker Heights into a smoldering expanse of greasy sand. Once in place orbiting Darkath, Cristobal would have a gun to Hara's head as well. With a word from him, the *Salvadore* crew would strike at Khaj Point, or The Eye of God as they called it. To hell with the hostages. She would never call his bluff anyway.

While he was disobeying Jimenez who had ordered the *Salvadore* fueled and stripped, standing by to evacuate the eighty or so personnel it could carry, he was not overly worried. Jimenez was a defeatist and a fat coward. At the moment of Cristobal's victory, he would arrange for the commandant to fall prey to a stray bullet or perhaps an overdose of sleeping pills. Nothing would stop him from wresting victory from the jaws of Jimenez's certain defeat. Twenty-four hours from now, Eduardo Cristobal would be Military Governor of Darkath, the savior of the colony and warder of an entire native population.

He felt so good he ordered his *tirav* to stop. Making sure he was in plain sight of several dozen civilians, he greeted a small boy, perhaps nine or ten years old, who was carrying water from sentry to sentry along the wall. He asked the boy his name.

"Ricardo," answered the boy who looked up at him with a dirty face and exhausted eyes.

"Why, that's my middle name, soldier. Do you know who I am?"

"Yes, you're *El Raton.*"

There was a muted round of stifled laughter along the wall. Cristobal flushed and looked around angrily, noting a Khaj soldier who was too slow in covering his grin. He replaced the smile on his face though it looked gaseous and cold. "I am Colonel Eduardo Cristobal and I would like to give you this medal for bravery." He reached across his left breast and removed a medal that indicated a medium rating in supply administration. He had acquired it five years ago on an orbital station around Ixtaya. It reminded him of tedium and humiliation and he only wore it because of a conspicuous lack of other decorations except the ribbons denoting the years of service any officer received automatically. This would all change soon.

As he pinned the shiny, thin medal to the boy's shirt, Ricardo cried out. Cristobal had pricked him. Flustered and wishing to extricate himself from the scene as quickly as possible, he kissed the crying boy on the cheek and squeezed his hand, still grinning skeletally. "There, there, soldier," he said. "Carry on. You are now a member of my . . . uh, personal staff. A private in . . . er, Cristobal's Rangers. How does that sound?"

"Okay," the boy said quietly. "Can I go now?"

"Of course, Private Ricardo. Yes, er, carry on." Cristobal saluted briskly and the boy ran away into the ranks of women, undoubtedly toward his mother.

Cristobal climbed hurriedly back into his car and whispered in the driver's ear, "Bring me that Khaj there." He pointed to the soldier he had caught laughing. "Arrest him. Put him in irons as soon as I'm out of sight. I'll take the car."

The driver saluted and stepped out. Cristobal drove on hurriedly, gauging the hours until nightfall when he could implement his plan.

* * *

The earthquake-ravaged church housed over one hundred Terran and Khaj wounded and while there was a shortage of beds, many would die in the next several hours or certainly by dawn, thereby creating more space. Already, the mass grave behind the church was nearly full of sealed bags containing the bodies of fallen Terran and Khaj. Jimenez himself had donated his own bed and all the beds in the governor's house. The commandant was standing over an amputee along with Doctor Castro and Padre Katanya, offering the dying Major Xavier what comfort they could when the Cappellan linguist, Moumya, entered.

Jimenez turned to the disconcerting looking alien and nodded. "How did it go?"

Sensing the commandant had no objection to speaking in front of the doctor, the priest and the severely wounded human, Moumya got to the point. "I found Sivran at the plaza of whores. He wants Cristobal's head. If he gets it soon, he may be able to effect a peace, maybe not. He offered no guarantee."

Jimenez turned to Major Jacinto Xavier who lay grimacing with his eyes closed, sweat covering his face. "Did you hear that, Major? They want the colonel's head. Should we give it to them?"

Xavier opened his eyes, clouded with painkillers and said through gritted teeth. "They killed my wife, my son, and my daughter." He coughed. "They have killed me, too. Send them all to hell, Commandant."

Jimenez said nothing, studying the dying man's face. After a full half minute he called for an aide. One of Fioricci's men came running to his side and saluted. Still looking at Xavier, Jimenez said, "I want an artillery barrage directed at the coordinates of the brothel plaza. Level it."

"Yes, sir!" The aide saluted and turned on his heel.

"Thank you, Commandant," Xavier said and sank further into his pillow, relaxed.

Moumya raised a pincer, placed it on Jimenez's arm and said, "Sivran would not be foolish enough to remain there. The plaza will be evacuated by now."

Jimenez stared at the repulsive limb of the Cappellan where it touched him and tried not to flinch. "Still," he said. "That should be answer enough for them. If I take Cristobal's head, it will be for myself, not for a traitor." He turned and walked out of the cloying atmosphere of the church, filled with groans and the crying of men, women, and children.

As he supervised the digging detail outside the church, he heard the heavy guns begin their barrage and thought to himself, *That was fast.* Glad for an excuse to escape the stench of death, he placed a handkerchief over his nose and walked around the edge of the building.

He breathed in the fresh twilight air, unladen with corruption and noticed that it had begun to rain lightly while he had been inside. As he crossed the compound he noticed that the *Salvadore* had begun its ignition sequence. Cursing, he attempted to run. His massive bulk and the gravity conspired to halt him. Within twenty meters he was winded and succumbed to leg cramps. He shouted for the nearest staffer he could find, but his voice was drowned by the engines of the *Salvadore*, and the deafening *crump* of the cannonade. None of his men were in sight. He waved frantically at one of the Khaj soldiers who had formed a protective ring around the shuttle at a safe distance. The Khaj remained immobile. Jimenez watched helplessly as the shuttle lifted off into the gathering rain and the lowering night sky. Flames from its thrust lit the compound and dust and smoke obscured everything as clouds of it swirled around him.

He saw beyond the cantonment walls to the darkened native streets below. Explosions erupted everywhere. The artillery was firing at random targets and not concentrating fire on the designated plaza.

He walked slowly, limping from the leg cramps as he crossed the parade ground to the administration building. His uniform was soaked with rain now. By morning everything would be a sea of mud. His eyes followed the trajectory of the launched shuttle: a streak of blue-yellow fire diminishing into the night. A gathering rage suffused his neck and face with blood. Wheezing with exertion he paused in his tracks, lifted his head to the night, and with rain spattering his face he shouted to the sky, "Cristobal!"

Several of his Terran staff met him with a groundcar and he got in. He issued orders that Cristobal was to be found and brought before him. "I want a squad of armed men to meet me in front of the administration building. When you find Cristobal, arrest him and disarm him, of course. The charge is insubordination, treason, mutiny . . . I don't care. Charge him with bad breath.''

Cristobal was in the communications center speaking with the pilot of the *Salvadore* when nine Terran soldiers arrived. The squad leader, a man named Kozlowski who was perhaps twenty-two years old, stepped inside and touched his helmet with his right hand in deference to the colonel's rank. He did not salute. He also did not draw a weapon. "Colonel Cristobal, I am to place you under arrest for insubordination. Commandant Jimenez's orders.''

Cristobal looked at the boy and smiled humorlessly. "Jimenez's orders are meaningless. I am relieving the commandant of command on Darkath.'' Outside, the steady *crump* and hollow *pooong* of the artillery delivering their outgoing shells sounded a counterpoint to the fitful falling of rain.

Kozlowksi looked back and forth from his men to Cristobal's men who numbered nearly thirty in and around the communications building. "Uh, sir, I must follow my orders from the ranking officer of the colony, the military governor . . .''

Cristobal drew his pistol and pointed it at the boy. Several of Cristobal's men, some of them Khaj, drew their weapons. The nine-member squad sent by Jimenez were completely covered. They stood by while the colonel's men disarmed them. Cristobal then waved his gun under the nose of the boy and said, "*This* is the military governor of this colony. Keep your hands raised and turn around. It seems that the time has arrived to persuade *El Gordo* of his retirement. Let's go.''

Forty men walked through the rain across the compound to the leaning administration structure now pouring mud from its broken ground floor windows that only an hour ago had been filled with the crests of sand dunes. The nine squad members marched ahead followed by Cristobal's men. Jimenez saw them approach and quickly assesed the situation. He stood with a dozen men; he did not think more would be necessary, but like so many other of his decisions on Darkath, he had once again been proven wrong. Jimenez had dispatched all possible personnel to vital positions during the emergency, it hadn't occurred to him that he would need to retain a small personal army against Cristobal's treachery. He quickly ordered five riflemen to take up positions in the upper windows of the building. He also sent a runner to order the cease-fire of all artillery.

Cristobal's party halted twenty meters in front of the muddy steps where Jimenez's soldiers stood. Cristobal ordered his men to fan out. They did until Jimenez shouted, "No one move!"

Cristobal's laugh came in reply through the chorus of rain and the erratic cannonade. "I see you have seven clerks armed with pistols, Manuel. I think you can see you are no longer in a position to give orders to me." He gestured at his men. He then ordered the nine prisoners to lay face down in the mud. "I am relieving you of command under section 78 of the Galactic Military Code. You are, in my estimation, disabled, Manuel. You are under the influence of drugs and drink during a time of combat crisis. Your decision-making ability is impaired to the degree that your command is endangered. I have, after painful deliberation, decided to take the necessary steps to insure the welfare of the Terran presence on Darkath. As second in command, I am well within my rights to do so. Please lay your weapons down and join these boys of yours. We will take a short walk to the detention facility where you will be treated as well as possible for the duration of the emergency."

A number of responses presented themselves to Jimenez, among them, "You won't get away with this" but he could not bring himself to utter such a banality.

Instead, what he said was, "What do you hope to accomplish by this, Cristobal?"

"I intend to bring the Darkers to their knees in the next twenty-four hours and keep them there. I can do it with the shuttle armed and orbiting. Your way is the path to disaster with possibly eighty survivors who will run out of fuel before they ever reach the edge of this system. You think small, Manuel. You think like a loser. You don't think very clearly at all, do you? How can you when you gobble pills like an old woman and drink like a swine and wallow in memories of your past dubious glories on San Miguel?" The outgoing barrage from the field guns suddenly stopped. A look of controlled anger crossed Cristobal's features. There was a momentary lull in the rain.

"You will hang, Cristobal." Jimenez said, "if this planet doesn't kill you first."

Cristobal laughed once more. "Come on, old friend. Let's get out of this weather."

Before either of them could speak again, the sky turned a bright white. The heavens were illuminated in a lingering flash that turned the night into day for a dozen heartbeats. Both men looked up and then met each other's eyes. They knew it was not lightning.

Cristobal was the first to break the silence. He watched a sputtering flame fall in a slow arc across the moonlit cloud cover. His voice was a ragged scream, "The shuttle!" he cried out. "The shuttle has exploded! God's blood! What. . . ?"

A shot rang out from one of the upper windows and Cristobal danced back several feet as the puddle in front of him sprayed mud and water into the air where the bullet struck it. Within a fraction of a second two more shots sounded from the upper floor and one of Cristobal's Khaj guards fell face forward, clutching the pistol he had aimed at the rifleman he had spotted above. The prisoners lying between Cristobal's men and those of Jimenez got to their feet and scrambled in different directions. Bullets whistled through the compound. The sharp repeating crack of gunfire and the chunk and thud of bullets hitting the administration building seemed muted by the thundering rainfall that had begun again.

Cristobal and his men were completely exposed to the fire from the upper windows, their only protection being the darkness and the rain. Jimenez and the men to either side of him took shelter in the mud behind the ground floor windows. They picked off three more of Cristobal's men before he called for the colonel to throw down his weapon. The reply was another burst of machine gun fire from the muddy compound.

The runner Jimenez had sent to order the artillery cease-fire returned in a groundcar armed with a rocket launcher and further equipped with a floodlamp. As the car approached Cristobal's position from behind, sending fountains of water from shattered puddles to either side of its great tires, the floodlight illuminated Khaj and Terran soldiers, both alive and dead, sprawled in muck at five-meter intervals to each other. One of the prostrate forms turned and fired a quick burst into the light. The compound was plunged again into darkness as quickly as it had been illuminated a moment ago. This caused a renewed crescendo of fire from both sides. Tracers whipped crazily through the darkness and rain. The rocket launcher on the car bellowed briefly. A flash and smoke from its back blast was visible for a second. In the next moment the field of fire between the car and the building became a nightmare of flying mud, metal and limbs. The explosion rocked the building and set the groundcar rolling backward several meters.

Silence, save for the rain. Running men and groundcars converged on the scene. Lights, voices, hesitant gunfire. When Jimenez emerged from the building, he ordered lights trained on the carnage in front of him. There were six badly wounded survivors of Cristobal's coup. The others were scattered in pieces mostly too small to identify.

"Where's Cristobal?" Jimenez shouted, "Find him!"

Lieutenant Kozlowksi called to him from a short distance away. "There's no trace of him, sir. But he couldn't have survived that rocket. There are . . . remains . . . all over the place. Some of them must be the colonel's." With that the young man clutched his stomach and doubled over as he retched.

"Find me something. Anything that might be Cristobal's. I won't believe he's dead until I see his teeth or his cojones. A piece of his uniform, anything."

They searched the compound until daylight, but found nothing that might be the remains of Eduardo Cristobal.

Chapter Sixteen

Amalia Dubois and Padre Gillermo stood at the crest of the mountain peak they had spent the day climbing. They stood in the high winds far above the sands that had assaulted them for most of the climb. They were bruised and bloody from falls and the punishment of the wind and rocks. One of their dragons had been killed in an avalanche and Gillermo had almost plummeted to his death astride it. He had clutched at a ledge and Amalia had thrown him a rope tied with scarves to pull him up. After that, they lashed themselves to the remaining dragon and negotiated the steep ascent against the wind. For hours they had battled the powerful mass of air that rushed downward from the mountaintops into the canyons while their dragon danced, hovered, was driven downward, losing precious meters they had gained and then slowly, with diminishing strength, gained purchase once again with its talons, steadying itself with its wings.

By midday they had yet another two kilometers of mountain to battle with an exhausted, old mount that seemed reluctant to continue and they despaired. They made themselves as comfortable as possible on a broken ledge barely large enough to hold them and then the wind died. It seemed they might make it on their own if the dragon were unable to continue and as they began to untie themselves from the beast, a sudden updraft from the long tunnel of canyon below and behind them, stirred the animal to its feet. It spread its wings and scooped once at the wind at their backs and once again began to climb. Amalia and Gillermo hurriedly remounted and the remainder of their upward progress passed with relative ease.

Now at twilight they stood on the sheer edge of Darkath's mountain range and looked out at the vast, featureless gray of the Nijwhol basin. It was as if God's creation of this world ended at this craggy line of high ranges and nothing but chaos, void, or antimatter existed beyond them. Amalia, despite all her efforts not to, clutched Padre Gillermo and began to cry. "We're going to die out there," she said.

Gillermo held her large frame with both arms and with bloodied hands patted her back. Even before he spoke, he knew how hollow the words would sound; nevertheless, he said them. "If it is God's will."

As abruptly as she had broken down, she stiffened and composed herself. "We must let the dragon rest. I can't go on myself."

"Yes," Gillermo agreed, "But just for a little while. The winds could blow us over the edge if we fall asleep here. We'll take an hour. If the dragon will not carry us down, we must find a passage ourselves."

And so they waited. As they sat in silence, the rain began to fall. Gillermo took inventory of the meager supplies he had managed to salvage from the ill-fated expedition. Five liters of water, enough dried food for perhaps three or four days if they ate little and, of course, the flare gun and Amalia's machine pistol. Gillermo had three flares, several pellet charges, and some smoke canisters. Amalia had two magazines of ammunition.

During a lull in the downpour, the clouds parted to the west and a patch of the Nijwhol basin to the north was bathed in a fiery rose color. Gillermo sat and stared at the beautiful play of light in the distance for some moments before he rose to his feet and shouted, "Amalia! Look!"

"What?" She got to her feet and looked to where he was pointing, but the sunlight faded and she could make out nothing except an almost indiscernibly lighter shade of umber that separated the sky from the horizon.

"The sandstorm. The wind has scoured patches of the basin clean of sand. I saw areas where the bedrock was exposed and there, far to the north on the horizon, I saw an irregular mass. Several . . . shapes . . . huge. Big enough to be the exposed wreckage of the ship I had hoped to find."

"Are you sure? It could be anything from this distance," Amalia sounded exhausted, but curious.

"Yes, but you see, there is nothing that size in the Nijwhol basin, not even a mass of boulders. At least that I'd ever heard of."

"Padre, even if we were to survive long enough to get there and even if it was your fallen starship, how would we return? How would you tell anyone about it? You have nothing to document the discovery."

Gillermo sobered. "That's true. But I traveled a long way to see this." He fixed Amalia with a challenging look, "And you came a long way out of your way to accompany me. If I am to die on this world . . . out there, I would like it to be after setting my eyes on the thing."

Amalia nodded. They agreed to set out at once, but the dragon had other ideas. Neither of them could rouse it from a deep slumber for another two hours. They sat in the rain, crouched under the foul-smelling right wing of the dozing beast which offered some protection, and Amalia recounted to Gillermo one of her colonial epics. It was a tale about a plain Altairan shopgirl who runs away to a small planet where she becomes queen of a race of golden-skinned, lotus-eyed men who adored her. The tension of the story seemed to reside in which of her languid suitors she would marry. Gillermo grunted and nodded and tried to keep his impatience and exhaustion from showing. Before she could come to the end of her story, the dragon raised its eyelids and bellowed hungrily, befouling the air around them for several meters.

"Come on," Gillermo mounted up. "Let's hope the beast can at least get us to the floor of the basin in one piece. I don't know how far it will go without food."

Dubois hurried onto the animal's back and dug her heels into its sides. The dragon unfurled its grayish-brown wings and arched on its legs. The animal turned its head sharply and spit a steaming gob of decayed vegetation at a nearby boulder. Amalia lifted her veil against the smell. Catching wind beneath itself, it lifted ten, then twenty meters, circling slowly. Amalia jerked the reins and pointed the beast's nose downward. They began to fall precipitously away from the edge of the mountain. The dragon rode a slight current that kept them from plummeting out of control, but they both hung on for their lives as they lost altitude at an alarming rate. Rain pelted them like buckshot. Gillermo prayed out loud. Amalia let out a long shriek that became a laugh. "By God's breath, this is fun, isn't it, Padre?" But the priest had his eyes shut, working an obsidian rosary through bloodless knuckles as he moved his lips.

The dragon leveled off after a full minute that seemed endless to Gillermo. They landed in pitch darkness on the floor of the Nijwhol basin. Muddy sand and water covered their ankles when they dismounted.

"I'm completely turned around," Gillermo said. I have no idea which way is north, where I saw the wreck."

"Can't reckon by the stars either in this weather. We'll have to wait till daylight." Amalia had to raise her voice over the din caused by tons of rain falling onto a shallow, but vastly wide puddle all around them. Gillermo agreed miserably and they both climbed onto the dragon once again to sit out the remainder of the night. Both of them were soaked through to the skin, but the night was warm and the rain only cool.

In the morning, they could see the bluff they had launched themselves from the night before and both of them recognized the configuration of mountains stretching away to the north. They set out. The rain was a steady, light drizzle that renewed its efforts periodically to flood the basin. If either of them dismounted from the dragon, the water would now reach their lower calves. They traveled continuously throughout the day, each taking turns dozing uncomfortably.

The second day of travel found them with a dragon that refused to go on. The animal simply folded its wings, retracted its talons, and allowed itself to float listlessly whichever way the wind would nudge it. Amalia decided the thing was weak from starvation and was preparing to die. Gillermo could understand, his own stomach rumbled wildly and he could barely summon the strength to move his feet under him and against the drag of water that now reached their knees. Before nightfall on that day, Amalia and Gillermo began to see the bloated corpses and flotsam of the Nijwhol convoy massacre. Bits and traces of the expedition, a glove, a helmet, a canteen, an empty plastic ammunition box, a swollen, fish-eyed body of a Terran private riddled with bullet wounds bobbed slowly past them. "The war has spread outside of the cantonment . . . all the way to Nijwhol." Gillermo said.

"Then there might be hope that some of our people are out here somewhere." Amalia tried to sound encouraging, but she, too, was showing severe signs of weakness and stress. Already, the formerly rotund woman had lost several pounds and traces of gauntness could be seen in her face.

It was in the middle of the second night that Gillermo accepted the fact that they would die in the Nijwhol basin. More precisely, he accepted the fact that *he* would die and relatively soon. The source of the fear he carried with him in the recent years of his late middle age concerning his own mortality was, he realized, a profound lack of faith. He hadn't identified it as such, but now knew that he no longer believed what he had been telling himself he believed. Oddly, this did not seem to alarm him, he did not go into a spiritual panic. In fact, the idea of a long deep nothingness after death seemed welcoming, restful. It was, no doubt, a measure of his physical weariness that these thoughts came to him, but they came to him nonetheless and he did not resist them. He was ready to die.

It was all right. It did not even matter that he was suddenly certain, with the force of premonition, that the God he worshiped was a chimera, a projection.

Gillermo tried to embrace the inevitable with grace, but even that was impossible. He slogged hip-deep in rising water that set up a choppy swell against his chest. He tugged at Amalia who had fallen silent and tended to slip under the small waves every few meters. At one point, he reattached them at the waist with the dragon tether.

The priest was slogging along in a daze, remembering a game of gravity ball he had played back at the University thirty-some years ago, in which he had scored five consecutive points in his opponent's gravity field, setting a record for amateur ball fielders, when he stumbled into a wall of cool metal. Stunned, he fell backward into the water and floundered around for several moments before recovering himself and making certain that Amalia was all right. He leaned her against the surface he had walked into and began to grope his way along the object to get some idea as to its dimension and texture. It was very smooth, pitted only slightly in fine, carbon-scored grooves. It bore no markings or identifying characteristics, but Gillermo knew it was the wreckage he had spotted two nights ago from the mountain peak. It was certainly the hull of a starship and of Terran origin. He edged along its surface until he found a breach in the side. Calling out to Amalia to make sure she was all right and waiting for her tired, but enthusiastic response, "I'm all right. We found it, didn't we?" he answered her.

"Yes," he said. "Yes, we did." And then he shouted, "Yes!" and began to chuckle to himself. The chuckle verged on hysteria and he steadied himself. "Can you make it over to me?"

"I'll try," Amalia answered. Gillermo then cautiously entered the hole in the side of the wreck. He had to climb, lifting himself by his elbows, and he was inside. He could see nothing and when he lowered himself slowly down into the ship's interior, he sank into a meter of mud. He waited for Amalia and when her form blotted out the paltry glow of the moon from behind a dense layer of clouds, he helped her into what he guessed to be part of a cavernous cargo bay. They leaned against the wall together, surrendering to the ooze and silt they sank into. The sounds of dripping water and loose components banging into the hull as they floated echoed in the chamber around them. Gillermo put his arm around the woman and said, "We'll be safe here. We'll rest until it is light." Within a few minutes they were both deep in sleep.

They slept only a few hours and woke to the movement of the wreck as it shifted on its bed of sand due to the level of water rising around it. They shared rations of dried fruit and powdered meal and set out to explore the interior of the vessel. In the gray daylight Gillermo quickly confirmed that the ship was indeed one of the Dreadnaught class starcruisers of the African Imperial expansion period. The ship was called the *Slovo* and Gillermo estimated its age between 1000 to 1200 years. There was nothing left except the skeletal frame, some loose metal that had rusted or otherwise eroded away from the main structure, and the OG bonded hull that could have been made of any of a number of alloys the Africans employed.

Gillermo had no means of making any further investigation, even if he had the strength.

Still he (and, of course, Amalia Dubois—*sangre de santos* not even a *lay* archeologist, but a fabricator of shopgirl fictions!) was the one to prove the Africans had reached the outer edge of the galaxy! The other implications were staggering, but only speculation. Of course, he would never be able to prove it. Even if he were to survive this ordeal by some miracle, he would not be able to produce one shred of evidence that what he had seen, what he was now touching, was anything more than a fevered hallucination brought on by heat, exposure, starvation or simply ambition and wishful thinking. Gillermo knew he would never have to deal with this particular problem because they were certain to die here. The water level in the basin had risen another foot and was now filling the interior of the wreckage.

Amalia waded slowly over to where Gillermo was brushing with his sleeve at traces of some kind of writing on the hull. "Padre," she sputtered in the rain that dripped more steadily from the top of the wreck, "we have to get out of here. Maybe if we get on top of this thing it will buy us a few more hours. You can use your flare gun. Maybe there are troops nearby, close enough to spot one of the flares."

"Even Darkhani troops?"

"Padre, who cares?"

They found an open hatch with rungs leading away from it to either side and climbed out into the leaden downpour. They resembled nothing so much as two survivors of a huge and overturned seagoing ship clinging for life to each other in a troubled ocean. Gillermo took his flare gun and fired into the sky. The missile rose, sputtered, and ignited high above them. They watched it fall in silence.

They waited. After perhaps an hour, Amalia insisted they try again. Gillermo fired his second flare and again they watched its erratic descent as it was buffeted by winds and rain.

After the second flare, they allowed nearly two hours to pass and then Amalia nodded at him. The waters sometimes closed over the top of the ruined vessel. They had no more time. Gillermo fired his last flare. He began to pray, more for Amalia's comfort than his own. His life had been fulfilled in a way, though not in the manner he had envisioned. He was not frightened or empty. He only felt a sadness, a sense of personal loss . . . all the beauty in all the worlds he had known . . . to think that it was over. As he prayed, Amalia prayed with him.

After a time, she spoke. "It would be a miracle, wouldn't it, Padre? I mean, if any Terrans were to see our flare and rescue us, that would be a real miracle wouldn't it?''

"It would be miracle enough if the rain stopped," he replied after some time. He wanted to tell her the words he knew he should say, the words that were his office to recite. At least to tell her that their whole lives had been a miracle. They held each other to keep themselves from being washed away and he was about to say that it was all right and not to be afraid of death when something in the sky drew their eyes upward.

It was a light or a series of lights. Something huge descended slowly, a great winged shadow studded with blinding pinpoints of brilliance like a colossal jewel-encrusted bird. The sound of its engines was a high-pitched chorus that disappeared off the upper and lower registers of their hearing, resounded in their teeth, skulls, and bowels. The priest and the dramatist looked at each other in awe. They both knew it was a space-craft of some kind and they both knew it was unlike any they had seen or heard of before.

When the craft had lowered itself to within a few meters of them, blotting out the sky and the rain, a portal opened and a blue metal ramp appeared like some glistening robotic tongue.

Amalia and Gillermo hesitated only a moment and then, with their hearts sounding in their ears and clutching each other's hands, entered the ship.

* * *

Jack Avery flitted from world to world like a starved hummingbird.

On a planet known to Terran astronomers as Illisandur, he watched the migration of creatures that looked like furred reptiles as they made their way from the northern hemisphere drifted with rainbow-colored snow to their equator where they would spawn. They were pursued, harried, and slaughtered by roving packs of humanoids armed with intricately fashioned spears and dressed in the skins of their prey. Jack was the first Terran ever to behold the events under the planet's dense cloud cover. Far from trade routes and strategically undesirable for any purpose, no Terran had ever made landfall on Illisandur.

He observed the ovoid race that called themselves the Arciiya as they moved on their towering stiltlike appendages and recounted the myths of their kind by emitting several hundred distinct and subtle odors in a pattern refined over thousands of years of their unique art. Their world was known to them as Hicia and completely unknown to Terrans. It was some five kiloparsecs from Illisandur, deep in the Coalsack where Terran vessels found it invariably fatal to venture.

He swam the seas of Marus, ate the fruit of the dream trees of Jocilindos, hefted a deadly Bulsivetta against the barbarians in the southern hemisphere of Karatava and saw his mother brushing the pelt of a calf pilder on Cygnus, his home. She sang a song he knew well from his infancy and she cried. When he reached out to touch her, she stopped crying and smiled, turning away to complete her round of chores.

Jack visited the pastel forests of San Miguel, stood on the deck of the Terran starship *Todos Santos* as it exploded into a million glowing fragments moments after it was rammed by a renegade Rigelian Tuskship, wept at the songs of the Wuutu on New Proxima as they played instruments made from their own bones.

Jack hovered and darted and immersed himself into the worlds, as many worlds as he could see and taste and touch and know, drawing from each of them some knowledge, experience, color and texture as if it were some vital nectar to his soul. Jack spread the wings of his vision and flew deep inside The Eye of God.

He wondered: *Is this the onset of my mother's legacy of psi abilities? Am I a Cygni in this way? Have I become the freak my father feared I would become?* And the realization was there. Yes and no. It *was* a legacy of psi but it belonged to every sentient creature. While it was sometimes masked by intelligence, it was never far from the abilities of any creature capable of thought and/or will. That it was pronounced in the Cygni was more of a cultural effect than biological. Whether his father considered it freakish or not seemed irrelevant. An image sprang to him of his father as the pitiful maniac he was and not the hero Jack had constructed from whole cloth. And he forgave him.

It was on the heels of that very thought/emotion that he heard his name being called. He broke his gaze from the pulsing worlds before him in the crystal, looked up and saw Sergeant "Ironblood" John Avery Sr. hovering outside the tower window on the back of a dragon. He looked at him blankly and calmly for a full half minute, waiting for the vision to resolve itself.

"Blood of the great whore, boy! Have they hurt you?" His father peered at him and reached a hand toward him. "Do you understand me, Jack? You must come with me now. Can you make it to the ledge, lad?"

It was not a vision, not an image from The Eye of God. His father whom he had thought of a moment ago as a pitiful maniac, was indeed before him now.

"Jack? Jack? Can you hear me?"

Jack nodded slowly, his world, the world of the here and now, Darkath, came flooding back to him. He looked around him and saw the Dhirn, Raith, seated cross-legged on his perch still entranced by Ayeia Alaikhaj. Beyond him was Martin Cain staring just as slack-faced into its surface. "What about them?" Jack called to his father.

"Get Cain. Snap him out of it. Hurry, they're shooting at me and they'll be at the top of the stairs in a minute."

Jack now heard the staccato popping of gunfire below, shouts and cries, the stuttering of a high caliber machine gun. He jumped from his perch and ran to the stone mount where Cain sat. He climbed and shook the Terran. "Mr. Cain! Mr. Cain! Please, we've got to go."

Cain turned and blinked at him. He looked over at

the sergeant at the window, controlling the dragon with his knees and gesturing with a drawn pistol for him to follow quickly. "All right," Cain said calmly. "Get Raith."

John Avery bellowed, "Bugger the Dhirn! There's not enough room."

Jack shouted, "Raith! Raith, you have to save yourself."

Cain climbed down from the stone and paused. He looked at the body of Juum, shot twice in the chest, the body of another Khaj, the sentry who had been on watch when they came in. In turn, he looked at Sergeant Avery.

"Never mind them. They're dead." John Avery seemed to find reproach in the eyes of the Terran correspondent and he shouted, "They are the enemy Cain. Casualties of war. You do know we're at war don't you?"

Cain turned silently from the bodies and stepped up the bone ladder to where Raith sat. He saw that his Dhirn servant and teacher had tears trailing down his black face. "Raith, come along. We must leave."

Raith turned and studied Cain. "No," he said. "You go. I will remain here." He put his hand on Cain's shoulder. Cain took the hand and pressed it into his own.

"Are you sure?"

Raith nodded once. "I have much to learn here. I am in no danger."

"Take care of yourself, then, friend."

"Go with God, Cain."

"Yes. You, too, Raith."

With that, the Dhirn turned once again to face the stone the Khaj called The Eye of God and Cain joined Jack at the arched window. Jack jumped into his father's arms and seated himself in front of the Sergeant. Cain stood on the ledge and leaped at the small space on the saddle behind Avery Sr. With Cain's weight the dragon lost ten meters of altitude almost at once

Avery wheeled the mount in midair, dug his knees into the beast, and turned to fire off three shots at the Khaj soldiers who had just then appeared at the spot Cain and Jack had leaped from a moment ago.

The soldiers ducked beneath the ledge and that bought the three riders a moment to gain distance from the tower. They swooped low over the plateau and scattered Khaj fired up at them. Bullets whined through the air, struck the dragon in several places without noticeable effect, and shattered the raised visor on Sergeant Avery's sunhelmet. He wrenched it off and threw it away, then pointed below them at a half dozen dragonriders, obscured now and then in the still raging sandstorm, in pursuit of a single Khaj on another dragon flying an evasive pattern. "That's Virik playing decoy for us down there." He turned to the opposite side of the dragon and pointed below and behind them to a litter of dead bodies, some smoldering vehicles, and billowing smoke pouring from the mouths of two caves. "That's my other lad, Rilia . . . something. Tore up the place with a sixty caliber with explosive rounds. Kept the Darkers jumping while we stole a couple of dragons. Still, I don't think we'd have been as lucky if most of the troops here hadn't been shipped out last night. Virik told me the bitch had ordered something like ten thousand troops to a staging area in the desert, north of the cantonment. It was her last order. Virik put two bullets into her while I tried to wrestle her with my hands tied behind me."

Jack turned to look at his father as Cain leaned out to the side to study him simultaneously. Wind whipped past them making it difficult to hear. Each hoped they had misheard the sergeant. Cain spoke first. "Hara is dead?"

Avery Senior nodded, smiling with uncontained pride. "We walked in here, killed their two honchos, sprung you two, and ripped the place up a little. All with just three of my men . . . and one of them turned his coat on me, joined the bloody religious war or whatever it is.'' At that point he placed a hand on his son's shoulder and squeezed. The boy looked at his father's hand and gripped the pommel on the saddle tighter. His breath caught in his lungs and he wondered what it was he was feeling: elation, relief, sorrow, love, hysteria? Confusing emotions moved through him like a powerful electric current.

Cain maintained a serenity he had never before enjoyed in combat or crisis. His experience with Ayeia Alaikhaj had reawakened the knowledge within him that fear, anger, sorrow, any conditioned emotional response, like mania or exuberance, laughter and ecstasy were a matter of choice from moment to moment, neither being necessarily correct, appropriate, useful or better than the other. He chose instead to simply *be*, registering, without identifying too closely with, the sensations that careered through him. Like awareness of his breathing, he noted the clamoring of his mind and the tugging of his heart in a stew of emotion. That Hara was dead filled him with a sense of loss, shame and anger and yet in another part of him, the part reawakened in The Eye of God, he was certain that Hara lived. He said nothing to Avery.

The dragon flew at a low altitude through the winding network of canyons. They had escaped the renegade stronghold and managed to lose the several dragonriders who had set out in pursuit of them. This was thanks to Avery's skilled, but dangerous maneuvering of the dragon in sudden turns, loops and twists through the maze of wind tunnels. He flew half blind through the sheets of sand that blew up from the canyon floors, manipulating the dragon's wings with the reins like a sailor frantically sheeting canvas in gale. For a long time, conversation was impossible.

Avery led them to a shallow cave behind a ledge that protruded high above the floor of one of the mountain passes. They dismounted and tethered the dragon. ''Virik will rendezvous with us here. We'll wait an hour.'' He turned to his son. ''Are you all right, Jack?''

"Yes, I'm all right." He looked at the face of his father—it seemed to have been sandblasted—the ravaged skin, the wizened eyes that seemed to register awkward affection. "Why did you come?"

"I came for you, boy. I thought you might be here. We searched the cantonment and Darker Heights, the desert. You had to be a prisoner, I reckoned."

They stood measuring the years and distance between each other. It was Jack who moved to his father first. He put his hand on the sergeant's and clutched it. He said "Father" so quietly he wasn't sure he said it aloud.

After a moment his father spoke in a low, gravel voice, "Jack," and then turned away. In an abrupt change of tone, he asked Cain, "What were they doing to you in that tower with the crystal?"

Cain opened his mouth to speak, closed it. Here was an opportunity to practice his profession. For the first time since his arrival on Darkath he had a story, the most important news he would ever be asked to report. This would be the most crucial test of his communication skills ever presented to him in his career, and he found himself bereft, speechless, robbed of words, tongue-tied. A parade of cliches passed through his mind.

"It's . . . it's staggering, Avery . . ."

"Staggering." The sergeant repeated. "What's staggering?"

"It's a kind of shrine . . . and a learning device . . . and a communications medium of a sort." Cain began to babble. He told Avery about the Xi and their breeding with humans, breeding for consciousness, for evolutionary acceleration. "They have become like gods. They travel at light speed *without ships,* Avery. They can *become* stars." He realized how thoroughly he was failing. He would never be able to articulate his experience and what it meant to the reality they knew. He opted for the bottom line, the most vital and immediate intelligence. "The war must stop," he said. "We need the Darkhani and the Andromedans. This thing, The Eye of God, must be studied. I can't really explain . . .''

While Cain was speaking, the winds had died and a light rain had begun to fall. Avery looked at him as if he were a man possessed, a prisoner of war who had snapped under pressure. His look was a mixture of pity and sympathy. "Steady, Cain. You've been through a lot.''

"I know how it sounds to you, Avery, but I am not mad.''

The sergeant turned to his son. "Is that what you were looking at, son? Andromedans turning into stars?''

"No," Jack said. "I don't know anything about that, but Mr. Cain is right, it is a wonderful thing. I traveled across thousands of light-years. I saw worlds no one has ever seen. I saw Mother on Cygnus.''

Avery recoiled as if from a blow. He peered at his son with alarm.

"You see what you focus on," Cain explained. "I saw the Andromedans, the Xi, because they exist in a spectrum I could make out to some degree because of the optical augment surgery I underwent on New Proxima. Jack saw what *he* focused on. The point is, I must get to Jimenez and tell him to stop before this world is destroyed.''

"Surrender?" Avery snorted.

"No, not surrender. A cease-fire. A peace. We must make contact with the Xi.''

Before either of them could say any more, a dragon swooped into the canyon and made a hard landing onto the ledge outside the cave. The animal's wings sent rain flying around them and Virik half climbed and half fell off his mount. He was wounded in several places and seemed more dead than alive. Avery rushed to him.

"What happened to Rilia?''

"I couldn't get him out. I had to leave him. They were closing on both of us. He was hit with a spring-lance. There's nothing left of him. You've got to get out of here. I was pursued. There's a dozen of them that followed me. Take my dragon.''

"We're not going to leave you here, Corporal.''

"I'm a dead Darker, Sergeant. Don't waste your time. Don't make it all for nothing. You'll have a chance on two dragons. Here,'' Virik handed Cain his automatic rifle and gave Jack his machine pistol. "Go on, get out.'' Blood had filled his mouth. He coughed harshly and lay back, moving his lips as in prayer.

"You heard him,'' Avery said and mounted his dragon. "Let's go.''

Cain looked from Virik to Avery. "Ironblood Avery.'' Cain said.

"He knew the risks and he knows what he's doing now.''

Virik pulled a small pistol from his tunic that barely filled his hand. "I have what I need. Go on. Now.''

There was no time to debate the point. Fast moving shadows appeared overhead. "That's them.'' Avery said. "We'll wait until they pass. Put some distance between us.'' In the cave they were safe and further hidden by the rain that had become a downpour. "Move out,'' he said after a minute of silence.

Cain gave one last look at the corporal who no longer moved his lips or anything else. He bent to feel for a pulse and found none. He stood and then climbed onto the second dragon. As he sat in the saddle he said aloud, "Find your way into the heart of the sun, Corporal Virik.'' And with that he allowed the dragon to take him into the sky, holding on unsteadily.

Cain did not know how to handle the mount, but he didn't have to. The dragon was trained well and followed Avery's lead. They flew over the tops of the mountains and to the south. They flew all that day over the roof of Darkath in the rain that threatened to loosen Cain's grip. The tethers dug into his calves and hands. By midnight they had crested the escarpment that looked out over the Terran cantonment. In the dead of night they descended under a white flag Avery had fashioned with his undershirt.

Cain was exhausted to the point of death. He held on to one thought like a dog worrying a rag doll. *The war must stop.*

But fifty kilometers to the north it was just beginning in earnest.

PART III
GIATA

"He is invisible: he cannot be seen. He is far and he is near, he moves and he moves not, he is within all and he is outside all."

—Bhagavad-Gita 13.15

"Praise belongs to God, the originator of the heavens and the earth, who makes the angels His messengers, endued with wings in pairs or threes or fours. He adds to creation what He pleases . . ."

—The Koran XXXV.1

"Perfection is daring to embrace the universe itself as our true dimension, daring to steal the fire of the gods, to walk on water or fire unafraid, to heal, to claim plenty in time of dearth, to behold boldly that desired and become what we have need to be."

—Joseph Chilton Pearce
The Crack in the Cosmic Egg

Chapter Seventeen

Hara sat up, leaning on her left elbow. The painkilling compound that Nos, the Dhirn shaman, had mixed for her had taken effect and at last she could move without grimacing. She saw that her right arm was in a sling and her right thigh bandaged and protected by a small Terran cast made of silicone foam. Her chambers were crammed with both Khaj and Dhirn looking on anxiously. Nos spoke to Hara, but in a voice loud enough to satisfy the curiosity of everyone in the room.

"You will recover completely, Hia Hara. I have removed the bullet that lodged in your pectoral muscle and will cause you pain for some months. Your chain mail stopped it from passing into your lung. The other wound was very clean: the bullet passed out of your leg on its own. You have damaged muscles there and again you will experience much pain for some time. Still, if there is no infection that develops, none of us need worry for you." He smiled broadly.

Agitated shouting and relieved prayers passed through the chamber and reverberated through the hall, down the corridors and echoed up from the crowd gathered in the courtyard below. *She lives! She will recover!* Hara looked at Nos with a drugged fuzziness. She was about to ask him what happened, but the memory of wrestling with the Terran sergeant and lieutenant returned to her along with the silhouette of the Khaj who burst into the prison chamber and shot her. "The prisoners. . . ?"

Karsha leaned forward from behind Nos and answered her. "One dead, the other escaped. He took the boy and the man, Cain, from Ayeia Alaikhaj. Hara . . . he killed your father. I am sorry. My prayers . . ."

Hara looked down at her bedding hides as if she suddenly found some source of fascination there. Abruptly she lifted her gaze. With no emotion in her face or in her voice she said, "What are you doing here, Karsha? I ordered you to supervise the deployment of our troops in the desert."

"Everything is as you ordered. The captured groundcars, hovercraft, and six hundred mounted Grea' ka are in the staging area to the north of the cantonment. Our right flank is to the west of the spaceport, mostly infantry. The left flank is getting into position now in the mountains. They are waiting for you to command them, Hia Hara. I am here because a rider came to me with the news that you had been gravely wounded. I could do nothing else but come to your side. If I must be punished for leaving my post, that will leave Takyri in command of the center and left flanks and I do not think he has the fire of Alaikhaj himself in his heart as I do. I can deliver a victory to you, Hara. I know it."

"Yes. Yes. It's all right." Hara rotated both of her legs out perpendicular to the couch she lay on. She put her feet beneath her and Nos cautioned her that she needed several days' rest. "That is out of the question," Hara said. "You will provide me with whatever medicines are necessary, but nothing that clouds my head. Is that understood?"

"I will do what I can." Nos looked doubtful.

She turned to an aide and to Karsha, "Tell me everything that happened since I went to speak with the prisoner."

Karsha, since he himself had not been present at the stronghold, let the aide speak, a former infantry scout for the Terrans whose name was Livok. He told her of the three Lancers who had accompanied the Terran sergeant and how one of them, by the name of Jaralaj had immediately joined the ranks of Giata's children. The other two had wreaked much havoc, they blew up two ammunition supplies, started numerous fires, set off smokebombs and captured a repeating cannon that alone claimed the lives of twenty Darkhani. They had killed that one. The other one escaped on a Grea' ka along with the sergeant, his son and Cain, but he was most certainly mortally wounded. All told, the sergeant and his two Khaj had inflicted serious damage to the stronghold and killed some thirty personnel, including Hara's father and some women and children. There were many more injured, some of whom would join the ranks of the dead soon.

Hara listened to all of this impassively. When at last she spoke, it was to Karsha. "Return to your troops immediately. I will join the air armada in the mountains and wait. Advance on the cantonment two hours before dawn. By the time your army arrives at the gates I will be in the air with our ships. I intend to leave nothing standing."

Hara was escorted to the plateau where six air balloons waited. She painfully lifted herself into one of the puhlcalf baskets. The fire beneath the Grea' ka bladders was being tended to by two Khaj who greeted her silently with their fingers splayed over their eyes. The rain threatened to extinguish the flames and high, shifting winds promised to send them tumbling across the plateau. They waited for a prevailing southern wind for nearly two hours. When it looked as if the force of the storm might favor their direction, Hara ordered them to lift off.

They lost one airship immediately as the pilot could not release enough weights in time to gain elevation. It was smashed repeatedly against a jagged peak, spilling its passengers, and then drifted across the face of a mountainside tearing itself into splinters. Only the balloon of tightly stitched bladders remained intact and it drifted from sight into the black, turbulent night. Useless.

They were accompanied by a squadron of riders on the backs of ten Grea' ka bound to the airships with a series of long hide ropes to aid in navigation. All attempts at steering the crafts had met with failure except this cumbersome method. Still, they did not have far to travel and Hara was reassured that the remaining five ships had arrived at the rendezvous point above the escarpment overlooking the cantonment intact on the preceding day. Each balloon was manned by three soldiers, each armed with automatic rifles or machine guns, various grenades and handmade bombs. Hara hefted a springlance in her left hand, a machine pistol tucked into her belt.

It was nearly dawn when they arrived at the sheltered landing site overlooking the Terran settlement. Karsha's main force and right flank would have been advancing for an hour now and there was little time. She ordered the ten airships and twenty-seven Grea' ka into the sky during a lull in the rain when the wind had abated. She prayed to herself that they would not be suddenly blown back into the cliffs once they had crested the peaks and were in plain sight of the Terrans when daylight came.

Hara had been informed that the squadron had encountered three Terran patrols in the mountains above the cantonment. They had been dealt with and there were no survivors. The Terrans might be looking for hostiles on "dragons" coming from this direction and they would not be disappointed. The plan was that while the Terrans were occupied by a diversionary assault of the Grea' ka, the ten airships would follow, spread themselves out over the cantonment and deliver their payload of destruction at whatever targets presented themselves. She had requested that no intentional bombing of the hospital or Terran church take place (her intelligence had informed her the building was being used to house civilians), but was too experienced a warrior not to think that they, too, would be likely casualties in the heat of battle.

Sixteen Grea' ka took flight and Hara saluted each rider, with both hands to her eyes, as he or she mounted. She then gave them ten minutes to crest the mountains and descend. When she heard the popping and cracking of weapons in the distance, she gave the signal and the remaining Grea' ka lifted off, tugging the airships behind them. They rose effortlessly over the peaks and then, as planned, played out the lines between the ships. The craft were supposed to separate as the Grea' ka pulled them apart, but three of the airships drifted together, tangled their lines and could not seem to disengage. Daylight was a violet-gray smear on the horizon.

Hara drifted downward. Too fast. She released the stone and sandskin weights and slowed her descent, hovering over a series of campfires surrounded by troops. The soldiers were being served something from hot cauldrons by women and children. She immediately rejected these targets, silently cursing herself for her weakness. "When we get within range of those sheds, destroy them. They must hold equipment, weapons, or machinery. Perhaps communications devices." Her two companions looked at her and at each other, down at the easy targets they passed over and again at Hara. They nodded, puzzled or frustrated. Explosions lit the landscape below. Already the other ships were finding targets and the bombardment had begun. In the gathering daylight Hara could see smoke and running figures everywhere. It would now be impossible to distinguish soldiers from noncombatants. So be it, as their priests would say. She set down her springlance and picked up a fragmentation grenade and an incendiary device.

Hara pulled the strip of wire that armed the explosives on each of them simultaneously and tossed them onto the cracked and buckled roof of the building below them. The others in the balloon did the same. The airship glided neatly past the building as it threw itself into the morning sky with a staggered roar. Shrapnel whipped past them and heat from the rushing flame seared the air. Hara noted the sensation of motionlessness for the first time. They traveled at the same velocity as the wind and this created the illusion of stillness even while the ground sped past them.

Hara could not tell what might have been in the building and there would never be a way of knowing now. Gunfire stitched the bottom of the balloon and ruptured several bladders, causing them to descend again slightly. The Khaj soldier who was not tending the gas flame had taken a bullet in the crotch and bled profusely. She cried out once, slumped to the bottom of the car, and died. Hara lifted her and threw her over the side with a quick prayer.

The craft gained altitude again.

To either side of her, Hara could see the progress of their assault. They had achieved their objective of chaos if nothing else. The Terrans were posted around the walls in preparation for a siege from the direction of the spaceport and through the streets of the Darkhani villages stretching away from the high ground of the cantonment. There were token antiair defenses at intervals, but few of them were manned. Now, Terran troops were haphazardly leaving their positions on the walls and frantically trying to find shelter or regroup around the antiaircraft guns. Two of these guns had been taken out already by Hara's balloons. Still, the assault might be more short-lived than she hoped.

Two of the balloons were down, their crew dead. The three tangled craft had drifted against the mountain wall and hung there: fixed targets taking heavy fire and returning none. The free flying Grea' ka swooped and circled, dropping charges and firing at will toward running figures below. It was almost full daylight now and the heavy Terran artillery was barking its protest at the advance of Karsha's troops making their way through Darker Heights. The rain renewed its forceful drive on winds that had shifted east. Hara's craft drifted back in the direction they had come.

Despite the pain in her shoulder and thigh, Hara fired her machine pistol at a gun emplacement they drifted past quickly in the high wind. The balloon was too low for the awkward cannon to swivel and fire without hitting their own people across the compound. Hara shot the three gunners who attempted to man it and tossed a handmade concussion bomb at the heavy weapon. The charge fell short, but buried the swiveling mechanism in several kilos of mud.

From the rooftop of the Governor's mansion, a flock of Grea' ka mounted by Terran and Khaj cavalry soldiers took to the air. She counted eight of them. Two homed in on her craft and she threw the remaining weights from the balloon. Her ship rose quickly and caught another air current that pushed it farther east and closer to the rockface where the three other craft had met their end. The Terran riders maneuvered easily and gave pursuit. Hara and the soldier with her fired a long burst at both the riders. One of them flew from his mount, but the other bore down on them firing rapidly with a heavy rifle. The rider closed within fifty meters of her and she could see the sunburst tattoo around the eyes of the Khaj. The sensation of killing one of her own people who rode against her sickened her. As the rider's head and chest blossomed with bullet holes and he fell from his dragon to his death, Hara fought down the rising bile in her throat and the wail that threatened to escape her.

Her ship was flying low past a row of groundcars that were in the process of being equipped with mounted machine guns. Her remaining crew member was poised to lob an explosive over the side and demolish one or two of them when she shouted, "No! Wait!"

She quickly calculated the odds of running the balloon into the mountainside, if not the cantonment wall beneath it, and decided it was likely. The rain was driving them groundward too forcibly. The nine cars beneath her were draped with dead or wounded Terrans who had tried to use the small but powerful guns against the strike from the air. Another handful of Terran soldiers, including two women, were starting the engine on one of them while three others fitted the guns with magazines the size of their chests. "There!" Hara pointed.

The Terrans looked up at Hara's craft. They swiveled the guns and one of them erupted with a deafening metallic cough, puncturing several bladders. Hot air spilled over Hara's face from the escaped gas. The craft sank suddenly. Hara and her companion fired at the enemy beneath them. Hara killed two men and one of the women. The soldier/pilot, whose name she suddenly realized she had forgotten, shot the other woman and tossed a grenade into the second car. Hara hadn't had time to tell her comrade in arms that they were going to need those cars in the next few moments. The car shook itself into pieces and tried to levitate itself several meters off of the ground. Bits of gore flew through the rain. Hara was close enough to be spattered with blood.

The balloon hit the ground at a speed neither passenger was prepared for. The basket was dragged for several meters and caught fire. Hara leaped and rolled beneath one of the Terran groundcars and watched as her flight companion rolled in mud to extinguish the flames that licked his head and torso. By the time Hara reached the Khaj soldier/pilot, his teeth were rattling, his skin and hair smoldering. There was a long piece of puhlcalf lodged in his throat and blood bubbled from the wound and out of his mouth. She could hear his breath escaping in an eerie, atonal wheeze. Hara put her pistol to his head and fired into his skull, ending his horror for him.

She climbed into the groundcar that hummed with a live engine the Terrans had so thoughtfully started and looked over the controls. There were two foot pedals she could identify easily enough marked in Terran Standard, ACCELERATE and RETARD. She gripped the steering mechanism in one hand, her pistol in the other, releasing her arm from the sling with no little pain and absently wondered if she could recover her springlance. She decided there was no time. She released the brake handle and spun the tires for a moment before launching the car forward and sending arcs of muddy water to either side of her.

She ran down a Khaj soldier in a Terran uniform who fired a pistol at her and missed.

Hara could see that those who had abandoned their siege positions at the walls were trying to fall back and reman the perimeter. This meant that Karsha's army had made its way through Darker Heights and were close to the cantonment. She pointed the car at a collapsed section of the cantonment wall that was manned by two very young and very frightened looking Terran soldiers. They were engaged in the task of throwing sandbags into the breach in the wall that crumbled during a quake and then sagged further with the rain. Several other breaches in the wall were in evidence; some of them were from the hasty, misdirected fire of the Terran's own antiaircraft guns. A Khaj soldier dressed in a blue waistcloth ran after her waving a rifle in the air. For a moment she assumed it was a Terran loyalist and she aimed her pistol at him, then quickly realized it was one of her own from a downed dragon or balloon. She slowed the car and the soldier hopped in. As they sped at the wall, Hara's passenger setting up a steady stream of bullets ahead of them, the young Terrans threw down their weapons and ran in different directions.

The car easily climbed the low hill of sandbags and sailed through the opening and down the hill. Two of the tires exploded as they crushed concertina wire beneath them, but Hara didn't slow. She drove for another kilometer and then stopped when she saw

Karsha's troops advancing through the streets ahead of her and below. No one had fired at them since they left the cantonment.

Hara got out of the car and said, ''We'll wait here for Karsha. Tonight we'll take the cantonment.'' The soldier nodded, his hands over his eyes. Hara slumped against the sagging left front wheels and hung her head between her knees. In a moment, the soldier joined her and when he saw that she was shaking, put his hand on her shoulder.

* * *

Cain hurried alongside Jimenez's car as the commandant rolled past the gun emplacements and the firing positions along the wall. The older man ordered the car stopped at intervals and he would speak with the men, women, and children who now made up the Terran Imperial Army. Smoke wafted in dense clouds everywhere. The unexpected strike from the air that morning had been devastating and though all the fires were now under control, their ammunition, food, water and medical supplies had been reduced by half. There were more than one hundred Terran personnel dead, almost as many wounded. The attack had been repelled, but the cost had been high. The rain had stopped for the moment and Cain, who had managed to grab a few hours' sleep, shouted over the ground-car's motor as he ran, his lungs billowing painfully. At last, Jimenez ordered the vehicle to a halt and he turned to Cain.

''All right, Mr. Cain. Slow down. I can give you a minute, no more. I don't have much time for Andromedans. I have more pressing concerns. I think you can see that.''

''There's nothing . . . more pressing . . . than this. . . .'' Cain wheezed, trying to catch his breath. ''Sergeant Avery has already reported to you?''

''Yes. Under normal circumstances I'd have him arrested for what he did. Unfortunately, I need him more than ever now.''

"Then he told you Hara is dead.''

"He told me his man shot her and that he personally saw her go down, yes. I also have over a half-dozen witnesses who swear they saw her this morning during the air raid.''

"One female Khaj soldier . . .'' Cain's words were punctuated by his ragged breathing as he tried to find air to fill his lungs. ''. . . may look pretty much like another . . . to some Terrans, Commandant.''

"That's what I figure, Cain. If she's dead . . .'' Jimenez inclined his head briefly to indicate the enemy beyond the gates, ''then they might not know about it. They're organized as hell and that's got to be her influence. If she's alive, she's probably twice as determined as before to have every one of our heads. Either way, her army doesn't seem to be falling apart with either a dead or wounded figurehead. Get on with it, Cain. Say what you came to say.'' Jimenez seemed intensely distracted. His eyes twitched and his hands shook which he tried to cover by wiping them continuously with a handkerchief.

Cain tried to outline the story Raith had elicited from the dying Dhirn who had crashed in the shuttle. He spoke quickly and sparingly. This recaptured Jimenez's attention as Cain thought it would. He then told the commandant what had happened to him since then. His sentences were terse, impressionistic. Even if he had had the breath, he would not have been able to find the right words. Still he tried.

Jimenez looked thoughtful and vaguely put out, as if he were trying to digest something disagreeable. "I don't understand, Cain. You mean to say that this thing, this shrine the Khaj have up there is some sort of communications device. A link-up with the aliens on Darkath's moon who, you claim, originate in the *next galaxy*?''

"Yes, in a way. It is much more than that, but yes,

I was able to communicate with them. Or at least they communicated with me. They are essentially human, or at least enough like us . . ." Cain groped for a way to convey the magnitude of what was happening. He heard his own voice, his choice of words tumble from him like so much doggerel.

". . . exist in different ways, like light can exist in different spectrums . . . exist *as* light itself . . . what light is . . . what a star is . . . not a burning ball of matter and gas in a vacuum, but an event of consciousness . . . potential simultaneously being, decaying, forming, growing, dying . . ." Cain trailed off when he saw the look on Jimenez's face.

"Cain," he said quietly, "what in the name of God are you talking about? Did that thing up there bake your brains somehow?"

Cain shook his head. He realized he had a week or more growth of beard, his hair was matted, his clothes disheveled, he stank and sounded like a raving lunatic. It occurred to him the Xi might have been mistaken in selecting him as their messenger. He could hardly tell Avery what he needed to tell him and now, having even more time to think about it, still found it maddeningly difficult. Perhaps the Xi had sensed in Cain such an eagerness from transcendental experience, they assumed he would herald their coming with evangelical fervor, act as a kind of salesman for them. If so, they had underestimated the jaundiced view he lived with like a wound that could never heal. He was in awe of the Xi certainly, and part of him was so very eager to weep with relief, throw his hands in the air and shout, "Hallelujah!" But he had lived through too much to mistake, what was in essence, an invasion, a conquest, for anything else.

He tried once again, choosing his words carefully and relying on his correspondent's instincts for the salient facts. "They are capable of destroying every Terran on this planet instantaneously and they will do it, Commandant, to protect the Darkhani.

"Over a thousand years ago they did some kind of genetic engineering with themselves and the Africans. They have returned to follow up their experiment—the Darkhani are their experiment, Commandant. Their goal is to create a race of ultimate sentience, existential perfection: unlimited power over the environment, the physical universe. They are pretty damned close to it as it is. I can only guess at what powers they have. They will stay out of it as long as the Darkhani are winning. If it looks as if their victory will cost too much, though, the Andromedans—the Xi—will step in and . . . I don't know. It won't matter. There will be no Terran presence of any kind, that much I *do* know."

"Are you telling me to surrender, Cain? Is that your advice?" Jimenez remained expressionless. Cain could see that the man had lost weight. His eyes were ringed with exhaustion and his skin seemed a moldy paste color.

"The Terrans are finished here. No one can win this war. Even Hara knows that. You can hold out for a few days, but it will cost you too much.

"It's finished, don't you see? The Empire's reached its end here. For all we know, there is no Empire anymore." Cain needed more words, but didn't find them. He relied on Jimenez's ability to know certain defeat when he was confronted by it. Any combat soldier could and Jimenez was, if nothing else, a combat soldier. At least he was once.

Jimenez smiled with more than a trace of bitterness. "So this is 'their colony,' eh?" He harrumphed, but without bluster or even energy. "This command was my last chance, Cain. My career has taken one blow after another. The Quadrant Staff calls me 'unlucky.' Did you know that? That's worse than being called incompetent. How can I hand over our flag to a primitive rabble we already conquered one hundred years ago?"

Cain allowed the military governor his momentary self-indulgence. He suspected that ultimately Jimenez would not give weight to his own career destiny, would know that that was finished for him. He hoped that the man's priorities were simply not to make things worse.

Jimenez roused himself from some personal abyss and skewered Cain with a querulous look. "And you are the spokesman for these Andromedans, eh? You are the emissary for these supermen or . . . angels?"

"I suppose so. In a way."

"Was it these . . . Xi that shot down the second shuttle? The *Salvadore*?"

"I don't know for sure, but I think it's a safe assumption."

Jimenez nodded. It *was* a safe assumption.

"Cain. Get this and get it right. I can't risk laying down our weapons, rolling over belly-up for this Hara and her legions of religiously outraged killers. They have the taste of blood now and they want more. I've seen this kind of thing. What you're suggesting is a kind of suicide and I can't choose that option for the men, women, and children here. My duty is to protect them as long as I can in the best way that I can. No offense, Cain, I think you're a decent sort, but I can't take your word for something like this. You have a long history of bizarre behavior on fourteen worlds, always something to do with aliens and their religions. You are a strange bird. A little too strange. I'm sorry."

Jimenez paused, seemed about to order his driver on, then added. "I'll tell you what, if these Andromedans have some business with me or some concern about the situation here, why don't they make themselves known to me and not some unbalanced holo correspondent who has gone native? Answer me that?"

But Jimenez didn't wait for an answer. "Since you're such good friends with this Hara, why don't you find out if she's alive, go to her, and speak for me? Arrange a meeting. If peace is possible, then in the name of God, I'm for it. Tell her that. Tell her Cristobal is dead and that he was responsible for the insult to the Dhirn without my knowledge. As for the solar project, well, she got her pound of flesh there, didn't she? If she is dead, then maybe you can talk to Sivran. Tell him he could have Cristobal's head if I could find it. The colonel was pulverized with a rocket at close range. If you can stop this war, do it, Cain. In the meantime my duty is clear for the first time since I've been on this bloody impossible asylum of a planet: I will protect the people I am responsible for."

With that, Jimenez ordered an aide to escort Cain to the groundcar with the white cloth draped over the hood, the one Moumya had used to cross lines and meet with Sivran. "Good luck, Cain. I hope you make it. I really do. Get a shave and a bath first . . . if you can find any water."

With that, as if on cue, the rain began again and Jimenez continued his rounds.

A crowd of forty-some people watched Cain leave alone in the white-hooded car that glowed eerily in the momentary moonlight a break in the clouds afforded. It was near midnight. Among those gathered around the side gate were Jack Avery and his father. Jack wanted to go with Cain, but his father forbade it. They both wished him luck. Jack watched the car, like a pale, slow saurian, negotiate its way down the broken streets and through the hastily rigged barbed wire that defined the fire zone around the siege perimeter.

Jack turned again to his father and they made their way back to Sergeant Avery's position with the lancers. For the first time since his arrival on Darkath, Jack felt little fear. His father's gesture and what he had seen in The Eye of God had eclipsed and transformed that emotion into a kind of fulfilled acceptance of the universe's economy. He felt and *knew* that fear and courage weaved their way in and out of existence with an inexorable rhythm, like happiness and grief, love and hate or life and death itself. All of it to the complete indifference, or complete acceptance of the stars. And it was the stars, he suspected, the stars themselves that were the key to anything worth knowing.

He didn't know exactly what that was, but he knew it was vital. It was more important than his own brief life and the lost and regained gift of his father's love. He looked at his father and saw him for the first time. A hard, ugly man who battled his own fear and loneliness with defiance, rage, and violence. His scars were testimony to a fraction of what his battles had cost him. The fact that he had come for Jack, that Jack stood by this impossibly gnarled man now and walked with him, was a testament to the victory his father had achieved over those same demons. It was also an affirmation to Jack that despite the cold equations of the universe, there were the random factors, kinds of magic. And the most powerful of these originated in the human heart.

"Ironblood's Lancers" had taken up an observation post on the roof of the administration building. Here Sergeant Avery and a newly promoted lance corporal, Kavril, took turns on watch and slept on saddles beneath hastily erected tarpaulins. After seeing Martin Cain off through the gates on his dubious mission, Jack fell into a fitful sleep for several hours. He woke, soaked to the skin and shivering, to the sounds of shouting and the scurrying footsteps of booted soldiers across the rooftop. Jack sat up and grabbed the rifle his father had placed next to him. He worked the bolt and slid a bullet into the chamber. He saw his father peering through the nightscope, pointing agitatedly into the distance and issuing orders.

"What is it, Father?" Jack asked squinting into the predawn dark and rain. He could see nothing except dim fires in the distant streets of Darker Heights.

"They're moving up, Jack. This is it. By God, they've got good looking cavalry moves, too. Wouldn't be surprised if Jara had something to do with that. Taught him everything he knows." The sergeant had genuine pride in his voice. This struck Jack as only slightly odd, he was beginning to know his father a little. The fact that he was something of a wongheaded swine was just something else to accept . . . and Jack thought he could.

"I'm going to have half my men in the air before they get within a kilometer of the fire zone. They'll come in from behind them, from over the spaceport. The Darkers have mostly Dhirn infantry on that flank. This isn't going to be as easy for them as they think. Because they outnumber us ten to one, they've got to be cocky as hell. Think they'll just roll over us like a log. I don't think so, Jack. Do you?" The sergeant turned to his son, rubbing his hands with gleeful anticipation.

Jack smiled at his father. "No," he said.

"Are you afraid, boy?"

Jack hesitated only a moment. Finally, he said. "A little."

"Good. Nothing wrong with your brains, then." John Avery let out a sharp laugh and slapped his son lightly on the back. "Stay close, Jack," he added with a lower voice and a slight squeeze to the boy's shoulder.

"All right," Jack said. He would.

* * *

Alaikhaj rose through a break in the clouds on the horizon. The rain had stopped and the heat from the red giant turned the landscape into a watercolor of mist and steam. Terran artillery pounded the quickly advancing ranks of insurgent troops. The boom and crack of the guns was a constant background tympany that deafened the huddled residents and combatants in the cantonment. Once accustomed, or inured to the barrage, the pervasive silence became apparent, as if the planet was holding its collective breath in preparation for the clash to come.

Karsha's hovercars moved ahead of the infantry and

groundcars that got bogged down in the mud. The advancing front line arrived at Hara's position in staggered formation. The Dhirn walked alongside the Khaj under the plain blue flag. Already, casualties from the artillery barrage were being carried back on dragonsleds and groundcars.

Sivran had located Hara during the night and they shared tea together in the hazy dawn while they awaited Karsha and the order to advance against the walls. Neither of them spoke. They each studied a map of the cantonment marked by daubs of paint that signified weak points, feints, concerted infantry concentrations, cavalry positions, objectives, and a timetable for each of these notations. They agreed that the war could be fought and won in a day. Two at the most.

Karsha disembarked from his hovercraft and splayed his fingers across his eyes. He politely touched his chest to Sivran and joined them for tepid tea. "We are behind schedule," he said. "We relied too much on the Terran guns and groundcars. In the rain and mud, they work against us. One more hour and I'll give the order to take the walls. It may take most of the daylight."

Hara and Sivran nodded. They sat on Terran folding chairs while they waited for the train of troops to slog their way through the calf-high mud to the staging area. When an hour had passed, they were still short nearly five hundred soldiers, but they agreed to order the cavalry in.

Led by the defector Jaralaj, formerly of "Ironblood's Lancers," the first frontal assault of Grea' ka riders, some two hundred Khaj, most of them with some Terran training in siege maneuvers, lifted into the air. The objective: to cause the Terran riflemen on the walls to fall back into the cantonment and to effect as much damage as possible to the artillery emplacements.

Hara raised her hands and led the troops in the prayer to Giata. When it was concluded, the cry of battle rising from over 8,000 throats cut the morning stillness and for a moment drowned the barking of the Terran guns. The cavalry lifted off and to themselves, Hara, Sivran and Karsha began to pace off the hours remaining in the day.

None of them foresaw that it would, in fact, take five days to breach those walls.

Chapter Eighteen

The Army of Giata might have overwhelmed the cantonment walls in one massive surge, but it became apparent to both Hara and Karsha that the cost would be too high. The casualties inflicted by the Terran artillery had been massive. It was decided to break up the assault into stages. Infantry and armored cars, followed by cavalry, regrouping, and then infantry again. The large Terran guns had run out of ammunition by the middle of the second day and Sivran pointed out that it was now wiser to wear down the Terrans: wait for their food and water supplies to diminish, morale to drop and for the ineluctable fact of defeat to sink in to those behind the walls.

Other unforeseen setbacks delayed the fast victory Hara had envisioned. Only two balloons remained functional after the first air attack from the escarpment. While they continued to set out over the mountains and drop explosives from a high altitude, they, by necessity, had to remain too far above their targets to achieve any accuracy. The Grea' ka that accompanied them to fly interference were kept busy by Avery's cavalry who engaged them in aerial combat with discouraging effect. The rest of the Terran cavalry flew missions from a staging area far to the west of the spaceport and behind Giatan lines. They wreaked havoc up and down their right flank, diminishing the pool of both infantry and cavalry they could draw on from that quarter. Still, time was on their side.

The concertina wire around the perimeter was strung

with extremely effective anti-personnel mines and while most of them were neutralized by the end of the second day, they had decimated the first three waves of infantry assault troops.

It had become a war of attrition. Hara had time and thousands of soldiers, but the Terrans had more and better weapons, higher ground and a grim, unshakable determination to survive.

* * *

Cain had found his way through the mines and wires only to emerge in a barricaded plaza of the heights where he was pinned down for several hours under machine-gun fire. He called out to the gunners that he was Martin Cain, on an errand of peace and that he wished to speak with Hara if she lived, or any superior officer. He was ignored except for a flurry of bullets. The car was riddled with holes and would have exploded if Cain hadn't shut off the fuel supply, detached the canisters of neoline and tossed them as far as he could. A fragment of flying metal from the hood had caught him over his right eye and cut him deeply. He lost much blood as he lay in a crater, in a meter of water, under the car and waited.

When the first Giatan infantry charge began, he was taken at sword point and marched back, blindfolded and tied, to a flooded trench where he could smell cooking. He heard many voices and kept repeating his name and his mission, but he was ignored. He lost consciousness for a while, how long he couldn't say. When he woke again he was lying down on dry bedding. He heard a familiar voice.

"Sergeant Avery went to so much trouble to rescue you. Is it possible you don't wish to remain rescued?"

Cain opened one eye, "So you are alive, Hara?" he said.

"Very much so."

* * *

The onslaught of rain caused the foundations of the Terran buildings to resettle themselves with resigned shrugs, groaning sighs: the slow silent sinking of sick men into their bedclothes. The building housing the detention facility was no exception. Dug deeper than many other Terran structures into the rock itself beneath the many meters of sand, it was not the first to be affected, but not the last either, for even the bedrock beneath Darkath's sands were situated with a permanence that was, at best, dubious.

The tracks that contained the sliding doors to the cells and the floor beneath them, fell away gradually, almost imperceptibly from the walls and cells they supported. The tectonic trembling of the ''bedrock'' had not ceased with the rains, but became, if anything, more pronounced as if lubricated by the flooding and mud.

The sole prisoner in the detention facility watched this process with desperate fascination. Weak with hunger to the point of dizziness, kept alive only by the need to see Darkath's sky again and the mountain passes flow with Terran blood, he waited. Each hour he tested the door of his cell against the distance from its track. He counted thirty-two hours, thirty-two tests. It was on the thirty-third try that the door swung away with sufficient space to allow his shrunken frame to pass through to freedom.

* * *

Nigel Wilson tapped the belt of holocassettes he wore around his shoulder like a bandolier. In a sense they were in fact ammunition, all he would need. Each was filled with unprecedented footage of the uprising and would serve him the rest of his days. If he could survive somehow for six months, a year at the most— and he had no doubt he *would* survive, one way or another—until a Terran ship arrived, these little cubes would be worth as much as fifty billion cruzeiros apiece. To the fax networks they might be worth, conservatively, half of that; but Wilson suspected that the inevitable tribunal hearings back at Quadrant HQ as to what went wrong on Darkath might very well pay much more. They would want to know what happened and they would also want to insure that no one else ever did. The footage would be edited down to some harmless stock stuff, but Wilson's name would be forever up there with the greats.

He would certainly be more famous than Martin Cain and deservedly so. What was Cain doing anyway? The man was wandering around looking for playmates among the enemy. Since his arrival as a correspondent, Cain hadn't corresponded a damned thing. Wilson had some good shots of Cain going out the side gate in the middle of the night on his "desperate and courageous mission of peace" as he had termed it in the voice-over and in that way, he could use him. Cain would almost certainly never return alive and sometime later Wilson could do a little memorium piece; "a fellow correspondent fallen in the attempt to save lives, etc." But Wilson would have to give a little more thought as to how all that would make *him* look.

As he thought about that, he leaned against the pole supporting the civilian mess tent and played his viewfinder absently over the parade ground. It was in between the assault waves and he was thinking about getting a few more shots of the exhaustion, grief and fear on the faces of the besieged colonists. Some movement in the shadows over by the lock facility gate caught his eye and he swung the viewfinder back.

A filthy, emaciated figure scuttled out of the gate and lifted a blanket from a sleeping woman who leaned against a wall to his right. Before he threw the blanket around him, Wilson could see plainly that the figure was a Khaj, but a skeletal caricature of that warrior caste. He watched the Khaj slip a knife from the belt

of a Dhirn who was among those who remained loyal
(for one reason or another) to the Terrans. The Dhirn
noticed nothing as he studied the walls for signs of a
new attack. Wilson could see that the Khaj was a skill-
ful thief and then it dawned on him: he was witnessing
the escape of the last of the hostages. He had heard
that Cristobal had executed the two Dhirn after their
uprising and had left the Khaj who was said to have
been a thief as well as a spy.

Wilson quickly turned on the holocorder and rose
slowly to follow the progress of the escaped prisoner.
He tried to remember the name. He knew he had heard
it, had filed it away back there in his reporter's memory for possible use. He walked slowly, inconspicu-
ously across the compound, his lens on three-quarter
telescopic magnification and watched the blanketed
Khaj climb the walls of the administration building like
some sort of withered, caped monkey. It occurred to
Wilson that the prisoner was after a dragon. Ironblood
Avery had some mounts up there at his observation post
and the prisoner must have seen them. It didn't occur
to Wilson to shout, "Stop him!" Or "Escaped prisoner!" Or "Look out up there! An enemy soldier with
a long knife is sneaking up on you fellows!" What did
occur to him was the prisoner's name: Dalak.

Jack leaned backward over the edge of the roof and
stretched his spine and neck. While it wasn't raining
at the moment, he was wet through to his bones and
had begun to believe that he would never be dry again.
He was tired and hungry and still wondering what it
would be like when the time came for him to use his
weapon and kill someone. Until now they had held the
enemy at the walls and Jack hadn't fired a shot. He
was no longer so much afraid for his own life, but
afraid of his own behavior; of freezing up at a crucial
moment and in sight of his father.

Across the rooftop, the commandant was conferring
with Sergeant Avery and three aides. He was straining

to hear what they were discussing when a hand clamped over his mouth and a short sword was placed at his throat. A rasping voice, the voice of death itself urged him, "Be silent!"

Jack smelled his assailant, a bitter stench. He felt the rough cloth of an army issue blanket pressed against him, saw the jet black hand that clutched the blade. He allowed his rifle to be taken from him and the sword was removed from his throat. Next, the hand released his mouth and the voice said, "Remain still." He felt the muzzle of the gun at the base of his spine and heard the bolt click home.

One of Jimenez's aides saw him and pointed, lifted his pistol and aimed. The gun was placed on Jack's shoulder and the odoriferous Darkhani behind him pulled the trigger. Jack's ear burned and he went deaf. He saw the aide thrown backward from the bullet. All eyes on the rooftop were on Jack and the figure behind him that he could not see.

"Drop all your weapons and move away from the Grea' ka!" The voice behind him said.

Everyone obeyed except for Jack's father. "If you harm that boy, I'll have these Grea' ka pull you limb from limb across the desert. First, I'll pluck your eyes from your head with my own . . ." Avery never finished. The escaped Khaj fired another shot and struck the sergeant in the arm. Avery went down, grimacing.

Jack was hurried to the closest of the dragons and told to mount. He did so as Jimenez, his aides, and several lancers backed away. "Father!" he called out.

"Silence!" The rifle muzzle jabbed him painfully in the back of the head. Jack winced and as he did so, he could not see that Commandant Jimenez had palmed a very small pistol from his sleeve and brought it down. Before Dalak could swivel the rifle barrel around, Jimenez had fired two shots and sent the Khaj flying off the dragon.

Dalak hit the ground, still clutching the rifle. With one hand he fired three shots in rapid succession. All three of them hit Jimenez and the commandant clutched himself, swayed on his feet and before he fell, managed to fire twice more at Dalak. The second bullet found its way into the Khaj's left cheek. He lay back, fluttered his eyelids, and went still.

Jimenez fell with a hollow flat sound against the roof. His aides rushed to him and lifted his head. Jack climbed off the dragon and ran to his father.

John Avery was conscious and biting his lower lip until it bled. His right shoulder was shattered. Bits of bone flowed with the stream of blood running down his arm.

Jack looked over at the fallen commandant. He heard one of the men say. "He's alive, but he's dying. Get him downstairs."

He looked at his father, turning pale. "I'll be all right, Jack. I will."

Jack nodded. He *knew* his father would be all right where another man might not. He knew something else now, too. He now knew he could kill the enemy.

Nigel Wilson appeared on the rooftop out of breath. He swung the holocorder wildly around trying to take in the scene, but he was too late. He got a few shots of men carrying the tremendous burden of the fallen commandant and a shot of a young boy clutching the prostrate form of his father, "one of the heroes of the Darkhani uprising." With the background story, the stowaway angle, he could work up a nice little bit there. He had missed the main show, but, still and all, not bad, not bad.

"Excuse me," he turned to one of the lancers, training his holo on him. "Could you tell me exactly what happened just now? In your own words." The lancer placed his fingers over the lens and wrenched it away from Wilson's face. The next thing Wilson saw was a hammy fist growing huge in his field of vision at an alarming rate. He didn't see anything after that for nearly an hour.

* * *

Something less than five hundred Darkhani remained behind at Ayeia Alaikhaj, most of them mothers and children and noncombatant Dhirn. A rearguard of some seventy Khaj and Dhirn warriors patrolled the hills, mountain passes, and plateaus or sat in caves over fires eating, drinking, and tossing bones for gems.

In the tower, before The Eye of God, Raith had sat transfixed for three days. The escape of Cain and the boy, the gunfire, and ensuing chaos were only momentary distractions. Only when hunger and exhaustion had caused him to topple from his stone pedestal, did Raith resign himself to returning to his people. After finding some food and sleeping for a full day, he inventoried his reserves of spiritual strength and found them wanting. The revelations he had experienced at the shrine in the Ceremony of Light had been profoundly disturbing and yet uplifting at the same time. He had undergone a transformation, a kind of mythocide and rebirth. His lifelong devotion to the precepts of the Dhirn, his unwavering worship of the mother goddess, Darkath, he now believed to be only a shadow of a larger truth.

He had been wrong. The Dhirn had been wrong. It was not so much a question of the Khaj being right as it was the degree to which their truth approached a more universal reality.

Now he walked among the people, seeking out gatherings of Dhirn and he would speak to them. "I am Raith," he would say, "of the Dhirn. I am the son of Lijhar the beverage maker and Halia, a healer and teacher of children. I have been a servant and laborer of the Terrans and an abidingly religious Dhirn who treads the sands of the mother with reverence and love. I have been to the god of the Khaj who is not the god of the Khaj, but a light that pervades all things. A veil has been lifted from my eyes and my heart and I wish to tell you what it is I have been given to understand.

"We are the descendants of two races. One of them is the Terran race, what they call the human race. The other is a race known as the Xi from much farther away than the Terrans. When the Xi first made planet-fall here, they encountered the survivors of a Terran starship and coupled with them. Their offspring became known as the Darkhani. The Xi had been traveling so long through the empty spaces between stars, had endured such hardships in their small ship on its long journey that the ground beneath their feet, the world upon which we stand and have called Darkath became a God and mother to them. This is the genesis of the Dhirn belief and teaching.

"Those who retained the wisdom and teachings of the Xi became the Khaj. And though much of those teachings and disciplines became transmuted during the centuries of survival and brutality, it is their worship of our star, Alaikhaj that most resembles the blinding truth that transcends all others.

"The Dhirn worshiped the ground because of the belief that evolved, quite understandably, that the fundamental tie between all living things is pain. Darkath, with her rivers of molten rock, her violent thrashings that give birth to mountains or turns them to desert, takes life or gives it with her khat and puhlcalf is a model on a great scale for the things that terrified us or nurtured us. Darkath seemed to be the source of life and death, birth and pain. She became our mother. When the khat is plucked, it bleeds life-giving water. When the *ika* is cured with the flowers of Darkath, we are given visions that take us to the heart of the goddess. We see her recesses, her mysteries, her womb. We could as easily have turned our visions upward and seen much more.

"It is not so much that we have been wrong, but that we have glimpsed only a part of the truth. The Khaj held yet another part of that same truth. We have needed each other all these centuries and it is a divine occurrence that the Terrans have united us, forging our alliance in hate and tempering our fierce differences, unwittingly preparing us for a more majestic reality.

"The Xi have returned. They are the angels the Khaj seers spoke of who will come from the dark side of Giata to vanquish our conquerors. They are real. Some of you have seen them as creatures of light in the sacred caverns of Darkath while in deep meditation. The time has come to transcend the idea of fundament as pain, the bowels of the planet itself as God. The time has come to let go of the old ways, the ways born of necessity and violence. We must now embrace the light the Khaj have spoken of. The light of our star and others. The light inside of us that we can become and must allow. The Xi will show us. We must learn."

Raith gave variations of this sermon to several groups of Dhirn. At first he was met with puzzled stares and indifference. The third group he spoke to shouted him down and called him a heretic and traitor, a madman. He walked through the mountain passes in the rain and found yet more huddled groups of Dhirn waiting out the war beyond the peaks. In one cavern, above a steep ravine that had no name and fell away to such a depth its floor was shrouded in mist, he found several families and among them a shaman that he knew. He spoke his message and as he did, they shouted him down. He continued to speak and one of the children threw a stone at him that glanced off his shoulder. He raised his voice and continued. More children threw rocks. The shaman told him to leave and when Raith remained, the shaman picked up a stone and hurled it. Raith was struck on the head and he fell. He put his arms up over his face to protect himself from the rain of missiles, but there were too many of them and they were thrown with too much anger.

When Raith lay unmoving in a pool of his own

blood, they picked him up and threw his body into the chasm below. Some listened for the sound of him striking the rocks below, but it was too far. They were rewarded only by silence.

Chapter Nineteen

On the fifth day of the siege, Jimenez still lay on the two beds that had been wired together to contain his bulk. He had two bullet wounds in his right thigh and one in his stomach that had ruptured his spleen. He was dying, and dying painfully. Avery, accompanied as always now by his son, had just visited to assure him his own wounds were on the mend. The sergeant wore his arm in a sling and seemed pale, but otherwise fit. The boy no longer seemed to be a child; it was as if he'd been forced to manhood in a very short time. In spite of what they said, their reassuring appraisal of the situation, the look on both their faces told Jimenez everything he needed to know: not only that he himself was dying, but that the defense of the cantonment would not be possible for much longer.

Jimenez conferred briefly with aides that came and went with dispatches from the walls until they were chased out by the ranking surgeon, Doctor Castro. Castro was half dead himself, his eyes ringed with lack of sleep, his apron splashed with blood like a butcher's. On Castro's heels was the tireless priest, Padre Katanya. Jimenez allowed last rites to be administered to him and then lay back and closed his eyes as pain-killing medicine coursed through him.

He could not have slept for more than a few hours when he thought he heard his name being called as if from a great distance. His eyelids fluttered open and he looked up at a group of faces surrounding him. None of them came into any focus except that of Martin Cain, the correspondent who had come to him with the story of the Andromedans and who had set out to negotiate with the enemy. "Cain?" he said weakly. "Is that you?"

"Yes, Commandant."

"Who else is there?"

"Members of your staff: Fioricci, Sergeant Avery, Padre Katanya. They are here to confirm what it is I am going to tell you." Jimenez could barely see Cain or the others, but it seemed to him that Cain looked somehow . . . insubstantial. Pale, almost translucent.

"Yes? What is it?"

A pause stretched beyond a single moment and then Cain told him. "The Andromedans have arrived. Their ships are over the cantonment, the spaceport, the heights, the mountains, everywhere. They have not landed yet nor made any hostile gesture, but sir, unless the war stops now, I believe they will destroy us. That is, isolate us more effectively than even the siege. We would die, most certainly, of starvation and thirst— possibly turn against ourselves."

To Jimenez, it seemed as if the correspondent were trying to relate something hideous he had seen, some prescient, grotesque vision of some possible future.

"You don't sound as . . ." Jimenez spoke through the pain, trying to find the words, ". . . as suffused with rapture over these 'angels' as you did. You sound scared, Cain."

Cain didn't respond to that, but went on. "Hara is still alive. Sivran as well. They have agreed to accept surrender and they guarantee the lives of Terran survivors and Darkhani who have remained loyal to Terra."

"How can I accept their word?" Jimenez breathed with difficulty.

"Manuel, it is I, Padre Katanya. You must accept their offer. There are less than two hundred Terran survivors, perhaps another hundred or so Darkhani who have remained with us. We have no more food.

Medical supplies have been destroyed and there is something odd out there . . . perhaps Sergeant Avery will tell you.''

Avery looked at the faces around him, seemed flustered. He clutched his helmet beneath his arm and twisted it nervously. ''Yes, sir, something odd. Since those ships arrived, sir. No one can get in or out of the perimeter. I've only got a few mounts and riders left and I was using them to cover men repairing breaches in the wall or to recon activity on the eastern peaks, but they can't get outside ten meters of the wall in any direction. Not only that, but the Darkers can't get *in* either. Bullets won't penetrate whatever it is. The war is in stalemate for now, sir.''

Jimenez tried to rise on one elbow. Castro urged him back down on the bed. ''What is it? What is he talking about?''

Captain Fioricci leaned forward. ''Sir, Major Joxbov, the Rigelian scientist who designed the solar project?''

''Yes, what about him?''

''He thinks that the barrier is a field of charged mass, small particles made several thousand times more dense than usual . . . like some kind of ion curtain.''

''There's no way around it?''

''I don't know, sir.'' Fioricci said, ''We have certainly tried everything we can think of.''

''I wonder if Major Joxbov has any suggestions?''

Cain interrupted. ''I don't see what difference it makes, do you, sir? If we don't settle this, the Andromedans . . . that is, the Xi, are going to show us some more of their tricks and I don't believe they will be as . . . neutral about it.''

Jimenez turned to him. Again it struck the commandant that Cain had some sort of difference about him, a lighter presence, as if he weren't altogether there. It must have been the drugs. ''How did you get through this curtain, Cain?''

"I just walked through. They . . . permitted me to pass. I was detained and unconscious for a while, but I spoke with Hara and Sivran and they agreed to peace. The siege has cost them many lives. As soon as I was able to, I returned. I had no difficulty getting here."

Katanya spoke again. "It is clear that Mister Cain is the messenger of these Xi. I believe there is no alternative, Manuel."

Fioricci said. "We can't keep fighting."

Avery added reluctantly, "And we can't just wait it out. We'll starve."

Cain said, "The Xi want peace and they want to talk to us. It is safe to believe that much."

Jimenez breathed with difficulty or perhaps exasperation. "Then why don't they show themselves? Why aren't they here in this room to say what they have to say?"

Everyone looked at Cain. He said, "First, an end to the bloodshed. They feel we might be distracted while they were talking to us if we were busy killing each other."

"Can these ships be seen from here?" Jimenez wanted to know.

"Yes, sir." Fioricci replied. "Right out the window you can see a few of them."

"Wheel me over there."

Castro protested, but Jimenez ordered him to continue his rounds.

As they lifted him onto a gurney, his stomach wound bled heavily again. He grimaced but demanded to be taken to the window. Fioricci, Cain, and Katanya did as he asked.

The first thing Jimenez noticed was the devastation in the compound. Bodies littered the parade ground. Bomb craters filled with small lakes and floating, bloated corpses dotted the cantonment behind the walls. The sandbags and makeshift barricades crowned with barbed wire and twisted metal were manned by scarecrow figures, most of them civilians. Jimenez hung his head, closed his eyes. He could not bear to look and so he forced himself to raise his head and look skyward.

The clouds had settled over Darkath's northern hemisphere with a leaden solidity. Rain fell in a fine, dense drizzle. Silhouetted against the clouds were three winged shapes that Jimenez at first took to be hovering dragons until he realized they were at a very high altitude, were very large, and glistened with barely discernible winking lights. Cain pointed, "Xi ships, Commandant."

"They look like dragons hanging there," he commented.

Avery agreed. "Exactly like 'em. Only bigger."

"Can you make out any weapons, Sergeant?"

"I don't reckon I have to, with all respect, Commandant. If they can freeze the fire zone around us like we would trap sand wasps under a bowl, seems to me they might have devised a weapon or two."

Jimenez began to cough. He cried out with the pain that followed and he relaxed suddenly.

"Is he dead?" Fioricci asked.

No one answered, but looked at each other. Cain sent for Castro.

They moved him back to his bed and the doctor came running over. He told them to leave Jimenez in the gurney as he quickly ran thin tubes down the commandant's throat. He waved them all away.

"Wait a minute," Cain said. "We need an answer from him now. If he's dead, then who's in command?"

Doctor Castro snapped. "He's unconscious. You won't get an answer from him. Get out of here."

"Who's next in command?" Cain demanded.

"That would be me," Fioricci responded. "But the commandant might come out of it."

"We can't wait." Cain took Fioricci's arm. "Let me go back to Hara and bring her Jimenez's sword."

Fioricci looked to Avery. Avery snorted and said, "I'm commanding half-starved women and boys out there. That's not soldiering and there's no honor in watching them starve or die from fever. Give Mr. Cain the sword, sir. Let's end this.''

No one noticed the figure who had stepped from the darkness of the church/hospital arches beyond the surgical lamps. The shrouded form was draped in layers of Khaj robes and wore a ceremonial scarf across the face, exposing only a pair of shadowed eyes.

Fioricci took the sword from the clothes, boots and effects laying in a pile next to Jimenez. He drew it from its scabbard and turned to Cain. ''Will you take it, Mr. Cain? Tell them it's over.''

''Nothing is over yet!'' The voice from the shadows echoed through the church. The figure stepped into the light and brandished a pistol at the men gathered around the motionless form of the commandant.

''Who are you?'' Cain asked.

''The one you're looking for,'' came the reply. ''Next in line for command.'' The voice was familiar to everyone in the room. ''Drop the sword, Captain, and please don't reach for your weapon, Sergeant Avery, or I'll blow your good arm clean off your shoulder.'' He removed the veil from the lower half of his face.

''Cristobal,'' Cain announced.

''Colonel,'' Fiorrici said and let the unsheathed sword fall onto the bed next to Jimenez.

''El Raton,'' Avery said. ''Back from the dead.''

''Not at all. Quite alive actually. I've been in a sort of bunker I took the liberty of having constructed beneath the church for just such an occasion. Well, I've given you all enough time to realize Jimenez can only lead you to defeat. I can lead you to victory. You see, I have light weapons secreted down there. Just a few, but enough to rout the Khaj and, I'm certain, give your Andromedans, Mr. Cain, pause enough to reconsider threatening us. It would certainly cost them a ship or two to annihilate us.''

''You're out of your mind, Cristobal. No one will

follow a mutineer. At least I won't.'' Avery turned and walked away.

"Then I'll have to make do without you, 'Iron-blood.' '' Cristobal took a few steps forward until he was positioned next to Jimenez's gurney. He pushed Padre Katanya out of the way and aimed his pistol at Avery's back. He pulled back the hammer.

Cain shouted, "No!" and made to close the distance between himself and Cristobal. Before he could get more than a few paces, Cristobal's gun jerked upward and discharged into the ceiling. The colonel made a surprised, breathless sound and looked down at his mid-section. A swordpoint, red with blood, protruded from a spot just beneath his rib cage. Cristobal touched it gingerly with one hand. The other hand, the one holding the gun, began to tremble. Soon both arms began to tremble. Colonel Eduardo *El Raton* Cristobal staggered forward, tried to speak and instead fell to his knees. He said, "Gaaadaah . . . " and collapsed. Jimenez's sword rose from the colonel's back, a grisly skewer.

Avery had turned around. Everyone was now looking at Jimenez. The huge man lay breathing in staggered, labored stages. "Take the sword, Cain . . . Take it to Hara . . . tell her . . . tell. . . . "

Though his lips moved, no one could make out what he might have wanted Cain to tell Hara. They waited another moment, but Jimenez never spoke again. He joined the legions of dead on Darkath.

Chapter Twenty

The Xi ship lowered itself slowly, coming to rest a few meters from the ground in the middle of the fire zone between the Terran perimeter and Karsha's infantry lines. Since Cain's appearance at the main gate holding the sword in two hands over his head, the curtain that had separated the two factions was no longer in evidence. Whereas before it had been partially visible as rain flowed over it in a miragelike effect, now only a light vertical downpour tinted the air a crystal gray. Anyone could now come and go and could, presumably, fire weapons at each other, but no one did. Only Cain crossed the distance between the enemies.

He stood before the ship holding the commandant's sword out like an offering. Behind him a thousand paces stood a crowd of Terrans, Darkhani who had remained loyal to the Terrans, a few Rigelians, and Cappellans. John and Jack Avery, Fioricci, Katanya, and Doctor Castro stood closest to Cain at the head of the gathered survivors of the siege.

The ship was large, larger than any of the buildings on Darkath, but no larger than a Terran starship. Its surface was a flat black that seemed to absorb or negate light through gleaming sources of brilliance that winked randomly at varying intervals around its hull. Two gracefully curved extensions, symmetrically balanced, seemed to grow out of a slightly bowed nose or prow, giving the entire ship the effect of a great jeweled bird frozen in a gesture of reverence.

From the bow of the ship, a tonguelike ramp extended to the ground just ahead of Cain. Cain hesitated. Was this an invitation to enter? He looked behind him at the Averys, the doctor, and the priest; even Nigel Wilson had his holopack trained on the Xi ship. As he turned back to face the ramp, he saw Hara and Sivran approaching from the lines of their army. He waited until they stood before him. Hara seemed depleted, her movements were the slow deliberate dance of the aged, a combination of stunned sadness and resignation. She accepted the sword Cain presented to her with no visible relish. With her other hand, she took Cain's and squeezed it, a Terran gesture. Cain was a little startled. As quickly as she had taken his hand, she let it go. She said, "Thank you."

Cain only nodded, not knowing what to say, what she was thanking him for. The sword, he supposed.

Sivran spoke to Cain. "The sword is blooded."

"Yes," Cain answered and told him of Jimenez's final act in slaying Cristobal.

"What now?" Cain asked Hara. "Do you wish to negotiate terms with Captain Fioricci? There hardly seems any point. He commands a handful of soldiers and another handful of half-dead women and children."

"No." Hara was peering into the darkness of the starship. So far there had been no movement or sound from within. "They won't be harmed. They are free to do as they wish." Hara spoke distractedly. "There is a carving of this ship at the Cave of the Angels near The Eye of God."

"I'm not surprised," Cain said. "It was probably a ship much like this one that brought your ancestors."

"So you say," Hara responded and then her face stiffened, her eyes narrowed. "Who is that?" She pointed to the top of the ramp.

Cain looked up into the ship and saw a heavyset Terran woman in a simple cloth shift of a faded rust color. It was that woman, the dramatist, Dubois. *How? . . . What? . . .* Next to her appeared the archeologist priest, Gillermo. He wore a similar garment, only blue.

It was Gillermo who spoke first. "Hello, Mister Cain. Hara, I presume? and Sivran, of course."

"Padre Gillermo," Cain said. "How did you. . . ?" He trailed off, gesturing.

"The Xi saved Doña Dubois and myself from certain death in the flooded Nijwhol basin. We discovered the African craft. I was right about that and the Xi have confirmed it." Gillermo's voice sounded calm, cheerful, reassuring.

"The Xi. . . ." Cain seemed to be having trouble speaking aloud. He sensed his thoughts were being monitored, by the Xi, as if telepathically, and he had never felt comfortable with the phenomenon of telepathy before. Until his experience in The Eye of God. Now, whether he was comfortable or not seemed to have little to do with anything.

Amalia Dubois spoke, "They are essentially human, Mister Cain, Hara, Sivran. If anything they are . . . more so than we are."

The crowd from the Terran cantonment began to move closer to the ship. Those Darkhani soldiers in the closest ranks behind Hara also approached to hear what was being said. Khaj, Dhirn, Terran, Rigelian and Cappellan, who hours ago were fighting savagely for each meter of the fire zone they now stood on, seemed oblivious of whose shoulders they brushed as each jockeyed for a view of the portal at the top of the ramp.

Sivran spoke up, "Will they show themselves?"

From the crowd, Nigel Wilson shouted around his filament mike, his one eye pressed against the viewfinder of his holocorder. "Yes, tell them to come out!"

In response, another figure appeared between Amalia and Gillermo. The alien was short. Shorter than the average Darkhani, but quite obviously the genetic prototype: well defined muscles, though nowhere near as massively developed as the average

Darkhani. (Cain knew that a remarkable trait of the Xi in their primary bodies was the capacity to assimilate necessary evolutionary changes in a fraction of the time it would take most species: a matter of several generations, not several millennia. This trait, along with everything else about the Xi, seemed to complement human genetics when introduced to its equation.)

The visitor from the Andromeda galaxy—or nebula—wore long hair and had the familiar masklike membrane over the eyes. Two striking differences were immediately apparent: the skin was albino, pinkish white and the long hair, a blush rose color that seemed to shimmer prismatically. Cain later learned this was merely a cosmetic effect, a fashion—their natural hair being colorless, gray-white or silver. The alien stood before them naked. The similarities between the Xi and both humans and Darkhani were apparent: along with bilateral symmetry, opposable thumbs, and upright posture, a male sex organ, hairless and white but nonetheless familiar, depended from the creature's groin.

"I am Schen." The creature's voice was androgynous: either husky female human or effeminate male. The word "Schen" came out like a bitten off whisper. Still, it was a human voice speaking standard Terran Galactic. "We have not hidden ourselves from you. You have been looking at us. This is how you see us." Schen was no longer visible. A small explosion, like a concussion grenade going off, resounded as air rushed into the space Schen's body had occupied a moment ago. Neither Dubois nor Gillermo seemed alarmed at this. They stood still and Gillermo gestured at the point of light, like a glowing ball with a shifting corona that hovered between them.

"This is also Schen," Gillermo explained. "In fact this is more Schen's natural state. You see the other identical points of light on this ship and the others. Well, those are not navigational lights or weapons, they are Xi, existing as pure consciousness . . . consciousness become light. This is their mode of existence; it is also their mode of travel.'' With that, the ball of brilliance that was, presumably, Schen, disappeared and reappeared several meters away. It/he did this several times before returning to his physical form between the two Terrans. ''It is also their technology, their religion, their science, their recreation, and art form. We can learn this from them. The spaces between stars or galaxies mean nothing now. The Xi are masters of the environment, the physical universe and the nonphysical universe. They are offering us an opportunity to join them, allow ourselves to learn . . . or perhaps the term is *remember* this reality, this birthright . . . divine right if you will.''

Padre Katanya stepped forward and shouted, ''Gillermo, what the devil are you talking about?''

Gillermo looked pained, or perhaps just disappointed. ''Padre Katanya, how are you? It is very difficult to contain what I am saying, on the tongue, in any language. But I assure you, Padre, I am not talking about the devil. I would not waste your time.''

Hara had turned to Cain. She whispered to him. ''Yes, you are right. They are the angels in the carvings. The angels the Khaj seers have described. The Dhirn have called them demons. You saw them, perhaps, because of your special eyes when usually they are only visible to seers while staring through The Eye of God straight into the light of Alaikhaj. We *are*, then, the Darkhani, distant cousins of these creatures. We share the same ancestors.''

''Yes,'' Cain replied. ''And that makes you part Terran as well. The Xi seem so human in their physical form. The fact that they could successfully mate with humans as well has . . . so many implications.''

''Vast connections,'' Hara said.

Cain wasn't sure he heard her. ''We are distant cousins. You and I.''

''Not so distant, I don't think.''

"I want to go with them, Cain," she said. "I think you do, too."

Cain was about to say, "Of course," and then realized something. Here was the promise of transcendence he had sought most of his life, here were the keys to thousands of mysteries, the doorway to a billion worlds all offered to him freely, requiring only a simple act of will to board the ship. Why then was he hesitating? Or rather, why wasn't he running up the ramp? Why wasn't he already up there, his arms thrown around Schen's knees in sobbing relief? And it occurred to him that it was because his quest was over. It had been since he had looked into The Eye of God and beheld himself as the center. He had, at that moment, wanted nothing nor did he reject anything and to his own amazement, he found he still possessed that freedom. The search was over. The emptiness, the yawning, driving, sucking, searching, yearning, desperate, wanting, needing emptiness had gone. The desire for his experience to be anything other than what it *was* had evaporated like a dream. And so he turned to Hara and was about to say, "I don't need to go." But he stopped himself.

No, he didn't need to go. He didn't need anything any longer and that filled him with a peace that can only be understood at its center. But there was something else, another feeling he noted that tickled and tingled not unpleasantly. Curiosity. He would *like* to go. He was interested. It would be fine to know what it was like. Yes, he *was* curious. There was no reason not to go, simply because he had no overwhelming compulsion to do so. He could *choose* to go. . . .

But there was time.

All the time there ever was or will be.

Maybe it would be better to spend some of it getting to know the man whose skin he had been trying so desperately for so many years to escape from. Maybe it was time to explore and make friends with Martin Cain the man instead of Martin Cain the aching wound.

Perhaps the Xi could still use an emissary, a bridge from their reality to that of the fading Terran Empire. A guide beyond the Empire's horizon from the old universe to the new. Surely there were billions of souls out there, creatures of a thousand races who would need someone to communicate, give them a choice. And what else had his life been if not a rehearsal for this? All the species he had sought out, all the cultures he had immersed himself into as if it were some kind of dye that would transform him, all served to point out to him what would be appropriate now, what would be *perfect. Now.*

And so he said to her, "Someday I will."

There was no question. It would be what he had always done: his life was a pilgrimage and before long he would miss that aspect of it. But when he left again it would be with a considerable measure of peace.

To Hara, he said, "Their universe isn't going to disappear, but in the meantime I believe I have things to do. I will stay right here for a while."

"On Darkath?" Hara seemed surprised.

"Yes. This is an important place for me. It marks the end of one thing and the beginning of another, both for my own life and for the world I come from. Your world, too, no? Besides you will need someone to take care of Ayeia Alaikhaj while you are making love to the stars."

"When you put it like that," Hara lifted her face into the rain that began to fall again with renewed force, "it makes it even harder to stay behind."

Cain looked over at Hara in surprise. He had, somehow, assumed she would leave with the Xi, that her desire to close the gap between the mundane and the eternal, the finite and the infinite, was as strong as his. It was something he had sensed unerringly in her since he had first seen her in the dungeon; a fuel that burned bright and true within her and refracted itself through her outwardly as charisma. "Stay behind?"

he echoed. He couldn't be sure he had heard her in the gathering downpour.

"All my life I have longed to escape who I am, what I must be, what was expected," she said. Her choice of words struck a note of familiarity and sympathy in Cain. "Now that I am offered this opportunity, on the heels of the kind of victory I and all of my people have always dreamed of since I was a girl, a victory that now seems to mean nothing with the Xi before me and all the bodies at my feet—now it is clear to me that I am needed here more than ever. I love my people, the desert, this world that is my home. Someday I will be ready to let go of it, and it will be ready to let go of me . . . and then I will follow the Xi and . . . How did you put it? Make love to the stars." She smiled at Cain and he returned it. "In the meantime, my children need a mother."

Cain nodded. He understood. Completely.

Hara said, "I offer you my desert, my world and for as long as you wish to stay . . . my home at Ayeia Alaikhaj, Martin Cain."

"Thank you," Cain bowed a little. "I'm honored. And maybe when the time comes for each of us . . . maybe we will set out together."

"Maybe, Martin Cain." Hara smiled and returned Cain's small bow. "Maybe."

* * *

The Xi had enough ships, enough room for over one thousand passengers. Less than three hundred boarded their craft. Eighty-three Terrans, two Rigelians, three Cappellans (including Moumya), and two hundred Darkhani. Jack and John Avery booked passage for Cygnus, John stiffly skeptical and nervous around the Xi.

The night before the Xi were to depart, Cain and Hara, as well as anyone else who cared to, had been invited on board to tour the ship. They walked the pastel lit corridors lined with small, spartanly furnished passenger berths, common areas for dining, excercise, meditation, reading, or viewing. The ship's interior reflected an atmosphere of temporary convenience as if no one were expected to spend much time there.

Sivran was on board and looking forward to the journey. He laughed and, it seemed to Cain, appeared much younger than on the previous occasions he had met the Dhirn. It was as if Sivran were somewhat giddy with relief at the end of the war, the end of the role he must play. In fact, he seemed a far too eager participant in an event that would take a long-held and unwanted responsibility from his shoulders and his heart. He hoped the old Dhirn would not find himself going mad, cut off from the life and world in which he had invested so much. He hoped he would not be cheated.

He hoped none of them would.

On the glowing list of names of those who were to lift off the following day, Cain was mildly surprised to see Nigel Wilson's. He saw the Starfax man taking holo footage near the control chamber in the bowels of the ship. Wilson seemed to have come through the difficulties with nothing more serious than a black eye. Remarkable. He told Cain he would rather not wait for the next Terran ship when he was sitting on the most spectacular documentary footage in the history of media. The Xi had agreed to take him to Puerto De Estrella where he could file his material and catch a Hub-bound vessel. Cain did not bother to point out to Wilson that, if he were to ask, it would probably be of no particular bother to the Xi to take him directly to Sao Paulo on Terra if he so desired. Wilson was going on about this milestone for his career.

"Yes, well, congratulations, Wilson." Cain had said as he studied the bridge of the Xi ship which seemed to be comprised of mandalalike controls that suggested magic rather than science, though Schen had assured him this was not so.

"Thanks, Cain. Decent of you not to carry on about me scooping you. Those are the breaks of the game."

"What? Oh, well, That's just fine, Nigel."

When all the ships lifted off the following evening, Martin Cain, Hara, Captain Fioricci, and Padre Katanya stood side by side just outside the cantonment gate watching. The ships lifted silently but brilliantly into the night. A tremor shook the ground beneath them as if the planet were shrugging off the unwanted burdens of old gods.

The priest said, "The church will survive them. Just as it has survived all the others." He said it as if it were a threat born out of some deep and unforgivable insult.

The captain looked at him and grunted noncommittally. "What do you think, Cain?"

Cain couldn't think of anything to say. The comment seemed extraordinary somehow in its irrelevance. He watched the closest ship again and thought about the new, strange brand of imperialism all of this suggested, the alarm he felt initially in the presence of the Xi. He thought/foresaw/remembered the blunders ahead, the inevitable misunderstandings. What occurred to him was the coldness with which these angels played with worlds and races, lives; and the trace of blind egoism he sensed in this species who had, possibly, come too far, too quickly. He thought about the price that is paid for being God.

After all, he did not think that pain and horror and error would be erased from the equation for anyone, anywhere.

The phrase "Spiritual imperialism" occurred to him and he wondered what that meant. He had time to think about it, and memories, analogues to draw on.

For the moment, he suspended disbelief. Anything was possible now and, in fact, always had been. After all, he stood on a world where dragons existed and people communed with the planet herself.

And the craft looked elegant as it ascended toward a widening break in the cloud cover. Stars peered through at them, multiplied, grew brighter. Quickening shades of an impassioned sunset colored the fleeing cumulus and nimbus configurations around them. Giata, a plum and pomegranate crescent, rose to meet the ships. And so, turning to Hara, he said only, "It's beautiful."

Hara put her hand on his arm and answered him. "Yes," she said. "It is."

Cain added only one thing. "All of it," he said.

They watched until the lights of the Xi were indistinguishable from that of the thousands of other stars in Darkath's sky.